Kim Lawrence lives on a farm in Anglesey with her university lecturer husband, assorted pets who arrived as strays and never left, and sometimes one or both of her boomerang sons. When she's not writing she loves to be outdoors gardening, or walking on one of the beaches for which the island is famous— along with being the place where Prince William and Catherine made their first home!

Susan Stephens was a professional singer before meeting her husband on the Mediterranean island of Malta. In true Mills & Boon style, they met on Monday, became engaged on Friday and married three months later. Susan enjoys entertaining, travel and going to the theatre. To relax she reads, cooks and plays the piano, and when she's had enough of relaxing she throws herself off mountains on skis or gallops through the countryside singing loudly.

THE SPANIARD'S SURPRISE LOVE-CHILD

KIM LAWRENCE

A BRIDE FIT FOR A PRINCE?

SUSAN STEPHENS

MILLS & BOON

First Published in Great Britain 2020
by Mills & Boon, an imprint of HarperCollins*Publishers*
1 London Bridge Street, London, SE1 9GF

The Spaniard's Surprise Love-Child © 2020 by Kim Lawrence

A Bride Fit for a Prince? © 2020 by Susan Stephens

ISBN: 978-0-263-27810-1

MIX
Paper from
responsible sources
FSC® C007454

This book is produced from independently certified FSC™ paper
to ensure responsible forest management.
For more information visit www.harpercollins.co.uk/green.

Printed and bound in Spain
by CPI, Barcelona

THE SPANIARD'S SURPRISE LOVE-CHILD

KIM LAWRENCE

CHAPTER ONE

THE CLASSICAL MUSIC playing through the sound system—gifted by a famous old girl after her first platinum album—was almost drowned out by the combined din of young voices, the shuffle of feet and the scraping of chairs on the ancient wood floor as uniformed pupils filed into the school auditorium.

Though several of her colleagues were frowning at the noise levels, Gwen barely noticed the racket that echoed off the high rafters of the school's Tudor hall. Her thoughts were wandering, though not far. The crèche—which had been the deal clincher when she was offered the job at Mere Grange—was not five hundred yards from where she was sitting beside the rest of the staff on the stage.

Despite a disturbed night that had made Gwen fear the worst, Ellie had seemed fine this morning. True, she had been a bit clingy when Gwen had dropped her off in the crèche earlier but her temperature had been normal. Gwen had checked it twice, but still the vague anxiety lingered. Was it maternal instincts or just guilt?

The former she'd always assumed to be an urban myth but she was now certain really did exist, and the latter, though she knew it was irrational, she had come to appreciate as a fact of life. Was it just her or perhaps single mums or maybe all mums? She couldn't be the only mum who felt that guilty tug every time she left her child in the crèche. For some reason even knowing that Ellie was well cared for and happy there didn't lessen the feeling.

'She'll be fine. Stop fretting.'

Ellie turned to her friend Cassie, the head of English, with a rueful smile. 'How did you know I was worrying about Ellie?'

'Love, you're always worrying about Ellie. You make parenting look easy but it must be tough doing it all alone.'

Gwen brought her lashes down in a protective sweep that shadowed her blue eyes. She had opened up more to Cassie than anyone else, but the other woman still only knew the bare minimum—just that Ellie's father was not English and he was not in the picture.

Her slender shoulders lifted in a shrug as she pushed away the image of Ellie's father that had slipped through the mental barriers she had erected, though, as she thought of him every single time she looked into her daughter's beautiful eyes, it hardly seemed worth the effort.

Before she could be drawn into an internal debate on her past mistakes and awful taste in men—or at least *one* man—a shout emanating from just below the stage made her turn her head.

The same noise had caught Cassie's attention.

'I'll have to go and help,' Gwen said after a moment. Her classroom assistant, Ruth, was struggling to contain the energy and boredom of a class of twenty five-year-olds who, thanks to someone who hadn't considered their lack of attention span, had been seated first in the auditorium.

'Good luck,' Cassie breathed, tacking on a low-voiced warning. 'The head will notice you're not sitting here with the rest of us and he won't be pleased. He said "*all* staff",' she quoted, adopting the man's distinctive clipped delivery.

'I doubt if one less bowed head is going to stop Lady Moneybags donating the money for the library extension. Anyway, he'd *notice* a lot more if one of my lot escapes—now that would make a bad headline.'

Gwen reached the front row just in time to cut off an adventurous member of her class before he slipped through a fire exit.

'This way, Max,' she said, touching the top of his curly red hair before she firmly took his hand and led him back to his seat. 'Oh, you're sitting next to William...*not* such a good idea.' A fact that Gwen had learnt the hard way, and in class she now had them sitting on opposite sides of the classroom. 'Move over, Sophie. Max can sit next to you. Excellent, now don't move,' she admonished, before moving down the row to where Ruth was sitting. 'You almost lost one there.'

'Sorry, Miss Meredith,' Ruth said, smiling her gratitude.

Gwen smiled back, though it never made her feel anything but ancient to be called Miss by the young woman who was actually a year older than her. The prestigious fee-paying school was very keen on defined roles and did not encourage use of Christian names in the professional setting or, for that matter, romantic relationships between staff, although blind eyes were turned so long as people were discreet.

Gwen wasn't interested in being discreet; she was simply not interested at all. In the odd quiet moment she wondered if her libido was dead, but not for long.

Those moments were rare and the rest of the ninety-nine per cent of the time she was too exhausted to even think about it.

Even had she trusted her own judgment with men after her experience with Ellie's father, romance was a pretty low priority for her these days. Now sleep, and maybe finding a few more hours in a day to sit down and read a book or do her nails—these were the things she lusted after. Gwen had well and truly left physical lust behind and she didn't miss it one bit.

'No harm done, Ruth.'

'Max is pulling faces at me, Miss,' Sophie complained.

'Max!'

Gwen's glance moved over the red head of the culprit, who was now looking angelically innocent as she scanned the faces of her charges occupying the first two rows, waiting until she had their attention before she widened her eyes and raised a finger to her lips. The result was nothing approaching calm, but the imminent possibility of someone swinging from a chandelier or making an escape bid receded.

'It's a miracle!' she heard Ruth breathe. 'How do you do it?'

Gwen rewarded her charges with a nod of approval and, more importantly, promised them a nature walk because they were being so good. She usually found the carrot a lot more effective than the stick. But before she could make her way back to the stage, the sudden lowering of the hum of youthful voices in the room indicated that she was too late to slip unobtrusively back to her seat, so instead she sat down on the bench next to Ruth as the head walked on the stage with their VIP guest speaker.

The head had a voice that filled the auditorium without effort and silence immediately fell. Barely listening to the introduction, Gwen kept her attention on her pupils, while hoping the guest speaker didn't turn out to be as fond of the sound of their own voice as the head. A five-year-old's attention span was limited, especially when they were bored, but hopefully they would fall asleep rather than run amok.

'And now I give you Mr Bardales.'

Bardales... No, surely it was the *Cavendish* Prize that was being given by the benefactor that the new science block was named after? *Bardales* was a very different name with very different connotations for Gwen.

On the surface nothing changed. Outside she was a serene swan, with only the fluttering of the long curling lashes that framed her sapphire-blue eyes and the faintest quiver of the fine muscles beneath the skin around her wide mouth betraying that under the surface she was frantically duck paddling to stay afloat, a heartbeat away from...*who knew*? Total panic? She'd never gone there and she never intended to—it was all a matter of control.

Breathe, Gwen, she told herself. The breath left her parted lips in a slow, uneven, near-silent hiss as, like someone who had jumped in the deep end of the pool by accident, she kicked for the surface, leaving panic behind.

She brushed her forearms hard with her hands, rubbing the rash of goosebumps that had broken out over her skin. She despised her stupid overreaction, the first in a while. It had to have been a couple of months ago the last time she had experienced the dry-throated, heart-racing sensation of stepping off a cliff in the pit of her stomach. On that occasion it had been triggered when she'd seen a dark head standing out from the crowd in the middle of the busy shopping centre, but a moment later she had realised there was no definitive arrogant angle to his jaw, no big-cat fluidity to his stride. The sensation hadn't lasted longer than a moment before her common sense reasserted itself and was followed by the sigh of relief that left her feeling foolish and annoyed with herself for allowing her overactive imagination to take control, even for a second.

The annoyance with herself was already kicking in hard as she tipped her head back to see the cause of her flashback. She had to tip it back some more as the guest was tall, the cut of his dark suit not disguising the power of his lean muscle-packed frame.

No, it hadn't been a flashback; *this* was a flashback! And pulling free of it was not an option. Nearly three years suddenly slipped away and she was back in New York.

The bar was as cool and sophisticated as its clientele and Gwen, sitting perched on a tall stool, fitted right in; she was cool, she was sleek and she belonged...or at least she *looked* as though she did and that was what counted, she'd discovered. She imagined there would be a time when it didn't feel as though she were playing a part. It would come; she'd only been in New York three months and she knew it couldn't happen overnight. She focused instead on the positives, the most positive aspect being that her five-year plan was already off to a flying start.

The first month at work she'd been finding her feet, so anxious to make a good impression that she had been unable to hide it. She did what she'd done all through university, when she had known that if her plan was to succeed she needed a good degree—some people could party and still get good results, but Gwen knew she couldn't do that; she had to focus solely on work. So she kept her head down, sacrificing a social life to achieve what she needed. It had taken her a few weeks before she'd realised that the same method was not going to work here. Simply putting in extra hours at the office was not enough; you needed to network outside office hours too.

The first time she had accepted an invite she had stood out like a sore thumb in her office gear, but now she'd become something of an expert at making a seamless transition from day to evening and had it down to an impressive five minutes in the ladies' room to make the necessary adjustments.

Like anything in life, it was about organisation: first make-up refreshed, lips highlighted for the evening by a bold red lipstick, then her hair, released from the sleek ponytail secured at the nape of her neck; one quick shake and it fell in glossy waves down her narrow back. All achieved while she was exchanging the discreet studs in her ears for a pair of art deco jet chandelier drops.

The tailored jacket that had seen her through the day's meetings was removed and the stark simplicity of the little black dress it had covered was jazzed up with an oversized art deco pendant tonight. The jacket, neatly folded, was inside her capacious designer bag along with the moderate heels she had swapped for a pair of spiky ankle boots; that part took two minutes, tops.

It was amazing what you could do when you were organised and Gwen was incredibly focused. That was how she had made it this far. She didn't allow herself to be distracted; she knew what she wanted and then figured out the quickest way to achieve her goal. People had quickly started to notice. She'd overheard a conversation in the ladies' room once, and she had wondered, curiously, who this *ruthless* person was that they were discussing.

Then she'd found out it was her.

'You're just jealous, Trish, that Gwen has got the face and body to sleep her way to the top,' had been one of the cruel comments she'd overheard.

Crossing one slim, shapely ankle over the other, she turned her head and laughed because everyone else was. The anger she had felt that day in the Ladies was spent now, but the memory still had the power to make the tension climb into her shoulders. She put her hand on the back of her neck and rotated her head from side to side to ease it.

In one aspect they had been right—she *was* determined to succeed—but the totally unfair implication that she ever would demean herself by sleeping her way to the top… It had hurt and made her want to rush out and challenge the women cattily bitching about her, but just as well the tears streaming down her face had made her reject this impulse, because it was far better to make them eat their words by simply being better than them, and proving herself.

Blurting out that actually she was a virgin would not have improved the situation; it was almost easier all round to be considered an ambitious slut with no morals.

'You look fierce!' Louise, who had been the new girl in the corporate finance department before Gwen had arrived, looked at her with raised eyebrows. 'Do you want another drink?'

Gwen shook her head and smiled as she held her hand over her full glass. She turned and caught sight of herself in the mirror that lined the wall behind the bar. Her loose hair had a mirror gloss, but the cost, which had initially seemed enormous, of having her thick chestnut waves tamed by the hand of someone who was a superstar in the world of hairdressing had proved to be a good investment, she decided, taking a sip of her wine. She intended to make it last all evening—the buzz of being here in this city was all the stimulation she needed.

Gwen leaned in to catch what the woman beside Louise was saying.

'Your Scots accent is just so cute, everyone thinks so.'

When they're not thinking I'm sleeping my way to the top, Gwen thought, hiding her flash of bitterness behind a smile. As she had to virtually yell to make herself heard above the competing conversations, Gwen decided it required less effort to smile and nod rather than correct the woman's mistake over her nationality, even though it felt as though she was betraying her Welsh roots.

Not that anyone back home would have recognised her—the once awkward, intense swot with the glasses—in this place, she thought wryly, leaning in again to catch what Louise was saying.

'Don't look now but *he* hasn't taken his eyes off you since he came in.' Louise's eyes widened as she tipped her head towards the smoky glass wall that screened the bar from the street. 'I said don't look!'

'I wasn't going to.' Gwen was not averse to the idea of romance, at the right time, but it wasn't scheduled at this point in her life. Right now it came under the heading of a distraction she didn't need. Still it was always good if someone appreciated the effort she had made with her appearance.

Louise took a sip of her cocktail and sighed, leaning sideways to look over Gwen's shoulder. 'He really is totally…oh, my God!' she yelped, before hissing, 'He's coming over, don't panic.'

Gwen heard his voice before she saw him, deep, with a light gravel underlying the velvet and an intriguing hint of an accent. It made the half-smile she was wearing in response to her friend's antics quiver and fade as for some inexplicable reason a deep shiver that made her toes curl passed through her body.

It was that same voice that dragged Gwen away now from the New York bar and the exact moment when her five-year plan—*My God, was I really that arrogant, or was I just incredibly young and naive?*—had started falling apart. She was back to sitting in the school's assembly hall where for some inexplicable reason Rio Bardales, billionaire heir to the Bardales empire, was holding his audience in the palm of his strong brown elegant hand. Gwen had a sudden unwelcome image of that hand, those tapering fingers sliding over pale skin…her skin… She gulped and blinked to clear the unwanted images dancing in her head.

Everyone was clapping, except Gwen. She couldn't have, even if she had wanted to. What she actually wanted, what every cell in her body was screaming at her to do, was to run as far away as she could.

Her head turned fractionally from side to side in mute denial—*this cannot be happening!*

'He looks like a film star.' Ruth's awed whisper brought the past back with a rush she had no defence against. She remembered thinking exactly the same thing that night in the stylish New York bar where they'd met. He'd been wearing a suit then too but it had looked as though he might have slept in it, yet he'd still looked absolutely gorgeous—how could he not? Even if you discounted his physical attributes—several inches over six feet tall; long-limbed without being in any way lanky; lean and muscular with broad shoulders and a natural athletic elegance—Rio's strong-boned symmetrical features were arresting enough to be a conversation-stopper. His eyes, dark and almond-shaped, were almost black, framed by dense long lashes and set beneath strongly defined flyaway brows, his carved cheekbones sharp enough to cut, and his square chin had the hint of a cleft, but it was his beautifully cut, overtly sensual mouth that did the most damage to her nervous system.

Gwen felt dizzy as the image from the past was overlaid by one of the man standing on the stage, his words just sounds that had a physical effect on her, sending successive shivers over the surface of her suddenly too warm skin.

She felt as though everyone *must* see what was happening, that they were all staring at her, but crazily they were completely oblivious. Now they were laughing, an appreciative ripple of sound that wafted like a breeze through the vaulted room—Rio was being amusing, entertaining. She knew full well, though, that he could get a *lot* more entertaining than this, especially when there was skin-to-skin contact involved.

Jaw clenched, lips compressed over the cry trying to escape her lips, she closed her eyes and thought, *Do not go there, Gwen...* But too late—she was already remembering that first shock of feeling skin-to-skin contact after he had unfastened her bra for the first time and, holding her eyes, had pulled her hard against his chest...

* * *

The myriad impressions made her dizzy: the warmth
of his skin, the clean salty tang she'd breathed in, the
tingling of intense pleasure as her hardened nipples
pressed into the barrier of his naked, muscled chest.

His eyes didn't leave hers for one moment, the hot
desire burning in them making her limbs go boneless,
silencing the voice telling her she needed to explain to
him that she didn't have a clue what she was doing. It
had seemed a matter of simple politeness only a few
minutes ago, but now she found herself thinking in a
hazy way what did it actually matter...?

Why shouldn't her embarrassing inexperience remain on a need-to-know basis? After all, he'd not
twigged yet so why should it matter? She could suddenly see all the advantages of sleeping with a stranger:
you didn't owe them anything, including explanations...
Ironic, really, when this was precisely what *he* pointed
out to her a few days later in a frigid voice filled with
icy contempt she would never, ever forget...even though
she had tried.

'I owe you nothing, certainly not explanations. We
had sex; we are not in a relationship.'

The brutal words carried the impact of a sledgehammer, each individual scornful syllable adding fresh lay-
ers of hurt as she clutched his shirt around her. Unable
to match his marvellous unselfconscious attitude to nu-
dity, she had pulled it on to walk to the bathroom, and
it retained the scent of his skin but it didn't give her a
warm feeling of intimacy; she felt mortified and stupid
and very, *very* cold.

She lifted her chin, struggling to salvage a tiny shred
of pride. 'I... I didn't think we were.' It wasn't totally
a lie; she knew that a few nights of passion did not add

up to a relationship. It nearly hadn't even made it this far after he'd found out he was her first lover and hadn't exactly been thrilled about it, and he'd been quite clear then that this was not the start of anything; it was just casual fun he was offering.

Pride and the determination not to give him the satisfaction of knowing that she had just begun to believe that they'd developed a deeper connection made her stand her ground rather than run away. She felt stupid even imagining for a moment that when he'd told her she was the best sex he'd ever had, it meant he thought she was different and what they had was worth more than a quick fling. It was easy to see *now* that it had all been wishful thinking on her part.

Maybe he'd known anyway because in case she'd missed the point he drove it home with brutal honesty.

'We are not exclusive, you and I. You do not have the right to interrogate me.'

The chill in his eyes, the hauteur in his body language, the expressive curl of his lip did not require the addition of the snap of his fingers to tell her she was being dismissed, not just from his bed or this room, but from his life.

'Who I sleep with…and, let me tell you, it is never *knowingly* anyone who would rifle through my private correspondence…is none of your concern.'

She tried to defend herself, tell him that wasn't what she'd been doing, she really did, but she failed. Basically, because the bottom line was that it was true she *had* read his letter, but not intentionally. She'd picked up the incriminating piece of paper off the floor along with the pile of other correspondence that had landed on the carpet when she had caught it with her elbow. She was unable to replicate the precision of the neat stack but, tongue caught between her teeth, she had been making an effort to do so when the letterhead had caught her eye. She had scanned a sentence before she had realised what she was doing and…she really *should* have stopped; that was why she knew the guilt had been shining in her eyes when he'd caught her in the act.

She had considered pretending she hadn't read it, but it would have looked foolish.

As it turned out that wasn't even an option as the awkward words just blurted out of her mouth in the face of his accusatory glare.

'I only said, "So you have a child…" I didn't know, that's all. Are you and the mother together?' She felt the blood drain from her face. 'You're not…not married, are you?'

He arched a brow. 'Would it have mattered to you if I were?'

She wanted to slap him then, and she had never struck anyone in her life, she couldn't even crush a spider, but it took all her control to keep her clenched hand at her side, refusing to rise to the insulting provocation.

'What is his name?' There was no reason he shouldn't have a child, several children, in fact, and no reason either that he should have mentioned it to her…because he had made it quite clear that what they were enjoying had a shelf life. She was the one who had decided something had changed—and now it had.

He was the sort of man whose response to the news that he was a father was to demand a DNA test; he was the sort of man who, when asked his son's name by her, replied that he couldn't remember! The irony was that she'd learnt more in the last twenty seconds about this man than she had in three whole days…or, rather, nights.

He arched a dark brow and regarded her with frozen distaste. She had caught glimpses of the hauteur before but had never been on the blighting, chilly receiving end of it.

'What business is it of yours if I have a child?' His voice carried no expression but it didn't need to as his eyes said it all.

'None at all,' she agreed as the paper in her fingers that outlined in black and white a DNA match fluttered to the floor. 'So it confirms you're a father, so what? It takes more than a piece of paper to become one of those, doesn't it? Paternity has very little to do with being a father—that's all about a lifetime commitment, not just donating your genes—so I really hope this kid has someone else in his life who doesn't need proof that they're related to him, and someone who actually remembers his name.'

With a sneer of contempt that was aimed as much at herself as at him, she gathered her dignity around her as she removed his shirt and, with a grimace of distaste, she dropped it on the floor before she walked away with her head held high.

CHAPTER TWO

RIO WAITED FOR a polite ripple of laughter to die down before he moved on. His mother, who he was standing in for, could do this sort of thing in her sleep and she'd been genuinely upset that she couldn't attend today, which proved, he supposed, that there were some people who enjoyed their schooldays and wanted to be reminded of them. His glance slid over the young shiny faces turned to him.

Were there any lonely kids out there who cried themselves to sleep when the lights went out? Not that he'd been traumatised by being sent off at a ridiculously young age to an English boarding school, just stifled, perhaps.

The fact that he and his twin brother, Roman, were each other's support group meant he'd never suffered the sort of isolation that had afflicted some of the other children, and there had been enough foreign students at his school to make his own accent nothing to set him apart. Despite the fact he had survived the experience relatively unscathed, sending his children to boarding school was a tradition that he intended to break, not because he was rebelling against tradition, but because he didn't intend to have children at all.

He felt the phone in his pocket vibrate and resisted

the temptation to cut the obligatory amusing anecdote short. Nothing in his delivery would make his audience suspect he had moved onto autopilot and was working out how soon he would be able to make his exit. Instead of his speech, his thoughts were on the rescue package he was putting into place for a friend. Jake was so grateful to him, which made him feel guilty. It hadn't required much effort on his part to save Jake—the name Bardales inspired confidence and made those banks who didn't appreciate that his friend was a techno genius a lot more likely to extend credit.

'Again, thank you, Mr Jarvis, for asking me here to present the Cavendish Prize in my mother's stead.' Rio turned to look at the headmaster before he could launch into another speech. 'My mother sends her apologies for being unable to be present herself today, as this school still holds such a special place in her heart. However, she is here in spirit and I believe her presence is still marked on several desks where she left a permanent impression. So without further ado...' He took the crystal cup from the female teacher who held it out. 'I present this award to this year's recipient of the Cavendish Prize, Clarice Walker.'

Smiling, he watched a tall girl who was blushing as brightly as her auburn curls walk from the back of the room towards the stage, her progress accompanied by clapping.

He handed the girl the crystal goblet engraved with her name and the envelope that contained a more practical reward in the form of a cheque.

'Congratulations, Clarice. My mother is looking forward to meeting you in the near future when she is more mobile.'

In the meantime, his normally very active parent was being a predictably pretty impatient patient, frustrated by the plaster cast that was her souvenir from a recent skiing trip.

He took a step back and joined in the clapping as the youngster took her place in front of the microphone. 'Thank you, Mr Bardales. I do hope your mother is better very soon.'

His mother was fond of saying that being involved with young people kept her young, but being in this room filled with shiny idealism and even shinier faces made him feel old and not a little nostalgic for a touch of youthful rebellion—if there were any mavericks in the room, they were hiding it well.

It was hard to disguise his inner cynicism as he scanned the sea of faces staring up at the stage listening to the earnest speaker, wondering how long it would be before the real world would kill off all this youthful enthusiasm.

His thought stream was interrupted when the room suddenly erupted into sniggers at what he could only assume was an 'in joke' from Clarice. Rio fought an eye-roll, recognising with a jolt that he was displaying all the characteristics of a grumpy old man at only thirty-one—it did not bode well for the future.

Rio let his eyelids droop, the silky mesh of his lashes hiding the gleam of cynicism shining in the dark depths. *Perhaps,* he mused, *I need a day off...* Or a night in with someone smart and beautiful who had no interest in what made him tick, but just wanted to use this body that was actually in better condition than he deserved, considering the schedule that had left very little time for the punishing exercise regime he had once enjoyed.

His mobile mouth curled into a smile that flattened

out as a movement in the periphery of his vision interrupted the pleasant fantasy before he had even begun to weave it, dragging his wandering attention to the rows of children sitting nearest the stage.

Finally a bit of rebellion! He didn't fight off his grin as he watched one of the tiny occupants of the low bench just in front of the stage making a determined bid for freedom.

Rio silently willed him on, but inevitably he didn't get far. The culprit was captured by someone who displayed a great deal of agility and also a really good bottom…actually, it was truly excellent, he decided, studying the curves outlined by conservative trousers that were wide-legged but pulled tight across her bottom as she stretched. The tall, leggy owner of the rich chestnut hair and excellent bottom released her hold on the kid's arm, bending a little lower to say something that involved a wag of her finger, and, although he dragged his feet, the sulky little boy retook his seat.

He was attempting to pull his attention back to the proceedings on stage when the woman straightened up, one hand smoothing her glorious hair, the other smoothing the fabric of her trousers over long thighs. He was on the point of looking away when she lifted her head and they made eye contact.

The connection lasted seconds before she turned away, head bent to the child, but it only took a fraction of that time for his self-possession to fragment into a million pieces as recognition shuddered through him with the force of a sledgehammer blow that continued to send aftershocks throughout his body. He lowered his eyelids to shield his eyes as he nodded, mainly because everyone else was doing it in response to something the headmaster was saying.

Confusion was not normally part of Rio's mindset, as confusion required an uncertainty, a hesitancy, an inability to cut through all the nonsense. None of these were attitudes he possessed, and he was rarely confused, but as he stood there questioning the evidence of his own eyes Rio was extremely confused.

It was the sort of confusion that came from seeing a familiar face out of context. Rio struggled to kick start his brain and think past the sense-limiting testosterone rush.

What the hell was this high-flyer doing in a school for kids of moneyed parents, wearing an outfit that made it easy for her to bend over and grab the would-be escapee kid—wide-legged trousers cinched in with a belt at her slender waist and a shirt that might have been sexy had it not been buttoned up to the neck?

If he ever thought about Welsh Gwen, he pictured her in a New York setting, dressed with immaculate City gloss, in sharp-edged fashionable tailoring that made sure people took her seriously despite the extraordinary face that was always going to set her apart from the other ambitious women aiming to shatter any glass ceilings that got in their way. And good luck to them; he liked ambitious women, just not ones who thought they could control him.

If he ever thought about her…? *Who are you kidding, Rio?* he mocked himself as he fought to regain control of his stupefied brain. The dressed part was a lie too; he always pictured her completely naked and lying beneath him, her stunning legs wrapped tightly around him.

It had been nearly three years since he'd last seen her, and, despite the fact he was not someone to dwell on past mistakes, his subconscious had been known to drag him back to this particularly gorgeous mistake time and time again.

His eyes slid over her rear; he was thinking of the sleek curves under the clothes and an image flashed into his head of the last time he had seen her, walking away from him stark naked, anger and pride in her slow determined strides. He remembered every detail: her lovely long legs, her slender square shoulders, the graceful curve of her spine and feminine flare of her hips from a tiny waist. Thinking about the dimple just above her taut right buttock and the endless graceful legs sent a fresh flash of hormonal heat through his body.

He had spent considerable time and effort rationalising how their short liaison had left such a lasting raw impression on him, convincing himself that it was the element of unfinished business between them, thanks to that messy conclusion. All wasted energy as it turned out, as in reality he was unable to file the episode away in some dusty mental drawer marked 'Over' because he had never known a woman who had made him this *hungry*!

Though in his defence Gwen Meredith, with her melodic lilting voice, was not a woman a man forgot. *Any* man with blood in his veins could not be indifferent to the memory of the electricity that had been between them, the little whimpered purr low in her throat whenever he'd slid his tongue between her plump lips… He inhaled sharply. *Dios*, this raw hunger was something he had not experienced before or since her; in fact, the memory had made any encounters he'd had since Gwen seem pallid and boring in comparison. He frowned and pushed away the sense-paralysing fantasies before they took hold, focusing instead on the mystery of her presence—here, where there were no glass ceilings whatsoever to shatter.

How and why the hell had she transplanted herself from New York to the English shires and a private school in leafy grounds?

He'd always enjoyed the challenge of unravelling a mystery.

It wasn't until Max tried to twist out of her grip that Gwen realised she still had hold of his hand.

'Sit down, Max.'

Her voice was lacking its usual note of calm authority and sounded as though it were coming from a long way off. The fact the child had ignored her did not at that moment feel like something that Gwen could deal with, when standing up was taking all her focus, and her head was still spinning.

She pressed her hand to her stomach, and squeezed her eyes shut. She couldn't excuse the liquid heat of desire in the pit of her belly on ignorance, she was simply stupid and weak and...

Oh, stop bleating, Gwen, and deal with it!

A tiny sigh huffed between her clenched lips as her slender shoulders lowered and her chin lifted fractionally in response to the bracing inner voice that had zero tolerance for self-pity.

It was one thing to acknowledge you had a problem, it was another entirely to find yourself staring it straight in the face. It left little room to hide from the fact, mortifying and shameful but inescapable, that when it came to Rio her hormones were utterly indiscriminate, though in her defence there couldn't be many men who projected the aura of raw sexuality that he did.

She wasted one wistful moment wishing for a time

when she had sincerely believed that respect and liking were necessary for sexual attraction, when she had believed that being paralysed with lust by an obsidian-eyed stare had anything to do with a mystical connection. No, actually she wasn't wistful at all; it was scary to think how beneath her sophisticated facade she had been so totally vulnerable. She had had nearly three years to think about it and she had come to the conclusion that it had all been about her belated sexual awakening allied with her inexperience and timing. Yes, most importantly, it was always about the timing.

She'd told herself it could have been anyone who had sparked her desire; it had just happened to be Rio Bardales who had provided the catalyst, and the idea he wasn't special whatsoever had been oddly comforting.

Misplaced comfort, as it happened. The second she'd seen him again she'd felt sick to her stomach and scared stiff. He had recognised her too—she had seen it in his eyes. The question was would he be curious enough to seek her out, talk to her, try and find out why she was here instead of New York? She clamped her lips tight over a snort of self-disgust for the idiot she had been. The simple fact was, she might have known a whole lot about financial forecasting, but when it came to life and men she just hadn't had a clue.

Maybe she was paranoid after all, thinking he'd recognised her? She bore little resemblance to the sophisticated career girl on the fast track to success, with her designer clothes and strong sense of self-belief that she could achieve whatever she set her mind to.

Right now her mind was set to getting the hell out of here, as soon as humanly possible.

'Max needs the bathroom,' she hissed in Ruth's ear.

Ruth started to get to her feet but responded to the

pressure of Gwen's hand on her shoulder and subsided back down.

'I don't want—'

Gwen smiled determinedly at the little boy. 'Yes, you do…'

Looking slightly bewildered but not at all unwilling to leave the boring assembly, he trotted along beside Gwen as she made her dash for the side door.

Once in the cool, emotional calm of the long corridor lined with photographs of sporting achievements down the years of pupils past and present, she realised that she had really not handled that very well at all. In fact, probably the only thing she'd achieved was to draw attention to herself.

'Miss…?'

'Oh, yes, right.' Her heels tapping on the floor, she led the boy to the nearest cloakroom.

'Off you go. I'll be waiting.'

Her excuse for escape vanished inside the boys' cloakroom and Gwen let out a sigh as she leaned back against the wall.

This isn't the time to panic, she told herself.

If not now, when?

She ignored the unhelpful insertion of her subconscious and reminded herself that Ellie was safely in the crèche, where it was most unlikely their VIP would be taken—the redbrick addition to the listed building was only a selling point to members of staff. No, he'd be taking the well-trodden route beginning in the photo gallery of alumni who had gone on to success and fame or, in some cases, had just had it handed to them on a plate, taking in the new state-of-the-art science block and then heading back via the restored, historically listed gardens for refreshments in the headmaster's office.

She was safe and so, more importantly, was Ellie.

But she didn't dare relax; people didn't when night-mares started happening for real. Hand to her mouth, she straightened up and began to pace up and down until the trembling weakness in her legs made her stop. She placed her hands on the window sill, staring out at the quadrangle with its borders of herbs she had supervised her class planting last week.

It *was* going to be fine but she had to prepare for the worst, and hope...*really* hope for the best. Her smooth brow furrowed. The most important question was, how bad could the worst be?

This was a situation she had never anticipated hap-pening when she had made her decision not to make contact with him after she'd discovered she was preg-nant. It hadn't been an easy choice to make or one she had ever foreseen she would have to. Having children had been something she had seen for herself, but only in the distant future when she was in a secure, loving relationship and had got far enough up the career lad-der to be able to afford to step off the escalator tempo-rarily and then afford excellent child care afterwards.

She was very conscious of the argument that mor-ally a man had a right to know when he'd fathered a child and a child had a right to know who her father was, but what if that father had no interest in being a father? He'd demanded DNA proof of paternity once, she thought scornfully, so why would this time have been any different?

During her pregnancy there had been moments when she knew she wouldn't ever tell him and others when she had come so close to making contact. She'd even composed emails she'd never sent. They'd generally been along the lines of I thought you should know, but don't worry, it's fine that you're not going to be involved in our child's life, but any relevant family medical history would be appreciated.

She had see-sawed back and forth as she wrestled with the difficult choice throughout her pregnancy. There had been a deep sense of relief when she had finally made her decision while looking down with a sense of wonderment at her perfect newborn daughter, experiencing a swell of protective love she had never realised existed until that moment.

Why was she worrying about the rights of an accidental father who thought parenthood was just about making a genetic contribution? Presumably he'd ask her for DNA proof too. How could a man like that, a reluctant father, be good for her daughter? After all, this was all about what was best for her baby. Holding the warm, perfect person she had given life to, the cold-bloodedness of Rio's attitude to being a father chilled her. She decided then and there that this baby would never know she had a father who didn't want her.

After all, Gwen knew exactly what that felt like. She might have no siblings but growing up she hadn't been the only child in the house. Her father was a man who expected to be the centre of attention at all times. Gwen had learnt not to compete with him for her mother's attention, but it hadn't stopped him resenting her existence.

She didn't know how old she had been, or even how she had found out that her serial-adulterer father had had his first affair when her mother had been pregnant with her. In his eyes that, at least, was an excuse for his behaviour. After that it seemed things had gone downhill, although to the outside world they had continued to present the image of a happy, perfect family—and it had all started with the birth of the baby he'd never wanted anyway.

And now Gwen's decision not to tell Rio he was a father, which had seemed so right at the time, was being severely tested. She had made it assuming that their lives would never intersect again. Because what were the odds? They lived in totally different worlds. She remembered the day she had seen a missed call on her phone and recognised his number. It had been a very weak moment and if she'd picked up she might, just might, have told him. Though imagining his face if he had seen her the way she was that day, attached to a drip in a hospital ward unable to keep any fluids down, made her very glad she hadn't. She hadn't felt lucky at the time but now she knew that some women suffered that sort of debilitating nausea all through their pregnancy. For her it had only lasted five months, which had been more than long enough.

'Miss… Miss…'

Gwen shook her head and turned to the little boy standing there. He'd washed his face a little too enthusiastically and his hair was wet, as was the front of his uniform shirt. She felt a tug of affection and smiled. She had fallen into teaching through a mixture of accidents and necessity, but she loved it.

'What have you got there?' she asked, looking at his cupped chubby hands.

'A bee, a big, big bee! It was stuck on the window.' He lifted his hands to his ear. 'It's still buzzing but he won't sting me. He's a nice bee.'

Gwen sincerely hoped this *nice* bee lived up to expectations and hastily opened the window, letting in a waft of warm scented summer air and the murmur of young voices as pupils began to file out of the hall and through the wide stone arch at the far end of the quadrangle. She picked up her damp pupil and she smiled encouragingly until he opened his hand, giving his captive freedom.

'Ah, there she is now.'

Gwen's smile became fixed as she froze, only the child in her arms preventing her from humiliating herself by ducking down out of sight. The headmaster didn't appear to notice her deer-in-headlights pose, framed in the window as he looked at the man standing beside him.

'Mrs Meredith, I was just telling Mr Bardales…'

'Rio, please—'

The headmaster tipped his head in pleased acknowledgement. 'How *interested* his mother was when I was telling her of your enthusiasm for outdoor teaching.'

'I share her enthusiasm,' Rio lied without a flicker and bared his white teeth in a smile that did not touch his eyes as they drifted down her body, or what he could see of it.

Self-preservation kept her expression blank as the shock, guilt and fear that paralysed her were virtually obliterated beneath a shameful hot thrum of sexual awareness that made her legs tremble. Her nerve endings were screaming out in recognition as she turned away from the window and, after taking a deep soothing breath, opened the adjacent door and stepped outside.

The headmaster beamed, blissfully oblivious of any undercurrents seething around him. 'Excellent…well, we have the expert here to explain.' He gave an impatient little shake of his head. 'Come along, Mrs Meredith.' He paused and lifted a hand. 'Ah, here is your class now.'

She huffed out a sigh of relief, saved by the bell—

or at least by the scuffle of twenty pairs of small feet as the reception class, with Ruth bringing up the rear, came filing out of the hall into the archway.

All she had to do now was to walk past Rio and she was home free. She clenched her jaw and with determined optimism told herself that this could still turn out all right.

'There you go.' She put down the child still in her arms, took his hand and led him towards the arch, where, the moment he saw his classmates, he took off, ignoring the headmaster's bellow of 'No running!' as he pounded across the gravel to join his friends, the tiny stones scattering in his enthusiasm.

It was an enthusiasm to get away that Gwen shared.

Careful not to make eye contact with Rio, her heart pumping frantically beneath her pale blue cotton blouse as she struggled to channel calm indifference, she nodded towards the head and made to join her class.

'No, Mrs Meredith.'

She stopped and sighed, her eyes following her class as she thought wistfully, *So near and yet so far,* before squaring her shoulders and turning back, an expression of polite enquiry painted on her face.

'Come and explain to our guest about your initiative. I admit I had my doubts initially but I have been won over,' he said graciously. 'We have even included it in our new prospectus and the parents are most enthusiastic…but now I'll allow our expert to explain,' he added to Rio as Gwen joined them, struggling to hide her reluctance. 'I will leave you in her very capable hands.'

'My class—' Gwen protested, clutching at straws.

'If you could bring our guest to my office at two-thirty, the governors are joining us there for coffee.'

'I shall look forward to that,' Rio, who up to this

point had been fully intending to find himself regretfully having to leave long before any convivial chat over coffee, assured with plausible sincerity.

Gwen pulled in a breath and, thinking it was now or never, forced herself to meet his stare head-on. She had chosen to forget about the skin-tingling effect of his proximity, because, until you were actually feeling it, the aura of raw masculinity he exuded was hard to quantify.

She struggled to think past it and waited.

His expression was one of unstudied cool, a calmness contradicted by his hands, which were clenched into fists at his side. 'So, *Mrs* Meredith, this is a surprise.'

'Yes,' she agreed, relieved and slightly amazed that she sounded so calm. Now all she had to do was string two words together in the right order and make an excuse to leave, after finding someone else to dump him on. That shouldn't be too difficult, as she was certain she wasn't the only female who couldn't see past the packaging.

She allowed her eyes to sweep up scornfully from his toes to his face, but midway through their journey the scorn got lost. All right, in her defence, it was *very* pretty packaging.

CHAPTER THREE

'So, you're married?' She had not adopted her husband's surname, but that was not unusual these days. The thought that she was married lay in a tight knot in his belly, his own reaction surprising him. Or maybe like his own mother she was divorced and now went by her maiden name?

A speculative crease appeared in his brow as she looked at him like a cornered animal and said nothing…which suggested that perhaps things were not all smooth sailing on the marriage front.

'Does your husband work at the school too?' he asked, instinctively disliking with a vengeance this unknown sexist jerk who had asked her to give up her dreams for him, leave her high-flying career and bury herself here…in sensible clothes.

His nostrils flared in outraged contempt as his glance slid to the flare of her hips below the cinched-in waist. The undeniable fact was she would look desirable in a sack. He didn't probe too deeply into the question of *why* the idea of her falling in love with some guy deeply enough to give up everything she'd worked so hard for made him so angry, then decided that it was the waste of talent. It was her choice, obviously, but she'd probably end up resenting the man at some point in future.

You didn't want her but you don't want anyone else to have her, suggested the sly voice in his head.

'It's been lovely to catch up,' she said brightly.

He laughed. 'Is that the conversational version of fake news?'

Gwen's polite mask slipped. What did he want her to say?

The truth was a luxury she didn't have, which narrowed her conversational options. Veiling the animosity she knew he had to be seeing in her eyes, she lowered her lashes to half mast and continued doggedly as though she hadn't heard his sarcastic insertion.

'But I really should get back to my class. They'll be running riot, and—'

'I thought you were going to explain to me about your outdoor teaching scheme.'

'Because you're *so* interested.' And she was so in trouble, if the head overheard her talking to the guest of honour that way. She saw the flare of interest in the glitter of his dark-framed eyes…the lush eyelashes his daughter had inherited…and wished the words unsaid.

'Absolutely,' he came back, not missing a beat.

She tightened her lips and this time didn't react to the provocation. 'Fine.'

'Outdoor learning sounds a bit New Age and *out there* for a place like this.' His eyes swept across the black and white Tudor building behind her.

His sneering attitude really riled her, despite the fact she knew full well that his interest was feigned. She could only assume he was enjoying making her feel uncomfortable. She snorted. As if *he* weren't born to a life of privilege.

'Because you went to an inner-city school, of course.' The words popped out before she could stop them. Flustered, she slid her eyes from his, her cheeks burning with embarrassment that she'd lost her cool.

'Did you?'

Surprise brought her eyes back to his. Dizzied by the direct eye-to-eye connection, she brought her lashes down in a protective shield that cast shadows across the curve of her high, smooth cheekbones. She gave her head the tiniest of shakes.

'No, I was brought up in a smallish market town in mid Wales.'

The primary school had been overcrowded after several large estates had mushroomed around the town. After that, she had taken the bus with everyone else to the red-brick comprehensive in the nearest large town.

He had asked the question, she had answered, and he felt…?

What?

They had been as intimate as two people could be, he had explored every inch of her body and she had shown an endless fascination for his, and yet, other than conversations that involved work, he knew virtually nothing about her. But then this shouldn't be so surprising; intimacy outside the bedroom was not something Rio did.

It was a choice, and he didn't feel as though he was missing out on anything. If there were occasions in the cooling aftermath of satisfying sex that made him conscious of a nebulous feeling of something that could be called emptiness, he considered it a price worth paying to avoid drifting into a relationship where he'd be expected to profess feelings he didn't believe existed, or, even worse, might convince himself *did*. His own father had never stopped believing he loved someone, even when it had nearly destroyed the person he'd claimed to love.

She saw a flicker of awareness move across the dark surface of his eyes before he lowered his gaze, frustrating her curiosity.

And why was she acting as if that were a *bad* thing? Gwen told herself she didn't want to know what made this man tick. She wanted him and his disruptive aura the hell out of her life.

'So tell me about outdoor teaching.'

Her shoulders lifted in a fractional shrug and she began by hoping to bore him but then, despite herself, warming to the subject until she heard herself talking about key-stage attainment and came to an abrupt halt. There was boring and then there was being an anorak.

'So you're basically telling me that kids are more engaged when learning outdoors?'

It wasn't as if she hadn't come across the sceptical response before, and was usually tolerant of it, but in this instance her chin came up. 'Quite definitely,' she said confidently. 'Learning through direct experience gives a greater understanding and research shows it raises academic attainment and—'

'It's fun,' he cut in with a quirky smile that made her heart flip. He thrust one hand in the pocket of his trousers and pulled out a vibrating phone. Silencing the low purr, he replaced it without even glancing at the screen. 'Relax.'

Gwen almost laughed at the advice, and so would he if he knew about Ellie. No, he probably wouldn't be laughing at all, but what he would be doing remained something of a question mark, and she was quite happy for it to remain that way.

'I'm all for anything that doesn't involve falling asleep in a stuffy classroom, although it might be tough to do in a city. But here—' his glance took in the parkland that surrounded the school buildings '—you have the advantage in that you don't have to go far to find a green space.'

'It's very lovely,' she agreed gravely. Who would have known when she got up this morning that in just a few short hours she'd be discussing the countryside with the father of her child? How long would it be before they got onto the topic of the weather?

'But not a cheap place to set up home?' he asked, clearly digging for information on what job her so-called husband did.

'We live in a cottage in the grounds.' Now, if he chose to assume that the *we* she referred to was a husband, that was his business. She hadn't lied; not that she wouldn't if she had to in order to protect Ellie. The problem was she wasn't very good at it. For once she was thoroughly glad of the outdated tradition in the school—so far unchallenged—which meant that every female teacher, regardless of her marital status, was referred to as *Mrs*.

The muscles along Rio's jaw clenched and he had a sour taste in his mouth as her words conjured an image of bucolic domesticity. He had never craved for domesticity, bucolic or otherwise.

Being bound to your soul mate for life might be some people's dream, but it definitely wasn't his. Leaving aside the fact that soul mates occupied the same space in his brain as unicorns, to him the marriage contract was not a cause for celebration and certainly not one he ever planned to put his name to.

He was ready to concede that it was possible not *all* marriages were toxic—perhaps even his parents' marriage had had a honeymoon period—but why take the chance? He'd often been called a risk-taker in business, but his risks were calculated and based more on facts than speculation. Marriage was just a risk too far for him.

The sound of a child crying behind him provided a distracting respite from his thoughts, but, respite or not, the wail had a nerve-shredding intensity and brought an expression of pained irritation to his face. However, the irritation turned to speculation when he saw the expression on Gwen's face. She was frozen with fear, but this was the first time he had seen it. The only movement was provided by her long lashes fluttering like some exotic butterfly's wings against her bone-white skin and the rapid rise and fall of her breasts under the blue cotton shirt that looked like a paler version of her striking cobalt eyes. She looked so dreadful he was convinced she was about to pass out and he tensed, ready to catch her before she hit the ground.

Then, as he watched, she unfroze like a statue coming to slow life, her eyes swivelling from a point beyond his shoulder to his face. A tiny amount of colour seeped back into her skin, robbing it of its marble appearance, and her expression was now almost...*resigned*? The furrow between his darkly etched straight brows deepened, but before he could ask what was wrong an older woman dressed in a floral-print dress that looked as if she'd fashioned it out of the curtains of a small bungalow rushed past, barging him with her elbow as she struggled to soothe the child she was carrying. He was no expert but this tiny dark-haired bundle did not look anywhere near school age, although she did look as though she might be rather a handful.

'Gwen, I'm so sorry,' the crèche assistant gasped. 'We simply couldn't pacify her; she just wants you, I'm afraid.'

'Has she been like this for—?'

'No, it's only been the last half-hour.'

'Don't worry, that's fine.' Gwen held out her arms, and Ellie, still sobbing, wrapped her arms and legs limpet-wise around her. Hot and sticky, the heat of her small body penetrated through Gwen's shirt and made her think of that first moment when Ellie had been laid on her chest, so warm and heavy. 'Hush, sweetheart, I know...' She smiled at the other woman feeling oddly calm now the worst was actually happening and she had no other option than to just deal with it. 'Thanks and don't worry.'

'Poor sweetheart...' The motherly woman stroked the child's dark hair before turning away. 'I have to get back, Gwen.'

'Of course and thanks again. I had a feeling she wasn't right this morning and I wish I'd kept her home now.' She had time owing in lieu of the sixth-form economics after-school club she had filled in for last month. It was a role she'd originally arrived at the school to take up, covering maternity leave. She'd had nothing to go to afterwards and the offer of a six-month stint in the reception class had seemed like a gift.

At the end of the six months she had been offered a permanent contract and she had found her niche in a place it would never have occurred to her to look. The days when she imagined that monetary rewards and kudos would make her happy seemed a long time ago.

Rio found himself rooted to the spot as the cogs in his brain clicked incredibly slowly. He considered the facts in front of him, but, despite a reality that was literally staring him in the face, it still took him a few seconds for comprehension to dawn. He waited until the pretty floral woman moved outside hearing distance before he spoke.

'She's yours.' He ignored the twisting sensation in

his chest; the problem was all in his head, where Gwen had remained frozen in time as the incredibly desirable, ambitious young executive who had seemed so sweet, so open and honest, that he'd started to feel guilty, among other things, that their affair was only temporary, until he'd caught her reading his correspondence. It had instantly resurrected toxic memories of watching his father read his mother's mail, take her phone and check her messages, delete numbers *he* felt she didn't need. *Dios*, he'd only just got his head around Gwen being married and now it seemed she was a mother too.

'Yes…now, if you'll excuse us…'

'Hold on!' He bent down.

She ran her tongue across her dry lips and tightened her grip on the child, who now lay limp in her arms. It looked as if the crying had tired her out; she was almost asleep.

Rio straightened up and held out the dog-eared stuffed rabbit that the little girl had dropped.

'Is this yours?'

He waited as the child's head lifted from her mother's shoulder. She regarded him with deep suspicious eyes like velvety brown pansies before she snatched the toy from his hand and buried her face back in her mother's neck.

Several feet of air separated them but Gwen could still literally *feel* his big body clench and still. His intimidating concentrated maleness was even more pronounced than normal as the tension stretched the skin tight against his incredible bone structure. His eyes swivelled from her hand cradling the back of Ellie's head to her face.

It felt like years before he spoke but it was probably only seconds, his voice low and soft. He seemed unaware that he was speaking Spanish and, while she only had a schoolgirl smattering of the language, Gwen didn't need a dictionary to translate the stream of hoarse words.

He knew—of *course* he knew!

You'd have to be wilfully blind or stupid not to see what had drained the vibrant colour from his olive-toned face and dissolved his habitual aura of cool command.

He was seeing the same thing she had the moment she'd looked into her newborn baby's face. Previous to that day she had gone along with loving new parents who said their baby was the spitting image of one or other parent, while in her experience the soft infant features all looked alike.

But Ellie's baby face had borne a startling likeness to Rio from day one. She'd tried to tell herself that the likeness would lessen as the little girl got older, but seeing them together now dispelled that vain hope. If anything, being able to study their faces side by side made the likeness between father and daughter all the more striking.

He wouldn't need a DNA test to confirm his fatherhood this time, she thought bitterly. It was practically like looking in a mirror for him. It was all in the bones, the angle of the jaw, the hairline, the shape of Ellie's forehead and, most of all, her eyes, fringed by a double row of sooty eyelashes.

'The child…she is mine.' He sounded as shocked as he looked for a man who'd presumably been there and done this before. But maybe it was easier to deal with the facts on paper rather than be confronted with a real-life person. For all she knew he might never have even seen his son.

Or he might be with, or even have married, the

mother of his firstborn. Both were equally possible, she realised with a rush of shock.

Strangely she found the latter possibility more disturbing and her feelings could not be totally explained away by her natural sadness for the things his firstborn would have that Ellie wouldn't—like the love of his father.

She couldn't take her eyes off the muscle clenching and unclenching in his concave cheek. It didn't even cross her mind to lie—what would be the point now?

'Yes, she is yours. Her name is Ellie and she's just two.'

She could see he was struggling to string a sentence together and waited, stomach clenched, for what he might say next.

'Does your husband know the truth or does he think she is his?'

Her delicate jaw clenched as she eyed him with disdain. If she'd had a free hand she might have forgotten she was a committed pacifist—*again!*—and slapped his face! The question of why something about this man had bypassed a few thousand years of evolution and made her feel primal was for another time.

'Your opinion of me is so flattering, as always.' So not only was she the woman who went through his private correspondence, now she was the woman who pretended another man's child was her husband's. 'But I don't actually have a husband. All female staff here are referred to as Mrs, regardless of marital status.'

He dismissed the explanation with an impatient shake of his dark head. 'But you said—'

Her chin lifted to a challenging angle. 'Actually,' she countered, '*I* didn't say anything, you just assumed. Hush, Ellie, darling,' she murmured, and brushed a strand of dark hair back from her daughter's flushed forehead as the sharp voices made her start to cry again.

'You allowed me to think—'

'I don't owe you any explanations,' she hissed back quietly between clenched teeth for the sake of her fretful, feverish daughter. She really didn't have the time or energy to deal with his indignation or anger right now.

His eyes were on the poorly child who had settled a little now, and the expression in those dark depths was almost hungry. Gwen experienced a spasm of gut-clenching fear. Suddenly, for the very first time she encountered the possibility that he might *want* Ellie. He might actually want to take Ellie away from her.

'I think explanations are the least you owe me,' he intoned grimly, equally quietly.

She closed her eyes and gave her head a tiny shake of disbelief, the anger spilling through her pushing away the last vestiges of guilt. 'I owe you nothing and you owe me nothing. We are simply two people who… who…collided.'

Rio's eyes lifted to hers. 'Several times,' he murmured, the brief wicked gleam in his eyes fading as he struggled to clear the sound of a child crying that was still echoing in his head. It was disconcerting as the echo was playing in sync with the real thing.

The child…*his* child—and would that ever seem real to him?—had begun to sob and squirm in her mother's arms. As his focus widened beyond his own private drama involving the three of them, he became aware for the first time that they were beginning to attract attention. Some of the pupils and staff filing out of the hall had slowed to stare at them curiously.

'I can't believe that we are having this conversation.'

'What did you think would happen?' he bit out.

Colour stinging her cheeks, Gwen rebutted, 'What I mean is this was not supposed to happen.'

'What, getting pregnant, or me finding out I had a child?'

'Both,' she admitted removing a hank of her hair from his daughter's—*Ellie's*—tenacious grip.

'I'm no expert, but shouldn't you be taking her to the hospital?' He knew nothing about children but this one was...*his daughter*. He gave his dark head a shake, but, no, he was actually awake and this was really happening. It wasn't a dream. The shock he was experiencing was momentarily blanked out by a fresh wave of anger as he thought of all the moments he had missed with his child that he would never get back.

'That's right, you're *not* an expert,' Gwen pointed out. When had he last had a sleepless night? she thought, her contempt almost immediately vanishing to be replaced by a sick feeling in the pit of her stomach as she recalled some of the things Rio usually thought preferable to sleep.

It was a measure of how completely he took over her mind that this thought led seamlessly into an image imprinted and preserved in her head in perfect detail, the moment captured for ever, along with the nameless ache she had felt deep inside as she'd stared at him lying asleep on his back early one morning, one arm above his head, his face in repose. The lines that might one day be permanent had been ironed out, looking, not softer, exactly, but younger beneath the piratical stubble that emphasised the angles of his jaw and the hollow of his carved cheeks.

In the soft dappled early morning light that had filtered through the blinds on the open window, his skin had shone like dull gold against the crumpled white sheet that was bunched across his narrow hips, the shadows emphasising the muscular definition of his chest and ridged belly.

She remembered desperately wanting to touch him and so she had, her fingers moving along the line of dark hair that ran down his belly until her hand was caught and she found herself staring into black, wickedly gleaming and not at all sleepy eyes that were still looking at her as he pulled her down on top of him.

Breaking free of the vivid memories drew a tiny grunt of effort from her parted lips.

'This is neither the time nor the place for this conversation,' she said, a shade of desperation creeping into her voice because there was no time and no place where she wanted to have this conversation.

He glanced towards their growing audience. Clearly, it was the first thing they had agreed on. 'So where, and when?'

She looked at him in horror, the recognition dawning in her brain that there was going to be no escape route, no secret door, no alternative to them having a face-to-face discussion.

She tipped her head in acknowledgement and defeat. 'All right, my cottage.'

'Cottage?' His slightly confused expression cleared. 'The one in the grounds you mentioned? Right, I will find it.' He glanced at his watch. 'Shall we say five o'clock?'

Gwen shook her head. 'No, six.' By that time she ought to have been able to pacify Ellie and if not he'd just have to wait. She lifted her chin. Her daughter would always come first with her and the sooner he caught onto that fact, the better. The world might work around Rio Bardales's schedule but she had moved on.

CHAPTER FOUR

GWEN NOTICED ABSENTLY that her hand was shaking as she tried to coax her daughter to take the temperature-lowering medicine. When the toddler turned her head away for the fourth time and it spilled down her front Gwen felt the tears she'd so far held back begin to spill down her cheeks.

Taking a deep breath, she squeezed her eyes tight shut and told herself, *Self-pity, Gwen, is really not attractive.*

A moment later as she choked back a sob and forced a smile, perhaps her change of attitude communicated itself to her child, who stopped crying to watch her mother with big eyes.

Gwen took advantage of the moment of calm to spoon the mixture between her lips. 'Excellent, good girl…'

She sat back with a sigh as a wave of love so strong that it made her breathless washed over her. Before Ellie had been born she had worried about bonding with her, not able to imagine this swell of instinctive parental love. Suddenly, an image of Rio's face, the shock of recognition in his eyes when he'd seen Ellie, surfaced in her head.

What would it feel like to be hit by the reality you

were a father that way? The truth was she could not imagine that scenario any more than she could imagine how he was feeling now he'd had time to take it on board.

Or maybe he was wondering how to break the news to the mother of his son—his partner…his wife? Her life had moved on and it was only reasonable to assume that his had too.

Which Rio would arrive? Would he be angry? Cold? Businesslike?

Would he even arrive?

Another image flashed in front of her, of the expression in his dark eyes as he had stared at Ellie, and she shivered. It was definitely not the look of a man who had any intention of walking away.

Trying to shake the feeling of impending doom that weighed her down, she told herself her time would be better spent preparing a plan of action for a scenario that was never meant to happen.

She tried to reawaken the feeling of optimism, of liberation almost, that she'd felt the day Ellie was born and she had come to her decision not to tell Rio, a decision that had nothing to do with the months of arguing with herself and playing devil's advocate. The decision had been made because it felt right, and she could finally move on as a mother. It was a new, exciting and scary chapter in her life, but she could do it. Alone.

She didn't need Rio's help, and she was not going to beg or humiliate herself by submitting to DNA testing. She had mentally wiped him out of her life. Well, to be completely truthful, it had been a work in progress but she'd been getting there.

Sadly he didn't get the same memo!

With Ellie on her shoulder, she began to pace up

and down the small cosy living room humming softly, and after a few grumpy kicks and moans Ellie settled, soothed by the rhythmic motion. Gwen carried on humming, glancing at the clock on the mantle occasionally until she felt the toddler go limp in her arms and the baby breaths become deep and even.

She pushed open the only bedroom door with her foot. The lack of a second bedroom was one of those problems that she had left for the future, as for the moment the cot at the bottom of her bed worked and there was room for a small bed later on.

Pulling back the sheet, she laid her sleeping daughter down. Her cheeks were rosy but no longer feverish as the medicine was doing its job. Switching on the baby monitor even though there wasn't anywhere in the tiny cottage where she wouldn't hear her cry, Gwen drew the curtains and crept from the room, leaving the door ajar behind her.

Back in the living room, she glanced at the clock again, silently counting the minutes until Rio would appear. It was hard to rehearse what she was going to say when she didn't have a clue what he was going to ask, or demand or… She sighed and began to chew her plump bottom lip distractedly, fighting her way free of another wave of despair.

'For goodness' sake, Gwen, stop feeling sorry for yourself!'

Her eyes narrowed with determination as she began to whisk around the room, plumping the odd cushion, picking up a toy and lobbing it in the toy box beside the window. Yesterday she had been wishing she had the space for a playroom; today she loved everything exactly the way it was. Perhaps you had to have your little world threatened to appreciate a worn carpet or a shower that was only a frustrating trickle.

It was a struggle to visualise Rio in these surroundings; it really was *not* his natural environment. He was sleek and exclusive and—she released a quivering sigh—just the *thought* of him being here had the power to make her insides quiver. Shameful though it was, it hardly seemed worth the energy it cost pretending she wasn't still as vulnerable as she had ever been to his lethal sexuality.

It just proved that sexual chemistry was utterly indiscriminate. Ignoring the butterfly kicks still making their presence known in her stomach, she walked into her diminutive galley kitchen to get a glass of water to moisten her suddenly dry mouth.

It was the uncertainty, she told herself, that was really testing her. If Rio had gone into denial mode she could have dealt with it, or at least dealt with it more easily. Of course, he might still go that way once he had got over the initial shock.

He might just want confirmation that she was not going to make any future demands on him. Well, she could happily give him that—she'd sign anything if it meant he'd leave them in peace.

Gwen tiptoed back into the bedroom, checked on Ellie, who was sleeping peacefully still, and jumped at the sound of a rose branch scratching the window as the freshening breeze caught it.

You need to relax, Gwennie girl, she told herself, before grinning at the sheer impossibility of this. Absently fishing a lip gloss from her pocket, she smeared it over her lips before closing the door behind her.

By the time she had sat down and then jumped up again she had chewed the strawberry moisture off.

Would he be on time?

Should she have contacted a lawyer?

As if she had one on speed dial! She gave a small snort of self-mocking laughter and tried not to think of the access to top legal experts that Rio had.

Discovering a stray brightly coloured building block behind a cushion that had escaped her whirlwind round of frenzied tidying, she headed for the overflowing toy box when the knock on the door made her leap like a startled deer.

She took a deep breath and schooled her features into neutrality, or as close as she was going to get to that, and opened the door. Her eyes travelled upwards as she took a half-step outside, her elbow brushing the roses around the door.

His jacket had gone and the fabric of his tailored shirt was fine enough to suggest the drifts of body hair on his torso. Or maybe she was just seeing them because she knew they were there. Her cheeks heated guiltily at the thought.

'You live here?'

She didn't pause to think of a sarcastic response, just nodded.

He didn't respond to the social cue so, after an awkward pause, she added, 'It's convenient.' Less convenient was noticing for the first time the coiled tension in his lean body. It wasn't just his masculinity that sent a fresh shudder through her body, it was the predator barely disguised by the perfect tailoring.

One dark brow lifted but he still didn't say anything. Gwen tried to ignore the grab of some emotion that felt like a hand in her chest as their eyes finally connected, the moment she had been avoiding.

She wanted to look away but the moment dragged,

hampered by the mind-fogging hormonal flare she felt. She resorted to stiff formality as she finally managed to slide her eyes to some point over his left shoulder. Sexual chemistry had no place here; she owed it to Ellie to keep a clear head. She had learnt from her mistakes and it was more important than ever not to repeat them.

Chance would be a fine thing!

Ignoring the shame-inducing reaction of her inner voice, she gave a faint smile. 'Come in.' She stood to one side and, after an equally stilted and blank-faced pause, he stepped past her directly into her sitting room.

In the confined space his sheer physicality took on an extra resonance, as did the predatory undercurrents that had made her hormones leap.

Rio discovered that the cottage, which looked like a chocolate box outside, was more like a doll's house inside. He supposed it was charming if you liked low beams and leaded windows, but he didn't; he preferred light and space. His eyes moved over the toys spilling out of a box in the corner and they darkened. He was still desperately struggling to assimilate the knowledge he was a father, but the emotions were so complex and intertwined that the anger kept colliding with the shock and the sheer gut-wrenching wonder of it all.

It was a situation that he'd not asked for but one he was certainly responsible for, which equated to this combined anger and guilt. Being a father was one thing, but having the fact hidden from him, leaving him an outsider in a process he had been so intimately involved with, left him feeling...what, exactly?

Of course, the irony and the massive degree of hypocrisy his reaction generated was impossible to duck. How could he blame Gwen when he had done the very same thing to his brother? His twin, his other half, who still didn't know he had fathered a son… The guilt Rio had lived with every day since he'd agreed to the deception hadn't gone away, but it had been easier to bear because he had been so sure that he'd made the right decision.

Today's events made him feel far less secure about that. Had Gwen thought she'd made the right decision too?

Had she thought his daughter was better off not knowing her father? And could he really blame her? This degree of reluctant understanding of her possible motives didn't lessen his determination to be an ongoing part of this child's life, to be the best father he could, but the next step was convincing Gwen of this. Of course, his advantage in all this was that he suspected she had a strongly developed sense of fair play whereas he was quite *flexible* about such things, especially when the stakes were this high.

He had no intention of taking no for an answer.

He looked around the room again and glanced at her, wondering if she thought he considered it to be shabby and cramped. She was clearly bracing her shoulders in a defensive attitude and when he suddenly turned, she jumped, taking a nervy involuntary step backwards. She bit down, her white teeth sinking into her plump lower lip, distracting him for a moment. Then she cleared her throat loudly, and he wondered if she'd noticed.

Rio frowned. He could see that the blue-veined pulse at the base of her slender throat was throbbing nervously, and the possibility that she was scared of him made him feel like a monster.

'Are you all right?' he asked when she lowered her hand from her mouth.

She nodded. 'Can I get you anything to drink?' she offered.

'It sounds like *you* need a drink,' he said, wondering if that would relax her a little.

She shook her head.

'I'm okay, thanks.'

'Is she… *Ellie*…?' He paused after pushing out her name slowly as if he was still trying it out for fit. 'Is she feeling better now?' he asked, grimacing faintly as he heard the accusatory note edge into his tone. He could tell by the stiffening of her posture that Gwen had too.

She nodded.

'Can I see her?' His jaw clenched, the fine muscles quivering, as the request brought home just how wrong this situation was. He was asking permission to see his own child.

The look of alarm that flickered across her face as she desperately tried to think of an excuse to say no only added to the feeling of *wrongness*.

'I'm not going to snatch her, you know,' he said with impatient irony.

He saw a guilty flush rise up her neck until her face looked as if it were burning. 'I never thought you were,' she protested defensively.

His expressive mouth twisted. 'But you are now.' She was as easy to read as a neon headline.

'She's sleeping.'

For a guilty moment he acknowledged a flash of relief. How did you talk to a person who was little more than a baby? What did you say to your own child? But the hunger to see her again remained stronger than his self-doubt.

It made him think again of Roman, his twin, who had a child he would never know, and the guilt he lived with every day tightened as he promised huskily, 'I won't wake her.'

For a split second he thought she was going to refuse and the hell of it was there was not a thing he could do about it. He had fathered a child and yet he had no rights… His taut jaw clenched, dragging the skin tight across his slashing cheekbones at the prospect of having to beg to see his own child.

Gwen kick-started her brain, ashamed that for a few vital moments she had allowed herself to get sidetracked by the small jagged scar she had noticed on his forehead, white against his golden-toned skin.

'Fine,' she mumbled, except of course it wasn't. 'This way.'

She didn't look at him but she was very conscious of his physical presence as he followed her through the door she pushed open. She wondered where she drew the line—when did she say no? There had to be guidelines, limits…didn't there?

Gwen turned and saw straight away that his attention was almost immediately riveted by the cot that stood at the foot of the small old-fashioned brass double bed in the bright-yellow-painted room. She wondered if he could feel the quivering tension coming off her but she said nothing, just stood to one side as he walked towards the cot cautiously.

Gwen hung back, hands clenched, not wanting him here and particularly not wanting to see the conflict in his face as he looked down into the cot. Yet it was the wonder that flickered into his eyes, and something close to longing there too, that she really didn't want to see the most.

She looked away. She couldn't let this situation be all about him and his feelings. This was about her and

Ellie; they were a unit of two. Rio had to stay on the outside of that unit—she'd be fair but firm and if necessary selfish in order to protect Ellie.

'I'll be just through there.' She nodded her head to indicate the other room and left, but she didn't think he noticed.

It was five minutes before he joined her. Gwen was staring out of the window blindly and didn't hear his soft-footed approach. It was only the prickling on the back of her neck that alerted her to his presence.

She turned and saw him standing just inside the doorway, but his expression told her nothing. 'Sorry, I didn't hear—'

'I didn't wake her...' he said at the same time, and hesitated. Then, as she stayed silent, he added, 'Is she well?' He dragged a hand through his dark hair and moved further into the room. 'What did the doctor say?'

'She hasn't seen a doctor.' Before he could express the outrage she could see tauten his face she quickly explained, 'The next appointment the surgery has is not for several days.'

Rio snarled out his opinion of this situation in a flood of blistering angry Spanish.

'Do you mind translating that?' she asked, bewildered.

His jaw clenched. 'That's outrageous!'

She accepted the more polite, shortened version, noticing with a shiver that he suddenly seemed even taller and more physically intimidating in the small room.

'What's the doctor's number?'

Her eyes flew wide in alarm. 'What do you think you're doing?'

He flashed her a look as he pulled his phone from his pocket. 'What do you think? Should I call him out? Or,

better still, I'll tell him you need a second opinion—
except you haven't even had a first—'

Feeling her temper spurt at the implied criticism, she
cut him off, her voice cold but controlled. 'For the record *he* is a *she* and this isn't your call to make in any
sense of the word.'

She could see him almost literally bite back a sharp
retort as her words sank in. Instead he threw her a look
that simply seethed with frustration.

She struggled not to empathise with how he must
be feeling, but she couldn't afford to allow herself to
soften towards him or show him any weakness, or very
soon it could be Rio telling her when she could see her
daughter.

This horrifying image hardened her resolve.

Rio already had a child, she just had Ellie.

'You may have been a parent longer than me.' She
saw his blank expression and tacked on sarcastically,
'Or had you already forgotten?'

He didn't respond verbally to that barb, but at least
she'd got some reaction. She supposed it was *something*
that he could clearly feel guilt, always supposing she
wasn't misreading the reason for the dark bands of colour across his high cheekbones.

'But *I've* been doing this for two years now,' she added
with quiet dignity. No point explaining that sometimes
she still didn't feel as though she knew what she was
doing. She was not about to tell him about her insecurities; it would feel a lot like handing more ammunition
to someone who already had a gun aimed at your head.

A frown flickered across her face at the over-dramatic
analogy—she *really* had to lower the levels of paranoia.
On the other hand she really couldn't see a downside to
Rio thinking she was an expert in child-rearing.

The seething silence lengthened while their eyes clashed, black on iridescent blue. The dark bands of colour scoring his cheekbones deepened and his eyes dropped as he finally slid the phone slowly back into his pocket, tacitly admitting a defeat she could see was alien to his nature and life experience.

'And that is my fault, I suppose,' he said bitterly.

Gwen recognised that this could easily escalate into some sort of war of attrition. One of them had to keep their temper, so she took hers tightly in hand and shook her head. If she lost it she might say things that she would undoubtedly later regret.

'I didn't say that. I'm simply saying that being a mum is a learning process and this isn't the first time Ellie has been unwell. Babies do sometimes become unwell and they can't exactly tell you what's wrong!' Belatedly aware that her voice had climbed shrilly and started to wobble, she took a deep, calming breath.

He didn't need to know about her doubts, about the nights she longed for someone to share the responsibility that came with being the parent of a baby, but there hadn't been anyone so she had made the unilateral decision that she no longer needed any help.

'Her temperature has already come back down. She had a cold last week and it's left her a little stuffed up. She's been pulling at her ear…she seems a bit prone to ear problems.' She pushed out the information quickly before explaining something no new parent, or indeed anyone who had never been ill, would know. 'They are reluctant to give antibiotics these days for something that is probably viral, and sitting in a crowded waiting room was not going to make her feel any better. They'd just tell me to take her home and do what I am already doing.'

'Which is?'

He listened in silence as she explained that she'd given Ellie medicine to lower her temperature and made sure she had plenty of fluids.

'And sleep,' she added, 'is really good, though she's likely to be a bit grumpy when she wakes up.' She really hoped this would be sorted and he'd be gone by the time Ellie woke up, but, being a realist, she could see that this might be optimistic, so it was best to prepare him for the worst. 'Or then again, she might be chirpy. It's not an exact science…'

'But in general she is a healthy child?'

Gwen was relieved he sounded calmer. 'She's fine and, yes, she's had no health problems beyond the usual.'

He nodded and she could see from the blank look on his face that he didn't have a clue what the usual was. Perhaps he didn't have much to do with his son?

'Right, then, is there anything else you'd like to know?' She paused, wondering if she should tell him straight off that she wasn't going to make any financial demands on him. Just cut the polite and painfully awkward chit-chat and get to the point?

'This must have been a shock for you,' she said, remembering how much of a shock it had been to her to discover she was pregnant.

She'd run home—that had been her first mistake.

Ironic really that her parents, who had never really believed in her five-year plan and her career, had suddenly been absolutely emphatic that she not give it up. Her father, they'd said, had already told everyone at the golf club about her success, and they were impressed— as if this clinched the argument. Except she wasn't arguing, she was just letting them talk at her, feeling her heart freeze over as she listened to them in increasing horror.

'So you want me to "get rid of it"?' She remembered hearing her father's hiss of exasperation as she sketched sarcastic inverted commas in the air and finished, 'Just so that you can continue to have bragging rights at the golf club?'

'Well, you've finally done something for us to be proud of.'

Ironically, once her parents' pride in her would have mattered so much; it was what she'd been striving for all her life.

'Gwen, dear, you must see your life will be ruined. All your plans will come to nothing—and what will people say?'

'And that's what really matters, isn't it? What people think! The only thing that matters to you is appearances. There is no disgrace, no shame involved, in having a baby alone these days, Mam.' Gwen's glance flickered towards the towering presence of disapproval that was her father. 'But there is plenty of shame in living a lie.'

Unable to meet her eyes, her mother looked away and whispered, 'I only want what's best for you, *cariad*.'

'I know, Mam, but—'

'How dare you talk to your mother like that? And don't call her Mam—it's common!'

As he planted a beefy arm around his wife's shoulders Gwen found herself wondering when she'd last seen any display of physical affection between them.

'If you keep it, we want nothing to do with you.'

Gwen looked at her mother, who just shook her head and looked away.

It was the exact point when Gwen knew she was totally on her own.

Her mum looked small, like someone who'd had the life sucked out of her. Gwen knew that at one time her mother would have been strong enough to resist her father's demands that Gwen get rid of her baby...and her mother was probably paying a silent price ever since for not standing up to him, but she'd had no more fight left.

Gwen shook off the heavy empty feeling that came with the unhappy memories and forced a smile.

'Do you want to sit down? Oh, not that one,' she added quickly, gesturing at the overstuffed armchair he was standing next to. 'The legs are a bit wobbly.'

He probably thought the whole place was a *bit wobbly*. After all, he had just been escorted on a tour around the school, including state-of-the-art laboratory facilities, where no expense had been spared. Despite this, the employees lived in accommodation that could only be called basic.

He shook his head and walked across to the second armchair but, instead of sitting, stood behind it and placed his hands on the back rest. 'I'm fine.'

Gwen assumed his dark brooding scowl was directed at his surroundings and lifted her chin. Ah, well, it would do him good to slum it, she decided, struggling to hold onto her angry contempt as an image of his *cottage* on the Cape Cod island off Martha's Vineyard flashed into her head. When he'd first asked her to dinner, she'd assumed he was staying in a hotel, but she had learnt that it was never a good idea to *assume* with Rio.

His version of a cottage was the incredible sprawling seafront property set in the middle of lush, beautifully tended acres. The fact they had arrived in a private plane that he'd piloted himself should have been a clue to how ridiculously wealthy he was, but the sight of his house—or, more correctly, his estate—had brought it home to her for the first time that she was dealing with someone who lived in a completely different world.

A world where *wonky* had no place, just as she'd had no place in his.

She absently smoothed a throw that she had positioned to hide the worn patch on the arm of a chair. This was her world, hers and Ellie's, and she was not ashamed of it, she was *proud* of what she had achieved with no help from anyone and she wouldn't allow him to make her feel any different about it.

For years she'd watched her father blame her mother, or even sometimes her, every time he'd strayed—which had been often. But it had always been their fault for not understanding him, for not being *enough* for him.

The moment Ellie was born Gwen had vowed that she'd be a good role model. That her daughter would never have to feel ashamed of her the way Gwen had eventually become ashamed of her mother, who had been unable to break free of the cycle of emotional abuse doled out by her father.

Ellie would never feel that she was not *enough*!

CHAPTER FIVE

RIO WATCHED GWEN STRAIGHTEN, the cushion she had picked up still pressed to her chest protectively, her expression distant but wary as she focused on him. The idea that she felt she needed to protect herself from him made the muscles along his jaw quiver.

He admired the way she'd made this small house into a home, despite its worn appearance. He thought less of the school's headmaster, not Gwen. The employer in him considered this bad working practice. Loyalty was a two-way street; you treated staff well and they in turn were willing to go the extra mile.

The newly discovered father in him found the idea of his child not enjoying the luxuries that he took for granted felt wrong on so many levels. His child, but except for today's chance encounter he might have walked past her in the street and not known her!

'Why didn't you tell me, Gwen?'

Thrown by the directness of the question, she blinked. 'It was my decision to go ahead with the pregnancy, my body, my baby,' she intoned solemnly. 'What would have been the point telling you? What were you going to do, after, of course, I'd submitted to a lie detector and the prescribed range of DNA tests? Marry me?'

He winced but she didn't notice.

'People marry for less,' he observed carefully.

'Love, you mean?'

'You think a transitory chemical attraction is more important than having a child together?'

'You make love sound like a selfish indulgence,' she said.

He arched a strongly delineated brow. 'I wasn't talking about maternal love.'

'You asked what I think, well, I think that Ellie and what is best for her are the most important things to me,' she told him fiercely.

'Until you meet a man?' His broad shoulders tensed as a flash freeze image formed in his head of a faceless male in Gwen's bed and being a father to his child. The constant tug of sexual attraction he was fighting paled beside this raw and primal response to what was only an imaginary scenario.

She released a scornful laugh. 'Because I feel incomplete without a man in my life? Hardly! I have Ellie, and my work, so I already have everything I need.'

But did she have enough money? he wondered.

'I suppose that contacting you to keep you in the loop was an option, but not one that filled me with joy and positivity after our affair ended the way it did. And quite honestly I was too busy throwing up for several months to worry about it that much.'

He felt a kick of guilt that was totally irrational because he hadn't known she'd suffered that badly, but, as they said in every courtroom drama, ignorance was no defence. Something twisted inside him at the thought of her being alone and suffering.

But she wouldn't have been alone, he realised with a sense of relief. Not all families were as dysfunctional as his.

'You went home?' As his glance drifted over her sinuous curves, it was hard for him to imagine her heavily pregnant.

Gwen's eyes lowered. 'For a time,' she said, moistening her lips. 'I had some savings.'

'You packed in your job right off? I'm sure they had a very generous healthcare plan.'

'I was living in America and I was still on a probationary period, so there was no way they were going to give me a permanent contract if I was pregnant.'

He cleared his throat and gave a thoughtful nod. 'So not good timing, then.'

She gave a sudden laugh. 'There's never a good time to have a baby and yet people still do.'

He would have found this conversation more comfortable if he'd been the target of her resentment and anger, but she appeared remarkably calm about having her life thrown upside down. 'This was hardly a planned pregnancy.'

'The statistics on that make interesting reading— fewer than you'd think are planned.'

'At least you had a support network back home.'

Gwen said nothing. The less said about her *support network*, the better. She smoothed back her hair and gave a casual shrug.

'I have friends and I like to be independent. Also, as luck would have it, I had a small win on a premium bond my late godmother bought me years ago, so money wasn't a problem.' It was important to her not to come across as a victim—not of anything. 'Look, I'm sure you're not really interested in my finances, so let's just get to the real reason you're here.'

Something flickered at the backs of his eyes as he arched a sardonic brow. 'And that would be?' he prompted with a display of gentle interest, though there was nothing anyone would describe as gentle in the headlight stare that she found uncomfortably intent.

'I am not going to make any demands on you. I don't expect any involvement from you at all.'

A nerve in Rio's cheek clenched. She said it as though he needed reassurance, while her attitude strongly suggested that the news that she didn't expect him to be any part of his own child's life was meant to make him *happy*! *Dios!* He would have been the first to concede that he might have given her reason to think he was not exactly a saint, but did she really think he was such a rat as to walk away from his own child?

'What sort of demands are we talking?' He kept his face locked in a mask of polite indifference that became increasingly hard to maintain as an image of her making some very pleasant demands of him floated through his head, her soft, husky laugh, her long, extremely flexible legs, her lips. His gaze sank to her mouth, which he assumed was about to say something far less pleasing than, *Again, please, Rio*!

His indolent drawl had nothing to do with the flames flickering in his mesmeric eyes, and for a moment Gwen lost her verbal footing as waves of distracting heat thrummed through her body.

She stammered out, 'I-I'll put it in writing if you want…? I expect you have lawyers on speed dial?' She faltered, her voice drying up as she encountered his furious glare. She could literally *feel* the anger vibrating off him.

'You think that's why I'm here? To have you sign some sort of nondisclosure agreement and pay you off!'

'I don't want your money. I don't want anything from you!' she exclaimed in horror, pushing aside a small voice in the back of her head that asked if she was allowing her pride to get in the way of Ellie's best interests.

But she was getting ahead of herself. Rio hadn't offered her anything yet, with strings or otherwise.

He sighed and dragged a hand through his hair, his eyes flicking to the half-closed bedroom door. 'It appears as if you're coping.'

As he gave the grudging concession—perhaps it was even a compliment?—her shocked, widened eyes flew to his face. But the expression in his own hooded gaze as he continued talking had her quickly back-pedalling on the compliment idea.

'But why should my daughter have to just *cope*? I realise it can't have been easy for you.'

Not even slightly mollified by the acknowledgement, Gwen ground her even white teeth. 'I'm not a victim.'

'I didn't mean to suggest that you are.'

She looked at him sideways and thought, *Yeah, not much?*

'I have a job I love, a daughter I adore—I consider myself extremely lucky.'

Rio's slender grip on diplomacy slipped through his fingers as he ground out a frustrated imprecation. This woman really was the most aggravating and touchy female he had ever encountered.

'Well, you would say that, wouldn't you, because you're too damned stubborn and independent to admit you needed help, even if your life depended on it, but this isn't just your life, is it? It's Ellie's, my daughter's…' He caught the flare in her eyes but ignored a stab of guilt for his below-the-belt blow. He still had a point to make. 'Our daughter does not even have a room of her own and she is left in the care of those who, although I am sure they are admirable, are little more than strangers…'

'Not to me!' she countered. 'And sometimes a child is better off with a stranger than a real parent.'

'You think my daughter would be better off with a stranger than me,' Rio said flatly.

Her blue eyes flew wide. 'That wasn't what I meant.' She heaved out a sigh and lifted her hands, palm up, as she admitted, 'I didn't have the best relationship with my father.'

His clenched air of tension relaxed somewhat at her admission. 'And now?'

'There is no relationship at all.'

He tipped his head but to her obvious relief didn't push it, instead murmuring a soft, expressionless, 'It happens.'

'Look, this could get very complicated. You already have a child and—' Something flashed in his eyes and she stumbled to a halt. 'Obviously your relationships are none of my business, and if you wanted to put something to one side for Ellie when she's older, for her university education, that might be a nice gesture.'

His head reared back, his high cheekbones standing out on a face that was rigid with offence, which she clearly found bewildering if the confused look on her face was anything to go by.

'You think I make a habit of impregnating women and walking away?' And why shouldn't she? he thought bitterly. After all, that was exactly what he had done, even if he'd only done it the once, rather than twice, as she believed.

Rio was not a person who had ever felt the need for the good opinion of others and he rarely, if ever, explained himself to anyone. Some people called him arrogant and he was fine with that—people took him at his word or they didn't, and it was not something he ever lost sleep over.

So it came as a shock to have to fight the impulse to tell Gwen the truth about his brother's child, but it was not his secret to share and he had given his word to Marisa. It was a promise he couldn't break, even if he had regretted making it many times.

He sometimes wondered if the agreement with Marisa and his guilt over that had been partly responsible for the intangible distance that had grown between him and his twin. There was no question in his mind that, despite the kick in the gut that it had been at the time, he still hadn't accepted his brother's out-of-the-blue decision to walk away from the responsibilities they'd shared controlling the Bardales empire.

'I have no idea what sort of arrangement you have with—'

Rio cut across her, choosing his words with care. 'That child you speak of is not in my life.'

'I suppose fatherhood is not for everyone,' she muttered, looking at her feet.

'Your efforts to be non-judgemental could do with some work,' he said drily.

Her eyes flew to his face. 'I'm not judgemental,' she said huffily.

His eyes narrowed on her flushed, angry and quite heart-stoppingly beautiful face and he felt his blood heat with inconvenient but inevitable lust. 'I'm sure you're the epitome of tact and political correctness.'

'Things nobody is going to accuse you of!' she fired back.

His sensual lips twisted into a smile. 'Well, at least we've stopped being painfully polite to one another.'

'*I* am polite.'

'I'm starting to get the idea that you'd be happier if I wanted to escape my responsibilities.'

'I…we are not anyone's *responsibility*—' She stopped mid angry flow, her eyes widening to their fullest extent as she stared at him in dawning horror. 'You mean you're not?'

'What do you think I've been trying to say?'

'I won't know until you say it.'

'I want to co-parent Ellie. I want to be fully involved in her life.'

'Co-parent?' she parroted as though the word made no sense to her. 'You *want* to be involved?'

'Why are you so shocked? I may not have given birth to her, but half that child's make-up is mine.'

Gwen's bubble of laughter was half a sob. 'That's hard to miss.' She shook her head. 'But you have said that you don't have contact with your son so I assumed—'

'You mean you hoped?' he said cynically.

Her eyes slid away from his.

'Look, I'm not going to force you into anything. I just want to get to know my daughter and I think you owe me that at least.'

Any brownie points his placatory manner might have won was clearly cancelled out by that *owe* and he could see Gwen's temper fizz. '*Owe*? So are you keeping some sort of score card? You know, you might think I'm dim, but I can't for the life of me think what I could possibly owe you!'

'Ellie's first steps?'

He watched an arrested expression steal across her face. She was so easy to read that he wondered how she'd got this far without someone taking advantage of her.

She hadn't. Because you did.

'First smile,' he ground out, pushing away the guilt. 'First word… In fact, you owe me for all the things I have already missed, all the milestone moments that I will never experience!'

The emotion that thickened his normally slight Spanish accent obviously shocked her deeply.

'I didn't think you'd want to experience them.' Honesty rang out in her voice.

'I have told you I want to be a part of her life. I meant it.'

Rio paused, tilting his head to shield the expression that flashed into his dark eyes as the dark irony struck home. He was fighting for a role that he had colluded with another to deprive his twin of.

He tensed, ready to quash the guilt and nagging doubts that inevitably accompanied the acknowledgement of his role in the deception, given an added knife twist now that he had discovered he was a secret father too.

But the two situations were different, he reasoned. Roman's relationship with the mother of his child had been over long before she had come to Rio asking for his help.

You never had a relationship with Gwen, though, the voice in his head contributed unhelpfully. *You just had sex.*

His jaw clenched. He did not need reminding about the sex. He remembered every touch, every gasp, every soft sigh… With an effort he dragged his thoughts away from the warm distractions filling it and focused on the facts that had influenced his decision.

The mother of his brother's child had approached Rio at a time when every media outlet had been delivering

a new image of Roman, a now famous bestselling author who was as daring and handsome as his fictional
hero on an almost daily basis. In every image the same
woman was with him, frequently gazing lovingly up at
him. His twin was happy, or appeared to be, with another woman. His life had clearly moved on.

Had Rio's own ever really moved on from the short
torrid affair with Gwen?

The furrow between his ebony brows deepened as
he closed down the inner dialogue. Not being in a relationship didn't meant that he hadn't moved on from
Gwen; not being in a relationship meant he was doing
something right. Living his life the way he always did.

A fleeting image of his brother's ex-lover floated
into his head. Despite his initial natural inclination to
side with his twin, Marisa's story and her genuine desperation had touched him, and brought home how far
he and his twin had grown apart. There had been a time
when they discussed everything.

He asked himself what would be achieved by telling
Roman now. At the time, he couldn't for the life of him
see anything positive in doing so. But his eyes drifted
to the half-open door behind which his own child lay
asleep and he realised that now his reaction might have
been very different. But that had been then, he told himself, once more squashing down his guilt. Marisa's child
had got the bone marrow he'd so desperately needed
to save his life and that was what mattered the most.

'And every child deserves a father?'

He arched a brow, wondering if he had imagined the
tense undercurrent in her question. 'You don't think so?'

'It depends on the father. If I think that you're not
good for Ellie, I will cut off all access and I don't care

if you have a tribe of lawyers throwing money at it.' Her eyes shot blue warning fire at him.

His lips twitched at her ferocious tigress act, except of course it wasn't an act. He was pretty sure she'd make anyone who hurt her child regret living. 'That seems reasonable.'

Suspicious of Rio's sudden, easy capitulation, Gwen folded her arms across her heaving breasts. 'So how do you envisage this working?' She was pleased she sounded calm and businesslike, and glad he couldn't hear the panicked thud of her heart. Although maybe he could—it was pretty much all she could hear.

Gwen couldn't help wondering if Rio was secretly regretting having no contact with his son and whether Ellie was going to be some sort of consolation prize. But as much as she hated the idea, Gwen knew that he was right to ask for the opportunity to get to know his daughter. She *owed* him a chance, at least, to establish some sort of paternal relationship with Ellie.

'I understand there is a week left of term and then you have a long summer vacation?'

She nodded cautiously. Even the most devoted staff were counting down the days.

'You have any plans?'

Gwen was not fooled for a moment by the seeming casualness of the question. 'I thought we might take a few trips to the beach. I might even buy a tent when Ellie is a bit older and try camping.' She had always wanted to camp when she was a child but her father had been too busy for family holidays and her mother came out in a rash at the idea of being that close to nature.

'That sounds enjoyable, but I have another idea, although I'm afraid it does not involve canvas. Come to Spain with me. I have a place with a private beach where

you can relax and I can get to know my...*our* daughter,'
he swiftly corrected in response to the warning flash
from her eyes. 'And you can get used to me being part
of your life.'

'You can't be a part of *my* life!' she snapped.

He arched a brow. 'Isn't that inevitable when we
have a child together? Don't make me fight you on
this, Gwen.'

She found the absence of anything in his expression
or voice more intimidating than if he'd yelled at her.

She swallowed, but her chin stayed lifted to a defi-
ant angle. 'Are you threatening me?'

He gave an impatient shake of his head. 'Don't be
so dramatic. I am simply telling you that I intend to be
part of my child's life.'

'*Our* child's life.'

He smiled, all silky confidence and even white teeth.
'Exactly the point I have been trying to make.'

'I could send you reports...photos or—' Under the
relentless unblinking gaze of his deep-set eyes her voice
trailed off as she felt like a drowning man going under
for the last time. 'Spain in the summer might be a little
hot for Ellie and she can be quite fussy about her food.'
The former was a relevant concern; the latter was a
downright lie. Ellie happily munched through everything that was set in front of her.

'We have air conditioning and adequate sunscreen,
plus she appears to have inherited my colouring...'

Her attention was immediately drawn to the vibrant
deep gold of his skin. She shrugged while her treach-
erous hormones went wild as she struggled to dispel
the image that seemed imprinted on her retinas of him
standing in front of her naked, the formation of long

bone and deep muscle giving him the look of a classic statue brought to warm, rampant life.

'It's hard to tell at this stage,' she mumbled.

'I have read that introducing children to new tastes early on influences healthy food preferences later on in life.'

Gwen wasn't sure that was completely true but it certainly sounded plausible, and while she was thinking about it, he added smoothly, 'So I will make the necessary arrangements and pick you both up on the last day of term. I'll be in touch soon to let you know what time.'

CHAPTER SIX

RIO TRAVELLED LIGHT. Packing was not something that he wasted time and energy on. Like most things in life it all came down to good organisation.

That morning it had taken him five minutes between returning from his run, getting out of the shower and sliding suited and booted behind the wheel of his car, coffee cup in hand. His laptop and his bag containing all the essentials was slung in the boot of his car, a boot that up until about fifteen minutes ago had seemed capacious enough for his needs.

'Don't worry, we'll find Ant,' Gwen was saying to Ellie.

He knew it had been a mistake to get his hopes up. Struggling to cling onto his calm, he watched Gwen, holding the child by the hand, vanish back into the cottage…and ignored the odd twisting in his chest as the dark curly head tilted up to her mother.

The child said something that made Gwen pause before she dropped into a graceful stoop and swept the toddler up into her arms with practised ease.

He set his shoulders against the gatepost and wondered who Ant was. But he wasn't going to ask, because by now he was pretty sure this performance was all about making a point, just because he had arrived ten minutes earlier than they'd agreed in their email exchange. Gwen had already told him he couldn't come inside because they weren't quite ready.

He stood outside, feeling very much like a taxi driver with the meter running. It astonished him that a woman who could be totally calm in her professional life could be so disorganised when it came to getting one small child in a car.

Was she trying to show him that parenting was not all fun and games? Well, he'd never thought it was. Actually, it was not a subject that he'd spent much time thinking about—up until now.

Now he was thinking about it a lot, when he wasn't thinking about what he had done to his brother in depriving him of the opportunity to know his son. The rationalisation that he'd done it in good faith no longer worked, not since he had looked into his daughter's face and realised that blood really *was* thicker than water.

Guilt was his constant companion, and it was eating away at him, depriving him of a single moment's peace. It was sending him to the gym, where he'd worked himself into a sweat-soaked state of exhaustion in the hope of gaining some respite that deep down he didn't think he deserved.

What if he was as bad a father as he was a brother? His own father hadn't been a bad *father* as such, but he'd had little time for his sons because he had poured all the love he had to give on his wife. Or at the very least, it was his version of love—but it had been the kind of poisonous, stifling, controlling, jealous love that had made it a relief when she had finally summoned the courage to leave.

He wouldn't be like his father, that was the most important thing. So ever since he'd discovered Ellie, he'd read everything he could on the subject of parenting. He'd immersed himself in it, had pored over what people who were considered experts wrote about what made a good or bad parent until, frustrated by all the conflicting opinions, he had put the research aside.

Sometimes there was no replacement for hands-on experience, and he was about to be thrown in at the deep end. His eagerness was counterbalanced by a fear of failure that he had never encountered in his life before.

It was a new feeling for him and not one that he liked. Also, he could see no rational reason why he felt this way. It wasn't as if he didn't regularly put himself in positions outside his comfort zone. He believed in pushing himself to avoid becoming smug and stale, and he generally thrived on the exhilaration of new challenges.

All this attitude required was a belief in yourself, and Rio did. It didn't mean he didn't mess up on occasion, but he never stressed over the chance of this happening ahead of time, and if and when it did he never made the same mistake twice.

The problem was there were generally no second chances with parenthood and you weren't dealing with figures on a spreadsheet. He knew that many would consider that there was pressure involved when a wrong move could wipe billions off a share value, a bad investment could make your brand toxic.

But those consequences paled into insignificance beside the possibility that something you did could harm your child.

'We're done!'

Finally! He relaxed his shoulders as Gwen appeared in the doorway, holding the toddler by the hand. She was wearing pale blue jeans that clung in all the right places, emphasising the long, sinuous length of her legs. Her tee shirt, tucked into a narrow red belt that emphasised the narrowness of her waist, was white with an abstract colourful print on the front.

The sunshine caught her chestnut hair, which she wore tied back from her face by a bright blue silk scarf, bringing out the incredible cobalt of her eyes.

'Oh, sorry, I forgot to check the fridge!'

He watched in disbelief as she opened the door, vanishing inside—*again*!

His teeth clenched as he silently counted to ten before crossing one shiny booted ankle over the other. He leaned against the gleaming paintwork of the low-slung limited-edition model and secured the open passenger door with his hand as a gust of wind caught it.

He glanced inside the car. The child seat now fitted in the back was not what he would have termed intuitive but he had eventually figured out the mechanism. It wasn't as though he hadn't had time. He flicked back his cuff to check out the watch on his wrist, beginning to wonder if she had some form of OCD... After all, how hard could it be to grab a suitcase and get a two-year-old out of the door?

'That's it, we're all set.'

Rio knew better this time and didn't get his hopes up.

Gwen revisited her mental checklist before she walked out of the front door, Ellie, clutching a plastic bucket in one hand and a spade in the other, trailing one step behind her.

'Beach now?' the little girl said for the tenth time in as many minutes.

Gwen tried very hard to be truthful with her daughter but this was not the time for a temper tantrum. So instead of correctly saying no, she smiled and opted for a distraction rather than a fib that would undoubtedly come back to bite her down the line, thanks to her daughter's very good memory.

'Oh, my, isn't that a big shiny car?' Gwen knew zero about cars but she knew what this wasn't and that was a family car. However, it was extremely shiny and no doubt eye-catching—much like its driver—to people who cared about such things.

It had probably cost as much as a small family house. Rio knew as little about the life normal people lived as he did parenting. She felt a tiny pang of guilt for taking some pleasure from the impatience he was struggling to disguise.

Ellie looked unimpressed. 'Want a twactor.' She turned to look at Rio, who was standing beside an open door concealing his impatience very badly. 'A pink one, or wed.'

'Red,' Gwen corrected automatically.

'Wed,' Ellie repeated obediently.

'Good girl,' Gwen said absently, trying not to breathe in the warm scent of Rio's skin that was making her stomach muscles quiver. This, she decided, stifling a deep sigh, was going to be a very long journey. She stood to one side to let Ellie climb into the narrow back seat. Leg room for rear passengers had clearly not been a priority for the designer.

'Climb in, sweetheart, and be careful of the seat.' Cream leather and small children were not a match made in heaven.

'Here, let me,' Rio offered.

'It's fine.' Gwen elbowed him away and, leaning inside, clicked the belt in place. 'There's a knack to it,' she said defensively when she straightened up.

Gwen and Rio got into the front seats and clicked their own belts into place.

'She's not car sick,' Gwen remarked as the car drew away.

'That's good to know,' Rio said gravely, despite the fact that she could tell he'd never even considered this factor.

'How far—?' she began then stopped, horror spreading across her face. There were still several cars parked on the grassy section that had been reserved for parents picking up boarders. Several of the latecomers were gathered in a huddle near the school gate chatting.

She froze for a second, then slid down the seat, ducking out of sight.

'Don't stop,' she hissed. 'Just drive past quickly. Go! Go!'

'Are you going to stay there for the entire journey with your head on my lap? I just feel I should warn you that being seen in that position might be...er... misinterpreted?' The image that flashed into her head at his remark instigated a slow-burn heat in her belly.

Struggling to ignore his silky observation, she eased herself back up in the seat she had just slithered down, pressing her spine against the leather backrest and feeling as mortified as it was humanly possible to feel.

'What do you mean?' she choked.

He arched a sardonic brow and she realised it *was* possible to feel more mortified. Her already hot face flamed with a fresh rush of embarrassed colour.

Once more in an upright position, she stared straight ahead at green hedgerows flashing by as she sat, hands clasped in her lap, waiting for him to say something sarcastic.

He didn't.

'I suppose you think that was funny,' she muttered.

She shot a look at his enigmatic profile and looked away again quickly. Now she knew what a silence that spoke volumes sounded like.

'I thought everyone would already have left.' She could have kicked herself for being overconfident. The Harker parents were notorious for being late picking up their boys. She bit her lip. 'If I'd been a bit quicker on the uptake, we could have gone out the back gate.'

'Because being seen with me would be—?'

'Have you any idea how fast gossip travels in this place?'

'I know two-year-olds still believe that closing their eyes makes them invisible, but...'

'You think they saw me?'

'I'd say that's a distinct possibility.'

She bent her head and covered her face with her hands. 'Oh, God I know they did and I looked straight at them too...it was just instinct.'

Rio had had women he'd never seen before literally fall at his feet to drape themselves all over him in order to sneak a selfie with him, some fainting theatrically so that he could catch them and they could see the image go viral on social media the next day, but to have a woman ashamed to be seen with him was something of a first for him.

Clearly if he wanted his ego kept in check, Gwen Meredith was the right person for the job.

'I take it you've not told anyone where you are spending your vacation?' he said drily.

'No.'

'So I am your dirty little secret. How...charming.'

'I'm a private person.'

'Surely that is being paranoid? Do you not think it's inevitable that the identity of your child's father will eventually become public, or would you like me to wear a false moustache, possibly a full beard?'

'I have to work with these people,' she protested.

'Actually, you don't,' he said pointedly.

'I need to work, Rio. I'm not rich.'

'But I am.'

The suggestion that she would allow him to keep her brought her head up. 'I intend to be a role model for my daughter. I want her to be proud of me.'

'You do not think that being a mother is a job to be proud of?'

'Yes…no…of course I do, but I need to work for my own self-respect.' She glanced behind a little nervously, but Ellie was busy holding a conversation in gibberish between a teddy bear and a toy horse.

He looked thoughtful but said nothing.

Then he commented, 'She seems to have an active imagination.'

'Most two-year-olds do.'

'And most two-year-olds…' Rio couldn't understand a word Ellie was saying right now but struggled to tactfully ask Gwen what he wanted to know without causing offence. 'Do they have much vocabulary?' he wondered casually.

'She is actually considered bright for her age.'

'Ah… I don't know many two-year-olds…or any, actually. So here we are.'

Gwen looked around as they drove through some tall gates. 'This is a private airstrip.'

'Yes, it avoids the congestion of the bigger airports and the facilities are quite good,' he explained as he drove directly onto the tarmac.

Her eyes widened. So this was flying, but not as she knew it.

Once he'd brought the car to a halt he jumped out and started to talk to a man who had come out of the nearest jet. A few minutes later Rio walked around the car and opened the passenger door.

'I have a couple of last-minute details to sort out.'

'With the plane?'

He shook his head. 'No, there is no problem with our flight; it's just work. Ramon will board you.' Like an actor in the wings waiting for his cue, a uniformed figure came hurrying across the tarmac. 'He will make you both comfortable and I will join you presently.'

He did, but only for a moment; the pilot, it seemed, was a friend of his and he chose to travel up front with him, having first checked that she and Ellie were all right.

'We're fine,' Gwen assured him, glad of a respite from the nerve-shredding effect of his close proximity, no matter how short.

The flight went without incident and, thanks to a very attentive crew, she didn't really have to deal with Ellie, who they seemed to enjoy entertaining, though by the time the jet circled to land night was falling and Ellie's eyelids were drooping.

By the time they were preparing to get into the car that waited for them, a big four-wheel drive with plenty of room, Ellie was sound asleep.

Gwen really hoped she stayed that way although she felt as though sleep might be a long time coming for herself. Gwen's body was still taut with anxiety and self-doubt as she had spent most of the journey staring out of the window into blackness, wondering what awaited them in Spain and asking herself if she had made the right decision bringing Ellie here.

But what other option had she had?

Did he *really* want to be part of Ellie's life? She frowned; there were far too many questions and no answers. The only thing she was sure of was that, even though her romantic fantasies about him had been shattered, she was still far from immune to his potent brand of masculinity.

'Let me help with—'

His deep voice jolted Gwen free of her introspection and back to the moment, and an instinct she didn't question made her lurch forward. She virtually elbowed her way past him to block his access to the sleeping child, but it wasn't all win, win... The fleeting collision had made the prickle under her skin even more intense.

How she was going to survive the constant exposure over the next few weeks to this permanent adrenaline overload, she had no idea.

'No, I can manage.' Wincing inwardly at the defensive quality in her own voice, she flashed him a quick look through her lashes.

She looked away quickly because he was standing uncomfortably close—was there even such a thing as comfortable when it came to him? From the electric effect he had on her nervous system she wasn't sure what the safety-zone perimeter was—or even if there was one.

She found her weakness to him disturbing, though not as disturbing as the insidious warmth that was even now spreading through her body at his nearness. Her only defence was to pretend it wasn't happening and hope her hormones would go back into hibernation some time soon.

The absolute worst, most shameful part was that she was pretty sure he knew exactly what his physical proximity did to her—she just hoped that he was so used to women going weak at the knees when he was around that he barely noticed any more.

She lifted her lashes to flash him another look through the dark mesh and found her eyes connecting with his. Her eyes grew wide for a moment before she dragged them away—no, those intent eyes of his noticed absolutely everything, she decided. It was the thoughts that might be going on behind their deep, dark surface that raised the question mark because, although she had the distinct impression he could read her like a book, she struggled to see past his mask.

'There's a knack to this,' she husked out as she bent to the task of unfastening the sleeping child's restraint, biting her lip as her trembling-fingered clumsiness contradicted her claim. Pushing her hair back impatiently—she had lost the velvet ribbon that had secured it at her nape at some point in the journey—she gritted her teeth, told herself to man up and completed the operation without waking Ellie.

'So you already said about the car seat,' he replied in the tone of a man who was not amused. 'But I'd like the chance to learn.'

'If she kicks off you'll be glad you're not carrying her. She can be pretty cranky when she's tired.'

The attempt at conciliation slid off Rio like sea water off a seal and his jaw clenched. He wasn't keeping count—actually, that wasn't true; he was. He remembered each and every time she'd rebuffed any attempt he made to help with Ellie. Once he might have put it down to Gwen's bloody-minded independence but that wasn't what this was about. When he went anywhere near the child she went straight into guard-dog mode.

'I'm fine with you not trusting me.'

Except you're not, are you, Rio?

Recognition of the fact flickered in his eyes before he half lowered his heavy lids and went on to incise with heavy irony, 'But I think even I've already grasped the basic concept that dropping a child is not a good idea.' *His* child that she would have kept from him her whole life so they'd have ended up as complete strangers to one another... Through sheer force of will he stopped feeding his anger, drawing a veil across the relentless stream of pointless *could have* scenarios, and instead heaved out a sigh and all the anger with it.

He could carry on being angry with Gwen but it wasn't going to move them on from this point if he wanted this child in his life. He had let the resentment go, even though at the moment that remained a goal rather than reality.

'It's got nothing to do with trust. Why do you have to make everything so personal?' she asked.

His ebony brows hit his equally dark hairline and his eyes slid to the face of the sleeping child before returning to Gwen's. 'She's my child—does it get more personal than that?'

Gwen hated the flush that she felt climb to her cheeks and hated him for making her feel guilty. 'Just how long are you going to punish me for? I only ask because children tend to pick up on tense atmospheres and—'

'So you want me to pretend that everything is sweetness and light between us?'

Her eyes flew wide in rejection as she ejaculated in utter revulsion, 'Oh, God, no!'

Her parents' life had been and presumably still was

one long pretence, her mother pretending to believe her serial adulterer husband every single time he promised his latest fling was over and he'd never stray again. Her father pretending he had every intention of forsaking all others for his wife.

The only thing that seemed to unite her parents was a determination to maintain appearances, appear happy, pretending to be the perfect loving couple in front of their friends and neighbours.

Belatedly aware of Rio's speculative stare, she lowered her gaze and took a deep restorative breath. 'I intend to be honest with my daughter.'

'So what honest answer were you going to give her when she asked you who her father was?'

She glared at him in defiance.

'Or hadn't you thought that far ahead?'

The fight drained away, leaving her feeling weak and vulnerable and unable to think of any retort that sounded smarter than the truth.

'Sometimes I rarely think beyond the end of a day.'

'That's not an answer.'

She gave a weary sigh. 'Yes, I had thought about what I'd say to her and to be honest I...' Her voice cracked and she swallowed hard. 'I just know what I *wanted* to be able to tell her. I wanted to be able to tell her that her father loved her.' She compressed her quivering lips, her blue eyes lifting to his. 'Maybe now I can?'

Looking into her exhausted white face, he felt something twist hard inside his chest and looked away, unwilling to acknowledge the surge of emotion he hid behind a gruff response. 'You won't need to tell her anything now. I'll be there and she'll know it first-hand from me.'

As Gwen stared up at him the sudden hum of tension that had filled the air between them evaporated and he placed a guiding hand in the small of her back, leaving her unsure if she should interpret his words as a promise or a threat.

'This will save for another time. You look shattered. Just try and remember that the object of this exercise is for me to get to know my daughter, which you agreed was a good idea. But that is going to be kind of hard if you won't let me get within ten feet of her without going into "protective tiger mother" mode.'

My daughter... The possessive inflection in his voice dispelled the embryonic, uncomfortable stirrings of guilt she had been experiencing. 'I think *agreed* is overstating it, but obviously I'm fine with you holding her...' she lied with stiff, unfriendly formality.

He snorted and she blushed. 'I'm only thinking about Ellie.' She stopped as she recognised the untruth in her claim. It was her own life with him in it in *any* role that she was thinking of. She gave a tiny frustrated shake of her head and bent down to pick up Ellie. 'I'm just not used to—' She straightened up with a little grunt of effort that she had noticed was getting louder. She looked down at the sleeping toddler with her thumb in her mouth and gently settled her head on her shoulder to follow Rio off the plane towards yet another car, wondering how much longer she would be able to carry her daughter this way.

There was an ironic twist to the wistful half-smile that curved her lips. Gwen had smiled politely when people told her to enjoy these early years with her child because they flew by, but she hadn't really believed them—it was just something that people said. But she was starting to realise that they said it precisely because it was true. Those early months had already flown by but she still had precious memories to sustain her.

Rio had never had that time with Ellie, and he had no memories. The guilt came rushing back in a nauseating wave—anger was so much easier to bear.

It seemed like only yesterday that she had been wishing away these early years, dreaming of a day when Ellie was older and not needing the amount of childcare she required now. Being less hands-on would leave her with some time to herself. She would prefer not to identify the urge that had made her push Rio aside moments earlier as something perilously close to jealousy—she really didn't want to be that person!

Rio scanned her upturned features, watching the flow of emotions across her remarkably expressive face, and felt a strange twisting sensation in his chest that took him unawares. Maybe it was the contrast between the tilt of her stubborn chin and the purple shadows beneath her incredible eyes that had dragged this unexpected—no, *unheard-of*—response from him.

Or maybe it was because he was closely examining her beautiful face with its soft, smooth skin and he could feel his libido pounding against the iron leash of his self-control. It was not something he normally had a problem with as his control over his emotions was always what had set him apart from his brother. But now it seemed as if the heat in the pit of his belly, the pounding of desire, was something he was going to have to learn to live with when he was around Gwen.

'I suppose I've got used to not relying on anyone,' she admitted and, despite his iron grip on himself, he flinched slightly.

CHAPTER SEVEN

WITHIN SECONDS THE air between them was thick and thrumming with a different kind of tension this time... Their eyes remained connected, sealed, and Gwen couldn't have broken free if she had wanted to.

She didn't want to.

Did his molten hooded stare hold some sort of hidden message? She didn't know and she couldn't breathe as he seemed to be leaning into her. Her head lifted as his mouth lowered and she could see the tiny silvered flecks deep in his dark eyes and felt the equally dark thrum in her blood as her knees went weak. But then Ellie shifted in her arms and let out a whimper.

The spell was broken, the small cry shattering it like splintering ice, or maybe it had all been in her fevered imagination, Gwen mused, glad of the sweep of hair that hid her too warm cheeks, as she laid a soothing hand on her daughter's head before placing her gently in the car and getting in herself. Unfortunately there was nothing imaginary about the trickle of moisture pooling in the valley between her breasts and, despite the air-conditioned cool of the car, her clothes were sticking to her hot skin.

Not magic, Gwen, just sex, she told herself. The brutal truth hurt, but then so did discovering that fairy-tale happy endings only happened in, well, fairy tales. She was still feeling ashamed of that little rush of excitement that had left curls of heat in the pit of her belly when he spoke.

'I think you've already proved your point that you are Super Mum,' he said.

The smooth skin between her delicately delineated brows formed a tiny pleat. 'I…what do you mean? I'm not trying to be super anything.' She classed a good day as one when she didn't feel utterly inadequate. Her eyes flickered wider, suspicion settling in the cooling blue depths as she looked over at him as he drove fast with an effortless skill. 'Have you been asking people about me?' Looking for dirt, fuel for a highly paid lawyer who would paint her as a hopeless mother?

He rolled his eyes. 'Now don't go getting all paranoid on me again,' he drawled.

Her mouth opened. 'I'm not…' She closed it with a snap and a sigh before tacking on reluctantly, 'All right, maybe I am being a little suspicious, but have you been telling people that you're Ellie's father?'

'Would it be so terrible if I had?'

Gwen compressed her lips over a retort and reminded herself that it was always good to choose your battleground. This, she decided, looking around the confines of the car, wasn't it. Glancing out of the window, she realised that they had left the motorway behind them now and they hadn't passed a car for miles.

His jaw clenched as he met her combative blue stare. 'Relax.' It was advice that could have equally been directed at him as well, she thought, noting the tense muscles across his shoulders. 'I haven't said anything; you just came up in the conversation.'

Which told her absolutely nothing. She compressed

her lips and glared at him. 'Conversation with who, exactly?'

'Being a VIP guest involves listening politely even when you're bored. The headmaster of your school spoke highly of you, as did the head of lower school, and before you go all conspiracy theory on me I didn't ask about you.' But Rio had listened rather than tune out what they'd been saying. 'It seems that among your colleagues it is an accepted fact that you have no flaws,' he said, eyes swivelling in the mirror to touch the curve of her neck where in the gathering darkness the skin there had an opalescent sheen that was indeed flawless.

The effort of dragging his attention away from her and back to the road added another groove to the frown lines between his brows.

No one he spoke to had mentioned that mouth of hers, though he was pretty sure several of them had noticed it. But they had stuck to less inflammatory subjects like her devotion as a parent and her incredible teaching skills.

'I don't appreciate the sarcasm.'

He cut off her protest with a disarming smile. 'Not even a little bit…?' He held a thumb and forefinger a whisper apart. 'Don't worry, I'm exceptionally subtle. I forgot your name twice to put them off the scent.'

She gave a snort. 'Sledgehammer-subtle.'

His mouth lifted in one corner in a half-smile. 'Why would it bother you when no one had a bad word to say about you?'

'Maybe you asked the wrong people.' Her parents would have told him what a disappointment she was to them—they told everyone else in their social circle. 'Some people think that having Ellie ruined my life.'

He arched a brow. 'What people?'

'My parents…or, at least, my father.' But then she shook her head, remembering how her mum had not defended her when her father had insisted she get rid of her precious baby.

Her nostrils quivered as she pushed the memories away, swallowing hard before she looked directly at Rio with defiance shining in her eyes. Her father had made her choose between them and her baby and it truly amazed Gwen that he had been shocked when she had told him she had every intention of keeping her baby.

'I'm not trying to steal her away from you, Gwen. I just want to share her.'

The quiet assertion took her breath away, and returned the shadow of wariness to her eyes, as once again his ability to read her thoughts and feelings was unsettling.

'I'm not afraid of you, Rio.' Perhaps she ought to be?

'But you don't trust me.'

It was a statement.

'You have Ellie's interests at heart and so do I—we are on the same team, and we need to work together,' he added.

'You sound so reasonable.' *Which obviously makes me the unreasonable one and in a moment I'll even be apologising*, she thought irritably.

'She isn't going to love you any less when new people come into her life.' He sensed her eyes were on his face but the road had narrowed at this point, as they joined the mountain track that led down to the beach house, and it took all his attention.

'Well, thank you for those words of wisdom, Professor. What sort of selfish, possessive, *needy* idiot do you think I am?' The car jolted and she grabbed for the door handle to steady herself.

'Sorry, we had the track resurfaced last year but there were some bad storms last winter.'

'How far is it?' she asked, clinging on as they jolted along.

'Not far now.'

'Is it a big resort?'

He flashed her a look before turning his eyes back to the road. 'Not a resort as such, just a beach house, and the mountain road meant that the area has remained totally undeveloped. My brother and I used to come here during the summer with our parents, and when they divorced she moved in and renovated it, pretty much rebuilt it.'

'So did they remarry other people, your parents?'

'My father died a few years ago.' There was *something* in his voice, but his expression gave away nothing of his feelings.

'Oh, I'm sorry to hear that.'

'We were not close.'

'And your mother? Did she—?'

'My mother is making up for lost time.'

'Lost time?'

'Her marriage to my father was not good at all. He was a jealous bastard who tried to manipulate and control every aspect of her life.'

'Oh!' It seemed a pretty inadequate response but Gwen couldn't think of what else to say.

'Right, here we are.' They were drawing into the courtyard, which surrounded the house on three sides.

'It's beautiful.'

'It looks even better in daylight and I can't take responsibility for the landscaping. The honour goes to an ancestor from a couple of centuries ago but my mother rediscovered the skeleton of the original garden lost

under a lot of neglect, and she had it restored.' One of
his earliest happy memories was of his mother wearing a straw hat on her head and holding a trowel in her
hand, bossing around the gardeners.

As they came to a halt the lights came on, presumably activated by sensors, illuminating the low-lying
stone building. One side of it, which overlooked the
sea, seemed to be made entirely of glass, and the sea
itself reflected a silver sheen off the dark shadows of
the hills either side of the sheltered bay.

'It's beautiful.' His idea of a beach house was very
different from her own!

'Yes, it is.'

'Not at all what I was expecting.'

'I will show you around once you have settled in.'
He stepped out of the car and walked around to the passenger door, opening it for her.

She climbed out, enjoying the fact that the warmth
was far less oppressive here than it had been in the air-
port. The light breeze smelt wonderfully of the sea and
the wild thyme that grew between the cobbles underfoot.

She hesitated, half anticipating an army of staff to
come running out to greet them.

'I hope you don't mind but for the first few days I
thought it might be helpful for us to be alone here. I
gave the staff some time off, though, if you prefer, I
can recall them?'

She shook her head, some of the tension leaving her
shoulders.

'The food is arranged, the kitchen is stocked with
provisions, and there are meals already prepared in the
freezer. Estelle is a very good cook, and she is also the
housekeeper here. She supervised the arrangements
before she left.'

'Arrangements?'

'The house has not seen children for a long time, not since—' His eyes wandered over the high stone wall to the right; he was clearly lost in memories.

'Since?' she prompted, wondering at an expression that was close to wistful that had drifted across his hard features.

He turned to look at her. 'Since I was a child. May I?' He tilted his head towards the sleeping child still in the car.

She nodded. 'Go ahead.'

She felt her throat tighten as she watched how carefully he bent and picked Ellie up, as though she might break. She grabbed the bag that contained the baby essentials that she had packed separately and followed him down the cobbled path and under an arch of clematis and honeysuckle.

'The pool,' he said, rather unnecessarily, indicating the infinity pool cut into the rock, which was surrounded by a terrace of flowers.

Ellie nestling on his shoulder like a baby animal, he punched numbers into a keypad and as if by magic the entire glass wall slid apart silently, the glass seeming to vanish inside the walls.

'Wow!'

'It's pretty much open-plan.' He pressed another button and the room was illuminated by recessed lights in the ceiling and tiled floor. The massive space stretched the entire width of the house, incorporating several seating areas with massive sofas, a long polished oak antique table that could have seated twenty, a grand piano that took pride of place one end, with bookshelves the other, and a modernistic wood burner hung suspended from the ceiling in the middle of the room.

She'd already said wow so she just stared.

'Kitchen is that way, study's off to that side and the bedrooms are in the other two wings.'

Gwen heard him but she was too busy staring at a corner of the room where there was a tall doll's house, several tubs of toys and a doll's pram.

'If they're not the right kind of toys, you can—'

'They're absolutely right. She'll love them all.'

'This is the nursery,' he said. There was a wooden child gate across the doorway and a faint smell of paint as they walked into a bright square room with a frieze of rabbits around the wall. The bed in the corner was painted to resemble a castle and there was a cot at the far end of the room.

'I wasn't sure if she needed a cot or a bed.'

Gwen looked at the bed with the safety sides, a little girl's dream. 'This looks perfect as she's already started trying to climb over the sides of her cot. Thank you, this is all very thoughtful.' A lot seemed to have been achieved in a short space of time.

She had thought it was impossible but Rio actually looked embarrassed.

'Your room adjoins this one, and there is just the small corridor that way. The child monitors are in every room and the volume control is on the pad by the door.'

He looked at the bed and hesitated. 'Shall I put her to bed?'

'Yes, please.' She took a deep breath and thought, *You've got to let go some time, Gwen.* 'I'll leave you to it, while I'll explore a bit if you don't mind.'

It was a gesture but a start and he seemed to recognise it as such. 'Thank you,' he said quietly.

Gwen made her way back to the car, popping her head around the door of the incredibly appointed modern kitchen on the way. They were clearly not going to be roughing it in any way!

At the car, she selected the bags that contained her essentials and some more stuff for Ellie and made her way back to the house. She was halfway there when she was intercepted by Rio.

'No, I'm fine.' Her fingers tightened around the handle of the heaviest bag.

Her stubborn determination to retain her grip brought her up against his chest and as his fingers curled over her own, it wasn't just the unexpected impact that made her gasp. She knew she should be doing something else rather than standing there panting, her small gasps now less to do with exertion and more to do with the buzz of expectation that tightened like a fist in her belly as the last remaining resistance drained from her body in one slow shuddering breath.

Gwen's eyes drifted closed, Rio's lean male body and the support of the hard breadth of his chest the only things keeping her standing. She was vaguely conscious of the bags hitting the floor but much more aware of his fingers pushing into her hair, his hand sliding to her waist and the words of husky Spanish as his hot breath stirred the skin of her cheek.

'I want you...'

Did I just say that to him?

She must have done because he was replying to her, but in Spanish, the words sounding as fevered as he felt. She leaned in at the waist, increasing the pressure of his erection against the softness of her belly. He was still murmuring against her mouth, her lips parted, willing the words to be lost in her mouth.

It took a couple of seconds for either of them to react to the sudden racket that cut through the still of the night. With a soft cry that was lost in the deafening sound of a helicopter flying incredibly low over their heads, Gwen sprang back, her hand pressed to her trembling mouth, her eyes wide and shocked.

Rio hadn't moved. He stood as still as a statue, Gwen's bags dragging around his feet, his face raised to the sky as he raked a hand through his dark hair. He let loose a string of fluent curses in several languages as he followed the helicopter lights above them with unfriendly eyes.

The noise diminished as the flashing lights moved farther away, remaining loud but no longer deafening.

Gwen was shaking like someone who had just stepped neck deep into a pool of ice water. 'Does that happen often?' she asked desperately, trying hard to sound normal, although it was incredibly difficult when her entire body was thrumming with frustration.

What was it about Rio that turned her into a totally different person, a person she barely recognised?

'No.'

'What's wrong?' *Beyond the fact you dissolved the moment he touched you,* she thought with dismay. There had been no gradual build-up—the passion had simply exploded between them and she was still shaking inside and out.

'We have a visitor.' He took his narrowed eyes off the distant lights where the helicopter had just put down. 'The only question is, is it my mother or my brother? I didn't expect either of them.'

The idea of meeting a member of his family at any time would have bothered her, but now, when her emotions felt so exposed and raw, and when all she wanted to do was... No, she didn't want to think about what she wanted to do right now. An interruption was a good thing, she insisted to herself.

Delaying the inevitable, Gwen?

Ignoring the goading voice in her head, she lifted her chin. 'You have a brother?'

Looking distracted, Rio nodded, a faint frown line pleating his brow as he gave her his attention. Or at least he looked at her mouth, as pink and swollen as though he had got as far as kissing her. 'Didn't I mention him before?'

'There's no reason you should have, is there? I should go inside and check that the noise didn't wake Ellie.'

'Fine. You do that and I'll go and check out the visitor.' He half turned, then paused. 'Don't worry, they won't be staying.'

'You can't make them go!' she exclaimed in shock.

He flashed a white grin. 'Oh, I can be very persuasive.'

Didn't she already know it!

Not that his persuasive powers were all that tested where she was concerned. Because all he had to do was touch her and she was lost. 'But what will you—?'

Her words were addressed to thin air as he had gone, his long legs quickly distancing him from her until the dark swallowed him up, leaving her wondering what the hell was about to happen. What was he going to tell their unexpected visitor?

With a deep sigh and a last resentful glare into the darkness, Gwen made her way to the nursery, where Ellie, oblivious to everything going on, was still sound asleep. Gwen had no excuse to linger in the nursery although she was tempted because, despite Rio's very inhospitable stance, she couldn't imagine that their visitor would not be staying the night at the very least. Of

the two possibilities, she would have preferred it to be
Rio's brother who had arrived. He might be less judgemental about Ellie and was less likely to view her with
the maternal suspicion she felt sure his mother would.

Gwen made her way back to the sitting room and sat
down on the piano stool. She was still sitting there five
minutes later when Rio returned, pushing a wheelchair.

Feeling like a guilty schoolgirl caught some place
she wasn't allowed, Gwen shot to her feet, but her ap-
prehension dissolved as she met the smiling and teary
eyes of the woman sitting in it.

Despite the chair and the plaster leg extended before her, this wasn't a frail figure. This slim woman,
her dark hair flecked with silver, instead projected an
air of vitality despite her confinement and certainly
did not look old enough to be a grown man's mother.
The mother of *two* grown men, she silently corrected.

Lady Cavendish extended her hands and without
thinking about it Gwen found herself walking towards
her, her own hands held out until they were enfolded in
the cool grasp of the elegant older woman.

'My dear girl, firstly I must apologise. I came looking for one son and found the other.' Her head turned
towards Rio. 'And not just a son but a granddaughter
too.' Her voice thickened with emotion. 'I can't tell you
how happy I am and I know you will forgive me for in-
truding like this.' She threw her son another look, this
one satirical. 'Even though Rio will not ask you, but…
could I see her? For just a moment or two? Oh, I promise
that I won't wake her. But just to *see* her…' She swallowed, visibly moved by the prospect. 'My grandchild.'

Gwen felt herself relaxing and responded to the
charm and appeal in those lovely velvety eyes without thinking.

'Of course you can,' she said warmly, contrasting this stranger's reaction to becoming a grandparent to that of her own parents.

'And then I will be gone. You won't even know I've been here and I'll only be a moment, I promise.'

She was actually five minutes, and when she and Rio returned there was evidence of more tears on her cheeks along with a few streaks of mascara.

'She is very beautiful. You must be so proud of her.'

Gwen nodded. 'She looks like Rio,' she said, and immediately felt embarrassed, not because it was a lie, but because *he* was beautiful too and a few minutes earlier she had wanted to touch and love every beautiful inch of him. Now she was talking to his mother, whose eyes were enough like Rio's to make her wonder if she could also read her mind.

'Yes, he and Roman were beautiful babies too.'

Standing behind the wheelchair, Rio said something that sounded impatient in Spanish.

'Yes, Rio, I am just going—but am I allowed to ask for a glass of water first?'

'Because there is no water on board?'

'Because I need to take my painkillers.'

The quirk of Rio's lips was immediately replaced by a downward tug of concern. He said something in Spanish and vanished.

'Are you in pain? Can I do anything?'

'Oh, heavens, no, it's only a little discomfort and I'm rather frustrated because I thought I'd be up and around by now…but things are not healing as they ought. I'm booked in for surgery, a new pin and…but enough of that. No, I'm actually not in any significant pain, it was just a little ruse to get rid of Rio for one moment so that I could talk to you in private.'

'This must have been a shock for you,' Gwen said, feeling her way cautiously. It would be a lot easier to navigate this conversation if she had a clue what Rio had already told his mother about them.

'A marvellous surprise! I never thought I'd ever have a grandchild. My sons...can I be frank with you?' Without waiting for a response, she pushed on, speaking quickly. 'Well, I don't know how much you know, but my own marriage was not a good one, and while we were together my boys were my champions. They should not have needed to be and the knowledge shames me greatly. I am afraid that witnessing my marriage has left scars for them both. Not the kind of scars you can see,' she added, glancing at her own leg. 'Though in the past I always knew that at least then they had each other to lean on. But now one is...' Her smile suddenly flashed out, soothing away the lines of worry on her face.

'But no matter,' she husked, brushing away an emotional tear from her cheek. 'Rio has you and Ellie now.'

Gwen realised with dawning horror that Rio's mother had got the totally wrong idea about them. 'Rio and I, we are not really—'

'Oh, I realise that you have been apart for a while. The whys of that are not my business, although if ever you need to talk about anything, I am here. But it's not the past that matters, it's the *now* that is most important. Rio has moved on, he has found happiness, which makes me so very happy. He has been so lonely, I think.'

Gwen kept her expression neutral as she thought about the countless covetous female eyes that followed Rio whenever he walked into a room. If his mother thought he led the life of a lonely monk, it was not for Gwen to disillusion her.

'The boys were so young when the responsibility

of the business fell on their shoulders, and then when Roman walked away and left it all for Rio to manage, it must have been very hard. But he has never complained, you know, and he never did. He was such a *loving* little boy.'

Rio a little boy…a *loving* little boy! The images planted in her head by the poignant words made Gwen's chest tighten.

'And so spontaneous, before he sadly became so closed off… Their father used to pump them about me for information. What I was doing, who I was doing it with, if you get my drift?'

Gwen, who did and was horrified, nodded. The story explained a lot of things about Rio and her tender heart ached for him.

'There was one occasion when Rio blurted something out the way boys do in excitement and his father used the information to…' She shook her head sadly, not completing the sentence. 'From being spontaneous Rio became very self-contained—they both did, which was all right while they had each other. So, you see, that is why I am so glad Rio has his own family now.'

Gwen felt a wave of helplessness. She simply didn't have it in her to wipe the glow of happiness from this lovely woman's beautiful face by telling her the truth about her relationship with Rio.

An image of Rio watching Ellie sleep flashed into her head. 'I think he'll be a good father,' she said, and found herself meaning it.

'Your glass of water, Mother?'

Gwen jumped guiltily and turned to see Rio standing there. How much had he heard, if anything? His expression told her nothing. It seemed that the lessons he'd learnt as a child had been perfected during the in-

tervening years. There was very little in his face of the
young boy who'd blurted out the wrong thing to his father about his mother and then blamed himself for it.
This was the man who, it seemed, shouldered his brother's burdens along with his own with no complaints and,
as far as she could see, with no expectation of thanks.

'Oh, I managed to swallow the pills without water,'
she said airily. 'It has been so nice to meet you, Gwen.'
She raised a cheek, a gesture that Gwen correctly inter-
preted, bending to awkwardly kiss her.

'And you, Lady Caven—'

'Call me Jo—everyone does—and I hope to see you
all very soon.'

Gwen followed mother and son outside and sat down
on a bench on the terrace. She was still sitting there in
the warm darkness when she heard the crunch of gravel
heralding Rio's return.

'Is your brother missing?' she asked as Rio came
within her line of sight. 'Is that why your mother was
looking for him?'

Rio dug his hands into the pockets of the well-cut
trousers that were moulded to his powerful thighs. 'Not
missing, just off the grid for a while like me.'

'Your mother seems worried about you both.'

'It goes with the job of being a mother, you should
know that. But Roman is a grown man, and is well able
to take care of himself.'

'So you're not concerned about him at all?'

'I am not.'

It wasn't concern she could read in his expression,
but there was definitely something—something to do
with a falling-out between the brothers his mother had
alluded to…

'What did you tell your mother about Ellie and me? She seems to think we're a family now.'

'I told her the truth, or a partial version of it, and it really doesn't matter what she thinks, does it? It doesn't matter what anyone thinks. This is about us and what *we* think.'

The reference to *us* gave her a little warm glow. It answered an unacknowledged need in her to belong, something she'd never really had before.

'Earlier...' she began awkwardly.

He took a step towards her and she got to her feet swiftly, her hand raised in silent protest. 'It's all too much, too soon, Rio. I need to think.'

A muscle in Rio's jaw clenched and he let out a slow breath.

'Thinking can be overrated, but fine.' His eyes moved across her face, the hunger in them morphing into something gentler as he noted the dark shadows under her eyes. 'You must be tired.'

'It has been a long day. I haven't even the faintest idea what the time is.'

'Ten-thirty.' He hesitated. 'Would you like some supper?'

'No, I had some sandwiches on the plane. I'm not hungry and, to be honest, I wouldn't mind turning in.'

'Of course.' He tipped his head. 'Goodnight, Gwen.'

She held her breath as he leaned forward but the kiss never came. He just brushed aside a strand of hair that had fallen in her eyes before he straightened up. There was nothing even vaguely erotic about his action but she was trembling as she walked towards the house, too ashamed to respond to his soft goodnight.

CHAPTER EIGHT

AFTER TWO HOURS of trying to bury the fact that the smell of Gwen's hair had aroused him to the point that even ten minutes of standing in a cold shower didn't work, Rio gave up trying to sleep. It wouldn't be buried and his ache just wouldn't go away.

In the end, he grabbed a pair of shorts and walked out into the warm, humid night. Ignoring the pool, he headed for the beach; he knew the tides quite well and felt safe swimming in the sea.

The repetitive action of swimming up and down eventually had the soothing mind-and-body-numbing result he had hoped for. He had forgotten to take a towel but the walk over to the house dried the moisture off his skin and he was dragging his hands through his sable hair to remove the excess water as he approached the house. He took the shorter route that cut past the pool, its turquoise depths still lit by the solar-powered underwater lights.

He was almost tempted to swim again but his body had achieved a level of relaxation that might enable him to actually get some sleep.

He was about to turn back to the house when he saw her, and all the benefits of thirty minutes of open-sea swimming vanished in a heartbeat.

Wearing a silky-looking cream nightshirt, Gwen was standing on the edge of the pool balanced on one foot, her other extended so her toes were dangling in the water. Presumably she hadn't been able to sleep either, maybe for the same reason he couldn't?

The possibility sent a fresh pulse of raw desire through his body.

She looked up suddenly as if she sensed his presence and he instinctively pulled back into the shadow of the overhanging trees but then stopped himself. It felt too voyeuristic to watch her when she didn't know he was there.

He swallowed and stepped forward instead. 'Are you thinking of swimming?'

'No, I'm just looking.' Gwen couldn't stop *looking* and there was nothing *just* about it!

Rio looked like a bronze god walking towards her, all rippling muscles and golden skin. He looked primitive, the very essence of maleness, his every move displaying a grace and raw strength that was simply mind-blowing. Anticipation made her heart thud, her legs were shaking... She was shaking all over, in fact.

He stopped a couple of feet away from her and by this point she could barely breathe, let alone think. She was simply suffocated by lust; her skin prickled with it, drawing the nipples of her round breasts into taut, tingling peaks. She wasn't in the water but she felt as though she were drowning.

'This would be crazy.' Her voice sounded as if it belonged to someone else.

A nerve clenched in his cheek. 'I don't care.'

She was shaking with excitement and as her passion-glazed eyes connected with his, the blatant sensuality of his stare sent a heavy throb of need through her body.

She gave a smile that sparkled with reckless energy. 'Neither do I.' Holding his eyes, she took the hem of the nightshirt she wore and pulled it over her head, tossing it away, oblivious to the fact it landed in the pool.

Watching through a haze of desire, he groaned and lunged, not in any specific order. One muscular arm banded around her ribs, the other behind her head as he lifted her until their faces were level.

Her lips parted eagerly under the pressure of his mouth, inviting the sensual invasion of his plunging tongue, and as he tasted her she felt as though he would drain her.

He lifted his head and she could see there were dark stripes of colour along the crests of his cheekbones. 'Trust me.'

'I do.' Crazily it was true.

He skimmed his tongue over the surface of her lips. 'I want to see you lose control,' he slurred against her lips.

She whimpered and panted as he put her down and slid down her body, his hands on her breasts while his mouth traced a path between them. The muscles of her belly quivered as he slid even lower, then as her legs gave way he pulled her down to join him, rolling her underneath him, pausing only to remove his shorts.

His hands were pressed against hers stretched high above her head as he kissed her, his hips moving against her soft belly, letting her feel the strength of his arousal as his erection grazed her stomach. But it only made her more frantic to feel him properly, with all of him inside her.

'Did I say that out loud?' she wondered.

He lifted his face from where it was pressed into her neck. 'You shouted it. Call me *cariad* again.'

'*Cariad...*' she whispered obediently even though she didn't know she'd already said the Welsh endearment once. Her eyes drifted closed as the mixture of sensations was just too much to absorb. The long, hot, drugging kisses were draining her of any remaining strength of will and they were just making her ache for even more.

'I want to touch you,' she gasped.

He groaned, his face contorted with an agonised expression. 'Later... Now I just need...'

'Oh, God...' she panted, and widened her legs as she felt him begin to enter her. 'Yes, please, Rio!'

She arched her back, losing every vestige of self-control as she cried out his name again, urging him on as he filled her full of him, absorbing the powerful, driving thrusts that aroused every nerve ending and pushed her towards a climax that wrenched a wild, raw cry from her throat.

He lay there panting on top of her while Gwen slowly floated back to reality, which was that she was lying on a cold, hard tiled surface. Until now she had not even registered the discomfort.

'Let's use a bed next time,' he whispered in her ear as he rolled off her.

'Is there to be a next time?' she teased lightly, kissing the palm of the hand that was still thrown across her chest.

His dark eyes glittered wickedly down at her as he raised himself up on one elbow. 'You know that I always rise to a challenge.'

Gwen resisted the tug that brought her surfacing from sleep, her reluctance finally overcome by curiosity, the feeling that something was *different*. And then it all came back with a rush that made her suck in a short shocked breath as a stream of images and sensations began to flow through her head.

Without opening her eyes, she now knew that the weight she felt across her waist was Rio's arm thrown across it and the warmth was his long hair-dusted legs that were tangled with her own.

She didn't analyse the sense of rightness or safety that it gave her. Who wouldn't feel right waking up entangled with a man who looked, felt and made love like Rio?

She lay there enjoying the moment. She had finally fallen asleep in the early hours with her head on his chest. It was still there now, and the sound she was listening to was the soft, slow boom of his heartbeat.

She remembered him asking did she want him to go back to his own bed.

She must have said no, but she didn't recall doing so.

She lay still, willing herself to absorb every detail, each impression, knowing she would want to relive this moment in her head later. She wanted to remember the feel of all the little whorls of chest hair that tickled her chin, the musk of his warm skin, the weight of his arm, and the way his fingers curved across the angle of her hip.

She wanted the moment to last for ever, but of course it wasn't going to. Her brain was not content with staying in neutral and her thoughts were already racing around like a frantic hamster on a wheel.

As the thoughts crowded in she couldn't lie still any longer. Holding her breath, she carefully pressed a hand into the mattress and eased her weight back, sliding out from underneath his arm. Balanced on the edge of the bed now, with just his thigh holding her there, she lifted her head and angled it to take a look at his face.

From this position she could see the perfect carved contours of his face, the angles and hollows emphasised by a night's worth of dark stubble, his long eyelashes lying dark against the perfect slashing angle of his cheekbones.

The ache of longing inside her as she gazed at him was frightening in its intensity. Lifting a hand to blot away the tears she felt on her cheeks, she eased herself carefully away from the confining weight of his hairroughened thigh, hating to break the contact with his warm body and shatter the lingering remnants of intimacy.

There was a very good reason Gwen hadn't allowed herself last night to think about what the morning would bring, and this aching hollow feeling in her stomach was it. Last night she had given herself over entirely to need, and she had accepted the *desperation* that had risen from the deepest part of her when he had touched her, not fought or questioned it.

This morning it wasn't the questions she was pushing away, it was the answers!

She reached down and picked up the gown she had folded across the end of the bed, which was now on the floor. Fighting her way silently into it, she tightened the belt and, without allowing herself a glance backwards, crept quietly along the small corridor that linked her room with Ellie's nursery.

She didn't go inside, just looked over the safety gate. This room was darker because of the blackout blinds behind the brightly patterned curtains. It took Gwen's eyes a few moments to adjust to the light cast by the two nightlights that projected a starry pattern on the ceiling and make out the dark curls above the low safety sides of the brightly painted castle bed.

Gwen could hear the soft sound of even baby breathing, and for a moment love banished the shadows lurking in her eyes. Did all mothers dream of the future they
wanted their child to have, a future without any tears?
Had her mother held her and thought that same way?

The guilt came as it always did, rational or not,
whenever she thought of her own mother. Her sadness,
the sense of betrayal she felt at her mother's actions,
was always tinged with guilt.

Of course she knew that her mother could have
walked away from her husband, but had *chosen* to
stay, just as she had chosen not to defend her daughter,
and that hurt the most. But despite everything Gwen
couldn't shake the feeling that she had deserted her
mam; she had chosen her baby over her mother.

She was momentarily tempted to go into the room
and hold Ellie, breathe in all the warm, comforting,
wholesome sweetness of her, but practicality won out.
So instead of risking disturbing her daughter she stayed
there a moment, just listening, before finally dragging
herself away. Her bare feet were silent on the cool tiled
surface as she turned and made her way into the massive light-filled living room. She touched a handle and
one of the full-height sliding glass panels that made the
outside and inside blend seamlessly together swished
open silently. Gwen slipped through and into the dusky
pre-dawn light.

She paused, breathing in the rich scents that filled
the air that was already pleasantly warm before making
her way through the garden that seemed to be planted
with sensory appreciation in mind. Her robe brushed
the sweet-smelling Mediterranean herbs, sending even
more intense aromas into the air.

Without any real plan Gwen found herself skirting

the pool, the memories of what they had shared there still too shockingly fresh. She felt like a different person when she was with Rio, a person she barely recognised.

By the time she'd walked down the broad steps onto the beach the sun was just rising over the horizon, spilling fingers of scarlet and gold out into the layered smoky grey and blue of the clear dawn sky.

Sinking ankle deep into the soft sand, she watched as the grey turned to bands of contrasting shades of blue split by red-gold that turned the sea a delicate shade of pale copper.

She felt her mood lift. It was hard not to feel hope in the face of nature's beauty, but her hope was tinged with confusion as the cool morning air washed away the last shreds of sleepiness and the light breeze blowing in off the water tugged at her hair. Gwen closed her eyes and lifted her chin, letting the breeze blow the heavy strands back from her face while the floor-length robe she had pulled on flapped against her bare legs.

There was nothing to hear but her heartbeat and the soft swishing murmur of the waves as they hit the white sand. The utter peace and serenity of her surroundings contrasted dramatically with her internal chaos of churning emotion.

The truth was meant to set you free, wasn't it?

She opened her eyes and gave a tiny self-mocking laugh that floated away on the breeze. Truth was overrated, especially when the truth of her feelings for Rio was simply tearing her apart.

Or was it *denying* them that was doing that? asked the voice in her head. She shoved the question away, convinced it had more to do with self-preservation than rationality. That if she gave those feelings a name it would give them a power over her.

Last night they had made love...no, not made love, *had sex*, she reminded herself. Truth, she decided, wiping away a silent tear that was tracing a salty path down her cheek, was *definitely* overrated.

The tide had started to turn while she stood there and she jumped backwards as the water washed over her feet. She supposed she ought to go back. Ellie might wake soon and Rio... Would he wake and miss her or would he be relieved she'd left the bed to avoid the awkwardness of any morning-after pillow talk?

Perhaps he wouldn't feel awkward at all? Perhaps last night meant nothing to him except as a temporary convenience, because they were both there, available and willing? She threw up her hands and turned her back on the sea. God, when had life got so complicated?

Since you fell—

She choked off the thought, strangling it before it formed as she stormed up the beach. The spurt of temper had only got her as far as the steps when she stopped.

Before she saw Rio she needed to decide how she was going to play this. How did he feel about last night?

Did she want last night to happen again?

Her white teeth ground together as a wave of disgusted impatience with herself washed over her. Why was she even asking these questions when she already knew the answers? Rio had not made it a secret in the past that all he wanted from any woman was no-obligation sex. He didn't do exclusivity or long term, and he didn't want permanent ties, but fate had introduced a game-changer to his life in the shape of Ellie who, against all the odds, he was clearly already madly in love with.

The only thing Rio was committed to was being a father to his new-found daughter. It would be dangerous for her to assume anything else had fundamentally changed between them.

The question remained—did she want last night to happen again, knowing that for him it had been as basic and uncomplicated as simply satisfying a carnal thirst?

No, she didn't want it, but, God, she *needed* it. She was still wearing the memory of last night's lovemaking like a second skin. It felt like a dream but the ache in several parts of her body told her it was all too real. A deep shudder ran through her at the skin-peeling intensity of it, the sheer overwhelming pleasure that had made her feel she was about to lose consciousness.

Without her realising, her steps had taken her right up to the beach house, which in the sunshine was now lit up by the golden light bouncing off the expanse of glass. She blinked in confusion. She still hadn't decided what she was going to do. She supposed she had to ask herself what price she was willing to pay for the exquisite pleasure of being back in his bed, albeit temporarily.

He'd share his body but was that enough for her? Did she even want what he would only ever give grudgingly, which was a deeper connection between them? He would no doubt say that they were now and always connected by their child, but Gwen wanted more than that and only a fool would fall for a man who was incapable of giving anything of himself beyond his body.

She had always sworn that she would never settle for a man who could give her any less than everything. She wanted love, and she wanted to be in a man's heart, not just his bed, but she also wanted Rio. Because she already *loved* him.

She was a fool.

'This is impossible!' she yelled loudly enough to drown out her own thoughts, and luckily there was no one to hear her other than the gulls drifting on warm air streams above her head.

She squeezed her eyes tight shut and clenched her hands, wishing with all her might that she could look at Rio and not feel so damned...*needy*!

Her eyes flew wide as a noise from inside the main living room, loud enough to penetrate the closed door, made her start, a noise that was the unmistakable sound of breaking glass.

Responding to a protective instinct deeply embedded inside her, Gwen was already moving, her first thought inevitably to check on Ellie. Even though logic told her that her daughter was safely tucked up in bed, even though she knew she'd turned up the volume on the monitor beside her bed so high that it would have woken someone in a coma, let alone a sleeping Rio!

In a few breathless seconds she had flung open the silent sliding doors and stepped inside. Her panic receded, the thud of her heartbeat slowing, when she spotted the cause of the noise. Shards of a tall cylindrical, dramatically hand-painted glass vase that had sat on a lamp table to the right of the grand piano were now scattered across the terracotta-tiled floor.

His broad back to her, Rio was bent over picking them up, swearing fluently in Spanish as he did so and paying scant regard to the fact that they looked razor sharp.

'Be careful,' she warned, alarm sharpening her tone. 'You'll cut yourself.'

At the sound of her voice Rio straightened rapidly and spun around, several shards of glass in one long-fingered hand. He looked struck dumb by the sight of her standing there. For once he was the one acting thrown by her presence, though displaying more shock than the situation warranted, it seemed to Gwen.

A frown flickered into her blue eyes as his dark stare swept upwards from her feet. She couldn't put her finger on it but he was acting very strangely. Perhaps his behaviour was linked with the previous night? Was he regretting it already?

The thoughts were flitting through her head when their eyes finally connected. The hand she had slid into her heavy chestnut hair to pull it back from her face fell down by her side.

She had unconsciously steeled herself for an emotional explosion, tensed in preparation of containing her usual reaction to him. The anticlimax was extreme: there was no explosion, no charge in the air between them, just air.

She felt… Actually she felt nothing at all. Her pulses were not leaping, there were no butterflies running riot in her stomach and no warm feeling in the pit of her stomach.

She felt…not needy!

Her first thought was that her prayers had been answered, her second was that there looked like a lot more than one night's stubble on his chin and under the stubble he looked paler than usual.

'Too late, I already have.' He extended his hand towards her, letting the blood drip unchecked from his thumb onto the white grand piano, before he blotted his hand against his trousers and then, as an afterthought, smeared the red blob off the piano with his sleeve.

Gwen, who was less indifferent to blood than he appeared to be, felt her stomach muscles quiver in sympathy with the injury.

His grimace implied indifference as he proceeded to rub his hand against his shirt, leaving a bloody smear to match the one on the piano before giving up with a shrug. 'Never mind. I'm sure Estelle will clean away the evidence.'

'She's not here.'

Gwen didn't add, *You sent everyone away so you could have some time getting to know your daughter before you shared the news with the world,* because at some point over the last few moments she had realised that she was talking, not to Rio, but to his brother. And not just any brother, but his *twin.*

His *identical* twin.

Rio's twin—Roman, wasn't it?—tilted his head to one side and for a moment looked less like Rio. In a similar situation Rio would have scrunched his forehead and—

'So who are you?'

Gwen discovered that her scrutiny was being returned by a very curious pair of familiar dark eyes, the difference being that in his gaze there was nothing even vaguely sexual or challenging or a thousand other things Rio managed to communicate to her with just one look.

She found herself gathering her robe a little tighter around her, feeling awkward. She felt many things when she was with Rio but awkward was not one of them.

There hadn't been time for Rio to contact his brother so this had to be a coincidence.

'I'm Gwen,' she said, even though she knew he would probably be none the wiser. 'You're Roman?'

'Hello, Gwen.' He gave a grin that was almost but not quite the same as Rio's. She noticed for the first time that he looked tired, and maybe she was being fanciful but to her it seemed there was a darkness, a sombreness behind his eyes that Rio didn't have.

Maybe she'd finally got used to being able to read

Rio's expressions, or maybe she could just see clearer when she wasn't being blinded by the mad impulse to throw herself at his beautiful mouth like a suicidal rabbit when she saw a fox, which was something of a relief.

Her light musical trill of self-mocking laughter made Roman's eyebrows lift, which made her laugh again and think, *Just like Rio.*

There had to be at least half a dozen PhDs in it for the academics. Two men, so identical to look at, and while one had awoken a deep primal passion in her that she hadn't known she possessed, the other was just an *extremely* good-looking man who physically left her completely cold. It really was inexplicable.

'You actually *are* identical.' The moment the words were out of her mouth she felt foolish. How many times must he and Rio have heard that line? Luckily he was too polite to comment on her lack of originality, but she was sure that Rio wouldn't have shown a similar restraint.

'So people tell us, *Gwen*...?'

She nodded. 'Meredith.'

'Meredith or Gwen?' She knew Rio would have accompanied the question with a mocking gleam in his eyes, but his brother didn't.

His brother seemed a more *intense* sort of person, this man who'd walked away from power and responsibility leaving Rio to shoulder the entire burden of their inheritance. It spoke of a certain selfishness to leave your brother holding the baby—though not that baby. Roman didn't know about Ellie yet.

Or did he?

Did they tell each other everything?

She knew that often twins were closer than ordinary siblings; some even claimed to have a telepathic connection—if one stubbed their toe, the other felt it.

Was that just an urban myth? She sincerely hoped so!

'My name is Gwen Meredith.'

'Are you Welsh?'

She nodded. 'I'm impressed. Not many people outside the UK would get the accent first time.'

'I'm the intuitive one, or so they say.'

Gwen, who had always found Rio uniquely intuitive, lowered her gaze rather than challenge his claim. It crossed her mind that perhaps people assigned twins' roles early on in childhood—bright twin, athletic twin, leader, follower, and so on—and they stuck to them unquestioningly throughout their whole lives.

She lifted her gaze and caught him yawning. He intercepted her look and grinned. 'Long drive, a last-minute decision to come. I thought I'd be here for the party. And you are staying here with...?' One dark brow floated upwards the same way she had noticed in Rio a hundred times, the likenesses as much as the differences between them fascinating Gwen. 'I am assuming that Rio is here?'

'He's in bed,' she blurted, then compounded her embarrassment by blushing like a teenager. 'That is... I mean...'

Rio's twin smiled wickedly and again Gwen was struck by the similarity of their posture and body language. 'I get the picture.'

She wanted to say, *No, you really don't because I hardly get it myself,* but stopped herself because he probably did, just not the entire picture! Still playing catch-up, she suddenly registered his earlier comment. *Party?*

What party did he mean?

'You should put something on that,' she said, changing the subject as she nodded to indicate his finger that appeared to be still oozing blood, though to her relief it was no longer dripping. Rio would be oozing blood too, she decided, if he had deliberately kept her in the dark about some sort of party. The idea that Rio was manipulating her for some reason brought a spark of caution to her blue eyes.

'I'll live.' She sensed Roman had to put some effort into his smile. 'Look, I'm sorry if my arrival is badly timed but I'm off to my bed. I'll look in on Rio first, so could you point me in the direction of my big brother's…usual room?' He was already moving towards the door and Gwen was still nailed to the spot; similarly her tongue felt glued to the roof of her mouth.

'No…yes… I think maybe…your mother was looking for you earlier,' she stammered.

His brow knitted. 'She *was*? She left?'

Gwen nodded.

'So you have already met our mother?' There was a new interest in his eyes now as he studied her. 'Rio finally fetched a girl home!' He gave a low laugh, amused by his private joke.

Before she could figure out how to respond to this the door to the hallway was pushed open, clearly with a foot, as that came into the room first, followed by a sleep-dishevelled Rio with a very wide-awake Ellie in his arms.

CHAPTER NINE

IF ROMAN HAD looked surprised when he'd first seen Gwen, he now looked like a man who had put chocolate in his mouth and tasted hot chilli instead. He genuinely looked as though he could not believe his eyes as his astonished stare went from his bare-footed brother to the child he was carrying.

If he was even half as quick on the uptake as Rio it would take him only about a heartbeat to fill in the blanks.

Rio saw Gwen and felt a sense of relief that could not entirely be put down to the fact he felt somewhat out of his depth entertaining a very unpredictable toddler whose speech patterns remained a bit of a mystery to him. Understanding what she said was pretty much ninety per cent guesswork on his part and his mistakes elicited a bad-tempered response in his daughter, who, he was learning, got even louder when she was frustrated.

The communication problem was a two-way thing. She didn't appear to understand his requests, or maybe she just thought it was fine to ignore him—like mother, like daughter. The irony was that when he'd finally resorted to speaking Spanish out of sheer frustration, she seemed to respond to it just as well as his English!

He couldn't decide if it was the novelty value or the proof that children mopped up new languages like little sponges at this age, but they had got there in the end after a fashion. When he'd recalled his lack of empathy and patience when Gwen had been packing up to leave the cottage he'd felt a twinge of guilt—it seemed there was nothing like a two-year-old to teach a man some humility.

Getting a child out of bed, picking her up and coaxing her to stop crying was a lot less straightforward than it had first appeared. People really did downplay the difficulty of this parenting role! In his career there had been moments when he had felt a degree of complacent self-satisfaction when he'd pulled off a major financial deal against the odds and despite the critics, but that emotion paled beside the glow of triumph when they had gone in search of Gwen to show her how well they'd managed by themselves.

'So there you are. I should warn you to speak up, Gwen—I might have lost my hearing.' The child's cries, amplified by the volume control beside the bed, had woken him, but even that sound had been drowned out for a few moments when he'd realised Gwen was gone. Panic wasn't the right word, nor even a feeling of loss, he mused, his expression sobering as he remembered reaching out to feel a cold sheet that still bore the imprint of her body instead of soft warm skin.

His eyes drifted over the shape and warmness he had missed earlier. The robe she wore outlined the fluid grace of the lovely long lines of her body, her vibrant glowing hair lying loose and wild down her back, making him think of how it had felt as he'd trickled it through his fingers last night before burying his face in it.

'Where did you get to? Couldn't you sleep?' His voice slid a few husky notes lower. 'You really should have woken me.'

She had definitely slept for some of last night at least. He knew that because he had lain awake himself for a while, just watching her gently breathing.

Her eyes were not closed now. They were urgently signalling some sort of message to him, but Ellie's curly head kept bobbing into his line of vision. He tilted his head to see around her and Ellie immediately yelled again, not wanting to be ignored.

Gwen stood there, silently discounting the twin telepathy theory. Rio clearly hadn't caught on to the fact that his brother was standing right behind him, but then he did have his hands full quite literally and she knew from experience that containing a wriggling Ellie took all your focus and strength, not to mention dexterity.

'Rio?' Gwen said, but the rest of her words were drowned out by an extra loud yell of complaint from Ellie. Rio went to put her down, probably thinking she wanted to run to her mother.

Gwen flung an arm out. 'Don't put her down yet, Rio. There's broken glass all over the floor!'

Rio swung her back up. *'Vamos en la piscina mas tarde—perfecto!'*

To Gwen's utter amazement Ellie stopped dead and looked at him.

'What did you say?'

'I said we'd go to the pool later.'

'She understood you?'

He shrugged and grinned. 'She is already fluent.'

She lost her fight not to respond to his grin.

'Will you be careful of the glass too?'

Rio was barefoot, but at some point since she'd left

him he had pulled on a tee shirt and boxers. His hair was sticking up in sexy spikes, which probably had less to do with nature than with Ellie, looking equally tousled but very cute in a pair of rabbit pyjamas, who was now running strands of her father's dark hair through both chubby hands.

'Where were you, Gwen? We both missed you, didn't we, my sweetest?' Rio crooned, bending his head towards the toddler, who grabbed another handful of the thick, glossy hair that seemed to fascinate her. 'Ah... please don't give her scissors... Hmmm, yes, thank you, Ellie—I think that's what she's saying?'

The warmth in his eyes as they lifted and connected with her own would have melted Gwen like ice cream on a hot day in any other circumstances.

'What do you fancy for—?' He broke off, a frown forming between his brows as he scanned her face, apparently seeing something there that bothered him. 'Do we need to talk?'

Roman, who had coped with the sudden appearance of a woman wearing very little, but who was coping less well with his ruffled brother carrying a child who bore a really startling resemblance to him, finally recovered his voice.

'I think maybe we do,' Roman mused.

Hugging a squirming Ellie, who had finally got bored playing with his hair, a little closer, Rio turned jerkily to where his brother stood.

'*Roman...?* What—?' The rest of his rapid staccato response was delivered in Spanish.

Roman patiently waited his twin out, watching the child in his brother's arms with a fascinated eye as he replied, 'I knew you'd be glad to see me.'

Rio ignored the irony. 'Of course I'm glad to see you,' he lied. 'But I—'

Reading the appeal in his eyes as he turned to her, Gwen moved forward, holding out her arms to receive Ellie, who cried shrilly in protest and held out her arms demandingly to Rio.

'I'll just leave you two to it, shall I?' Gwen said, not waiting for a response as she headed for the door.

'You don't have to go, Gwen.' Rio simultaneously registered his twin's expression of surprise and the revealing flicker of pleasure on Gwen's face as he spoke.

He also recognised it was impractical for her to stay, as the things he needed to say to his brother would be hard enough without an audience.

'Actually, it might be better, Gwen, if you just took Ellie to—'

'That's fine,' Gwen interrupted hastily with a throwaway smile that didn't reach her eyes. 'I'll catch up with you both later.'

Roman waited until she had gone.

'She looked hurt then, when you told her to go,' Roman said slowly.

Rio's jaw clenched. *Tell me something I don't know.* '*She* is the mother of my child.'

Roman wondered if his twin was aware of the pride in his voice or the challenge in his eyes. 'I did kind of work that one out,' he responded drily. 'So Mum was here, to meet her?'

Rio dragged a hand through his hair. 'Actually, she arrived looking for you. She is booked in for more surgery next Friday and she wanted to let you know,' he told his brother tersely.

'Is it—?'

'She said it's not serious but you know her.'

'So seeing Gwen and the baby must have made her happy… I am assuming that you two are together?'

'We will be.' Until he heard himself say it he hadn't really known that was what he wanted. But half-measure arrangements were no longer an option after last night. The recognition of that decision gave him a liberating lift and a moment's respite from the sense of impending doom that had descended when he saw his twin, the knowledge that there were no excuses left, he had to tell his brother the truth.

He'd known for days now that he had to do so, although Roman's sudden appearance had precipitated it.

'So what brings you here?'

You're only delaying the painful moment, Rio silently mocked himself.

'Thought I'd help out with the party, but I see you have it all in hand. So, does the surgery mean that Mum won't be here to host her party?' Roman looked at his obviously bewildered brother. 'It's July… You've forgotten about it, haven't you?'

Rio swore, which his twin took as a yes.

'I'll cancel it,' Rio said firmly.

'You can't do that—it's tradition and her way of saying thank you, even when she's not here in person.'

Rio muttered something indistinct about tradition that was probably unprintable, but Roman knew, they both did, that Rio would rise to the occasion. He could always be relied on to fulfil his duty and, on more than one occasion, Roman's too.

'So is the boyfriend going to be there to hold her hand again?' Roman asked.

'He's a nice guy, Roman,' Rio said as his twin sat down at the piano, lifted the lid and began a complex series of exercises. His brother had always struggled more than he had with their mother's ongoing relationship with a theatre director.

'This always did have a good tone.' Roman's hands fell away from the keys. 'And I'm still reserving judgement.'

'He's been around for two years now and she's very happy with him.'

'She'd better stay that way,' Roman growled and then changed the subject. 'So what's the story with you and Gwen?'

Rio exhaled. There was a story he had to tell his brother but it wasn't the one he was asking to hear.

'Just let me get this out before you...' Rio closed his eyes and clenched his jaw. 'Just let me get this out, Roman, before you say anything else.'

Gwen fed Ellie her breakfast before she popped her in the bath. Ellie loved bath time and Gwen, who like most single parents had become really expert at multitasking, had a micro shower with the door open so that she could still keep an eye on Ellie.

She had pulled on a pair of shorts and a cotton vest by the time Ellie was ready to leave the bath. A few minutes later they were both outside, Ellie wearing a cute play suit with a matching little sunhat and liberally plastered in sunscreen, though her skin had already developed a warm glow.

Gwen avoided the pool because she knew that Ellie would want to jump right in and instead made her way towards the dovecote that she had noticed when they arrived, armed with a bag of seeds she had seen stacked in the utility.

She sat on a bench and watched as Ellie threw seeds

for the flock of white birds, thinking about how Rio had asked her to leave the room.

She knew that she was getting this out of all proportion—she had no right to feel hurt and excluded from a conversation between him and his brother.

But she did, and her throat thickened as she felt the push of tears behind her eyelids. If Rio hadn't so unexpectedly seemed to want her to stay before then sending her away, it might not have been so bad.

'Yes, bad bird, darling, very bad bird!' she yelled back in response to Ellie's finger-waving at one of the doves who the little girl had decided was *'very, very geedy'*.

'Well, what did you expect, Gwen?' she asked herself crossly before pausing to blow her nose on the tissue she fished out of her pocket. 'To be included in a private family meeting when you're not family?'

She knew she was an outsider here but the reminder had hurt more than she wanted to admit even to herself.

'All gone.' Ellie tipped her empty paper seed bag upside down.

Gwen smiled. 'Come on, that's enough sun for one morning, I think. How about some juice?'

Clapping happily, the toddler skipped ahead. They had come within sight of the driveway when a car sped around the bend in the drive with a squeal, kicking up gravel. Gwen grabbed Ellie and pulled her back into her body, reacting to instinct rather than any actual danger as she watched the speeding car vanish with one hand shading her eyes.

Rio's brother drove like a lunatic—or perhaps a very angry man?

'It's none of my business,' she said, addressing her remark to a cloud of dust, which was all that was left of the powerful car driven by Rio's twin.

Like every other room in the house, the kitchen of the beach house was built on a palatial scale. There were free-standing units in a bleached wood down one long wall, with an old-fashioned range that was gleaming and unused, presumably preserved from the original building, on the opposite wall. Gwen opened a cupboard in the massive island and pulled out a plastic tumbler, and watched as Ellie headed like a heat-seeking missile to the corner where a brand-new playhouse, complete with a garden filled with plastic flowers, took centre stage. Ellie marched straight to the little gate and stepped inside.

Gwen went across to the nearest of the massive fridges, and swung a door open. 'Orange, apple or *yummy* water, darling?' she asked, but Ellie was already engrossed in her make-believe game and didn't respond. Before she could repeat her question a figure appeared in the doorway to the adjoining utility room.

A choking sound escaped her throat and her stomach took a sickening dive as she took in Rio's condition.

'Sorry, I'll just…' With a bloodied hand holding up an equally gory towel pressed to his face, Rio glanced towards Ellie, who continued to offer drinks from an invisible glass to dolls she had lined up in front of her.

'You carry on with Ellie. I was just washing up, then I might just…' He trailed off.

Rio's glance drifted back towards Ellie, who was animatedly talking to a teddy bear now.

'I don't want to alarm her.'

'You won't, although she might want to stick a plaster on you once she notices the blood.' Pity he wasn't so concerned about alarming me, Gwen thought acidly, trying to assess the damage behind the towel he was holding as she struggled to maintain at least the illusion of calm. 'What happened? Shall I call an ambulance?'

'*Dios*, no, it's just a nose-bleed. I'll wash up and get rid of this towel.'

Not fooled for an instant, she followed him into the utility area and asked her question in a firm tone that made it absolutely clear she expected an answer.

'What happened, Rio? And do not give me the nose-bleed story again. I'm not stupid!' Except she already was for imagining for one more moment that she could carry on pretending, even to herself, that she was not in love with Rio. The pretence had already grown thin, but seeing him standing there hurt and bleeding had peeled away the last of it, exposing the nerve of the truth. She had fallen for the father of her child, a man who would never love her back because he was too damaged from his own childhood experiences. 'What happened? Who did this?' There was only really one candidate to choose from but she wanted him to tell her. It was important to her for him to share at least this much.

'It's fine, don't fuss,' he said, his voice muffled by the towel.

'If you think all the machismo stiff-upper-lip stuff is going to impress me, you're very mistaken.' But then he wasn't trying to impress her, was he? She wanted to impress him; she wanted him to need her the way she needed him, and he wasn't going to, not ever.

'Let me see—'

'No!'

She ignored his protest and reached up to pull the towel away from his face. She swallowed a gasp, and thought, *Right, so your objectivity has gone out of the window; just wing it, girl!*

'That looks painful.' Turning so he couldn't see her own face, she walked across to one of the deep stone sinks inset into a smooth work surface made of the same material. 'I hope the other guy looks worse.' If it was Roman, as she fully suspected, he definitely would after she got her hands on him!

When Rio said nothing it only confirmed her suspicions. It seemed ironic that she had always wanted a sibling, but now she felt lucky she was an only child.

'Where's the first-aid kit?' It didn't even cross her mind that there wouldn't be one on his tick list when he had made this house a child-friendly haven.

'First door on the right.' He nodded to the open cupboard at the far end of the room. 'It doesn't matter. I'm fine,' he said, sounding irritated now.

She didn't have to feign anger to hide her feelings. 'You're an idiot!' she snarled, before muttering under her breath as she yanked the cupboard open. The label on the first-aid kit was in four languages just in case you made a mistake, and as she pulled it out and placed it on the work surface she opened her eyes wide.

'An EpiPen, *really*?' As a teacher, she knew a lot more than the general public about such things. 'You really did anticipate every disaster, didn't you?'

'Not me… I—'

'Yes, I know, you delegated the task,' she said in a flat voice. He might not give himself credit for getting this house ready for them, but she did. He hadn't personally painted the nursery or made every corner of this place as child friendly as was humanly possible, but he had instigated it all.

The effort he had made to accommodate a child into his life at incredibly short notice touched her deeply.

'What can I say? I was a Boy Scout,' he said, and she couldn't help but be aware of his intent stare following her as she selected the items she was looking for.

'Liar!' she denounced confidently. 'They'd have turfed you out after your first bad joke.'

Gwen gathered up the items she needed and walked back. Nothing in this place seemed to involve short distances. She sensed his eyes on her again and felt self-conscious. 'Sit down.'

Rather to her surprise, he did as he was told, straddling one of the tall stools that surrounded the peninsula work surface.

'This will probably hurt...' She took a deep breath and moved in closer, not realising until his thighs tightened on either side of her hips that she was standing between his legs. For once he didn't have the advantage of height, they were literally nose to nose, and the closeness was making her insides shudder. 'You more than me,' she added, avoiding looking him in the eyes, not liking the idea of what he might see there. She had her pride left if nothing else. 'Now, let me see...' It had never been more of a struggle to channel her inner un-flappable schoolteacher than in this moment.

He lowered his hand and the towel, setting it to one side on the counter top, revealing the full extent of the damage, which she was hoping might not be as bad as it looked.

His jaw was red, his lip was split and starting to swell, his nose bloody and there was already the sug-gestion of a purplish bruise under one eye.

On one level she registered that it could be a lot worse, on another she was trying to function despite the strength of her emotional reaction to his pain, which was making it hard to get words past the contraction in her throat.

But presumably losing all sense of proportion was part and parcel of loving someone.

She glanced away, too afraid he might see the tears she could feel standing out in her eyes. 'Where else are you hurt?' she asked, her husky tone falling way short of the clinical one she was aiming for, but at least she wasn't openly crying.

'I'm fine.'

'Of course you are and it shows,' she came back sarcastically.

'Are you crying?' he asked in a strange voice—or then again it might have just been his lip.

'I am not crying.' She sniffed angrily. 'I am *angry*. You want to know why I'm angry?' Apparently he didn't; he was just watching her with a veiled expression in his dark eyes. Taken unawares, he didn't resist when without warning she took both his hands in hers and closely examined them. There wasn't a mark on them; no signs at all that he had defended himself.

She could think of only one person that Rio would not defend himself from.

Her eyes lifted, the blue light in them grim and hard, and Rio could see exactly what she was thinking—that his brother was a bastard. He knew he should really put her straight and explain that he was the one with the bastard credentials, but he found himself dreading seeing the sort of angry condemnation and contempt shining in her spectacular eyes right now directed at him. Even though he fully deserved it.

He acknowledged his uncharacteristic desire to please her with a faint frown, but his head hurt too much to delve any deeper into the reasons that it was so important to him for her to think he was one of the good guys.

Maybe the headache was a good thing, Rio mused grimly. He had enough complications in his life without looking for more...or maybe even inventing some. The priority he needed to focus on right now was being a good father, or at least not a bad one, and maybe persuading his twin to speak to him again. After all, Roman had only hit him the once, on his jaw, and, although he had a hell of a punch, the rest of the damage to Rio's face had happened when he'd hit the corner of the coffee table on his way down. It gave him a thin sliver of hope that he still might be able to salvage some sort of future relationship with his brother.

A sound of frustration escaped Gwen's clenched lips. 'So who did this? And do not say you walked into a door because, so help me, I will hit you myself! Oh, sorry,' she exclaimed with a wince of sympathy as she touched the alcohol swab to his cheekbone and he flinched.

Their eyes connected and her fingers found their way to the uninjured side of his face, curving tenderly around his cheek. 'Did your brother do this to you?'

'I deserved it!' The words almost seemed pushed out against his will and hung there in the air between them as a stunned and confused Gwen finished cleaning up his face.

Once she'd finished, she shoved the gauze and antiseptic back on the work surface. The twisting motion unsteadied her centre of gravity and his thighs immediately tightened around her and his big hands went to her waist.

Suddenly breathing was difficult, and thinking was even harder through the fog of sexual desire that seemed to fill the bubble of air around them, and all her liberated hormones were running riot.

She lacked the strength and willpower to avoid his steady hot stare, the raw glow in his eyes making her insides dissolve into a pool of liquid.

'Thank you.' Her voice sounded as if it belonged to someone else.

'No, thank you,' he came back smoothly.

The effort to stay still in his grasp brought beads of sweat to her upper lip, but she managed to break the grip of his stare to glance down momentarily at his hands that rested on her hips.

'What did you mean you *deserved* it?'

In her eyes violence was not an answer to anything. 'Also keep in mind that the martyr look on you is very unattractive.'

His hands dropped away, and he suddenly looked so bleak that she was seized by a powerful urge to take his face between her hands and kiss him, except theirs was not a relationship based on loving kisses, was it?

'Did your brother do this?' she asked again in a low, dangerous growl.

'Yes, but like I said I deserved it.' The muscular support of his confining thighs loosened and she stepped back, feeling quite ludicrously bereft.

The air hissed through her clenched teeth as she planted her hands on her hips and looked across at him. 'Did you even try and defend yourself?'

He flashed a grin and immediately winced, lifting a hand to his split lip. 'Have you never heard of turning the other cheek?'

'I'm surprised you have.'

Not resisting Roman's fury had not been a plan, just a reaction to Rio's belief that he deserved everything he got, but in the end it was what had stopped the escalation of the fight. If he had fought back Rio was sure his twin would have kept going to the death and Rio, with his newly acquired knowledge of what being a father meant to him, understood totally.

He watched Gwen stalk over to the fridge, pull out a tray of ice cubes and dump them into a clean towel. He loved the way she moved; there was an inherent grace to it that was all the more seductive for being totally unfeigned.

'It might help the bruising,' she said, thrusting the home-made ice pack at him. 'And maybe an aspirin.'

'I'd prefer a brandy.' He looked at her mouth, thinking that, actually, a kiss might work even better!

'It's not even midday.'

Her outrage struck him as hilarious under the circumstances, but laughing hurt. 'Fine, then a cup of tea would be nice. Shall we?' He nodded towards the doorway.

She walked ahead of him back into the kitchen where Ellie was no longer playing. Instead, she was curled up fast asleep in the garden of her playhouse, her thumb in her mouth.

Rio watched with tender eyes as Gwen scooped her up. At least his daughter had a clear conscience. He rubbed a hand down his jaw on the uninjured side of his face.

'I'll put her down in the nursery,' Gwen said.

CHAPTER TEN

Rio nodded and watched her go, feeling the now familiar emotion tightening in his chest as he did so. The lightening of the heavy weight behind his breastbone had been only temporary. Once she had left the room it was back again.

He moved restlessly round the room. She was going to come back in a minute and then she'd be asking him questions again, and he'd end up telling her everything.

He felt he had to. The conviction that he shouldn't keep this from her any longer was deep but inexplicable. After all, it wasn't as though they were a couple, was it? They were just... His hands clenched as his handsome bruised features locked tight in a grimace of self-loathing and contempt.

Dios mio, they were not 'just' anything. That was the whole point, and if he'd needed evidence of it there was last night. He had gone past calling it mutual need, a chemical reaction. It was definitely *more* than that, but he didn't want more.

He wanted simple and clean cut.

Shaking his head and immediately regretting it, he headed for the living room. Tea might be nice in theory but he definitely needed something stronger and maybe two aspirin as well.

* * *

Ellie didn't wake as Gwen put her into her bed fully dressed; she was going to be hungry when she woke. Gwen kissed the air above her daughter's soft flushed cheek and pressed a button and the blackout blinds slid into place. Then she felt around to find the switch to turn on the night lights.

Her route back from the bedroom wing of the house to the kitchen took her past the open-plan living room that took up half the square footage of the entire building. She was determined to find out the truth about his fight with his brother if she had to physically drag it out of him.

She wouldn't accept a lie just because it made his life easier.

She had her argument in place if he was difficult, which was virtually inevitable, she reflected grimly. If he argued that it wasn't any of her business he might be right—it wasn't. But Ellie was, and she had a right to know about anything that could impact on her daughter. She intended to tell him that she wouldn't allow their daughter to stay in an environment where violence was likely to flare up.

There had never been any violence in her home. Her father had many faults but that had not been one of them. Instead, her childhood had been the story of a relationship based on lies, and lies destroyed trust and self-respect, which was equally destructive.

She immediately felt guilty for likening Rio to her father even in a small way. Her father had always been a weak man and Rio was strong, but she knew environment mattered and it wasn't about toys or beautiful clothes, it was about feeling safe. Children soon learnt to recognise the lies and half-truths inside a house.

She and Rio might not be in a relationship as such—although quite frankly she didn't know *what* they were doing—but any decisions she made going forward had to be based on truth, not lies, and if he refused to talk to her then it was a deal-breaker for her.

She was determinedly stomping along the wide hallway back to the kitchen when a distinctive discordant sound of crashing piano keys from the living room brought her to an abrupt halt.

She retraced her steps to the set of open double doors, her first thought that Rio's twin had returned. *In which case, you're going to do what, Gwen? Tackle him single-handed because his stupid brother wouldn't defend himself?*

Her shoulders sagged in relief when she saw that Rio was alone.

'What are you doing?' she snapped as her agitated heart rate began to slow.

Rio was sitting at the grand piano, glass of brandy in one hand, the fingers of his other now running up and down some intricate scales. He looked up as she spoke.

'I couldn't find the tea.' He raised his glass.

She walked inside. 'I didn't know you played.'

He crashed the keys again, producing a discordant racket that made her wince before closing the lid and surging to his feet. Even in a space this size he was a dominant presence, projecting restless energy under the frustration.

'Roman is the musical one. I was never more than adequate, according to our music teacher. I was the one who was better at boxing, a nice irony, huh?' he said, touching his jaw. 'Roman was always too emotional—it must have been a lucky punch.'

'Or maybe you just stood there waiting for it and then

took it like an idiot.' The image in her head made her as mad as hell. What on earth had he done that was so bad he felt he needed to be punished this way?

He gave her a sideways glance and didn't reply. 'Is Ellie okay?' he asked.

'She's fine, fast asleep. She missed her mid-morning nap, her routine is shot, so she'll sleep for a while.' Rio looked as if he needed to sleep too. She shook her head, impatient with herself. She had no idea why a tough man who was so obviously capable of looking after himself—except when it came to his twin—brought out such crazy protective instincts in her. She wasn't in love, she was insane!

'So you want to know what is going on?' His shoulders lifted in one of his inimitable shrugs and he conceded, 'You have a right to, I suppose.'

Gwen had been prepared to tell him just that and now felt as if the wind had been taken out of her sails. 'I didn't think I had any rights,' she said, struggling to keep the resentment out of her voice and failing.

'Well, you're part of this family now, so you might as well know the worst about us.'

Do not read too much into that, she counselled herself firmly. *He just means you're family now because of Ellie.*

'This isn't our normal way of interacting, Roman and me... There is no history of this sort of thing.'

'By this sort of thing you mean him beating several shades of hell out of you.'

'I love it when you call a spade a bloody shovel, Miss Meredith.' He expelled a deep sigh through his nostrils and looked at her. 'Yes, that is what I mean.'

'And is it likely to happen again?'

'If Roman is to be believed I'm not likely to ever see

him again—his last words to me were, "I'm finished with you!"' He gave a dry, unamused laugh. 'It sounded pretty convincing.' He continued to look at her, but as the moments stretched out Gwen had the impression he was not seeing her at all.

'That DNA match you saw nearly three years ago.'

His sudden words made her flinch. The memory of that day was etched deep in her psyche, and the wound was still barely scabbed over, even after all this time. 'Do we have to talk about that?' She was ashamed of her cowardly response but she couldn't help it.

'It's part of what happened today,' he said heavily.

'The argument was about your son?' she said gently. She could see the internal struggle on his face. This seemed to be something he had to tell her, or maybe he just had to confide in someone and she was here. But even if it was just an illusion it felt in that moment as if they were close.

'I don't have a son.'

A dozen meanings flashed through her head and she blurted a response to the only one that really fitted his words and the terrible bleakness in his eyes.

'I'm so sorry.'

He stared at her, bewilderment etched into his face as she surged to her feet and rushed over to him, taking his big hands in her own.

'I can't imagine what it feels like to lose a child.' Her voice was husky with empathy and emotion as she thought with a shudder that she never wanted to know!

Without a word he flicked his hands over so that hers were now pressed between his. 'No one is dead, and I never had a son. Roman did—he does—but he didn't know.' He released her hands and touched his face, a rueful gleam in his eyes. 'Until I told him earlier.'

'You don't have a son?' Her mouth fell open, her knees sagged and she sat down on the leather recliner behind her. She could still hear the echo of his words vibrating in her head but they made no sense.

How could what he was saying be true?

'I don't understand.'

'Two weeks before we met in that bar I had a visit from…well, her name isn't important. She'd had an affair with my brother two years before and apparently he'd proposed to her, which I have to admit fairly blew my mind at the time. I'd always thought Roman had the same mindset as—'

'You?'

'Well, anyway, she told me she was still married at the time but he didn't know.'

'She didn't tell him she was still married?'

Rio's hand, which had been raised to emphasise a point he'd been making, clenched and fell back to his side. 'Not until after his proposal. She had her reasons for that and they seemed right to her. Just as mine seemed right to me at the time. But that part is not my story to tell. Roman's proposal came with a demand that she get divorced immediately. She refused and…well, let's say their parting was not what you'd call amicable. A few weeks later, she discovered she was pregnant.'

'She passed the baby off as her husband's child?'

'He never knew about it because he died before she even knew she was pregnant. So fast forward now to the two weeks before you and I met in that bar. She turned up, made me promise not to tell Roman, then told me the whole story and explained that her son was seriously sick. He needed a bone-marrow transplant and his blood group was rare.'

Her eyes widened. 'The DNA results.'

He nodded. 'The thing about being an identical twin is that our DNA is identical, so I could donate instead of Roman.'

'You did?' He nodded. 'And the little boy...your nephew...he's okay now?'

'Fine, the last I heard.'

She gave a little sigh of relief.

'Marisa sends me a Christmas card and photos of the boy every year.'

He seemed unaware he had revealed the woman's name so Gwen didn't draw attention to it. He didn't need anything more to beat himself up over.

'Were you ever tempted to tell Roman? No, sorry.' She moved her head in a negative gesture. 'I shouldn't have asked.'

'Why not?' He seemed genuinely puzzled by her statement, which made her think how much their relationship had moved on during the past few days. 'And, yes, I was,' he admitted. 'There were several occasions where I was on the brink of breaking my word. If my brother hadn't taken himself off somewhere and turned into a hermit writer I might have done it, but instead it became an out-of-sight-out-of-mind situation.'

'But I don't understand——why didn't she just ask your brother to donate? Why didn't she tell him about his son?' She stopped, the irony of the recrimination in her voice hitting home. She was judging someone else...but what had this woman done that she hadn't?

She stared down at her clasped hands.

'I suppose pride played a part.' She looked up, a question in her cobalt-blue eyes. 'At the time she came to me, my brother was in a relationship, a pretty well-publicised one.'

'Oh...' Gwen felt a wave of sisterly sympathy for the

other woman. 'It must have been hard for her bringing up a child alone, especially a poorly one.'

Rio watched the expressions drift across her soft features and felt a strong wave of protectiveness rise up in him.

'You managed.'

'That really isn't the same thing at all.'

'No, it isn't, because you had no support network.' The idea of her parents abandoning her still made him see red and now he had a daughter of his own it seemed utterly inexplicable that Gwen had been cut off by the people who should have loved her the most. He knew that it didn't matter what Ellie did, he would always be there for her. 'And not much money to cushion you. Don't compare the situations, Gwen. You had to fend for yourself while she didn't have to worry about paying the rent.'

His unexpected defence brought a glow of pleasure to her face. 'But Ellie is not ill,' she pointed out, 'and I can't imagine how bad it would be if her life was in danger, especially when you have to make all the decisions yourself. That's the worst part really,' she mused.

'What is?' he asked, watching her closely.

'It's not just about the money though, gosh, yes, that helps. It's about not having someone to share the decisions with…someone to bounce ideas off and share the responsibilities with. Was she still in love with Roman, do you think?'

Rio shook his head. 'I'm not the expert on that subject,' he said. It was hard to be an expert on something when you'd spent your entire adult life running away from it. The love he'd seen up close and personal as a child had been a destructive force and the idea of embracing it had made as much sense to him as walking towards a tidal wave...knowing you would be completely helpless once you were in its grip.

Gwen's little glow of pleasure faded. Was she back to reality already? she wondered. The reality was that whatever future they had in front of them depended on her accepting the message in his words, and not expecting an iota more. Rio would never love her but he did love their daughter...which was what was most important, she reminded herself, ignoring the sinking feeling in her stomach.

'Is your brother still in a relationship?'

'Who knows?' he said with a shrug. 'He's walked out of the spotlight, and he's back to being his publicity-phobic self.'

'So he doesn't smile for the cameras like you, then?' she said, thinking sourly of all the online photos she'd seen of Rio with beautiful model types draped over him.

Rio didn't react to the jibe. 'It sounds as if his and Marisa's parting was particularly bitter and acrimonious. People say things in the heat of the moment that are hard to take back or forgive.'

Was he trying to say that he was sorry for the things he had said to her?

'You don't think your brother will forgive you, do you?'

A look of pain and self-recrimination moved across his face. 'No, I don't.'

'Maybe the question you *should* be asking yourself is would you forgive him if the roles were reversed?'

She caught an arrested look on his face before he turned and walked through the open doors onto the patio. She watched him standing there dragging his hand through his already tousled hair for a moment before joining him.

The smell of lavender and lemon thyme was strong in the warm air.

'He's my twin. I'm not suggesting we have some magical connection but in the past we have always been each other's support network, no matter the distance between us. I resented him walking away and leaving me with the business, and we should have had a bust-up about that then rather than let it fester. Who knows? It might have cleared the air between us... But then I was already feeling guilty...'

'So that's a yes. You would forgive him if the roles were reversed.'

He looked at her then with an almost smile. 'But I'd have hit him harder first.'

'So if you'd forgive him why wouldn't he forgive you—in time?'

He barked out a harsh laugh. 'You like happy-ever-after endings.'

She pushed away the knowledge that she was not likely to have her happy ever after because you couldn't force someone to love you. 'Doesn't everyone?' she said lightly. From this side of him his profile was un-blemished and, of course, perfect. You couldn't see the damage to his face, but her stomach muscles fluttered because she knew it was there.

'Is it still hurting?'

'I took the aspirin.'

Squinting, she looked up at him, lifting a hand to shade her eyes from a blazing sun that had climbed high in the sky. 'And the brandy.' There was a teasing note in her voice.

His eyes drifted over her fair skin, where she knew that a scattering of freckles had appeared across the bridge of her nose. His hand lifted briefly before it dropped back to his side, and she wondered if he'd had a sudden impulse to reach out and touch her skin.

'Come and sit in the shade.' Concern lent his tone roughness. 'The entire place is wired for sound so we'll hear Ellie if she wakes.'

'Oh, she'll sleep for a while yet,' Gwen said, following him across to an area that was shaded by a canopy. She hesitated to take the seat beside him on the sofa, but felt it would look too obvious if she sat half a mile away from him.

Nothing essentially had changed; she'd just faced up to a fact that she had been hiding from. He wasn't going to return her love.

'Your brother mentioned a party.'

'Ah, *the* party. My mother holds one here every year. A celebration of her divorce and a thank you to all the friends who stood by her through the years despite the best efforts of my father to alienate her from them. Yes, this is a family where we actually celebrate divorce.' He drained the last finger of brandy and looked at her over his glass, as if trying to judge her reaction.

'If my mum ever decided to divorce my father I'd celebrate.'

The admission made him laugh. 'So you don't believe in the marriage myth either.'

'I didn't say that.' She hesitated—did he want to hear this? What the hell? She wanted to say it, so she would. 'I know the statistics, but I don't see why it shouldn't be a goal... I don't know what makes a *perfect* marriage or even if such a thing exists, but I do know what is essential before a marriage can work.'

'And that would be?'

She responded without hesitation. 'There has to be ongoing open communication. You have to be able to talk to the person you spend the rest of your life with. I don't mean you can't be different—you shouldn't ever lose your individuality—but I suppose you should at least share common values. And there has to be honesty and trust.' She firmly believed that trust once lost was almost impossible to regain.

'You have obviously put some thought into the subject. So love is optional for you?'

She shook her head vigorously, defiance edging her words as she insisted, 'Love is essential but I don't think you can ever be complacent about it. It needs careful nurturing, and it won't survive if you lose all the other things along the way.'

As the silence stretched she began to feel embarrassed for sounding off like that, for giving such an intense response to a casual question. He was probably wondering how to change the subject.

'When Roman and I were kids we both vowed that we'd never get married or have kids of our own. I think the kid part scared Roman more than me because he was always afraid that he had more of our father in him and he always said why take the risk passing on tainted genes?'

A little sound of horror that escaped her lips brought his eyes to her face. He sketched a quick smile that left his dark eyes sombre as their gazes met and despite the matter-of-fact delivery she could feel the pain behind his words, the memories that had influenced his young life and still did.

'So I never thought that Roman would really want to know...'

'You thought you were protecting him,' she breathed softly.

He shook his head. 'Did I? I really don't know but

back then I had no idea, not the faintest concept of what having a child feels like. But now I do and I've deprived him of the opportunity of having the same joy.'

The simple sincerity in his words made her eyes fill with tears.

'Roman always said marriage was a prison and I agreed with him. I should have realised when Marisa said he'd proposed to her that he'd already moved on, had managed to escape the past even if I hadn't.' The self-contempt in his voice was corrosive.

'But my mother's marriage *was* a prison.'

She covered his hand that lay on the table with her own. 'I think your mother is a very strong person to come through it as happy as she obviously is.'

Rio looked from the small hand on his to her face, and the muscles along his jawline quivered. 'She is, but she still won't go back to the house, our estate, even though he's dead.'

Sympathy softened Gwen's blue eyes. Jo had given herself and her sons a new life but it had taken courage. She found herself wondering what her life would have been like if her mother had refused to tolerate her father's infidelities and left him years ago.

Perhaps none of us ever escaped our past, she mused. Certainly these revelations about his childhood explained so much about Rio, especially his avoidance of committed relationships. A deep sadness rose up in her for him and his brother, and an anger and disgust for the parent who had scarred them this way.

'How old were you?'

'When they split, twelve, when he died we were twenty. The years in between, or at least until we were eighteen, we had to spend alternate holidays with him. He used to try and get information out of us about Mum, who was she seeing, that sort of thing, and the things he said about her…'

Gwen just nodded and didn't tell him she already knew about that from Jo. She was touched by the fact he was confiding in her and trying desperately hard not to read too much into it.

'He wasn't just toxically jealous—he was coercive and controlling.' The look of revulsion that crossed his face made her heart twist in her chest with a painful pulse of empathy.

It seemed to her that although their mother had escaped from him, the twins hadn't. What a terrible thing to use your own children as weapons, though sadly she knew that it was not as rare as it should be.

'It was a relief.'

She realised he was looking at her as though he expected her condemnation.

'It was a relief when he died,' he expanded.

'Of course it was.' It seemed to her that guilt was Rio's factory setting. 'So when he died you were finally free?'

He hesitated, the direct question resurrecting his hauteur that Gwen recognised now as a defence mechanism to keep people at arm's length.

Their eyes met and the ice in Rio's gaze warmed and vanished. There was something about her quiet interest, the total lack of prurience, that made him continue.

'Free of him but not entirely. Over the years he had used our inheritance as a stick to beat us with, threatening to cut us off so often that we both assumed that he had. We both made our own plans. Roman was in his second year at Oxford, I'd taken the year out and was working on an outback station in the Northern Territory.'

Gwen blinked. 'I can just see you on horseback.'

He smiled, but it faded almost instantly. 'Then we found out he'd left us it all anyway, the family estate and the money and also the private equity firm that he had founded. He was a bastard, but a bastard who knew how to make money. So in a way he found a way to control us after all—we had to learn fast.' He stopped mid-sentence, an arrested, self-conscious expression freezing his features into a shocked frown.

Where had his initial reluctance to explain the skewed dynamic of his definitional family background to her gone? He'd had to fight, to begin with, against the habit of a lifetime to reveal the facts he felt circumstances decreed she should know.

Now here he was, acting as though he were in a therapy session giving her an unrequested tour of his murky childhood and psychological flaws. 'Sorry, this is not really relevant—you must be a sympathetic listener.' She was certainly a non-judgemental one, which was a lot more than he deserved.

'So you worked together, you and Roman?'

'Initially I thought we made a good team. Until he left.'

And now he was a man shouldering all the responsibility, Gwen thought. 'You miss him.'

His eyes slid from hers and she could almost see him retreating from her as he sketched a quick smile. 'We have never lived in one another's pockets or finished each other's sentences.'

'So what made your mother leave your father in the end?'

'Actually this house was the final straw. It had belonged to her family and she'd inherited it. In the early days we came here on holidays regularly, but then my father took against it simply, I think, because she loved it, and then he arranged the sale of it behind her back and he told her to sign on the dotted line.'

Gwen watched as a thoughtful expression drifted across his face as though he was reliving a moment in the past.

'She said it was like waking up after a long nightmare. She ripped up the contract, grabbed us and, the way she tells it, a bag of knickers, phoned the best divorce lawyer she could and brought us here. The rest is history. Oh, and the lawyer will be one of the guests at the party. They are a pretty eclectic bunch but I think you'll like them.'

'I assumed that you were going to cancel...' She stopped. 'I'll still be here, will I?'

'It seems the ideal opportunity to introduce you to the people who matter to me, and Ellie, of course.'

'You're going to go public about us?'

The brow on the uninjured side of his face lifted. 'I considered sliding down my seat in the car and hiding from it all but...'

The teasing reminder of what she'd done at school to avoid those parents made her flush.

'Perhaps,' Rio said, watching her closely, seeing the wariness in her eyes, 'I should be asking you if you're all right with going public.'

'Would it matter if I said no?'

'Yes, of course it would.'

His response looked as if it surprised her.

'I'm not ashamed I'm a father. I'm proud of Ellie and of you for making such a good job of it.' Her flush of pleasure at this unexpected praise hadn't subsided when he added, 'But you're not alone any more. I'm not asking you to marry me.'

The colour seeped from her cheeks, leaving just two

circles of pink on each cheekbone as her lashes came down. 'I didn't think you were.'

'I really doubt if I could fulfil your criteria for one half of a good marriage.' He'd be very surprised if any man could, but he found he really didn't want any man other than him trying. 'But I want to be part of your and Ellie's lives.'

Gwen knew he really meant just Ellie. She was only included because they came as a package deal. She ignored the heavy weight that had taken up residence behind her breastbone and said nothing; the aching lump in her throat would have made it hard anyway.

'I think we should live together for Ellie's sake.'

Gwen's expression hardened. She half rose but he caught her hand and after a moment she subsided. 'Live a lie, you mean,' she said numbly. Everything in her was repelled by the idea of taking the first step on the road her own mother had chosen.

'No lies, just an open and honest relationship. We both have Ellie's best interests at heart and I don't want to be an every-other-weekend dad.'

'By open, do you mean—?' She found she couldn't even finish the sentence.

'As it is I really don't want to sleep with another woman, but I don't want to make any unrealistic promises to you that I might not be able to keep. I respect you too much for that.'

His matter-of-fact confession of possible future infidelity sent a cold chill through her body, but Rio seemed oblivious to her reaction and continued to outline his plan in more detail.

'I own a house in London, and the one next door has just gone on the market. It has a lovely walled garden and there is a fantastic school close by. You could move in and we could see how things go, and who knows? We might end up getting on so well we knock down the partition wall.'

'Or you might move your girlfriend in next door,' she said flatly, fighting the childish impulse to stamp her foot and yell, *I don't want your respect. I want your love, you stupid man!*

She had dreamt of receiving proposals but not this one!

'Or *my* boyfriend might not want you as *our* next-door neighbour,' she added sweetly, and she felt a surge of savage satisfaction when she saw his expression darken, while fire not ice filtered into his dark stare.

He suddenly looked very dangerous and she knew it wasn't an illusion but, instead of feeling like running for the hills or at least closing her mouth over further inflammatory comments, Gwen felt a rush of exhilaration.

'I think that it's back to the drawing board, Rio, because that idea absolutely does not fly with me. I'm happy for you to have access to Ellie but I am not living a lie for anyone.'

There was a look of shock on his face, as though he wasn't used to anyone saying no to him, which he probably wasn't, but Gwen didn't feel sorry for him because she was too busy feeling utterly furious with him.

As the worst effects of the flash of mind-freezing fury sparked by the image Gwen's words had planted in his head, of her in bed with some other man, subsided, Rio recovered his voice.

'I'm not asking you to live a lie.' She was twisting everything, making it sound as though he hadn't thought it through, but he had.

'Just live next door to you, I know, and be on tap for

sex when there is nothing better on offer. They used to call that being a mistress.' Her chin went up and she glared at him through fiery cobalt eyes. 'Well, I am not mistress material and I have no idea where you got the idea I was.'

'Believe me, if I had a mistress it wouldn't be one who takes offence at absolutely nothing. At least I have a plan! What do you suggest we do?' he asked, feeling incredibly frustrated that she had turned down his idea point-blank, without even considering it.

'I don't have to *do* anything. Ellie is my daughter. I'm not going to give up my job, my life and move halfway around the country just so that it's more convenient for you.' Hands on the arms of the sofa, she pushed herself up.

'So are you holding out for marriage, then? Is that what this is all about?'

The sneer in his voice did it. She twirled back on him, for once able to look him in the face as she levelled her shaking finger at his broad chest. 'Obviously I'm desperately tempted,' she snapped with withering sarcasm.

Rio, who had regretted the words the moment they left his lips and blamed them on the image of her nameless future lover still residing in his head, felt the regret fade as she spoke. He reached up, his fingers curling around the wrist above the wagging finger.

She froze but didn't resist the light pressure he exerted to draw her downwards. Her only reaction was to reach out and brace a hand against the arm of the sofa to stop her body simply collapsing against him; as it was he was close enough to feel the heat off her body and inhale the scent of her skin.

One hand curved across the back of her head, fingers digging deep in her hair as he brought her face in close, feeling the tremor that ran through her body. Above the dull hammer thud of his heartbeat he could hear the soft hiss of her uneven breathing, and feel her warm breath on his face. Only a thin rim of bright blue remained visible around her massively dilated pupils.

This wasn't the normal scratching of a carnal itch; it was as if something in her connected with a deep inner emptiness inside him, and he wanted to fill it with her warmth. As he stared into her eyes the hunger inside him flared white-hot and any anger that had been in him seeped away as the tide of hot, humid desire rushed in to replace it. What shocked him the most was that in the middle of all the lust a tenderness surfaced. She looked so confused and so lost—the idea of being a person who would take advantage of that confusion repelled him.

With a growled imprecation of self-disgust he released her. It was so sudden and the sense of anticlimax so extreme that Gwen gasped like someone who had just fallen into ice water and staggered a couple of steps before she regained her balance.

She just stood there looking at him, her plump lips swollen as if he had just kissed them, and temptingly parted as she dragged in air in gulping gasps like someone who was drowning.

The strength of the passions he stirred inside her with such insultingly effortless ease was terrifying and yet it was also exciting. She didn't know who she was; the swift shift from angry resentment to all-consuming passion was utterly disorientating. She ought to be grateful he had stopped, that he hadn't kissed her, but she wasn't. She was angry.

She was aching.

She buried her humiliation deep behind a blank

mask. 'I'll go and check on Ellie.' She turned, head held high and narrow back straight, and walked back into the house.

The unstudied provocation of the gentle sway of her hips distracted Rio enough to make him forget to make allowances for his injuries as he dragged a frustrated hand down the bruised and battered side of his face.

He held in a groan of pain behind the barrier of his clenched white teeth.

CHAPTER ELEVEN

FIFTY PUNISHING LAPS of the pool hadn't even taken the edge off his frustration, although Rio hoped that if he punished his body enough it would stop punishing him or maybe the voice in his head would just switch off. Even turning the volume down would be a help at this stage.

He swam to the side and put his hands on the tiled surround to heave himself out and changed his mind. Falling backwards into the water again, he allowed himself to sink to the bottom, staying there long enough to feel the burn in his lungs before he kicked for the surface and the sparkle of the rejected multicoloured lights.

He broke the surface gasping, his chest heaving, and wondering if maybe the pool had been a mistake. The memories of the previous night were still too fresh in his mind.

Well, they're going to stay that way, aren't they, Rio, while you carry on reliving every glorious minute of it? He shook his head, sending a shower of silver droplets outwards onto the water, pebbling the still surface.

Let it go, counselled the voice in his head, but it wasn't easy advice to take when he didn't want to let anything go and desperately wanted a repeat performance.

He leaned back, letting the water support his body,

and he stayed that way for several moments, arms outstretched in a crucifix position, staring through half-
closed lids at the stars dotted in the midnight blanket
of the night sky. Except it wasn't midnight, it was three
a.m. and yet again he hadn't had a moment's sleep.

With a small grunt of effort he struck out, still on his
back, his body silently cutting through the water. His
arms and legs worked in unison as he cleaved straight
as an arrow through the water, pushing himself to the
limit and silently counting out each turn.

After another fifty lengths he stopped, treading
water before he finally hauled himself out. He stood
there on the rim of the pool, his lean brown body almost invisible in the darkness, water streaming down
his face and body, looking at nothing through the blur
of water droplets that pooled on the ends of his lashes.
The vigorous exercise had not cleared his head or tamed
his body.

He closed his eyes, head back; his chest lifted in a
deep soundless sigh. If he couldn't get rid of it he had
to live with it, he told himself as he headed for the outdoor shower. He revolved under the cold spray until
all trace of pool water was long gone and his skin was
icy from the prolonged exposure that he hoped would
offer him some respite from the relentless, pounding
desire that defied the iron control he had come to take
for granted. Rio was tolerant of weakness in others but
not in himself, and he hadn't allowed his body to rule
him since his hormonal teens.

He shook the moisture off his hair before he used
both hands to smooth off the excess, then grabbed his
towel, looped it across his shoulders and headed back
to the house.

They had spoken, just not to each other, barring the

odd 'please' and 'thank you' or frigid 'excuse me', while Ellie had glowed with all the attention that came her way partly to compensate for the silences between her parents.

It was childish, and he knew it, but he still hadn't been prepared to back down first and say sorry or whatever it took to thaw the frosty atmosphere.

The only full sentence she had directed at him was when she had asked if he'd like to put Ellie to bed. Had this been her way of meeting him in the middle, an olive twig rather than a branch? It was only a possibility that had occurred to him after the fact and then it was too late. Gwen had taken herself off to bed soon afterwards.

He didn't bother turning on the lights as he padded through the open-plan living area. The tiled floor was warm underfoot with the heat retained from the day's sun, even though the ambient temperature had been lowered to a comfortable level by the air conditioning.

He headed towards the bedroom wing, where the doors of the empty suites were open. One door beside his own was closed, and he found his feet stopping outside it.

He stayed there, struggling with the battle going on inside him, a struggle that was etched into the strong lines of his lean, sculpted features. His emotions were written on his face but there was no one around to hide them from. Gwen was behind the door. He stared at it, wondering if she was asleep or if she had lain awake thinking of him. He could picture her curled up in bed, her glorious hair spread out over the pillow.

What would she say if he knocked?

A sigh slipped from his mouth. He valued his freedom; he liked being answerable to no one. Yes, he was a father now but that wasn't going to change, because it didn't need to.

The problem was every time he looked at Gwen, when he smelt her skin, or touched her, a fragment of the wall of his carefully compartmentalised life crumbled, and he needed to stay in control.

What the hell was he doing?

Impatient with his own thoughts, and teeth clenched in a fierce grimace, he turned to walk further down the corridor to his room when the sound of a door opening stopped him. He swung back, his heartbeat accelerating, and she was standing there, all shocked big eyes, soft mouth and glorious tumbling hair. The tee shirt she was wearing clung to the high contours of her rounded breasts and just about reached the tops of her thighs, revealing the lovely tanned length of her long legs.

Like his brother's punch, he didn't try and block the flame of desire that scorched through him. He doubted that it would have made a difference even if he had; it would have been like trying to turn the tide with the power of his mind.

Shock nailed Gwen to the spot. 'I… I…wanted…' Her voice drifted away, and she forgot what she wanted to say. 'Milk…?' she said faintly, trying to think past the will-sapping fog of desire in her brain.

She swallowed, her eyes dropping as her gaze slid down the lean length of his powerful body. She had no time to prepare any defences and couldn't hide what she was feeling.

'Oh, my God,' she whispered, the words dragged from the deepest part of her as the fight drained out of her. She might as well have fought her own DNA than tried to fight the way he made her feel.

For several heartbeats neither of them moved, then

they fell into one another, kissing with a desperation that was almost feral in its intensity. Her hands were locked behind his neck as his hands moved over her shaking body, moulding her bottom and sliding down her slim thighs, then up under the hem of her nightshirt.

Gwen gasped, her head falling back as his lips made slow progress up the curve of her throat, and she arched into him.

Then her eyes filled with guilt and she lifted her head, pulling back a little as she laid her hand on his cheek. 'Your poor mouth.' She raised herself on tiptoe and kissed the corner of his injured mouth. 'I don't want to hurt you.'

He flashed a fierce smile and took her face between his hands. 'I'm a fast healer.' Holding her gaze, he very slowly fitted his mouth back to hers.

The slow, dreamy, sensuous kiss was blissful torture. His eyes burned with need as his head lifted, and the predatory glitter made her legs weak with lust.

'You're so beautiful,' he rasped with a strained grin before he trailed a kiss down her jaw. Then, reaching the corner of her mouth, he added, 'Are you going to invite me in?'

She didn't say a word, she just looked at him, silent longing glowing in her eyes. Rio was stunned by the need building inside him. The strength of it was like nothing he had ever known before.

She turned and Rio followed her into the bedroom and over to the bed, where the covers were thrown back and the pillows all over the place as though she had done a lot of tossing and turning. He found himself pleased that he hadn't been the only one suffering.

Her eyes were locked on his as she sat on the edge of the bed. He walked over to her and, still holding her eyes, caught the edge of the nightshirt. Without a word she lifted her arms and he pulled it over her head.

Gwen heard his raw gasp. Her eyes had drifted closed and she couldn't open them; they felt heavy, her entire body infused with languid weakness.

She felt the bed give a little as he joined her there, drawing her down beside him until they lay thigh to thigh, face to face beside one another.

The first skin-to-skin contact drew a deep shuddering sigh from her, and her eyes opened. She raised her head and kissed him on the mouth, telling herself that she didn't care about the future. All she cared about was now and being with this beautiful man who she loved.

He was stroking her everywhere, and she was just holding him. It felt as if she were floating outside herself but she had never felt so aware of her body, or so in tune with it.

'I want to taste you…all of you…' He slid down her body, his mouth warm and moist, his tongue drawing raw gasps of pleasure from her parted lips as she arched to his touch.

He drove her close to the edge twice before he responded to her pleas and allowed her to guide him into the tight warmth between her thighs.

'Look at me, Gwen. I want to see your face,' he urged. He was never a selfish lover, but she thought he'd never taken so much care with the pleasure he was giving her before.

They moved together, their gasps and moans becoming one part of the perfect whole until the frantic final moments of pushing to reach the heights. The release when it came shook her to her core…the waves of pleasure reaching her curling toes and continuing to rock her as she clung to him, pressing her face into his shoulder.

Finally he flopped over onto his back and lay there, his flat belly sucking in oxygen, his chest rising and falling until his breathing slowed, and he turned his head and looked at her.

'Shall I stay?'

She looked at him, her loving gaze moving over his beautiful bruised face, and she felt a debilitating kick of warm desire.

'Yes,' she murmured, rolling towards him, fitting herself to his hard angles. She hated the idea of him being in the next room, and being in the next house was even more unacceptable to her.

She was nervous in the run-up to the party, but not as much as she had expected. Then again, there hadn't been much time to get nervous, only forty-eight hours. Luckily Rio's mother had organised the catering, and all Gwen had had to do was open the door to the small local firm.

Though actually opening the door to anyone, and letting the world in, had not been an inconsequential thing. It had effectively shattered the feeling of isolation from the world that had enveloped Gwen ever since they'd arrived at the beach house.

Up to that point, for all the contact they'd had with the outside world they could have been on their own desert island, with the exception of the rather dramatic interruption afforded by first Jo's fleeting visit, and then Roman's.

Now the world was here, or at least a very small proportion of it. Rio had said it would be an eclectic mix of people and he hadn't been inaccurate. The majority

Jo had met through her charity work, and there were some well-known faces among them. Gwen's own concerns about what to wear had been dispelled as soon as people started to arrive, dressed in a wide variety of styles. When Rio had said she could wear *anything* she liked she had accused him of being unhelpful, but it turned out he was actually being literal.

At the moment he was being invisible. She glanced around with a slight furrow between her feathery brows, realising that she hadn't seen him for half an hour or so. He'd stayed by her side as he'd promised during the introductions and then left her to sink or swim. She was mostly swimming, to be honest, and if anyone was curious when Rio introduced her as *'Gwen, Ellie's mum'*, they were polite enough to hide it.

Ellie was represented by a framed photo that everyone admired. It was the same photo that Rio had emailed his mother at her request.

Rio had told Gwen that Jo was ecstatic about being a grandmother and she couldn't wait to meet her granddaughter again.

Ellie herself was in bed and asleep. Rio had agreed readily enough when Gwen had said she wasn't having her daughter paraded for inspection as well as herself.

Gwen joined in the ripple of applause when their most instantly recognisable guest, who was sitting at the piano playing requests, played the opening chords of one of his hits. He'd aged pretty well for a member of an iconic eighties rock band that had not been known for its moderation.

He was being accompanied by a woman wearing a fashionable jumpsuit who had arrived with her saxophone. Apparently, her day job was in the head office of a charity, although she looked like a model.

There were at least three men and a woman wearing jeans and a few men in tailored trousers and shirts like Rio and a smattering of women in formal evening gowns. A few were dressed as Gwen was, somewhere in between the two. In the end she had chosen a mid-length silk shift in a dramatic violet shade, cut high at the neck and dipping into a deep V at the back. She had worn it for every 'special occasion' event for the past three years but nobody here would know that, and she was just glad she had thrown it into her case as an afterthought.

She responded to a comment about her shoes from a woman whose name she had forgotten, and agreed they looked good but they were killing her.

'Where's Rio got to?' the woman asked.

'Not sure.'

'The last time I saw him he was with Rach and she'd had a few too many glasses of fizz, so the poor man will need rescuing.'

Now there was a name she remembered and the last time she had seen him with Rach he hadn't looked much as if he needed rescuing. On the contrary, he'd looked as if he was enjoying himself as the *tactile* curvaceous blonde in the sequined minidress had laughed her head off at something he had just said.

Gwen made her way around the outside of the room. She had been checking on Ellie regularly all evening and it occurred to her that maybe Rio had too. His absence could simply be explained by the fact that she had woken.

A smile tinged with pride tugged at the corners of her lips. Despite all her misgivings Rio was really trying to be a good father—actually better than trying. He *was* a good father. Anyone seeing them together would know that. Being a single parent, knowing that, if anything happened to her, Ellie would be alone had been a nightmare that had regularly woken Gwen in the middle of the night in a cold sweat.

She hadn't had that nightmare since her first day here. Even if she knew that the only place Rio wanted her was in his bed, he genuinely wanted Ellie in his life. Gwen told herself she had everything but his love, and while Ellie was safe she could live with that.

When it was fifteen minutes past and he still hadn't reappeared her conviction that he was trying to settle their daughter increased, so Gwen decided to check out her theory and relieve him. She managed to slip away unnoticed and once in the tiled hallway she stepped out of the admired heeled sandals that were murdering her feet. Dangling them from her fingers, although she didn't think she'd actually get them back on again, she hurried along the corridor.

Rio's job would be a hell of a lot tougher if he hadn't surrounded himself with a team of people he could rely on, people he was happy to delegate responsibility to. This was especially important after his brother had left for pastures new.

Up to this point he had never absented himself from work for this length of time, but he'd known that if he wanted to prove to Gwen he was serious about being part of Ellie's life he had to show his willingness to adapt, show he didn't want to be an absentee father.

He had not gone totally off grid; he had left an emergency number, but had made it clear to his second in command that when he said emergency he meant emergency.

So when the private number had buzzed earlier,

the timing had been lousy but he had known he had to answer it.

He was glad he had. The conference call had certainly had its tense moments but half an hour later he was able to sink back into the padded swivel chair, happy in the knowledge that a costly disaster had been averted.

The noise from the party was reduced to a gentle hum in the book-lined study where he had used to sit in a corner with a book, watching his mother write in one of the journals she kept. One day, she used to tell him, she'd turn the words on the paper into a book—he wondered idly if she still intended to.

Spinning around, he was about to lever himself out of the chair when a breathy voice made him freeze.

'Rio...so there you are, you naughty man. I've been looking for you everywhere.'

He sighed. Some people just shouldn't drink and Rachel was one of them. 'Hello, Rach, what brings you here?' The thing with Rachel was that, while perfectly charming when she was sober, when she was drunk the young widow was an octopus. He wasn't the only one of her friends to notice that she was drunk a lot of the time these days and as yet she hadn't admitted to herself that she had a problem.

'Were you waiting for me, darling?' she slurred as she swayed into the room on perilously high heels.

Rio's sympathy was currently tinged with impatience. He really didn't have time for this; he needed to get back to the party and Gwen.

'No, I wasn't.'

'Oh, I think you were... Are we going for that swim now?' She gave a little giggle. 'Oh, yes, that would be lovely. I don't have a swimsuit, but you don't mind that, do you, darling?'

'*Not* a good idea, Rach.' Alarmed by the speed with which this farce was developing and the potential for it becoming something worse, Rio moved forward, but was too late to stop her pulling down the zip on her sparkling minidress. The back sagged open and it slid half off her shoulders.

'*Dios mio*, Rachel, you need a coffee.'

She stood there swaying, her colour suddenly not good. He noticed the tears standing out in her eyes and his mood softened as he realised that on one level she had to know that she was making a fool of herself, and yet he and everyone else would carry on making allowances for her because you did cut some slack for someone who'd nursed the love of their life through a terrible terminal illness before being tragically widowed in their twenties.

'No, I need to lie down...' She blinked and the tears were gone and her seductive smile reappeared. 'Lie down with me, Rio...' She made a grab for his shirt and for a moment it seemed as if it was the only thing holding her up.

Grinding out a curse, he moved his hand to her waist to stop her slithering to the floor. She didn't, but the dress finally surrendered to gravity and lay like a pile of chain mail at her feet.

It was into this scene that Gwen walked, and his first reaction was relief that there was someone to help him cope with his sad, drunk friend.

He was about to say, *Thank God you're here*, when he saw her face, white as chalk, and her blue eyes frosted with suspicion and accusation.

He was ready to concede that at first glance this could look like an incriminating scenario, but she had to *want* to read it that way, he decided grimly, to carry on believing that. Unless, of course, Gwen really thought he was the sort of person who was likely to take advantage of a drunk and vulnerable woman.

Reacting to the direct hit to his pride inflicted by Gwen's silent accusation, he found that, instead of appealing for help, he'd angled a look of challenge at her. He was almost daring her to say what she was thinking as the woman he was supporting snuggled up closer to him, the sense of betrayal he was feeling stoking his spiralling anger.

She said nothing, but her silence spoke volumes. Rio remembered his father's toxic silences, meant to punish, and they had. They could last weeks after he had thought he'd discovered his wife having a non-existent affair that had been proven in his distorted eyes by a glance or even on one occasion, Rio remembered, a pair of shoes!

If Gwen could not trust him, that was her problem. He would not validate her jealousy by offering excuses, or demean himself by doing so.

But as she walked away, still without having said a word, he saw that Gwen was carrying her shoes, the same shoes he had earlier imagined her wearing with nothing else on as he carried her to their bed.

He still had Rachel in his arms, and getting her onto the couch while evading her attempt to grab his crotch did not improve his temper. Luckily for him the next person to appear in the doorway did not look at him with accusing eyes; instead, she was sympathetic and grateful. Rachel's friend May had come looking for her.

Her face was solemn as she told Rio to return to the party; she would stay with Rachel, she said.

'This isn't the real her, you know,' she added as Rio turned to go.

'I know, but she needs help. She can't go on like this.'

The other woman sighed. 'I agree. Maybe it's time we all stopped covering for her, before it's too late.'

Minutes beforehand, Gwen had been able to circulate and feel as if she belonged with all these amusing, entertaining people. Now, as she returned from Rio's study, she felt awkward and out of place, and whatever had made her feel she belonged, it was pathetic.

She was pathetic for believing that Rio had changed, not that he loved her, she wasn't *that* deluded, but that he cared a little, that fatherhood had changed him from the man whose socks had a longer lifespan than his lovers and probably more respect from him too.

He had actually had the gall to look angry at *her*! As if he were the victim... Her jaw quivered as she bit down on her full lower lip. Six feet five inches of muscle made a very unlikely victim in her book!

A smile painted on her face, she drifted around the room feeling the anger and disillusion building inside her. It hadn't been what he'd been doing—well, actually it had, she admitted, experiencing a flash of nausea as she recalled the scene she had walked in on—but the thing that was the deal-breaker was the fact that he hadn't been willing to unbend enough to explain himself, offer her the reassurance she needed.

Would she have believed him if he'd given her an explanation? She pushed away the irrelevant question, because he hadn't given her the option and she hadn't been forced to face her real fear, which was that she'd turn into her mother, pathetic enough to believe any lie in order to stay with the man she loved.

The worst part, the part that scared her the most, was that she had so badly wanted Rio to tell her it wasn't what it looked like, the same way she had seen her own mother beg time after time, swallowing her husband's stories, where somehow he was always the victim.

The idea that she might turn into a woman that her daughter would one day be ashamed of filled her with a stomach-clenching horror.

She hid her misery behind a wide smile, but no one seemed to notice that her laughter was brittle and her eyes too bright.

She was conscious of Rio returning, not that he made any attempt to talk to her. He probably expected *her* to apologise to him.

Of the blonde there was no sign—not until Gwen watched the last of the taxis drive away and she thought she saw a distinctive blonde head in the back of one.

Finally the last guest was dispatched and the last crate of crockery loaded up by the ultra-efficient caterers. Gwen wandered back to the kitchen, which showed no sign of their temporary occupation, and stood watching through the window as the tall figure walking up the driveway got bigger, until Rio, who had gone down to the gates to wave people off, was close enough for her to see the grim expression on his face.

He must have seen her because he changed direction and walked up the steps directly into the kitchen.

His face looked as if it were carved of stone, his eyes flat, expressionless and bleak.

She forgot her decision to be cold and distant the moment he walked in, and just fizzed up. 'If you're going to say it wasn't what it looked like, you can save your breath.'

He arched a sardonic brow and gave her a nasty smile. 'I wasn't.'

'So you admit it, then!' she shrilled out, appalled that he wasn't even showing an iota of shame.

Rio looked at her through narrowed eyes. 'Would it matter if I denied it?' He knew if he did, there would just be the next time and then the time after that, and he would end up spending his life soothing her insecurities, which would eventually ruin, not just her life, but his as well. He had seen how jealousy could poison a relationship and he'd been a fool, he could see that now, to believe that trust might be possible between them.

'I think I deserve an explanation,' she said tightly.

'I think I deserve your trust,' he countered.

'So if you walked in on me with a half-dressed man all over me you'd be just as trusting, would you?' she snapped. 'I thought we might be able to talk this through, but—'

'No, you didn't, you already made up your mind what happened. Oh, I'm not saying you wouldn't have minded seeing me grovel!' he flung back. 'But even if you saw fit to forgive me, you'd bring it up whenever I got out of line!' By the time he had finished his chest was heaving, and he was visibly shaking with the force of his emotions.

In Gwen's heart there had been a small corner that had secretly wanted him to say something to make her feel less angry, less betrayed. He would say it was all a silly mistake and they'd both laugh over it. She'd wanted him to talk her down from the ledge but he wasn't—if anything, he was pushing her further away.

He didn't just not love her; he actually seemed to despise her.

A block of ice had formed in her chest in the region

of her heart and she could not imagine it melting any time soon.

'I think,' she said quietly, 'that Ellie and I should go home.' She gulped and realised she had started to think of this place as home, not because of the beauty and the fine furnishings, but simply because Rio was here too.

'Go?' He looked shocked and then seemed to recover himself. 'Yes, fine. If that's what you want, I'll arrange the flight.'

CHAPTER TWELVE

As the taxi drew up in front of the cottage she felt none of the comforting sense she had anticipated she'd feel coming home.

'All right, love?'

She blinked and smiled at the driver. 'Fine, thanks.'

'Let me help you with this lot.'

The driver drove away with a generous tip in his pocket and Gwen put her key in the lock. The slight musty smell she had got used to made her nose twitch as she stepped inside, and it felt a lot smaller than she remembered.

She put Ellie down and walked across to a vase of wilted roses that she had missed during her rushed packing. The murky brown water in the bottom explained the smell.

'Right,' she said brightly to Ellie. 'We're home. Isn't that lovely? How cosy. We're going to have a wonderful summer together.'

'Swim?' Ellie said hopefully.

Gwen felt a stab of guilt. Was she being selfish in taking Ellie away from Rio? Shouldn't she be prepared to compromise to give her daughter the chance of a better life? She glanced out of the window where the gathering grey clouds seemed to echo her mood. It felt as if she were depriving Ellie of a life of sunshine and pools and… Her glance slid to the bin, where dead flower heads pushed at the lid, and she wanted to sit down and cry.

Instead she straightened her shoulders, lifted her chin and halted the creeping guilt and gathering self-pity. Her uncertainty vanished as she decided she had done the right thing—and Rio must have agreed with her because he'd not tried to stop them leaving. In fact he'd facilitated their departure.

Her determined smile was tinged with bitterness but she knew there was more to a happy child than swim-ming pools.

'I'll blow up the paddling pool,' she told Ellie, who didn't hear. She had tipped out a tub of building blocks and was sitting in the middle of them all, announcing her intention of building a beach house.

Later that afternoon Ellie was down for her nap, meaning it was the perfect time to unpack, but some-how Gwen could not work up the enthusiasm for the task. Instead, remembering her promise, she went to the small shed where a motley collection of garden tools and children's toys were stored.

She found the small plastic paddling pool she had bought during the sales last year, in the optimistic hope that they might have a heatwave before Ellie got too big to fit into it. There was no sign of the foot pump she had bought at the same time.

She took it outside and unfolded it, shaking the dust off it before choosing a spot in the shade of a flower-ing cherry that was no longer flowering.

Right. She took a deep breath and fitted her lips to one of the valves in the rim—how hard could it be? It wasn't exactly a big paddling pool.

* * *

There were reminders everywhere of their recent occupation. The toys, the bright mobile, the smell... Rio
wandered into the bedroom where, ridiculously, she
had stripped the bed, and found his nostrils flaring at
the evocative scent of the light floral soap Gwen used.

Por Dios! He strode outside, taking big gulps of fresh
air, but somehow the scent of wild thyme on the breeze
couldn't get that scent of Gwen out of his nose, or the
rest of her out of his head.

He hung onto his anger and reminded himself that
he'd done the right thing letting her go, but somehow
the statement didn't carry *quite* the same ring of conviction as it so recently had.

She was the one who had talked about trust but when
it came down to it, and trust was needed, she had none
for him. She hadn't been willing to listen to any explanations.

Did you even offer her any?

He frowned darkly at the unhelpful contribution of
the voice in his head. She should not have needed any.

*The same way you wouldn't have needed any if the
situation had been reversed? Wasn't she right about
that? Wouldn't you have gone into full Neanderthal
chest-beating mode if you'd seen her alone with a
nearly naked man? Doesn't being in love come with
some insecurities and primitive responses?*

His internal dialogue came to an abrupt halt as a look
of amazed realisation spread across his face. He'd been
running away from love all his life, believing that it was
the cause of his mother's hellish years, but that hadn't
been love, it had been a perversion of it.

Love was the way Gwen looked at Ellie; love was
what he felt when he... He groaned. Had he just let the

best thing in life walk away from him? No, he had actually arranged the transport for her, just because he was a coward who thought it was better to be lonely than take a risk on love, better to be alone than let history repeat itself.

But Gwen had crept into his heart despite himself. There, he'd admitted it, even though he knew it was a mistake to admit, even to himself, that he wanted a family and love, because admitting it laid you wide open to all this pain he was feeling right now.

Gwen paused, her head spinning dizzily from her efforts to inflate the sad-looking paddling pool. She dropped it and heard the hiss of air escape, leaving it looking pretty much as she felt.

Tears of self-pity pushed hotly against her eyelids and she blinked.

'You are being totally ridiculous,' she told herself.

'There's a lot of it going about.'

She spun around in the direction of the slow, deep, familiar drawl, her hair following her a second later, heart kicking against her ribcage drawing a loud gasp from her open mouth.

'You…here? How…? Why…?'

'In order: yes, I'm here. How: I chartered a jet because you had mine. And why: because I want to bring you home.'

Her face lost what little colour it had, and the wariness didn't leave her eyes; she was not about to misread this situation. 'You don't have to do that. I'm not going to try and stop you seeing Ellie and I've been thinking about it. The house-next-door thing; I'll do it,' she declared. It would hurt like hell to see his comings and goings with the beautiful women who drifted in and out of his life, and even more horrifying to contemplate the one that might eventually stay there with him. But what right did she have to deprive Ellie of a father as a constant in her life just because Gwen couldn't have him as one in hers?

Some emotion she struggled to interpret flickered in his dark silk-framed eyes. 'You would?'

She nodded. 'So long as she's not exposed to… Er… I mean, I'll need you to keep your private life quite separate from her—that's non-negotiable,' she told him earnestly.

'So no wild orgies in the nursery, then.'

'You know what I mean.' This was hard enough without him mocking her.

'Relax. That offer is no longer on the table.'

Her face fell and she half turned to hide her mortification but a hand on her shoulder pulled her back.

'I don't want a wall between us.' He curved one hand around the side of her face and looked deep into her eyes. 'I don't even want air between us.' He bent down and fitted his mouth to hers. The kiss was deep and hungry and tinged with a tenderness that brought tears to her eyes.

She emerged breathless.

'I know what you're thinking,' he said.

She looked at him with shiny eyes and thought, *That's more than I do!* Her mind was in a whirl and she barely knew if she was sitting or standing, but she was definitely floating, though a voice in her head was still telling her to be cautious.

'I'm not asking you to leave work if you don't want to. We can buy a house near this school. There's a small estate for sale within commuting distance and—'

She lifted a hand to his lips to quiet him for a moment, as her head was reeling. 'Are you asking me to move in with you...' she paused '...for Ellie?'

'No, I'm asking you to move in with me for me,' he said huskily, taking her hand and pressing it to his chest. 'I've a Gwen-sized hole inside me and if you leave me, I'll always feel this way. There was *nothing*,' he emphasised, 'going on that night with Rachel. She was grief-stricken and drunk, and I was cornered and actually relieved to see you.'

'I think I already knew that. I just wanted—'

'To hear me say it,' he completed with a deep sigh. 'And you deserved that.' He lifted both hands to his head and pushed his fingers deep into his hair. 'Just... just be with me, Gwen. I'll try to be the person you need. I swear I will. I love you and I've been trying to pretend I didn't because I was scared...a coward...but I'm not running from love any more. Marry me, Gwen, and be my family.'

By the time he had finished the sobs were shaking her body and tears were running down her cheeks.

'Please tell me that means you're happy,' he begged, wiping away the tears with the pad of his thumb as he bent in to kiss her salty lips.

She nodded. 'It's just I was so miserable and now I'm so happy! Oh, I love you so much, Rio. I think I always did right from that very first time we were to-gether. A lot has changed since then but not that.' She suddenly gave a little laugh of pure joy. 'Is this real? Is it really happening?'

'I know I'm not good enough for you, Gwen, but I promise I'll try to be. You will marry me?'

She nodded, her emotions glowing in her eyes. 'Oh, yes, I'll marry you—and you are good enough for me,' she declared fiercely. 'You're the best man I know and Ellie loves you too.'

He took her hands in his and lifted them to his lips. 'When I think of you being all alone it kills me, giving birth and no one to be there for you. It'll be different next time!'

'Next time?' she echoed.

He searched her face, a shade of concern in his eyes. 'If you want a next time, Gwen. For me, I already have everything I want in you and Ellie.'

'Well, actually, yesterday Ellie was saying she'd like a baby...'

A smile glimmered in his eyes. 'Really?'

'Or a cow.'

He gave a laugh, and she loved the sound.

'I love her but I draw the line at having a cow.'

'She'll be sad but I think she might be happy enough with a baby brother or sister.'

'Or one of each.'

She caught his hands and put them on her hips before stretching up to kiss his mouth. 'It's negotiable, but in the meantime make yourself useful and blow up your daughter's paddling pool.'

He grinned. 'I have a much better use for my breath.'

He absolutely did.

* * * * *

A BRIDE FIT FOR
A PRINCE?

SUSAN STEPHENS

To all my wonderful readers, editors,
publishing professionals, family and pets, who
inspire me every day, and who make writing such a joy.
Thank you!

CHAPTER ONE

He entered the restaurant at the front. The young back-packer rushed in from the alley at the back. They met in the middle at the bar.

More accurately, she crashed into him.

'Sorry! *Sorry!*' she exclaimed, bouncing off him with a yelp.

'No need to apologise.'

He took stock of the new arrival. Bright eyes, firm chin and a face smudged with dust from her travels. It was an interesting face full of character and not unattractive. The impression of soft curves yielding to his muscular frame stayed with him as he stared into eyes the colour of an emerald ocean on an uncomplicated summer's day—which this should have been. But when was anything as straightforward as it appeared?

'I'm gagging for a drink of water,' she gasped to no one in particular. Turning to study his face with engaging frankness, she added, 'Do I know you?'

'I don't believe so.'

'Are you sure?'

He thumbed twenty-four hours' worth of stubble. 'As I can be.'

She continued to stare at him intently, as if his face

rang a bell but her brain refused to yield the required information.

This break in proceedings allowed him to inhale her wildflower scent, and to appreciate more than a sweet rosebud mouth pursed in thought. Though, sweet was not a word he would use to describe her, he decided, noting the stubborn set of her chin and narrowed eyes as she ran his features through some internal search engine.

'I'm sure I know you from somewhere,' she insisted, still frowning. 'I just can't place you yet. But I will,' she warned with a smile that lit up her face. 'You're as out of place here as me, and yet you're totally relaxed…'

'Okay, Sherlock Holmes. Anything else?'

'You're obviously more used to eating in swanky eateries than I am…'

Undaunted by his silence, she turned to take stock of their surroundings. And gasped. 'Paint me staggered— I must have stumbled into Oz. Do people really drink magnums of champagne at midday?'

'It would appear so.'

She had freckles on her nose, he noticed as she wrinkled it with amusement. Having strayed off the alleyway behind the restaurant, she had landed in Babylon, where vintage wines were discussed in hushed tones, as if they were the answer to all the world's woes, while waiters served delicacies to clientele who, for the most part, couldn't care what they ate, so long as it was expensive enough to brag about. They were standing in a temple to excess on what was arguably the most stylish marina on the planet. He guessed the staff had left the rear entrance open to allow for the non-stop arrival of stock, as no place on earth could hope to keep sufficient food and booze on the premises to satisfy the appetites of the super-rich.

'Water and a job are what I need, and in that order,' the young woman announced, appearing to look to him for the solution. 'Do you know of anything going?' Chin angled to one side, she studied his face with brazen interest. Keen intelligence blazed from emerald eyes, and she had an eminently kissable mouth, he mused as she smiled again. 'Maybe I could get some work on board one of those huge boats in the marina...' She waited, and when he said nothing, she admitted, 'I've run out of funds. This trip has lasted longer than I expected. There's just so much to see, and so little time to fit everything in.'

'You're on some sort of deadline?'

'Not exactly,' she replied, 'but I do have to get back to work eventually—don't we all? I can't spend my entire life roaming. Though, I'd like to.' A wistful look crept into her eyes. 'At some point I've got to stop travelling and make a go of things again...'

'Again?' he probed as she stared off into the middle distance.

'Oh, you know what I mean,' she insisted with a careless flip of her wrist.

'I'm not sure I do. Have you travelled far?'

'From London, originally.'

'Where you live and work?'

She didn't answer his question, her gaze sweeping the marina. 'I adore the South of France, don't you?'

As attempts to change the subject went, that was clumsy. 'The Riviera's one of many places I like to visit.'

She pulled him up on his apparent disinterest right away. '*Like?* How can anyone *like* the South of France when it's so obviously gorgeous and fabulous? Don't you feel doubly alive when you're here?' Her face lit up, and all the tension he'd detected when she'd first burst into the bar dropped away. 'Music, food, heat, blue skies and sunshine—the way everyone throws back their shoulders and speaks out clearly instead of mumbling. People walk tall here with confidence and optimism, instead of huddling beneath raincoats in a grey, chilly drizzle—'

'You put forward a good case,' he conceded, shaking himself out of his black mood. 'Are you a lawyer?'

'No, but I've often thought legal skills would be useful.'

'In what way?'

'Oh, you know,' she said vaguely.

'If not a lawyer, are you a writer? Your descriptive skills?' he prompted.

She laughed and looked away.

'Why don't you ask here about jobs?' he suggested.

She swept a hand down her crumpled clothes. 'Like they'd hire me looking like this! And, anyway, I want to get as far away as I can. Out to sea would be my preference.'

'Are you under pressure to get away?'

'What makes you say that?' she asked quickly.

'I'm just following the ball of string as you reel it out.'

'So I'm not the only detective. I'd better be careful what else I say.'

'You'd better,' he agreed as measuring glances flashed between them.

Young, attractive, intelligent and feisty, she was a welcome distraction on a difficult day.

'I'm guessing you don't work here,' she said as she gave him a comprehensive once-over. 'Ripped shorts and a sleeveless top don't suggest to me that you're trying out for the job of waiter.'

'Me?' He laughed. 'No. I don't think they'd trust me at the sink.'

'A pot carrier, perhaps?' she mused. 'You've got the muscles for it.'

'I'm hired, then?' he teased with the lift of a brow.

'You wish.'

When she laughed a dimple appeared in her cheek, he noted.

'So how come they let you in?' she asked with an appraising look.

'Like you, I just walked in. If you do so with confidence, I find no one will stop you.'

'But you can't help me with a job?'

'Sorry. I'm afraid I can't.'

'Afraid?' she demanded askance. 'I've known you less than five minutes, but it's long enough to know you're not afraid of anything.'

He might have agreed with her at one time, but when the rock he'd built his life on tottered and splintered into pieces, all bets were off.

'Maybe you're the type of guy I should know better than to talk to?'

'Yet, here we are.' Making himself comfortable against the wall at the side of the bar, he spread his hands wide.

'Not for long,' she said briskly. 'All I need is a glass of water and then I'm out of here. I bet the barman could see you above their heads,' she hinted as she took in the crowd at the bar. 'Please,' she begged. 'You make the other men look like shrimps. They'll part like the Red Sea when they see you on the move. They wouldn't even notice me jumping up and down.'

'You flatter me.'

'Do I?' she demanded, opening her eyes wide. 'Entirely unintentional, I assure you.'

'All right,' he agreed. 'Stay there.'

'I'm not going anywhere without a drink of water,' she assured him.

She amused him, and had stormed his reserve with nothing more than a bold line in chat and an engaging smile. The pert breasts didn't hurt. Nor did a taut butt, displayed to best advantage beneath tantalisingly short shorts. It was all too easy to imagine those coltish legs wrapped around his waist, though they were tipped with a pair of battered old boots, which were possibly the ugliest he'd ever seen. He glanced back as he waited at the bar. Her face was a picture of puzzled concentration. She was still hammering away at the computer in her mind as she attempted to place him, he guessed.

Even windswept, she was beautiful. Smudged with dirt from the trail and make-up-free. Her hair, in particular, was an abundant, fiery magnificence. Its unusual shade of copper reminded him of sunset at sea. Held back carelessly with a few pins, it begged to be set free so he could tangle his fingers through the lustrous locks as he eased her head back to kiss his way down the long, slender line of her neck. But it was more than good looks that had captured his attention. She had character and spirit and gave as good as she got, which, in the world of sycophants he was about to inhabit, made her a welcome change.

He was on a deadline. Soon he would return to the principality of Madlena to take the throne after the death of his brother. The responsibility that entailed hog-tied him a little more each day. This might be his last trip on his yacht the *Black Diamond* before duty put an end to his freedom for good. The last thing he needed was a complication in the form of a sassy young woman with a seemingly bottomless pit of questions. No doubt sex would ease his tension, but his usual pick would be an older, experienced woman who knew the score, not an ingénue on a backpacking trip around Europe.

'Water! At last!' she cried theatrically as he handed over a misted bottle and a glass.

As she reached for it, her body brushed his, causing a riot she was seemingly unaware of, while his groin had tightened to the point of pain.

'Thank you,' she gasped on a grateful exhalation as she drained the glass.

'You could use another?' he guessed.

'You read my mind. But don't worry. I can handle it,' she assured him.

'Go to it,' he invited, standing back.

As she'd pressed against him, he'd been given more than a clue about the body beneath her shabby clothes. His adored *nonna*, Princess Aurelia, might have said this young woman was 'well made'. Although she was tiny like his grandmother, at least a head smaller than anyone else at the bar, which meant her repeated attempts to attract the barman's attention were a massive fail.

'All right,' she conceded finally. 'Seems I've got no option but to throw myself on your mercy again. Go to it!' she urged. 'I'll cheer you on from the sidelines—as much as I can with a throat that feels like sandpaper.'

Her voice was unmistakeably British, while her mouth was extremely sexy. An almost perfect Cupid's bow, it tugged up at one corner, which made the endearing dimple appear in her cheek. 'Hurry,' she begged, clutching her throat like the leading light in some amateur dramatic society. 'Can't you see I'm desperate?'

'You belong on the stage,' he commented dryly.

'Yeah, scrubbing it,' she agreed.

That she made him laugh on a day when laughter had seemed impossible pointed up the fact that this was no

overentitled drip. She wasn't helpless in any way. Here
in this preserve of the rich and famous, where labels
didn't just count, they were mandatory, and where a designer outfit would never dare to show its face twice, she
was as poised as a princess—and a lot more fun, if the
selection of po-faced contenders drawn up by his royal
council was anything to go by. She could also be a lot
more trouble, he considered on his return from the bar.
Her mouth had pursed disapprovingly when she saw him
served before anyone else.

'I didn't ask you to crash the line,' she scolded with
a grin.

'I didn't. The barman just happens to be supereffi-
cient.'

'Okay,' she conceded. 'Well, thank you. You've done
me a real favour, and I appreciate it.'

'I splashed out on two glasses of water,' he pointed out,
bringing her back down to earth. 'Hardly a good enough
reason to throw yourself at my feet.'

'You should be so lucky,' she assured him. 'Anyway,
sometimes a glass of water is all it takes. Do you know
everyone here?' she added as she glugged it down.

'No. Why?'

'Because they're all staring at you.'

'Perhaps they're staring at you.' When he turned,
heads swivelled away as the übersophisticated clientele
pretended they hadn't seen him.

'Hmm,' she mused thoughtfully. 'I don't think so.'
She downed the second glass in record time. 'I'm well
outclassed.'

That was a matter of opinion.

'Anyway,' she added with a gasp of relief as she put
the empty glass down, 'don't let these nosy parkers worry
you. You've got me to protect you now.'

'That's a joke?' he asked.

'Take it any way you want,' she said, 'but my suggestion is, just ignore them.'

Fiery hair was a fair indicator of temperament, he suspected, guessing she could be a little terrier if she was put to the test. There was no risk of overdosing on sugar when it came to this woman.

'So,' she added, barely pausing for breath, 'are you going to tell me who you are? I mean, apart from being the only person in here as badly dressed as me?'

There was no denying they were both showing a flagrant disregard for the dress code. As a minimum, patrons were required to wash the sand from their bodies before sitting down to eat—but who questioned royalty? And she was with him.

'My name is Luca,' he revealed. 'And you are?'

'Before we get to that—' she gave him one of her cheeky smiles '—I want to know how you've managed not to be thrown out when you look as if you've just stepped out of the sea.'

'Because that's exactly what I did.'

'Okay...' She drew the word out. 'My best guess, in that case, is that even if they combined their forces, security and the staff here wouldn't dream of taking you on.'

'More compliments?' he suggested dryly.

Pressing her lips together, she grinned. 'My mistake. But you still haven't told me how you get away with it.'

'Perhaps they like me here, and make an exception?'

'And perhaps pigs might fly,' she countered dryly. 'The maître d' looks like a regimental sergeant major, and I don't imagine he lets anyone slip by. You're either respected or feared,' she conjectured. 'So, which is it, Luca?'

Probably a bit of both, he mused. 'I have been here before,' he conceded.

'So are you crew from one of those floating office blocks?'

Following her stare to the line of gleaming superyachts moored up in a row down the quay, he shook his head.

'Not crew,' she reflected, 'yet everyone seems to know you, so are you the local criminal mastermind, or some fabulously wealthy billionaire out slumming it for the day?'

He raised a brow. 'I imagine I could play either role.'

'I bet you could,' she agreed. 'But not with me.'

'Has it occurred to you that it might be you that everyone's staring at?'

'Me?' she scoffed. 'I hardly fit the style brief here. Apart from a few disapproving glances when I first walked in, no one's looked at since.'

'Your fabulous hair might cause comment.'

'Why, thank you, kind sir,' she said, dipping into a curtsey.

'Did I let a compliment slip past me?' he mocked lightly.

She twisted her mouth before carrying on with her interrogation. 'It's definitely not me they're looking at. Now I've had my drink there's nothing desperate about me to suggest some sort of mystery attached to my coming here, or that might lead anyone to believe I'm seeking sanctuary in this steel and glass temple to excess.'

Sanctuary? '*Are* you running from something?'

Instead of answering his question she went off on another tangent. 'The trouble with Saint-Tropez is that it's so misleading. I'd never been here before, so when I first arrived it was hard to believe the town retained the charm of the original fishing village. There's such an abundance of megayachts and boys' toys—the dream cars,' she explained. 'But everything coexists happily. Bourgeois French life cheek by jowl with ostentatious wealth.'

'Don't you approve?'

'Of course I do. The contrast is what makes Saint-Tropez so special and fun to visit. But don't change the subject. We're talking about you.'

'*I* changed the subject?' he challenged.

She shrugged and laughed this off. 'So, come on—tell me. Are you a celebrity, or a fugitive from the law?'

'I don't fall into either category.'

'You might as well come clean. I'm very good at extracting information,' she told him with a comic accent. 'MI6?'

'I've always fancied being a sleuth,' she admitted, adding a comic face to the mix. 'I could never resist a good puzzle.'

'Perhaps I'm hiding out like you.'

'I'm not hiding out!'

The heat of her defence reinforced his growing belief that that was exactly what she was doing.

'You could hardly blend into the scenery with your looks,' she commented, making it sound like the worst insult possible. 'Simply stating facts,' she told him when he raised an ironic brow.

Some women simpered and preened when they met him. She did neither, but continued to stare at him narrow-eyed, as if he were an interesting specimen in a lab.

'The name Luca isn't much of a clue…'

'Can you put a name to everyone you meet?'

'Of course not, but I really feel I should know you,' she mused, still frowning. 'Anyway, let's forget that for now. I'm on my own, trekking around Europe, so I'd better be careful who I talk to. I think it's time to move on.'

'That's your choice, but if you're so concerned about safety, why strike up a conversation with a stranger in the first place?'

'You look trustworthy, and you don't frighten me.'

'Evidently,' he agreed, finding it hard to curb a smile.

Where had she been these past few months when his image had been splashed across the press? The tragedy of losing his older brother had resonated across the globe. First his grandmother, and then Pietro had raised him when their parents were killed in an air crash, only for Pietro to die in tragic circumstances. Two brothers cruelly torn apart, with the added fascination of great wealth and royal lineage, had made sure that their story reached everyone's ears.

Seeing him out of context must have thrown her. He bore no resemblance to the solemn man in uniform that had been pictured in the press. Those images showed a grim-faced individual, mired in sorrow, standing on a parade ground to accept the fealty of troops who were loyal to him now. That man didn't relax, or slouch on one hip, but stood sternly to attention, as he endured the unendurable, which was to accept that his beloved older brother would never brighten his life again. The diners who knew him here thought only that he was an aristocrat and a billionaire, with a megayacht worthy of mention. His vast three-mast rigger, the *Black Diamond*, was anchored off shore. Its modern take on a traditional design always caused comment, though no one fussed over him, as billionaires and members of the aristocracy were two a penny in Saint-Tropez.

The yacht was his pride and joy, and a guaranteed escape route from a news-hungry world. He'd bought it some years back with profits from a tech company he'd started in his bedroom as a boy. News had spread quickly that the Pirate Prince—as people liked to call him, thanks to his uniquely sinister yacht with its black sails and night-dark hull—was indulging in one last round of freedom before embarking on a life of royal circumspection.

'Since you're not afraid of me,' he told the young woman, 'I think it's time we became properly acquainted.'

'I'm honoured,' she mocked, bringing her hand palm flat to her magnificent breasts. 'My name is Samia. Samia Smith.'

'Exotic,' he commented.

'Me, or the name?' A smile tugged at her lips.

'What if I said both?'

'I'd say you were trying too hard and I don't think that's you.'

The name suited her perfectly. A bunch of contradictions, Samia was resolutely upbeat, but there was no mistaking the shadows behind her laughing eyes. 'Samia,' he murmured. Having tried the name on his tongue he found it rolled off like warm, sweet honey, much as she'd taste, he imagined. 'Very pleased to meet you, Samia Smith.'

'Also very pleased,' she said as they shook hands. She spared him another curtsey. But had she placed him, he wondered as she narrowed her eyes to stare thoughtfully into his. And would it change her attitude towards him if she had?

His best guess was no.

CHAPTER TWO

SAMIA'S TINY HAND in his big fist felt unreasonably small. Her grip was strong, her skin smooth and soft, as if she didn't work with her hands. She was in no hurry to remove her hand from his, he noticed, but stared directly into his eyes, giving the distinct impression that this was a woman who would bow her head to no man. Though, those shadows pointed to an event in her past that had driven her to travel in search of something different. Adding to his suspicions, there was a telltale mark on her wedding finger. A strip of pale skin showed where she had once worn a ring.

Forced to take hold of her shoulders to steer her away from a stream of waiters emerging from the kitchen, he was shocked by the bolt of heat that shot up his arm. This was matched by Samia's sharp inhalation of breath. As they swung around to stare at each other, something changed between them. No longer two strangers who'd met in a bar, they were a man and a woman reduced to their most primal state. There was a pulse beating rapidly in her neck, and her eyes were almost black, with just a thin rim of emerald around pupils grown huge. Some of the diners had noticed this bombshell, and were whispering about it, so he backed her into the shadows where they could talk unobserved.

'You don't want to be seen with me?' she challenged with a laugh.

'I don't want either of us to get in the way of the wait-staff,' he argued.

Of course there was another reason. Everyone with a smartphone was a member of the paparazzi these days, and shots of the Pirate Prince were priceless. How much more so, when the man in question appeared to be on the point of embarking on yet another affair? This was not the sort of thing he wanted his countrymen to see. They'd had enough upheaval, and must already be dreading the day when Prince Pietro's demon brother moved back home to take the throne.

'What brings you to Saint-Tropez?' he asked Samia. In unguarded moments, there appeared to be more than a backpack weighing her down.

'The name Saint-Tropez is magical, thanks to the film star Brigitte Bardot, who was just eighteen when she married the dangerously handsome Roger Vadim back in the fifties. They were lovers before I was born, but everyone knows their story and how they brought glamour to a small fishing village in the South of France. Who could resist that story?'

'Me,' he said bluntly. 'I see the place for what it is—a bustling, successful town.'

'You're a realist,' she confirmed.

'And you're a romantic, it would appear.'

'What's wrong with that?'

'Less than five years after they married, your glamorous couple divorced.'

'Don't spoil it,' she scolded. 'Why can't you think about the happiness they shared instead?'

'Because, as you pointed out, I'm a realist.' But he did

enjoy this woman's company. 'Doesn't your romantic life ever hit the skids?'

'Can we remain on topic, please?'

Her expression changed. Blood drained from her face. The dreamy expression had left her eyes. She looked almost frightened. 'What can of worms did I just open?' he enquired, pinning her with a shrewd stare.

'The one that says I'm hungry as well as thirsty…'

He didn't believe her for a moment, but they'd only known each other five minutes, which was far too soon for true confessions. 'How much time did you spend planning this trip?'

'It was a spur-of-the-moment decision,' she admitted.

'Who doesn't need a time-out occasionally?' he agreed. By taking things slowly, he might find out more about her.

'I'm happy to go wherever the wind takes me.'

He didn't believe that either. Everyone had some sort of plan. As she glanced at the door she'd used to come in, he wondered if she was running from something…or someone, and if the mark from the ring played a part in that. She hid it well, but she was jittery, reminding him of one of his highly strung polo ponies: always loyal, always willing, always ready to bolt. Beneath Samia's engaging personality, there was a story, and he wanted to know what that story was.

'So you always make a plan before you do anything?' She raised a brow. 'In that case, why should I believe that you just happen to be here, propping up the bar without good reason?'

If he told her he'd come to meet the man who had adopted his brother's child, would she believe him? Both the surrogate his brother had used and her husband wanted nothing from Luca, other than for him to know that his dead brother's child was safe and loved, and that they would never put a claim forward to the throne of Madlena.

Why would they? Maria, the child's mother, had demanded. Who in their right mind would choose to be royal?

Who indeed? he'd thought at the time, knowing only too well the restrictions that would place on the child.

Maria had decided not to go through with the surrogacy, she had explained, and had told his brother this before Pietro's death. Her husband was in full agreement. The child was theirs and needed no royal connections to improve his lot. What had hurt Luca the most was that Pietro hadn't felt able to share his longing for a family, and he blamed himself for being away while his brother had nursed this sad wound. All he could do for Pietro now was to keep his brother's secret. The people of Madlena needed reassurance, not another upheaval. 'I came here to settle some family business,' he told Samia.

'I think you're a bit of a romantic on the quiet,' she observed, smiling warmly. 'Family is—or should be—everything.'

There was a wistful note in her voice as she said this. 'It is to me,' he confirmed, more curious than ever about her backstory.

'Are you far from home? Judging by your accent, you're not French.'

'I sailed here,' he reminded her, 'I could have come from anywhere, but I guess my voice and my name tell their own story?'

'It's more about the tone of your voice,' she mused, eyes half-closed. 'Rich dark treacle with husky bass overtones...'

A laugh burst out of him. 'If I had a clue what you're talking about.'

'Just hum, but don't commit yourself,' she advised, eyes flashing open to spear him as she spoke. 'That's what I do when I don't want to answer questions—and it's obvious you're about as interested in answering questions as I am.'

'Point taken,' he said, interest spiking again as they stared into each other's eyes.

'I'll stop talking now,' she said, resting back against the wall next to him.

'Is that a promise?'

She turned her head. 'It's as close as you're going to get.'

The fact that they were still talking was nothing short of a miracle. Since Pietro's death, he'd had no patience for anyone or anything. Discovering his brother had wanted a family so badly, yet had not mentioned this to Luca, had rocked his selfish world on its axis. How could he have been so self-absorbed he had remained oblivious to his brother's distress? He had a lot to learn if he was to avoid letting down his country, as he'd let down Pietro.

'Where are you heading when you leave here?' his companion asked.

He turned to face her. 'I thought you promised not to talk.'

'It wasn't a forever promise, and you look as if you need a distraction.'

He smiled in spite of himself. There was something about Samia that forced him to see a lighter side of life. It also made him want to kiss that cheeky mouth into silence.

'Are you going home soon?' she prompted.

Home to him was either on board his sailing yacht, or on a bunk in a spartan barracks. A sumptuous palace with servants waiting on him hand and foot was his least favoured choice. That had been his brother's life, while Luca had joined Madlena's special forces where he had believed he could be of most use to his people. He had never imagined his parting from Pietro would be so final, or that the memories they'd shared would be tainted by the pain of knowing he'd let his brother down.

'You look sad and angry,' Samia commented with a frown. 'Is that my fault? Have I said something to upset you?'

'I'm not sad.'

'I'm pleased to hear it. Being Italian can only be a cause for celebration.'

He wavered between wanting to leave and ending their encounter, and staying to allow Samia to distract him from memories of his brother that threatened to splinter his mind. When his grandmother had been widowed and had gone off to live her own life, Pietro had raised him and cared for him, and where had he been when Pietro had so badly needed him?

'All that delicious pasta—'

'What?' His tone was harsh. Samia's intrusion into his private grief had jolted him—and even that was an indulgence. But seriously. Pasta? Of all the things she could have said about Italy—the art, the music, the architecture and stunning scenery—in her uniquely uninhibited way, she had gone straight for a decent plate of food. With a wry huff, he shook his head.

'There you are, you see,' she asserted. 'You're not so grim, after all. And I bet you're as hungry as me...'

'Are you hungry?'

'What do you think?' she teased. 'But I don't have enough money, and there's no chance we'll get fed here, even if I could afford it. With the best will in the world, the maître d' couldn't find us a table.'

He didn't disillusion her, though he only had to raise a brow for a table to be made instantly available.

'We're sunk,' she said.

'*We're* sunk?' he queried.

'Of course *we*. I'm hungry and you must be too. After your swim,' she reminded him.

Okay, he did have an appetite, and not just for food.

'Hamburger?' she suggested.

He followed her gaze to the public promenade where a hamburger stall was placed conveniently in the shadows.

Momentarily distracted as a text pinged on his phone, he saw that it came from the head of his PA team in Madlena. A Red Box, that indispensable piece of royal equipment designed to hold documents relating to vital matters of state, would be delivered to his study on board the *Black Diamond*.

He texted back.

I'd like you to look into something else—someone else.

Key points only, he added, after printing Samia's name.

'Finished?' she asked with a mildly disapproving look as he stowed the phone back in his pocket.

'My world never sleeps.'

'Poor you,' she said as he turned for the exit.

'I thought you were hungry. Aren't you coming with me?'

She shrugged and held back. 'I don't know you from Adam. Perhaps I should split.'

'Only you can decide. Are you hungry or not?'

'Hungry, but—'

'But what?' he demanded impatiently.

'If I do come with you, you have to take this.'

He stared at the ten-euro note she'd pressed into his hand.

'I know what things cost in this town,' she insisted. 'Great for keeping your ear to the ground, but not for eating out.'

'You're not a newspaper reporter, are you?'

She laughed. 'Why, do you have something to hide?'

'Do you?'

'Now we're both intrigued.' A smile hovered on her lips as she gave him a sideways look.

Warning bells started clanging loud and clear. Base instinct drowned them out. They had started leaning towards each other as their discussion grew more heated, close enough for him to detect Samia's wildflower scent, and to absorb the warmth of her body.

'I don't know how you can look so serious,' she told him. 'I find it impossible not to smile in Saint-Tropez.'

But with shadows in your eyes, he thought as she added, 'The sun is shining and the sky is bright blue. What's not to like?'

'A woman who never stops asking questions?' he suggested.

She laughed as she swung her bulky backpack off the floor, almost taking out a couple of drunks. Fortunately, they were too far gone to notice.

'I guess sailing isn't just work for you?' she said as she wove her perilous way through the crowded tables.

He glanced outside to where the bay of Saint-Tropez lay tranquil and glistening like a bright blue disc sprayed with silver in the trembling heat of late afternoon. 'No,' he agreed, remembering long, silent nights at sea beneath a blue-black sky littered with stars, and crazy, windy sun-lit days when dolphins raced ahead of the prow. 'Sailing isn't just work for me.'

'No wonder everyone's staring at you,' she com-mented when they reached the exit. 'They're jealous as hell, and I am too. What a wonderful life to work on board a yacht. Is the yacht where you work in the ma-rina? Can we go and look at it when we've had some-thing to eat?'

'It's moored out at sea.'

'Oh.' She sounded disappointed. 'Which one is it?' Shading her eyes, she followed his gaze. 'You are kid-ding? You work on board the *Black Diamond*? Everyone in town is talking about it. Isn't that one of the biggest sailing yachts at sea?'

'*The* biggest.'

'I read an article about the *Black Diamond*. If you could get me a job on board, it would be a dream come true.'

'I can put in a word.' It wasn't such a bad idea. A dis-traction like Samia was exactly what he needed before returning home to take up the reins of duty.

'I'm impressed,' she admitted. 'All the other yachts are scrubbed white to within an inch of their plimsoll line, while you sail the devil's own invention.'

'It's black,' he agreed.

'And massive.'

'Larger than average,' he agreed dryly.

'I'm glad you don't work on one of those floating of-fice blocks.'

'But rather the stuff dreams are made of?' he sug-gested with a cynical lift of his brow.

'Where I'm sure you fit right in. The pirate look?' she

prompted. 'You're only short of an earring and a parrot on your shoulder.'

Game on, he thought as they stared at each other and laughed.

CHAPTER THREE

SAMIA FROWNED AS she weighed the evidence. 'How did you get from ship to shore?'

Luca shrugged. 'Swam from the deck.'

Her frown deepened. 'That explains the thin film of sand on your skin.'

'You're quite the sleuth.'

'Just interested,' she admitted. 'But, surely that deck's too high for you to dive safely into the sea?'

'There's a marine deck at the stern where we keep the jet skis and power boats.'

'We?' She pounced on this right away. 'Does the owner know you make free with his possessions? I feel I should know who owns the *Black Diamond*. I'm sure I read somewhere that he's a tech billionaire with royal connections, and a reputation to make your toes curl...' Her thoughtful frown sharpened into an appraising stare. 'So you're no barfly, but a superfit member of the crew on a fabulous yacht. Who might even be able to get me a job on board,' she added with a winning smile.

Luca's mouth tugged slightly. It could have been a smile if his eyes hadn't been so calculating. She knew that feeling. Keeping a resolutely upbeat expression was making her muscles ache, but who wanted to employ a harassed-looking woman?

'Please tell your employer I'll do anything—within reason,' she added quickly. 'If you could arrange a meeting with whoever hires and fires, I won't let you down.'

Relief dashed over her like a great, drowning wave when Luca agreed. Impulsively, she stood on tiptoes to plant a kiss on his chin. Not her best decision, she realised when she saw the look in his eyes. She wasn't playing with fire, she was walking into it. She should be guarding her heart, not giving it away to the first man who offered to do something for her.

His overriding urge was to kiss her back. Which was crazy here in gossip central, aka the lobby of Saint-Tropez's most fashionable watering hole, but Samia's kiss was both a surprise and amazing. She felt so soft and warm against his hard frame, and smelled so good. He wanted nothing more than to kiss away the shadows in her eyes. Her zany sense of humour lifted him, while the sense of desperation he detected behind her jauntiness intrigued him.

'My priority remains finding a job,' she told him bluntly, in case he harboured any amorous notions, he presumed.

'You'd do better in an interview if your stomach isn't growling,' he observed.

'Then, you have my permission to feed me.'

And afterwards? She would join him on board or not. If she did, she would be one hell of a distraction from the ugliness banging in his brain that said he'd let his brother down. The world had judged Pietro a more than worthy heir to the throne of Madlena, while Luca was the spare, the bad boy, the rebellious teen; a dark and mysterious figure who was said to run dangerous missions, and who looked like a pirate, sailed like a pirate and, if the scan-

dal sheets were to be believed, rampaged through countless love affairs like a pirate. He had a lot of work to do
before he could convince his people that he was not the
devil to Pietro's saint.

Samia and her enormous backpack jostled him as they
reached the door.

'Hands off,' she said when he offered to carry it for
her. 'I'll have you know that this is a highly prized fashion item.'

'In whose universe?'

'And contains all my worldly goods.'

Why? he wondered. Her green eyes were dancing with
laughter, but the shadows were still there. Samia might
turn out to be an amusing coda to his trip, or a complete
non-event. Either way, he'd board his yacht and sail home.

'There's just one more thing,' she said as the doorman advanced.

'Only one?' He groaned theatrically.

'Any job I take must be lawful and respectable.'

'Of course. What do you take me for?'

'I don't know yet,' she said honestly.

Recognising him, the uniformed doorman flung the
door wide. *'Principe!'* he gushed, bowing low. 'What
an honour!'

'Principe?' Breath shot from Samia's lungs. *'What?'*

Numb with shock, she stared at Luca, and it took a
few moments before the pieces fell into place.

'I do know you… Of course I do. You don't work
on the *Black Diamond*. You own it. You're Luca Fortebracci, heir to the throne of Madlena since your brother's
tragic—' She stopped when she saw the expression on
Luca's face. 'I'm so sorry. That was clumsy of me. I've
been off the grid too long, but that's no excuse for not

thinking before I open my mouth. How insensitive you must think me.'

'Why should I think that?'

Nice words, but Luca's tone was frighteningly clipped and cold. She braced herself as he continued, 'Are you in a position to offer sympathy? Do you know me? Did you know my brother?'

In the space of a brief few moments, the sexy, laid-back guy she'd met in a bar had changed into a cold and distant prince.

'We need to clear the doorway,' he rapped. 'More diners are arriving.'

Cut him some slack! His grief was still raw, and she'd clearly poured salt on the wounds. 'I'm really sorry. If you'd rather I didn't come with you, I'll just go.'

Luca kept his hold on her arm and then she saw his need to hurry. *Photographs.* Those who had witnessed the mini drama between them were surreptitiously capturing the moment on their phones.

'Come on,' Luca gritted out. 'Let's get out of here. There's a time and a place, and this isn't it.'

She knew how it felt to be the focus of everyone's interest, and though in her case the scandal had soon passed over, forgotten as someone else came under the spotlight, for royalty it was remorseless.

'I understand your need for discretion,' she told Luca, 'and I get that everything needs to be calm and orderly in the enclosed confines of a yacht, but please don't let this stand in the way of you considering me for a job. I really need something, and I'll keep my head down and work as hard as I can. We've both relaxed more than perhaps we intended to over this past hour or so—equally, I think we both know playtime is over.'

Luca drew to a halt on the pavement outside. Narrowing his eyes, he pierced her with a stare, as if mining for truth, and then, as if he'd come to a decision, he jerked his chin, indicating it was time to move on.

Stay or go? Glancing behind them, she went with the best option.

She'd touched a nerve by mentioning his brother's death, but Luca knew that Samia wasn't responsible for his guilt. If he wanted her on board, he had to ease off. In her favour, having learned he was a prince, and no doubt recalling his colourful reputation, had made no difference to her opinion of him, and there was no doubt she was a welcome change from simpering princesses and spoiled celebrities.

'Hey! *Watch out!*' A surge of concern ripped through him as she almost stepped into the path of a passing coach. 'I get you had a shock back there, but there's no need to throw yourself under a bus.'

She looked at him, weighed him up, and then laughed. 'Wow, I thought I'd lost you there for a moment. Welcome back.'

He huffed something resembling a laugh as he stared down into her heart-shaped face.

'Are you sure this is good enough for your princely self?' she asked as they approached the burger stall.

'On the basis that your mouth will be too full of food for more cheeky remarks, I'd say it's the perfect choice.'

A rebellious glint fired in her eyes that promised more entertainment down the line. What had happened to his much-vaunted control? Wrecked, he concluded when he'd bought the burger and watched Samia lap red sauce from her fingers.

'So what do you think you know about me?' he asked

as a distraction from his body's urgent prompting to do more with this woman than eat burgers.

'Very little,' she admitted. 'Only what I've read in the press.'

'You mentioned being off the radar a while. Is that because of this trip?'

She confined her answer to a brief nod.

'I was hoping for more than that,' he admitted.

Flattening her lips, she said nothing, but her eyes told him firmly, *Back off.*

He liked that she stood up to him, but as he caught sight of the *Black Diamond*, apparently floating serenely on a tranquil ocean, when he knew all about dangerous currents lurking beneath, it was as if sailing was a metaphor for life. He didn't know this woman, or the harm she could do to him.

'Don't you want to share?' she asked, holding out the greasy bun.

His mind flew to the galley on board the *Black Diamond* where his Michelin-starred chef would be preparing some delicacy to tempt him. 'Thank you, but I'll pass.'

'Not up to your princely standards?'

He gave her a look, then thought of the unidentifiable sludge he used to eat in the army. 'I have a healthy appetite, and it will take more than a mouthful of meat to satisfy me.'

Her cheeks fired red, but she drove past her embarrassment to assure him she would remember that, if she got a job in his galley.

Or in his bed.

'Once you've had a chance to settle in, I'll assess what you can do.'

'Settle in?' she queried, pulling her head back to frown

at him. 'What do you think I've got in this knapsack? It isn't the Tardis. If I have to wear a uniform it would double the number of outfits I own. Will I have to wear a uniform?'

A number of options flashed into his mind. 'Not right away.'

She lightened him, he admitted silently, and no one but his beloved *nonna* could do that. A better state of mind was good for him, and could only be good for his people. Her banter amused him, and her quick wits kept his on point. Either she'd annoy the hell out of him when they were on board, in which case she'd leave at the next port, or she'd join him in bed.

'Will we be sailing straight to Madlena?' she asked as if reading his mind.

'I haven't decided yet,' he said as they approached his private dock.

'Aren't you due at an enthronement in a couple of weeks' time?'

His hackles rose. He didn't need a reminder that the gulf between the freedom he was enjoying now and the shackles he was facing then was closing. 'What's that to you?'

'Hold on to your hat,' she exclaimed. 'I'm just trying to work out your schedule, so I know where I stand.'

His schedule might have to undergo some radical changes if he was to fit in an interlude of pleasure before duty claimed him. That gap had almost closed already, he concluded as they approached the tight security cordon at the entrance to his dock. 'We might take a small diversion.'

'We?' she queried.

'The crew and I.'

The Fortebracci dynasty would have to wait a little

longer for its next Prince to forge some cold-blooded alliance with a po-faced princess. Spending time with a woman who gave as good as she got held far more appeal.

CHAPTER FOUR

HER HEAD WAS SPINNING. What had she done? Where was she going? Who was she going with?

Luca was a prince?

The facts kept bouncing around her head, while she went hot and cold, and her heart refused to stop pounding. She tried to act normally, as if she didn't care, but of course she cared. She cared for her safety. She cared for her heart, and Luca definitely provoked a reaction from her. It was impossible to be near him without feeling something. And what would he say when he found out what she did for a living? But she needed this job, and she'd be lying if she said her nose wasn't twitching at the scent of a story. How could two brothers who'd been so close end up with one being dubbed a saint and the other a sinner? Surely, the truth must lie somewhere in between? That Luca was complex, she had no doubt, but was he as bad as he was painted?

'You're having doubts?' he guessed as the guards at the gate saluted and stood back respectfully. 'Now's your chance to change your mind...'

'I'm fine.' Whatever she discovered about Luca, she'd keep it to herself. To broadcast details of his private life would be both intrusive and dishonest. Her heart was safe because he didn't want it, and he'd never find out that she was rubbish in bed, as her ex had insisted, because she had no intention of going there.

'Nothing serious, I hope?' she prompted when she saw that Luca was frowning at a message on his phone.

He hummed and said nothing, but his expression was like a storm approaching, and made her wonder if she was being too hasty in agreeing to this trip.

Once on board, she would untangle her thoughts. Beneath her blasé front she was still reeling from the effects of living with a bully. And yes, she'd been frightened of him...frightened of his power and reach. Divorce had not divided them, as she'd hoped, but had only made him more vindictive. Once on board, she'd be safe from him—for the duration of the voyage, at least. She must make the most of learning how the super-rich lived, and maybe write about it one day in general terms. There was no need to mention Luca specifically.

'Is this where we wait for transport to the yacht?' she asked, gazing around in wonder at the luxuriously appointed seating area, manned by uniformed attendants serving canapés and champagne.

'Not to your liking?' he teased while she trembled. The frisson was all due to him. Luca only had to look at her for her body to yearn for the excitement it had missed. Escaping the past was the light at the end of the tunnel, and she was eager to get there, desperate to march forward into a better future. 'A glass of sparkling water would be great.' Keeping a clear head would be better still.

Luca also refused champagne, saying he would be sailing later.

A pang of disappointment reminded her that a new recruit for the prince's yacht would hardly be at the top of his agenda. Regret still formed like a ball in the pit of her stomach, while Luca paced like a tiger with a thorn in its pad. They were both eager to get on board, but for different reasons. She might be hungry to continue the getting-to-know-you process, but he was returning to an activity he loved, and an unimaginably privileged lifestyle that defined him. *Grow up. Get real.* If she was lucky she might get that job, and occasionally see him in passing.

But she couldn't help herself. She never could. Her mother used to say she was born asking questions. 'So… Madlena?' she prompted.

'I'll answer questions when we're on board.'

Luca's tone was clipped, as if to discourage all further conversation. She couldn't blame him. He was a prince.

A prince in mourning.

He owned the yacht.

And soon his freedom to sail will be cut short.

At best, she'd be a lowly member of crew.

But I could still help him.

And how exactly would she do that?

I'll find a way.

'And when we're on board you'll ask no questions.'

She pulled back her head with surprise, then remembered he'd been hounded by the press, and must have had his fill of questions. When news of his brother's death broke, press opinion had been heavily weighted against the Pirate Prince taking over from Prince Pietro, who had never been known to put a foot wrong. Even she had to admit it would take something special to restore his reputation. Could she help him do that? Almost certainly not. Any influence she might have had in the press had gone down the tubes on the day she'd agreed to marry the newspaper mogul who owned the paper she wrote for. He'd used every threat in the book to make her change her

words for his, and after her mother's suicide, when she'd
thought it couldn't get any worse, his threat to ruin her
father's life had proved her wrong. She would have done
anything to save her father from more grief, and she had.

'You'll need to take those boots off when you board.'

'Of course I will.' She could have kissed Luca for giving her something so straightforward to think about. He'd
stopped pacing, and was standing close enough to touch.
Their hands were almost brushing against each other, and
hers were tingling, as was her thigh closest to his. Luca
was so overwhelmingly masculine, her body was acutely
aware of him. The power he exuded was very different
from that of her ex, but he'd been a bully, while Luca offered choices. Sex with her ex had been brutal and fast,
which had resulted in Samia dreading the act, while Luca,
for all his rampant masculinity, only filled her with the
yearning to be touched with tenderness and skill.

Maybe there was hope for her yet, she reflected wryly
as Luca, having noticed her interest, stared keenly at her.
Not *much* hope, she concluded, remembering she was
about to step into the unknown with a man she hardly
knew.

'At last,' he announced as a sleek black powerboat
cruised to the side of the dock.

Taking a risk had surely never felt this good. She was
excited. And why not? A threadbare, penniless nomad,
without a job or a home to go to, and a past so bleak it
threatened to swamp her, was on her way to a billionaire's yacht.

As Luca went to help his men, she took the chance,
while ropes were secured and fenders tossed over the side
to prevent the hull scraping against the dock, to do some
research on her phone. What she discovered about Prince
Luca Fortebracci only made her hungry to learn more.

The Pirate Prince had quite a history. Where romance was concerned, he appeared to be a generous lover, yet had never formed a lasting attachment. An entrepreneur almost by accident, who'd started his global business in his bedroom as a boy, whatever was written about him in the press—or whatever Luca thought about himself— he was considered a national hero in Madlena, so why was he so tense going home? For all his wealth and success, he seemed a solitary figure, apart from the beloved grandmother he so often quoted in the press.

'Ready?' he prompted.

Any minute now, she would be stepping from her world into his, so it was time to pull herself together, get ready to embrace whatever came next.

Don't get ahead of yourself, her nitpicky inner voice warned. *If you're lucky, you might get a job on the* Black Diamond *where Luca will most certainly be your boss, and so high above your lowly status you might not see him again. This is a chance to escape the shadow of your ex and plan the rest of your life, and that's all it is.*

And do a bit more research about Luca, surely—to satisfy her curiosity, if nothing else. Supposing her inner voice was right about not seeing much of Luca once they were on board, surely with her history in the bedroom she should be relieved. Anything more than a business relationship came with its own set of complications.

Shouldn't I, of all people, be wary of powerful men?

Turning for one last look around the shore, she saw so many things to reassure her—children playing, families sipping drinks—and yet the rope was playing out and soon she'd be leaving those familiar scenes far behind.

'I'll put a boat at your disposal if you change your mind once we're on board.'

Could he read her mind? Her anxiety must be showing.

'You'll have full Wi-Fi access,' Luca continued smoothly, as a boarding ramp was secured between the quay and the powerboat. 'If you lose signal, we have satellite phones. Why don't you ring your parents now to reassure them?'

'My mother's dead.' She clapped a hand across her mouth. The words had shot out before she could stop them. 'I'm so sorry. You must think me thoughtless mentioning something like that.'

'Why would I? I'm sorry for your loss.'

But he was frowning. 'And I for yours,' she said. Luca's face had grown closed and unreadable again. They had both experienced tragedy, and were both struggling to reclaim some semblance of normality in lives that suddenly made very little sense. The press had disclosed hardly anything about Prince Pietro's death, beyond describing it as 'a freak accident,' which was enough to rouse the curiosity of any investigative journalist, even one supposedly taking a lengthy sabbatical.

'How did your mother die?'

The shock of the question jolted her back to the present, and she decided to be equally blunt. 'She took her own life.' Rather than face the shame of Samia's father being brought before a judge. The guilt that hit was familiar. Could she have done more to save her mother? And now it was followed by a second thought: Did Luca have a similar demon to wrestle?

'We both have reason to grieve,' he observed in a clipped tone.

'And to go forward.' Every day she renewed her determination to return to the work she loved. Her fall from grace had been spectacular. One day her column was praised to the skies for its brave exposure of criminals, and the next, when her writing had inexplicably changed, from seeing both sides of an argument to only one, that of her ex, her readers had deserted her in droves. When she'd threatened to make his deception public, he'd promised she'd never work again, and when they'd divorced, he'd vowed to pursue her to the ends of the earth. That was why she'd left London with just the clothes on her back, and her mother's old hiking boots to keep her grounded. She needed space from evil to stand a chance of climbing back.

'Hang on. Sit down,' Luca said as he escorted her onto the powerboat.

Whatever they knew or didn't know about each other, Luca remained a comforting presence at her side as she took her place at the prow of the boat. To begin with, it was a comfortable ride—the skipper kept strictly to the speed limits—but once they were out at sea and the harbour police were left behind, he opened up the engines and the prow rose out of the water.

They hit a wake. She yelped and bounced onto Luca, who held her firmly, keeping her safe. Close contact was electrifying. He felt so warm, so strong like a rock. His hands were roughened by sailing, but that was another point in his favour. She was done with hands mauling her that had never done an honest day's work. Far from saving her father when she married her ex, she'd only made matters worse, given him more cause to threaten and bully her. She could only think now that she'd been reeling with grief after the death of her mother. Her father was weak and deep in debt, and she'd had to do something to save him. Her ex would keep him out of prison, he'd promised. Well, that had gone well. Her father was still in jail.

She noticed Luca was looking thoughtful as he read another text on his phone. Trouble? Could she help? She didn't know him well enough to ask. Did she care for him so much already? Was it even possible for that depth of connection to be instant? Had she already forgotten she had promised herself she'd guard her heart?

Enjoy the moment for what it is, her inner voice advised, *and stop worrying about what might happen, let alone what happened in the past. Live for now or you'll regret it.*

Turning her face to the sun, she smiled as the roar of the engines confirmed the distance they were travelling, from the mainland out to sea. It was as if she were flying across the ocean with a strong man at her back. How hard was it to be optimistic?

'This is amazing!' she called out, beginning to understand Luca's passion for sailing. Blue sky and a silver sea bathed in sunlight were nothing short of spectacular. The air was as pure as a new page waiting to be written on. 'I can't thank you enough for giving me this opportunity.'

'You'll have to work hard,' Luca warned.

'I'm ready.'

Was that a flash of calculation in his eyes? She didn't remain anxious for long. It wasn't possible with heat rippling through her veins like hot chocolate on a cold afternoon just from being close to Luca. Maybe she should be asking what jobs were available on board, but why spoil the moment when she felt properly alive for the first time in ages? Luca had reminded her how exciting it could be to pit her wits against an intelligent opponent, and offer opinions without constantly being mocked. She couldn't remember the last time she'd felt like this.

It was as if he'd read her thoughts. Taking hold of her hand, he stared at the mark left by her wedding ring. Removing her hand, she levelled a stare on his face. 'You must be wondering why I'm here. I know I am,' she admitted.

'You're escaping,' he said.

'Perhaps we both are.' She noticed he didn't deny it.

'Why are you so down on yourself?' he asked Samia. Beauty was so often marred by high self-esteem, but Samia was completely unspoiled. More of her bright copper hair had escaped her careless updo, while exposure to sunshine and wind from the sea had pinked up her face, adding to the sprinkling of freckles on her nose. She was lovely, and should be full of confidence.

'I'm not down on myself, but you're a prince and a billionaire, and I'm no one,' she said, 'so why take an interest in me?'

'*No one?* Did your ex tell you that?' He shook his head with contempt. 'Everyone's someone, and deserving of equal consideration.'

'In an ideal world, maybe,' Samia agreed with a rueful laugh. 'But not everyone's *someone* to the same degree you are.'

'If you're talking wealth and titles—' he spread his arms wide '—an accident of birth doesn't make me better than anyone else. Money? It depends what you do with it, but it's no guarantee of happiness. It doesn't make the bad times easier to bear.'

'I'm sorry.' She touched his arm sympathetically. 'I hardly know you, but your loss is so keen I can feel it.'

He blanked the comment. Unburdening himself to a stranger wasn't his way. What would it change? Nothing.

'I'm sorry, you must think me intrusive,' she added quickly, 'but if I can help in any way—'

'You can't,' he said flatly.

As the powerboat slowed beneath the shadow of Luca's yacht, Samia gazed up towards the yawning entrance that gaped blankly in its side. Borders she'd crossed had never intimidated her as much as this one, but she was determined not to show it as Luca stood. He was quite distant now, though still polite. Was that, as she had suspected, a sign of things to come? Employee and boss. Prince and civilian. The grief of losing his brother was shut away somewhere so deep she couldn't touch it. However strong an attraction she felt, they were strangers, and seemed destined to remain so. That didn't stop her feeling sorry for him, and wishing she could help. Luca might wield the power of a Caesar, but like everyone else on the face of the earth, when it came down to it, he was on his own.

He crossed the gap between the rolling powerboat and the comparatively stable yacht in one stride, and waited on the other side to steady her. His firm touch on her wrist was reassuring. Luca didn't frighten her like her ex, and it was a relief to discover she could still feel warmth, and be attracted to a man, and that—for her, at least—no amount of mistreatment could completely frighten off Mother Nature.

'Welcome on board,' he said as she leapt across the foaming gulf. 'I hope you find the experience worthwhile.'

'I'm sure I shall,' she said, matching him for politeness. She was eager to sample all the new things on board, and looking forward to meeting his crew.

The crew gave her a warmer welcome than she'd expected. Shaking hands firmly with each of them, she decided that she would like it here, with or without Luca's involvement. *Though with would be better*, she reflected as he touched her arm to move her on.

CHAPTER FIVE

THE EMAIL HE read on the powerboat was from the excellent team he had working for him. For now, the information they had on Samia Smith was enough for him. As requested, the answers to his questions appeared in bullet points, which they would send him a further list of soon.

A wife would go a long way to settling the distress in Madlena following Prince Pietro's death.

News of Prince Luca's marriage would silence the naysayers, proving intentions towards Madlena are both serious and long-term.

Arriving with a bride, followed by a formal blessing in the cathedral for everyone to enjoy, has been received with unanimous approval.

Good. It was his intention that the Pirate Prince would be seen as a man determined to change. At some point in the future, when confidence in his reign was fully restored, his wife could be discreetly let go with his blessing and thanks, together with a healthy pension for life. Any children, if there were any, would stay with him. There would be no repeat of his brother's misstep.

The magic of a royal wedding never fails...

A rather cynical take, to be sure, but he would not deny the citizens of Madlena the reassurance they so badly needed. His life no longer belonged to him, but to his people, who only knew him through his army career, and lurid rumours in the press. Trust took time. He accepted that, but an intelligent, lively bride he already found attractive was a good, solid start. He'd inform Samia that he intended to marry her when the time was right. She was the perfect solution to his dilemma. The fact this had happened so fast was no reason to doubt his decision. He would soon make her see the benefits of becoming his wife.

He skim read the rest of the email, which rambled on about plans for a wedding to a woman he hadn't proposed to yet. A detailed agenda for the ceremony would be found in the Red Box, together with a full CV of the woman he had asked his team to investigate.

If Your Serene Highness has an opportunity to review the biographies and photographs of the various suitable princesses that we've also included and let us know your decision, we'll move things along quickly and have your choice of bride delivered to the yacht for your perusal forthwith.

Forthwith? He curbed a smile as he glanced at Samia, wondering if any of these same advisors would have the courage to inform Samia she had been *delivered* to his yacht for perusal by the prince. The solution to Madlena's woes lay in his hands, not in a document contained in the Red Box, listing 'suitable' princesses.

He texted while Samia was taking everything in.

No princesses. I already have someone in mind.

Why waste time on unknown quantities when a challenging prospect was standing right in front of him?

Out of the frying pan, into the fire? Samia wondered as she gazed around.

She had never been anywhere like the deck of the *Black Diamond*. It was so vast, so clean and so very high-tech. Which she should have accepted, as it belonged to a tech billionaire who just happened to be a prince. Everything had gone so smoothly... *Too smoothly?* she wondered as Luca ushered her on. Did he have an agenda behind his generous invitation? There was no mention of a job yet, or even an interview.

Tell me I haven't blundered into trouble again!

She needed reassurance, and doubted she would get it. Luca would most likely go about his duties and forget she was around. Stiffening her resolve, she decided to talk to him while she could. Exploring the *Black Diamond* would have to wait.

He was issuing instructions to some members of the crew. 'Excuse my interruption,' she said politely, 'but I wonder if you could introduce me to your purser?'

The crew dispersed at a nod from Luca.

'Or whoever interviews candidates for jobs on board, please.'

'You're already hired,' he said.

'For what position?'

'Jack of all trades. Whatever you're called upon to do.'

'I need more than that. I need specifics.'

'Not now,' he stated firmly.

She was a grown woman with a phone and the ability to call for help if she needed to. She told herself to calm down and look at this sensibly. Having got herself into this situation, she could either see it through, or take a boat back to shore as Luca had already suggested. His crew respected him, and appeared glad to have him back. There were no funny looks, or anything to make her feel nervous. She could get to know him on board, and understand this incredible lifestyle.

'When?' she asked, softening the question with a smile.

'After dinner,' he suggested. 'Why are you still trembling?' he asked, frowning.

Was it that obvious? It was the Luca effect, but she wasn't going to tell him that. 'The breeze is kicking up,' she excused. 'Time to go below decks to my quarters?' She couldn't drop a hint any bigger than that.

'This is a sailing yacht,' he reminded her, 'and not one of those "floating office blocks" you referred to.'

'And it's lovely,' she said.

The quirk of one ebony brow warned her not to play with fire. No danger of that. She doubted she'd be on board long enough to get her fingers burned.

Samia remained uncharacteristically silent, which threw him. Inviting a woman onto his yacht within an hour of meeting her was not normal behaviour. The text from his team had endorsed his belief that a mix of gut instinct and feral lust could occasionally provide a solution to a problem. His next task was to convince Samia to become his bride.

Well, that should be easy, he mused dryly, taking in the stubborn set of her chin. Samia owed Madlena nothing, and him even less, and, while many might jump at the chance of marrying a prince, he doubted Samia would be the least bit impressed by either status or wealth. In-

dependent and feisty, she would determine her own route
through life. It was his task to make sure that route led
to him.

In pursuit of a seemingly ideal solution, he ran a list
of benefits due a royal bride through his mind: the throne
of Madlena, priceless crown jewels, front row seats at
every prestige event, private jets, superyachts, palaces
and homes across the world. Sycophants aplenty. He grimaced at this last thought. *Must try harder*, he reflected
with a tinge of amusement as Samia glanced his way. It
was hard not to be captivated by her enthusiasm as he
took her on a tour of the yacht. How long was it since
he'd witnessed such innocent pleasure, or that one of the
many visitors to the yacht had dared to admit that anything excited them? It was cool to be blasé, something
that seemed to have passed Samia by. She liked something, or she didn't, and she wasn't afraid to tell him,
whether her opinion was *cool* or not.

'Teams of stylists must have worked on this for
months,' she said as they crossed the grand salon.

'Years in the planning,' he revealed, amused to discover she was padding alongside him barefoot. But of
course, she didn't have anything with her, he remembered, apart from a few oddments in her backpack. All
that was about to change.

'It's a bit bland for me,' she admitted as glass doors
slid open at their approach.

'Bland?' he queried, a little taken aback.

'All this white and taupe is a bit dated, don't you
think? I like a splash of colour.'

'On board my black yacht?' he suggested with amusement.

'Why not?' she enthused.

Similar to the modern art in his quarters on board,

he was thinking. He'd never noticed the rest of the décor before, but seeing it through Samia's eyes gave it a new slant. As she took a closer look at a maritime map on the wall, his thoughts grew to encompass her soft skin beneath his hands, and the supple warmth of her body straining beneath his. The enticing scent of wildflowers and heat floated in her wake, and for the first time he could remember, he was stirred on board his yacht to do more than haul sail.

'First impressions?' he demanded.

'You are the master of all you survey,' Samia declared, 'and the *Black Diamond* is a billionaire's plaything.'

'It's a serious sailing yacht, not some toy.'

'You asked for my opinion.'

And unfortunately that was what she'd given him, straight up with no frills. 'Why don't you write a report?' he asked cynically.

'If that's what you'd like?'

She'd taken him seriously, and he couldn't bring himself to mock this straightforward woman. 'I would,' he said. What harm could it do?

'I've spent too long keeping my mouth shut in the past,' she explained. 'I've no intention of making that mistake again, so what I see is what I say, and if you'd like me to write it down, I'm happy to do so.'

'It's a deal,' he agreed. This microfact made him hungry to hear more. There was nothing he liked better than a challenge, and Samia would not agree with him simply to garner praise. This made her a refreshing change, and the perfect choice of bride for him. But he wasn't going to let her off too lightly.

'No wonder sailing is my passion,' he said dryly.

'Because the yacht doesn't answer back?' she suggested.

'Do I need a better reason?' From the blackest of moods earlier in the day, she'd lifted him, and it was a relief to discover he could still tap into feelings.

'I thought you were going to show me to my quarters?' she prompted. 'I sure as hell won't find them by myself. All this for one man,' she breathed in awe as they walked on.

'And one opinionated woman,' he added with an amused sideways look. 'I think most people would sympathise and say I badly need space between us.'

'Most people would sympathise with me, I think you'll find,' she countered with a cheeky smile.

He had the satisfaction of hearing her gasp when he opened a door leading into the burnished wood-panelled entrance to the suite of rooms he had chosen for Samia. 'This is more like it,' she exclaimed. 'Forget bland. I can't imagine anything more beautiful than this.'

'All my brother's design.' The words came out awkwardly, clipped and emotion-free. He still found it hard to talk about Pietro and this suite had been his brother's vision for guests on board the *Black Diamond*.

Guests? Luca remembered asking Pietro. *But this is a sailing boat.*

And you should not be such a loner, Pietro had insisted. *It's not good for you, Luca…*

In Pietro's trademark style, everything in the suite Luca had chosen for Samia was lavish and flamboyant. There were jewel-coloured rugs beneath their feet, and intricate hangings on the wall above a vast, canopied bed that was almost a joke out at sea. Only the most exclusive and vivid fabrics had been used for soft furnishings, and to dress the windows… Silks, satin, velvet and chiffon, the latter billowing lazily in the sea breeze blowing in from the balcony. Acres of lovingly polished wood and brass complemented these lavish adornments, and the setting was further enhanced by paintings of sailing ships through the ages, and good-looking men in a variety of impeccable uniforms.

'Your brother had great taste,' Samia commented as she trailed her fingertips across the arm of a comfortable chair lavishly upholstered in a luxurious velvet tapestry.

'He was a great one for history, and for design. Pietro could have had a great future ahead of him, had he not been a prince.'

'But surely, being a prince *is* a great future?'

'Not for Pietro.' The words were wrenched out of him and each left a jagged wound. 'Pietro always preferred a quiet life, out of the limelight. He enjoyed designing sets,' he reminisced, thinking back to the childhood concerts Pietro had enjoyed putting on. 'A quiet life was the only thing my brother craved, but that was not to be...'

Dragging his thoughts out of the past, he took a look around the suite again. It was every bit as grand and impressive as Samia thought it, though in his opinion the décor belonged in a museum, rather than a state-of-the-art sailing yacht that had been built to Luca's design. But he and his brother had always enjoyed doing things together, and he had wanted Pietro to be part of this too... *Dio!* How he missed him.

'You okay?' Samia asked.

'My brother was never a sailor,' he explained, clinging to cold, hard facts. 'Design was his strength and his passion.'

'At which he excelled,' Samia said frankly. 'He had wonderful taste.'

Her tone was quiet and understanding, and lacked pity, which was more important, as it allowed him to say without betraying any emotion, 'He was a wonderful man.'

'And you loved him, as I'm sure Prince Pietro loved you.'

Where had she sprung from, this woman fate had placed in his way? When he looked at her, he thought back to previous guests with their artfully tousled hair and intricate make-up, bringing on board cabin trunks bulging with clothes, only to discover that nothing they'd brought with them was remotely suitable for a sailing yacht. Naturally, they ordered more at his expense, prompting deliveries from Paris, Rome and Milan to arrive at ports ahead of them. Much of this forgotten inventory still hung in protective covers in Samia's dressing room.

'There's a swimming pool on board. Two, in fact,' he revealed. 'Feel free to use them.'

'There's one for your crew?'

'There are two pools you can use.'

'Wonderful…but I don't have a costume with me.'

'You'll find some in your dressing room that have never been worn. Help yourself. At least one of them should fit.'

'I'm not sure I'll be swimming.'

Who could blame her for not being thrilled at the thought of wearing a previous guest's clothes? 'The costumes are brand new,' he explained. 'Don't let pride get in your way. Consider anything you find in the dressing room a down payment for whatever job I decide you'll do.'

'I'd rather be paid a wage, if that's all right. I'm not very good at taking handouts.'

'So I remember,' he said, remembering the ten-euro note she'd insisted on giving him for the hamburger and the water. 'How about I pay you a wage too?'

She shrugged and smiled a crooked smile. 'It might be possible to come to an accommodation.'

When Samia looked like that, she was irresistible. 'Make use of any of the clothes you find in the dressing room. You'd be doing me a favour. All they represent to me at the moment is money down the drain.'

It was hard not to imagine her in one of the many evening gowns. How Samia would feel about that, though, was another matter. Most of them were extremely revealing, and she didn't move in the same brittle circles he did, packed with career courtesans making it their life's work to date rich, successful men in order to piggyback on their privileged lifestyles. Putting their wares on display in the full expectation of having them decorated with precious gems was all part of the game.

'I can wear anything I find?' she exclaimed with what appeared to be genuine excitement. 'Does that go for all your crew?'

He gave her a look that shut her up.

'Anyway, you're very generous,' she added. 'I always liked to play dress-up as a child, though that involved a thousand different ways with a tablecloth and things I borrowed from my mother's wardrobe.'

Seeing her grow wistful, he was more determined than ever to read the report on her that his team had sent over.

'Sorry if I'm holding you up,' she added as he turned for the door.

'You're not, or I wouldn't be here,' he said bluntly. The more he learned about this fascinating woman, the more certain he became that he'd made a good choice of bride. Samia would always be her own person, but he admired that. Her natural friendliness had already quickly endeared her to his crew, and vanity had no place in her life. His people would love that. She hadn't touched her hair once since they'd met, or fixed her lip gloss—if she was even wearing any. Understated, with personality to spare, she'd already proved she was kind and thoughtful, and the citizens of Madlena were hungry for a personal touch after his brother's shyness, which had manifested itself as apparent aloofness. She was funny and quirky, and who didn't like that? When he returned to Madlena, everything would be for the benefit of his people, and not for how it made him look. This *was* a politically astute marriage, just not the sort his people probably anticipated. How better to reassure the citizens of Madlena than to introduce them to his down-to-earth bride?

How can I be so sure she's so right for the role when I hardly know her?

With a full report waiting on his desk in the Red Box, knowing everything about Samia was only a matter of time.

'Where's your accommodation?' she asked out of interest when Luca turned to leave the suite his brother had designed.

'Down the corridor from yours, so if you need anything—'

'I won't,' she said quickly from a mouth turned dry. 'Surely, I won't really be staying here?' She stared around the elaborate room. First the clothes, and now this fabulous suite of rooms? Why wasn't she to wear the simple black rig all the crew wore, and stay in crew quarters? 'If you tell me where the crew sleeps, I'll be happy to find my way there.'

'You're staying here,' he insisted flatly.

'What?'

'Pietro designed this area to be used.'

'So I'm just filling a slot?' She felt relieved.

Luca shrugged his magnificent shoulders. 'Yes, you'll

actually be doing me a favour if you stay here, as there's no more room in the crew area right now.'

'Then…thank you.'

'And as I said about the clothes, you'll be doing me a favour wearing those too.'

Lots of favours, she thought. Would there be a price to pay eventually?

'Freshen up, take a shower and relax while you can,' he recommended.

While you can? What did that mean, exactly?

A frisson of excitement feathered across her skin. It would be churlish to refuse, she decided.

'Last chance to return to shore,' he added, then paused with his hand on the door handle. His lips pressed down. 'Too late.'

Hearing the unmistakeable grind of an anchor being raised, she couldn't keep the panic from her voice as she admitted, 'I didn't realise we were so close to sailing.'

'I made no secret of the fact that I needed to leave,' Luca said levelly.

'No, indeed—it's just that…' Plain and simple? She thought she'd have more time.

'Doubts, Samia? Better say so now.'

'No.'

'I can still get you back to shore in one of the small crafts we keep on board.'

'That won't be necessary, but thank you.' She'd made her decision and she wasn't backing down now, but what exactly had she agreed to…? Work as yet unspecified, and a suite of rooms fit for a princess located handily next to those of a prince. Was she really so naïve? Luca had shown little sign of wanting to romance her… Yes. She was that naïve. Was the Pirate Prince noted for his romantic nature, or was his calculating sexuality all he expected it to take to achieve another conquest?

She didn't have to do anything she didn't want to do. One thing she was certain of about Luca was that he didn't have to force himself on a woman, or mistreat her, or mock her, or do any of the things that she'd thought had put her off men for good.

'So you're happy to stay on board?' he asked.

Gathering herself, she confirmed this. 'If you'll still have me, but I do insist on making myself useful. Or how else can I pay for my passage?'

To his credit, Luca didn't say anything to alarm her, though his mouth did tug up a fraction at one corner. 'I'm sure we can find something for you to do,' he said as he opened the door. 'But for now I'm going to leave you to take that shower, which will give me a chance to decide exactly what to do with you.'

She got the distinct impression from his expression that her fate was already decided, but instead of alarm bells ringing, as they surely should have done, she felt incredibly excited by the prospect of whatever lay ahead.

CHAPTER SIX

HE DIDN'T RETURN to his suite right away, or even to his study where the Red Box was waiting. Instead, he retraced his steps to the grand salon to take a proper look at the space through Samia's eyes. And, following her verdict, it did strike him as insipid.

Nothing would ever be boring with Samia.

His yacht was state-of-the-art fierce, while this reception area was like a tepid bath, neither ice nor fire. And he craved fire, he thought, brooding on a pair of emerald eyes.

What is this grand salon used for? she must have wondered. Grand dinner parties where equally grand food and drink were served to grand guests.

He could almost hear Samia observing, *No invitation for me, then...?*

Those grand guests would all glut themselves at his expense. No one had ever been known to refuse an invitation from the notorious Pirate Prince, let alone offer the slightest criticism, or an opinion that might differ from his.

He'd rather eat a hamburger with Samia any day of the week.

She could hardly believe she was soaking in a king-sized tub in a pink veined-marble bathroom the same size as her bedroom at home, bathed in warmth and cloaked in shimmering, rainbow-hued bubbles. This was all incredible and new and fabulous—and it wouldn't do to get used to it.

What would it be like to live like this every day? Idle? Great to dream about, but a bit boring to indulge in all the time, though it did take her back to playing make-believe with her mother. Her father had gambled away their money, and her mother, a renowned beauty in her time, had been ill-equipped to deal with the harsh realities of everyday life. Samia had adapted quickly, because she was young and not used to much luxury, as that was reserved for her parents. She hadn't been very old when she'd started to see the cracks beneath the façade of their wealth—maybe six or seven. An empty larder, and holes in the soles of her father's expensive shoes, had told their own story. To begin with, her mother had made the best of things by acting out scenes she would have inhabited at one time, introducing Samia to a glittering world she could only dream about...*before now*.

How her mother would have loved this, she reflected as she trailed her fingertips through the bubbles and swished the warm water. Pressing her lips together hard, she remembered her mother's last note, begging for forgiveness, and saying Samia would be better off without her. Samia only wished they could have talked things through.

Closing her eyes, she sank back with a sigh. Things were rarely what they seemed. Even this incredible encounter with Luca might not be as straightforward as it appeared. More soldier than prince, he could play the role of laid-back charmer equally well. He'd set the restaurant alight with more than a title, good looks, or even his formidable reputation. It was the dangerously glittering

glamour he radiated that meant that even when he was
barefoot and casually dressed, he drew everyone's eye.

Luca was a powerhouse in every way, though
strangely, in spite of her past bad experience, she didn't
feel threatened by him. Quite the opposite. He made her
feel safe, which only made her all the more determined
to help him recover from his brother's death. If she got
the chance. Sometimes it was easier for a stranger to see
things clearly, and she felt sure that what the people of
Madlena needed was a strong prince to lead them forward into a bright and promising future. If Luca remained
locked in the past he wouldn't help anyone.

Take that as a lesson for yourself, she concluded. And
how exactly could she help Luca, with no job, no home
to go to, and a vindictive ex-husband? Looking back, it
was obvious her ex had married her for two things: her
column and some land in Scotland her father owned,
that he had hoped to farm one day. Her ex had said the
land shouldn't be farmed as it would make an excellent
golf course. She should never have married him, but
had run out of options when it came to helping her parents. And he'd seemed so kind at first, paying off her
father's debts, and buying her mother some lovely new
clothes. It was only later, in one of his drunken rages,
that he'd admitted that Samia was incidental to his goal,
and if she didn't allow him to edit her work, her father
would suffer. When she'd fought back in print, he'd accused her father of fraud, and mysterious funds had
started appearing in her father's bank account. When
her mother had discovered that the money she had so
enjoyed spending was a trap, she'd rapidly gone downhill, while Samia's bewildered father had barely put up
a defence at his trial.

Oh, yes, she was perfect princess material, Samia reflected with irony as she climbed out of the bath and grabbed a towel. While Luca was no longer a hot guy lounging in a bar, someone to chat to and spend time with, but master of this ship and a ruler returning to his country. Gaining in princely command with every passing moment. It was hard to see where she fitted into his plans.

Her stomach chose that moment to growl, which brought her down to earth with a bump. She couldn't wait until supper. She was hungry, despite the burger she'd eaten earlier. What were the chances of finding a light snack in the *Black Diamond*'s galley?

There was only one way to find out.

She was determined to remain upbeat, her intention being to quickly ransack the dressing room, find something suitable to wear, and go exploring to find the galley, but when she opened the first drawer and discovered a treasure trove of make-up, she couldn't bring herself to rush. It was as if someone had ordered a high-end cosmetic company's complete range, most of which was still in cellophane-wrapped boxes. This was dress-up with a rocket boost.

After that first discovery, it became a 'no holds barred' trolley dash through every cupboard and drawer. Scarves, purses, costume jewellery and handbags galore were soon scattered about—and how many swimsuits did one person need? Holding up a slinky turquoise number, she realised that whoever had ordered the clothes was about the same size she was. The wardrobes revealed another cache of riches, outfits and evening gowns of a quality she could never afford. Trailing her fingertips across the überdeluxe fabrics, she could only marvel that so many beautiful things had been discarded. Catching sight of herself in the mirror, she laughed. Still wrapped in a towel with her hair all over the place, she looked a sight. 'I am not worthy,' she murmured. But she could wear a cotton sundress…

Right at the back of the wardrobe, she had found a box packed to the brim with a selection of colourful summer dresses. Now it was just a case of deciding which one to wear…

She picked out the plainest frock. It was lovely, actually… Must have slipped through the style police's net: a bright cornflower blue with shoestring straps that tied on the shoulders. The colour matched her optimistic mood, while the dress showed enough of her body without revealing too much. Brushing her hair out until it resembled a fiery cloud, she added a touch of lip gloss and a good lashing of mascara. Why not? This was the first time in a long time she'd felt remotely feminine, or had access to such things. She couldn't do much about her freckles without a bucket of foundation, and she'd have to go barefoot, because none of the sandals she found were either comfortable, or suitable for walking on the deck of a sailing yacht.

Ready!

Staring at herself in the mirror, she wondered how the evening would end. The possibilities were endless—or they might have been, had she been a different person.

Which was the cue for her cheeks to heat up at the thought of Luca touching her…kissing her…

Enough of that! She had a job to do. He must find her one. He had to.

Picking up her notebook, she hugged it close to her chest, but then her grip softened and moved a little, as she began to imagine Luca mapping her breasts, and Luca teasing her promiscuously erect nipples.

Why was her body so eager to lead her into trouble?

Moving on down her ribcage and over her belly, she stopped when she reached the place where his knowing caresses could create a whole world of trouble. Leaving there reluctantly, she trailed her fingertips over thighs tingling just from thinking about him, and went on to rest her hands in the sway of her back, before allowing them to slip even lower to cup her buttocks.

Closing her eyes, she eased back her neck, as certain as she could be that nothing could compare to Luca's touch. Unfortunately, she was equally certain that she'd never find out.

So why not call a halt to all this unnecessary torment? Stop fantasising. Get real!

Not if she had a single functioning brain cell left. Who wanted tepid, when they could have excitement and fire?

Well, that was all well and good, but first she had to exit her make-believe life, and enter the real world where fingers got burned, and excitement could so easily lead to heartache.

A member of the crew dressed all in crisp black directed Samia to the galley. Air-conditioned to a comfortable temperature, the gleaming steel and white space was pristine. A man was lounging against the wall by the cooking station, chatting easily to a chef in whites. A big man. A big hunk of Pirate Prince, looking every bit as dangerous as his sobriquet suggested. He seemed unaware that she'd entered the room.

Wrong.

Luca knew the moment she walked in. 'Welcome,' he said, turning to look at her with a questioning smile. 'Hungry too?'

'One hamburger didn't fill the gap,' she admitted. 'Do you mind if I join you?'

'Not at all.' He scanned her from head to toe, his sharp gaze missing nothing. From his expression, she guessed she looked okay.

'Another hamburger?' he suggested with the hint of a smile that set her heart racing.

'If you just direct me to what I'm allowed to have, I'll sort it out myself,' she said, including the chef. 'I don't want to put you to any trouble. I hope you don't mind me invading your galley?'

My galley, Luca's black stare stated clearly. Pulling away from the wall, he positioned himself between Samia and the handsome young chef.

'I suggest something light,' Luca said, adding, 'and then we'll meet later for a formal dinner on deck.'

'Which will give me a chance to discuss what my job's going to be,' she agreed brightly.

Luca's expression suggested this was not part of his plan.

'Shall I dress for dinner?' she enquired, remaining determinedly upbeat, on the basis that no one wanted to hire a misery.

Luca's hard mouth pressed down and he shrugged. 'I imagine you'd like that.'

She would, but all the gowns she'd found in her dressing room were too sexy, and would put far more of her on show than she was used to. She'd face that problem later, she decided. 'Why don't I prepare something for us to eat?' she suggested. 'Give your chef some time off?'

A flash of something in Luca's eyes said, *This is my galley. This is my crew. Hands off.* Undaunted, she went to wash her hands, and by the time she turned around he'd dismissed the chef. 'I really do need to start paying for my passage,' she explained. 'I'll feel happier if I'm doing something.'

His shrug was one of acquiescence.

'How about pancakes?'

'You're hired,' he laughed.

Her eyes sparkled. 'Then move out of my way.'

Luca watched as she cooked, and then they ate their way through a stack of pancakes with lashings of sugar and lemon, eating at the counter, each with a bottle of beer. Conversation flowed easily, far more easily than she'd imagined, until finally Luca pushed his plate away. 'I'll see you later,' he said as she cleared up, determined to prove herself worthy of being hired.

They settled on meeting again at eight o'clock that evening. 'For dinner beneath a starlit sky,' as he put it with considerable irony.

Who said romance was dead? she reflected with amusement, allowing no emotion to show on her face. But then he did something she had not expected. Reaching across the counter, he brushed some sugar from her lips with the tip of his forefinger, staring into her eyes as he did so. To say her body gave an atomic reaction was probably understating the case. She remained motionless until he stood back, by which time she'd gathered herself enough to say, 'I'll be ready at eight. As will my report.'

'Your report?' he queried, turning on his way to the door.

Her mouth dried. He looked magnificent, such a dark, brooding presence in the steel and white space that she could hardly breathe. 'The report we agreed on? My thoughts on the décor?' she prompted.

He'd been humouring her, she guessed. It was easy to see why Luca had never formed any lasting attachments.

'Your only task tonight,' he informed her, 'is to turn up for dinner at eight o'clock sharp.'

'I'm looking forward to it,' she said mildly, determined not to sacrifice the chance of a job on the altar of her pride. This might be Luca's galley, his yacht and his crew, but she would work her passage, and never bow her head to a man again.

Samia Smith was turning his life upside down. There was such warmth and humour in her eyes, it was hard to resist, but there was also strength and challenge, and that threatened to drive him crazy. Perhaps he'd been spoiled long enough, and it was time to accept that human contact was what he'd been missing. Once he got over his affront, he could see that contact with someone who made no allowance for him being royal was welcome, and much needed. Samia gave her refreshing take on everything, whether he wanted it or not. He'd only really had that sort of understanding with Pietro before, but now this aggravating woman had slipped into his life with her hobnail boots, her flashing eyes, and her complete and utter lack of reverence.

It didn't hurt that she managed to look stunning in a simple blue dress, or that he found her banter appealing. She appeared to be comfortable in any situation, and with anyone, which could only make her an asset to the throne. He was pleased with his choice of bride; his only task now was to convince Samia that he would make her an ideal husband. As a seasoned seaman, he predicted stormy waters up ahead, but as he hadn't enjoyed himself or relaxed as much in a long time, so what?

Heading for his study to examine the contents of the Red Box, he was looking forward to reading about Samia. He needed flesh on the bones of what his team had told him. The two of them didn't have to be close to marry, but it was a bonus to discover a connection real and strong. Even with that, she'd have to realise that Samia would be the one making changes, not him.

CHAPTER SEVEN

WHAT TO CHOOSE...? What to choose?

She felt like a greyhound in the traps as she hovered in her dressing room, wondering what to wear. There were far too many contenders—most of which would make her feel ridiculous—for a formal dinner with Luca. Gowns with barely any fabric, held up on a wing and a prayer, were instantly discarded. The prospect of sitting next to him in one of those held zero appeal. She'd feel a right fool.

In a ferment of indecision, she thought about the hard-working crew. She didn't want to let anyone down by appearing not to care as they did. If they'd gone to the trouble to prepare a special meal, then the least she could do was to get the dress right. Obviously, Luca would look amazing, whatever he chose to wear. He could come wrapped in a towel and still look like a prince.

Actually, that wasn't such a bad idea...

Can the erotic fantasies! There isn't time, she told herself firmly.

Selecting an emerald-green gown, she slipped it from the padded hanger. It was quite bright, and revealing by her standards, but if she was going to do this, she was going to do it properly. She didn't want Luca thinking her a shrinking violet. What use would she be then? If she was going to work her passage, he had to take her seriously.

Stroking the cobweb-fine fabric, she shook her head with sheer bemusement that anyone could afford such intricately worked clothes. The beading alone was extraordinary...so many tiny crystals, and they must all have been sewn on by hand. She had never wanted to spend her ex's money, preferring to remain independent...until he fired her from her job with the promise that she'd never work again.

We'll see about that, she mused, firming her jaw. In clothes, as in life, she had always stayed beneath the radar, except in her column where she'd spoken her mind until her ex had replaced her views with his. He still hadn't destroyed her, as he'd hoped. She was done with apologising. Luca had given her an opportunity to see a new world that she could never have dreamed of, and if she wasted that chance, she'd only have herself to blame.

Finally dressed, she turned this way and that to check her reflection. It would be hard to look bad in such a beautifully constructed gown, and she had to admit to feeling surprised by what the mirror revealed. Now it just remained for Luca to pass judgement. He'd be shocked, she imagined, as this was somewhat different from her scruffy travel clothes and beloved ancient walking boots.

Closing the door behind her, she lifted her chin and strode out.

What a dress! What a night! What a man!

What a once-in-a-lifetime opportunity!

Stepping out of an ice-cold shower that had done little to dull his raging libido, he dried off, cleaned his teeth, parked a shave, and dressed in jeans and the first top he found in the drawer. He was itching to get his hands on the contents of the Red Box, but with a lifetime of Red Boxes ahead of him—and this one wasn't going anywhere—there was a task he had to complete first. He'd come back to dress for dinner after that.

Leaving his suite, he headed for the bridge to issue new instructions. His break from hands-on sailing would last a little longer than he'd intended, though the *Black Diamond* wouldn't be heading straight back to Madlena. First, they would make a stop at a small coastal town in Italy called Portofino, where he could speak to his lawyers to make sure everything was watertight for the prenup Samia would have to sign, as well as one more document she had made necessary. He was a planner who liked to make sure every loose end was tied up. The fiesta in Portofino was wild and fabulous, and he was confident Samia would relax enough once they were there to do as he asked, and for them to get to know each other better. This was essential before he took her to Madlena to meet his people.

Having given his staff new coordinates, he left the bridge and went to his study where the Red Box sat squat and square on his desk. Crossing the room, he extracted the key from his pocket, turned it in the lock, and tucked his finger under the lid. Swiftly riffling through the documents, he pulled out Samia's file. Opening it, he cursed his phone as it rang. Checking the caller, he took the call. A palace official wished to confirm some details concerning Luca's upcoming wedding—to the bride he had yet to propose to.

Accustomed to Luca's brother's much stiffer manner, the courtier asked tentatively, 'You do have a bride, Your Serene Highness? Only you haven't given us a name yet.'

'Discretion is always the best option,' he answered

smoothly. 'I don't want the woman in question hounded by the press. But rest assured my bride does exist.'

Having exchanged the usual pleasantries, he cut the line, then stared at Samia's file, which he had put down on the desk. He'd read it later. It was better to get to know her without bias. Tonight at dinner was the perfect opportunity to do that. In a few short hours, they would moor up in Portofino, where she'd have a chance to relax and reflect on their evening together, by which time he could add whatever she had to tell him to what he'd learn about her in the file. He didn't anticipate any surprises.

It was only later in his dressing room as he adjusted his bow tie that he changed his mind. Cursing at the fiddly strip of cloth as he messed it up yet again, he let it hang loose before finally ripping it off. Reverting to jeans and a shirt, open at the neck with the cuffs rolled back, he raked his hair, which was his one concession to formal grooming. Checking his watch, he saw there was time to read Samia's file after all. Maybe he would.

She felt great, even confident in the exquisite dress as she walked across the deck towards Luca. That was weird in itself, as she'd never worn such a provocative outfit in her life. Flimsy, transparent emerald-green silk chiffon, every inch beaded with tiny shimmering crystals and lined with a nude underskirt to give the illusion that she was naked underneath, was hardly her everyday wear.

She heated beneath his glance. Then he glanced at her again and this time his stare lasted longer. Her gown was split to the waist back and front, with only proper corseting holding it together. Her cheeks were burning red under his scrutiny, but she was determined not to falter. 'Good evening,' she said evenly, relieved she didn't have high-heeled shoes to contend with as well as the figure-hugging dress.

'A very good evening,' Luca agreed, though in a disappointingly cold tone, she thought. How could he be less than enthusiastic about a night like this?

Unless something had happened since she'd last seen him.

'I feel as if I've walked through a cloud of fairy dust,' she said, smiling as she glanced around at their opulent surroundings. The dining table laid out on deck sparkled with crystal and silver, and glowed invitingly beneath the light of flickering candles. If Luca was in a grim mood, it was up to her to bring him around. Being positive and upbeat was the best way to do that. 'What a beautiful evening,' she enthused. 'A velvet sky peppered with stars, and here I am on board a fabulous black yacht slicing through the ocean.'

'Like a steel knife through butter?' he growled.

'Exactly.' She refused to be put off. 'The creak of the sails and the snap of the ropes is the only music anyone would need to make tonight perfect.'

'You think?'

Swallowing deep, she asked, 'May I sit down?'

He made a careless gesture. 'As you please.'

But he did stand politely and hold her chair to see her settled before he sat down again. Then she realised they were alone. Where was the rest of the crew? Were they to serve themselves? That would be nice...

They sat in silence for a while, which gave her the chance to mull over another puzzle. Having told her to dress for dinner, Luca was wearing banged-up jeans with his feet thrust into a pair of simple sandals. But this was the Pirate Prince, she reminded herself, and with forearms like steel girders and his wild hair tossed this way and that, what did she have to complain about? But why didn't he say something? Was she supposed to make all the chat? At least he wasn't pacing the deck. And for once, she wasn't late. *Look on the bright side*, she chided herself. *Stop looking for trouble.* But she had hoped for more.

She picked distractedly at a freshly baked roll. It was hard to maintain her optimism in the face of such obvious disapproval. Why didn't he just tell her he'd changed his mind—didn't want to have dinner with her, didn't want to talk, eat, or even be remotely civil? It was such a comedown after the laugh she'd had in her stateroom, strutting around in the fancy gown, playing the role of supersiren. The only good thing now was the banquet of delicious food laid out on the table that she couldn't face. *Let's hope he lightens up soon*, she reflected, lifting her chin, as determined as ever to make this, her first evening on board the *Black Diamond*, a good one.

Did she have to look quite so beautiful? It was like salt in a wound. He didn't trust himself to react yet. What he'd discovered in her file kept on playing through his mind on a loop.

She was what?

Who?

With a vicious curse, he'd flung the file down on the desk. He'd brought Samia on board with the best of intentions—to make her his bride, a princess, and to lavish her with gifts and a lifestyle she could only dream about. She'd been welcomed with nothing but warmth and friendship, by him and by his crew, and had made the best of impressions within minutes of being on board. Now he felt he'd betrayed his crew, his people and himself, for falling for the oldest trick in the world, which was to be made to believe that everything was exactly as it seemed. Turned out nothing was as it seemed where Samia was concerned. Her wide-eyed, apparently guileless enthusiasm was just an act.

Her file had detailed every significant event in the life of Samia Smith, newly divorced investigative journalist. No wonder his team hadn't sent that news by text. Even worse, she'd been cruelly treated by her ex-husband, her column used by that sorry excuse for a man for his own ends, but what Luca had to ask was, did a leopard ever change its spots?

An investigative journalist?

After his brother's death, he'd tried not to feel anything. There was only space in his heart for grief and guilt. Then Samia had come along, loosening him up, and bringing him back with her zany humour. That humour had lost its appeal now he knew why she'd acted as she had. Having wheedled herself onto his yacht, she had lied by omission. He got that she needed to escape a vindictive ex. He would have helped her, anyway, if she'd explained the situation. But why hadn't she told him she was a journalist? There could only be one reason, and that was to profit from it. She'd seized the main chance like everyone else. Maybe she was not a career courtesan, but she was certainly an opportunist who believed she could take him for a ride. If she imagined she was going to get away with it, she was wrong.

'Luca…?'

The conflict inside him only increased when he drew back to stare into Samia's beautiful, lying face. How dare she look so appealing with that embarrassed expression on her face and a half shrug in her shoulders as she waited for his approval? It was dangerous to like someone as much as he liked Samia. Loving his brother, only to have him ripped away so cruelly, was the only proof he needed of that. It was better to feel nothing. Then there was nothing to lose.

'I look a mess, don't I?' she exclaimed, mouth pressing down in an apologetic smile. To make her point, she ran her hands over the figure-hugging fabric of her gown. 'Go on—you can say it,' she prompted. 'I can take it.' She pulled a comic face. 'This isn't exactly my style, is it?'

Samia thought his only problem with her was her appearance? She looked ravishing. Beyond beautiful, she was either the best actress he'd ever met, or she was seriously damaged, and he feared that the latter was the case, which meant he must protect her. The second part of the report had detailed her abuse at the hands of her husband, which angered him far more than Samia covering up her occupation ever could. But she had deceived him, and he could never forget that, though it was hard to reconcile this ingénue in her party dress with someone who would lie and cheat her way into his affection in order to get a scoop.

Don't the facts speak for themselves? Why else would she seek me out at the bar?

'I disagree,' he said curtly. 'You look beautiful.'

'Do I?' She blushed. 'Don't lie to me.'

Who was lying to whom? He prided himself on his straightforwardness. No matter what she'd done, he would not indulge in a cheap game of tit for tat.

'The gown is beautiful, as are you,' he insisted, though his tone was still clipped.

'The gown is outrageous,' she argued, laughing as her shoulders relaxed at his words. 'I'll probably fall over the fishtail train the moment I stand up.'

'I won't allow that to happen.'

'And as for getting out of it again…?' She grimaced,

while he, sensibly, kept his thoughts on stripping off the gown to himself.

'Please...eat,' he insisted. 'We can talk later.'

They would talk later.

At length.

Her blush deepened as stewards came silently from the shadows to attend them at the dinner table. How much had they heard? As bad as it was to suffer Luca's obvious displeasure, it was worse to think they'd been overheard. That was the price royalty, and those close to royals, must endure, she reasoned. Everything came with a price, and a complete lack of privacy was perhaps the highest price of all to pay.

'The champagne is open.' Luca indicated the misted bottle as a steward removed the cork with barely the faintest pop. 'Would you like a glass?'

'I don't think I should,' she admitted on a short laugh. 'I'm having enough trouble walking in this tight-fitting gown without adding alcohol to the mix.'

'One glass won't hurt,' he said curtly.

And might loosen her tongue enough for her to tell him the truth—that she'd had enough of his moody behaviour, and if he didn't want her here, he just had to say so.

'Thank you. I'll call you if I need anything else,' Luca told the stewards. 'We'll serve ourselves this evening.'

It was hard not to brood on Luca's mood, so to distract them both she produced the report he'd asked for.

'What report is this?' he demanded impatiently.

'The yacht's décor,' she reminded him. 'I'm no expert, but I do have an opinion. I wrote my ideas down longhand. I hope that's all right? My handwriting's not the best, but you should be able to read it...'

'You really have no idea, do you?' he asked.

'About interior décor? No. Honestly, I don't, but I have an opinion, as I said, and I thought that's what you wanted to hear. Anyway, here it is,' she said, pushing it across the table to him.

He brushed it aside. 'I've no time for this. I have something more pressing on my mind.'

'Can I help you with that?'

'Oh, yes, I think you can.'

'I realise you'd rather be sailing,' she agreed, 'than sitting here with—'

'An investigative journalist?' he bit out.

CHAPTER EIGHT

As Samia's jaw dropped on hearing his accusation, he wondered if the cause was innocent shock, or guilt? Either way, she had deceived him, and was continuing to do so. He had to sort this out before anything else could happen. 'Did you seriously imagine I wouldn't find out?'

She tensed as she closed her eyes, and then she released a long, steadying breath. 'It's not what you think.'

'Really?' he challenged, unmoved. 'And what do I think? Or, should I say, what would you like me to think?'

'That isn't fair,' she insisted hotly. 'We met by chance.'

'And I'm supposed to believe that?'

'You gave me the opportunity to get away.'

'Nice story, Samia, but it would have been more honest for you to tell me the truth from the start. Would you care to hear my version of events?'

'I'd like that very much,' she said, lifting her chin.

'Coming across me by accident in that particular bar seems unlikely. I think you were tipped off.'

'By whom?'

'Does it matter?'

'I didn't know anyone in the bar until I met you.'

'So you say.'

'Because it's true.' Firming her jaw, she fired back, 'Next question?'

'You wheedled your way onto my yacht with your story about wanting a job.'

'First off, I didn't *wheedle*,' she told him with a steely look. 'You invited me onto your yacht. And I don't *want* a job. I *need* a job,' she corrected him firmly. 'Which is something you seem reluctant to give me, though I noticed no reluctance on your part when you first invited me to join you on board.'

Not expecting this level of defiance from someone who was so clearly guilty, he leaned in. 'So you won't benefit from your voyage on board the *Black Diamond*? Is that what you want me to believe?'

'Believe what you like. I can't change your mind, but I'd like to know why you're so mistrustful.' Angling her chin, she waited for him to reply, as if he was being grilled now.

'Nice try,' he rapped crisply, 'but don't try and turn this on me.'

Rising, she planted her tiny fists on the table, and, lowering her head, she stared him straight in the eyes. 'I know your brother died, leaving you to pick up the pieces, but I'm not responsible for that tragedy.'

She might as well have slapped him across the face. He recoiled as if she had. No one dared to mention his brother's death to his face. No one intruded on his grief.

'I don't know who's responsible for the tragedy,' she continued grimly, apparently unaware of his mounting fury. 'Since we've met, I've looked back over the old reports about his death on the Internet. There was an embargo on the facts in the press, as I'm sure you know. I strongly suspect you lost your brother the same way I lost my mother, although I don't expect you to admit it. But whatever you've been through—and I know you've been through a lot—you're not the only one. I also know what it's like to lose a loved one—'

She broke off and her mouth worked. She said nothing for quite a while. Samia would be remembering her mother's death, and fighting down her feelings. He remained silent in respect for her grief, even as anger for her deception continued to seethe inside him.

'Whatever you went through doesn't give you the right to hold me to account for your feelings now,' she maintained.

Standing, he slammed his own fists down on the table. 'Enough! We end this now.'

'That would be too easy,' she countered fiercely. Craning her chin, she glared into his eyes. 'How about we both come clean?' she challenged.

Passion couldn't have been higher. The atmosphere they had created between them was thick with unresolved anger. Even the sea breeze that had stiffened into a gusting wind and lashed them remorselessly didn't stand a chance of cooling things down.

'You're hiding something too,' she insisted tightly.

'And you want to write the story,' he derided. One emotion crowned the other, until it was like a lava plug ready to blow.

'How shockingly mistrustful you are,' she accused angrily.

'Do you blame me?'

The tragedy of his brother's death had been shocking enough, but to discover Pietro had taken his own life, and that Luca had not been there to talk him down and help him, was a wound he would endure for the rest of his life. It had ripped the emotional rug from under his feet, leaving him shipwrecked with nothing to cling to but raw passion. And he was done with slamming fists down on a table. Samia had known enough violence in her life. She might rile him like no one else, but what-

ever else he was, or was not, he was no bully. What he'd
learned about Samia and her ex wasn't bland, it wasn't
regular, and it had forced him to balance his relief that she
had escaped an abusive relationship intact with the very
real threat that an investigative journalist presented to
the throne. No royal house could afford to take a cuckoo
into its nest, especially when that cuckoo had direct links
to the media.

'What else did you hope to gain, apart from your
story?' he demanded.

'What are you getting at?' she bit back.

The wind whipped them mercilessly as they stood
glaring at each other. 'Money from your story?' he suggested. 'Or perhaps it was even simpler than that.'

'Meaning?'

'Your ex was rich, but I am richer.'

Shaking her head, she made an incredulous sound.
'That isn't worthy of you, Luca. I'll freely admit my ex-
husband wasn't in your league, but who is? There's extreme wealth and then there's…' She glanced around at
all the accoutrements that went into making a billion-
euro yacht. 'Plus, you have the weight of history on your
side,' she added as she speared him with a furious look.
'As well as a duty to care for your people.'

'Which I fully intend to do,' he gritted out.

'And you think they need protection from me? Or are
you more interested in protecting yourself from a predatory woman?'

'Are you a predatory woman?'

'I'm whatever I need to be,' she admitted with the steel
he was becoming used to. 'But would I knowingly profit
from others? No. I stand on my own two feet, and have
done for years. I made a major mistake when I married
my ex, thinking I could save my parents. But I never

make the same mistake twice, so you can rest assured that if bread and butter is all I can afford, then bread and butter is all I eat.'

'So you're not after my money.'

'Didn't I just say that?'

'And you disapprove of all this…' It was his turn to gesture around.

'It's a completely different world for me,' she admitted, 'but do I disapprove? No. Why should I? You don't expect other people to pay for your pleasure. You've earned it.'

Silence stretched between them. At first it was hostile and tense, but then gradually they both came down from the peak of fury to a sort of understanding.

'I could only dream of sailing a boat like this when I was a boy,' he admitted. 'Madlena was impoverished when my parents came to the throne. They built it into the country it is, but at the start I had no expectation of being entitled to anything beyond what I could earn for myself. If you know anything about me, you should remember that my tech company was a start-up in my bedroom—'

'On a second-hand computer, which you restored,' she supplied.

'So you read up about me as well as Pietro.'

'You don't hold the monopoly on researching those you meet, and I applaud you for refinancing your country to the benefit of your people before you thought of doing anything for yourself,' she said coolly.

'I'm not so bad, after all?'

'Maybe that applies to both of us?' she suggested.

'When were you going to tell me what you did?' he countered. 'What you still do, or hope to continue doing, is my best guess. Or did you intend to hide the fact that you used to write for a national newspaper in the UK, and had an extremely popular and highly respected column?'

'*Used to* being the operative phrase,' she admitted with a rueful huff. 'My ex kicked me out when he had no further use for me, saying I had ten minutes to clear my desk. I was marched out of the building by his security staff like a common thief.'

'When were you going to tell me?' he repeated.

'When the time was right.'

'Pillow talk?'

'Does that sound like me?'

'I don't know too much about you,' he pointed out.

'Or I about you,' she conceded.

'Are you here to spy on me, Samia Smith?'

'No. I am not,' she stated firmly. 'I'll admit I was curious about you, and excited to learn how the super-rich live, but isn't everyone curious about that, and for purely innocent reasons? I didn't set out with the intention to share what I learned with the rest of the world.'

'How can I be sure?'

'You can't,' she said frankly.

'So, you're asking me to believe you came here out of idle curiosity?'

'And to escape,' she reminded him forthrightly. 'My ex was a bully, a very nasty, vindictive man. You don't have to believe me, but that's the truth.'

'And now I must consider the possibility that you have realised the many opportunities that have opened up since you met me, both to re-establish yourself and to further your career. You'd be a fool not to seize that chance.'

'Yet like you, I have principles,' she countered, 'so I guess we both have to learn to trust.'

'You're asking me to trust you not to write about me?'

'As I have to trust you not to hurt me.'

That shocked him more than anything else she might have said. He would never hurt her, but he had to put his country and its people first, which meant he must be sure that his choice of bride was as good as he'd first thought it. 'We'll have to come to an accommodation.'

'Meaning what?' she demanded suspiciously. 'I won't sleep with you to seal the deal, if that's what you think.' And when his brow shot up, she added, 'Sex means a lot more to me than that.'

'Fear and loathing?' She blushed as he said it. 'I've read your file.'

'You had my personal life investigated?'

'Of course,' he admitted. 'This is not just about my personal safety, but the well-being of a country and its people. Our original deal was for you to come on board the *Black Diamond* in search of a job. At no point do I remember inviting you to interview for the post of mistress.' As she visibly swallowed, he knew Samia must be wondering if she had left one bad situation only to walk straight into another. 'It's never been my intention to intimidate you, or force you to remain here with me. My plan has always been to fashion a deal we're both happy to subscribe to.'

'I don't understand what this *deal* is. What do you expect of me? You haven't specified a job yet.'

'For now I ask only one thing, and that is not to tar me with the same brush as your ex.'

About whom he knew everything.

'My lawyers will ensure that—' *that the self-important, pasty-faced barrel of lard my people have described to me would never beat up a woman again* '—he will never hurt you again.' His guts twisted at the thought of Samia trapped in a loveless marriage with such a brute.

'What have you done?'

She looked genuinely frightened, which for Samia was a rare loss of composure. The fiend she'd married had clearly done some serious damage to a woman who deserved so much more.

'Don't look so worried. I'm not a thug and I don't employ criminals so let's just say I have contacts in all the right places, and can promise you that, from this moment on, you will be safe from him.'

She let this sink in for a moment and then asked the obvious question. 'And what do you expect from me in exchange for your protection?'

He let the waters settle before explaining. 'This is not about protection. The word alone makes it sound as if you're a bird trapped in a cage, dependent on me for everything that keeps you alive, when I know you're a tiger that can care for itself perfectly well.'

It took Samia a few moments to realise he was serious, and then she thanked him with a perplexed frown. 'And you?' she said at last. 'How will you deal with having an investigative journalist alongside you on this voyage?'

Their association would last a lot longer than that, if he had his way. But she did have a point. For a stranger, let alone a journalist, to get this close to the Pirate Prince had been thought impossible, and anything Samia could find out would be beyond value to the press. She only had to use him as a headline for her credibility to be restored. She could name her price, choose any newspaper she liked, and have its top people begging her to put her byline on a column.

'I think you're ambitious,' he agreed thoughtfully, 'but not to snare a wealthy husband, or you'd have stayed where you were, and not just for a one-week wonder in the press. I think you're looking for a lot more than that.'

'Of course I am,' she agreed hotly.

'Self-fulfilment and independence,' he mused out loud. 'If you mean I don't look to anyone to support me or to validate me, and that I take pride in working and achieving, and loving and caring, you're right, but to do that I have to be free to be my own person, free of all influence.'

'And intimidation,' he added significantly.

Clouds invaded her eyes, as she no doubt thought back. 'Of course,' she whispered, but she quickly rallied. 'I can't live in a cage, however lush, and I won't *ever* live in fear again.'

There was quite a pause before he felt it was right to intrude on her memories, but then he asked the question uppermost in his mind. 'Could you be a princess?'

Samia gazed at him askance. 'I'm *sorry*?'

'What better way to restore your credibility than with your first-hand story of life with the Pirate Prince?'

'As your wife?' She gasped, incredulous as his meaning sank in. 'You really imagine I'd write about you, if I were your wife?'

An ironic smile crept onto his lips. 'Exactly.'

'And we were just starting to get back on an even keel. Why did you have to spoil it?' she demanded with a tense laugh. 'Except, of course, I know you're teasing.'

'Who said I'm teasing?'

'You are. You have to be. Unless you've gone completely crazy.'

'Portofino tomorrow,' he stated evenly. 'There's a fiesta. That should lighten things up.'

Samia's tolerant sigh said it would take a lot more than a party to persuade her that his suggestion was anything more than a joke.

CHAPTER NINE

'THE FIESTA WILL be hectic,' Luca had warned her as he stood up from the table that night. 'You'll need a good night's sleep...'

She was supposed to sleep after what he'd said? *Princess* Samia? It didn't even sound right. Turning over in bed for the umpteenth time, she punched her hapless pillow into submission. As she did so, she saw the glorious emerald-green gown, discarded where she'd stepped out of it. The beading glistened in the moonlight as if mocking her attempt to turn into an irresistible siren overnight. 'Well, that fell flat,' she muttered, flopping over so she didn't have to look at the gown. She'd had more success with a cotton dress!

A smile crept onto her mouth at the thought. Wasn't that a point in Luca's favour? He didn't even have to try. Snug-fitting jeans, and a shirt caressing his immensely powerful shoulders—why, even his feet looked sexy in a pair of cheap sandals he'd probably picked up at a market. But it was his eyes that really did the damage. They shot heat straight to her core. It was as if he'd cast an erotic net and she had swum right into it, she mused as she snuggled lower in the bed. Every part of her body had responded with approval, whether he chose to be pleasant or not. And they had got heated last night. Though, they'd mellowed out after he'd told her she would live fear-free from now on. That was worth everything. But then he'd had to go and spoil it with that ridiculous suggestion. Princess indeed! And he'd probably be sleeping like a baby...

That was all she remembered until someone hammered on her door.

'Get up, if you want to visit Portofino,' Luca called out.

'Give me half an hour,' she called back groggily. 'I'll see you on deck.'

'Ten minutes,' he called back, 'and then we're leaving with or without you.'

The day was young and undecided, but the sound of Luca's voice was the only encouragement she needed to leap out of bed and rush to the shower. She didn't even bother to dry her hair. Having towelled it, she raked it with her fingers and heaped it on top of her head. Shoving a clip in to hold it in place, she turned to the sink, where cleaning her teeth took a lot longer than doing her hair. *Well, you never know...*

Yes, she did, Samia lectured her inner voice patiently. Luca was indulging her with this invitation to visit Portofino, but that didn't mean there were kisses in store.

Worse luck, she mused wryly as she slicked on some lip gloss. She'd been dreading all contact with men, but Luca had succeeded in filling her with a simmering hunger, as well as a desperate need to discover if things could be different—if *she* could be different—when it came to full-on sex.

Perhaps it was just as well she had no time to progress those thoughts.

Slipping on another sundress from the hoard in the box at the back of the wardrobe, she grabbed a purse that sighed mournfully, rather than chinked merrily. It

couldn't be helped. At least she didn't have to pay for the
lift to and from shore.

Shoving her feet into a pair of flip-flops she'd found
alongside the box of sundresses, she headed out, by which
time she was bubbling with excitement at the thought of
spending the day with Luca, and exploring a new place
together.

Luca was cool. His crew was around, she reasoned,
and he hadn't exactly fussed over her last night. Which
was how she liked it, she told herself firmly. What he'd
said about keeping her safe was far more important. And
it meant she didn't have to face her greatest fear. It was
one thing fantasising about Luca introducing her to a
better kind of sex, and another thing actually doing it.
Anyway, he didn't seem interested in exacting that sort
of payment for the voyage, which was a relief.

Was it?

The Pirate Prince looked hotter than ever this morning
in a pair of black surf shorts and a form-fitting, sleeveless top that showed off his muscles to perfection. One
day, maybe she'd find the courage to forget the humiliation of failure as far as the bedroom went, and find
something fulfilling in the experience with someone she
really cared about…someone who understood her fears.
She could only dream that might be Luca. But reality
was never that kind.

As before, he took charge of making sure she was
safely transferred over the churning sea from the *Black
Diamond* to the rolling powerboat. He steadied her with
his hand on her forearm while she made the transition,
and his touch was like an incendiary device to her senses.
It made her pulse race and her breathing quicken—which
he noticed, of course.

'Are you scared or excited?' he asked as she staggered to the prow on the bucking boat under his guidance.

'I'm neither scared nor excited. Well, maybe a little excited,' she conceded.

'Only a little?'

Her body heated instantly at the sight of a glimmer of a smile on his mouth. Luca only had to look at her like that for years of doubt and dread to melt away, to be replaced by a throbbing yearning. Her dress was thin, and her body was a notoriously unreliable keeper of secrets, so, however much she tried to brazen it out, the brush of his arm against hers caused her nipples to tighten, while her lips felt swollen and tender beneath the tip of her tongue.

Clearing her throat, she told him briskly, 'You must tell me if I can be of any help on shore.'

'Fetching and carrying? Or did you have something else in mind?'

'I don't care so long as I'm earning my passage.'

'Keep me entertained,' he said in a disappointingly disinterested tone. 'That's your only job today.'

'Court jester?' she suggested.

To her relief, Luca's dark gaze flared briefly with something that might have been humour. 'If the cap fits.'

'I'll only wear it if it's got bells on it.'

'That can be arranged.' His lips twitched. He almost cracked a smile.

By the time they disembarked in Portofino, he'd decided to stay an extra day. He'd been on the move long enough, and so had Samia. The small town had lost none of its picturesque charm in all the years he'd been coming here, and he wanted to show her around. For someone who'd been trapped in London in a loveless marriage, the starburst of exuberance that unfolded in front of them could only be the best possible tonic. If he wanted a bride and he wanted that bride to be Samia, uninterested as he had always been in prolonging any relationship, or even working on it, this was worth it... She was worth it. Better used to *arrangements* swiftly made between him and an experienced woman—with no need for preliminaries, because they both chose to cut straight to the chase— he knew that would never be enough to convince Samia to marry him. In fact, it would probably have the opposite effect. She'd need more than a nice meal and sex. A lot more, he reflected, taking in her shining eyes as she viewed the scene.

The tiny harbour town of Portofino was bathed in sunshine when they arrived. The sky was unrelieved blue, while the fresh sea air was filled with the scent of blossoms cascading exuberantly over wrought-iron balconies. As they approached the main area lined with cafés, she was greeted by the signature scent of the region, which was lemon in all its various guises. Every table they passed seemed to be decorated with lemons and lemon leaves, both as a symbol of the region and to entice the customer to sit down and linger a while.

'Drink?' Luca invited.

'Yes, please.'

He ordered the ingredients for a local speciality, which was lemon juice, sugar, or sweetener, and fresh spring water, which the customers were left to mix themselves to taste. A jug of ice was delivered to the table, and half the fun was agreeing how much of each ingredient they should add. It was hard to be tense while she and Luca were arguing over the best recipe.

'Taste,' he instructed, holding the glass to her lips.

'Delicious!' He was definitely more pirate than prince today—and the drink was tasty too. 'But mine is better,' she insisted.

Leaning over, Luca took a sip. 'Not bad,' he conceded.

'Mine's better,' she threw back with a smile.

He leaned forward, his dark eyes smouldering into hers, and for the briefest moment she wondered if he was going to kiss her, but then he stood and went to pay the bill. Luca was playing her as a virtuoso might play a violin, she thought as she admired his back view. The Pirate Prince was impossibly attractive. As well as tricky to deal with, she concluded as she stood up, and he politely moved her chair away so they could continue their tour of Portofino.

She decided within the first hour that the fiesta was a full-on ravishment of the senses. The town was very pretty with its big wide square, cobbled streets leading off, and a walkway around the bay, lined with tiny boutiques, bars and restaurants. Festooned with bunting and banners, and with several bands competing for an audience, it was the noisiest and most wonderful celebration. Crowded with people of all ages, dressed in their best beneath mellow sunshine, and with stallholders calling out their wares, everyone was smiling. The scent of fresh bread, still warm from the oven, made her mouth water as they passed a stall, while other stalls boasted cheeses and cakes, as well as ice cream that made her sigh with anticipation. Having Luca at her side was like the icing on the thick slice of panettone, the sweet buttery fruit-filled bread he insisted she must try.

The crowds thickened as they walked on, and then he

stopped outside a lawyers' office. 'These people act for me,' he explained.

'Would you like me to wait outside?'

'No. You come in,' he said.

Nice of him not to keep her waiting on the street, she thought as he opened the door of a very traditional-looking office, full of mahogany panelling, tiled floors, and the evocative scent of beeswax. 'Do you have an appointment?'

'They're expecting me. And you as well.'

'Me?' she exclaimed with surprise.

'I'd like you to sign something.'

Of course.

She met his gaze and held it levelly. 'A non-disclosure agreement?' she guessed.

'Do you have any objections?'

'None.' But she wished he'd trusted her enough to discuss it with her first. But then again, why should he? She'd kept the truth about being an investigative journalist from Luca, until he'd uncovered the information for himself, so she could hardly refuse his request now.

The wood-panelled room they were shown into boasted no distracting views of the sea. Instead, it was a small space for a keen mind to work in. The lawyer explained exactly what she was about to sign, and insisted on taking her through the agreement line by line.

She was actually very happy to sign it, thinking it might release a lot of tension that had built up between her and Luca.

'I'm sorry I had to ask you to do that,' he said stiffly as they stepped back into the lemon-scented air.

'It's fine. I totally understand your reasons.'

'Well, thank you for being so understanding.'

It was tense for a while after that, and she felt it was

up to her to lighten the mood. 'Let's move on,' she suggested, meaning more than just walking down the street.

'Agreed,' Luca said.

For the rest of the day he was the perfect companion, and proved to be as competitive as she was, when it came to the shooting gallery and some of the other stalls. They tried all the games, even the coconut shy, where she proved to have quite an accurate aim, which meant they left the pitch laughing with their arms full of fluffy toys. 'This must be quite a change from your high-tech empire?'

'Something to remember when I return home,' Luca agreed.

'The children of Madlena would love something like this fiesta.'

Taking that as his cue, Luca began to hand out the toys they'd won to parents walking by.

'Job well done,' she said when he returned to her side.

'How about dancing?'

She had two left feet, but why not? There were a lot of things she wanted to do with Luca Fortebracci, but luckily she had more sense. Dancing was safe.

Or she had always thought it was.

The moment she stepped into Luca's arms, everything else faded away. There was barely time for the vague impression that they were standing close on a tightly packed dance floor to register before Luca's arms were wrapped around her with no pretence at keeping things the right side of safe. She couldn't think straight. She didn't want to think at all. All that mattered was remembering how this felt, and carrying those feelings forward into the future to keep her company when she was alone again. The rhythm of the band was sultry, and the melody tugged at her heart. It made her want things she couldn't have, like Luca, and like being part of one of the happy families milling around them. Why couldn't life be like this all the time?

Because then you wouldn't appreciate moments like these, she told herself impatiently, wishing she weren't such a softie beneath her protective shell, and could let her tears fall freely. She wasn't sad. This was too much happiness. No strings, no expectation on either side, no titles, no nobodies, just Samia and Luca enjoying a dance in the village square.

She acted cool, but was secretly thrilled when Luca kept his arm looped loosely around her waist as the band segued from one tune to another. Her imagination got to work right away... Luca tightening his grip, claiming her, caring for her, loving her.

'You okay?' he asked, as she gave an unintentional, but decidedly blissful sigh.

This girl doesn't do begging, she reminded herself as Luca stared down into her face, their lips just inches apart. But she did do a lot of dreaming, and no one could stop her doing that.

Having Samia in his arms as they danced had sharpened Luca's senses to an almost painful degree. Their bodies brushed lightly as they moved to the music. He made sure that was all they would do. He could wait. The longer he waited, the hungrier they would be, and pleasure should never be rushed. When Samia came to him, he wanted her wild with need and full of trust. He wanted to meet that tiger caged inside her and feel its claws. After another hour or so of the fiesta, they'd return to the ship. His lawyers knew to expect him again the following morning, when he would be ready to make arrangements to ensure that his return to Madlena would be with a bride.

Today was for relaxing, so Samia was in the right frame of mind when he made his formal proposal.

She sighed as the band stopped playing and laid down their instruments to take a break. 'I don't want this to end.'

She looked so innocent and happy, he could almost believe this was a conventional courtship. 'Would you like to return to the yacht for dinner?'

'More food?' She laughed.

'You could wear another of those fabulous gowns.'

'Or shorts?' she proposed as they began to stroll back towards the quay. 'To be honest, I feel silly in those dresses.'

'Well, you don't look silly,' he said firmly. 'You look like a princess.'

She gave an incredulous laugh. 'That'll be the day.'

He decided not to pursue the princess theme as they walked back. All that mattered was that Samia was happy and relaxed, her eyes bright with anticipation at the thought of the night ahead. He realised he was beginning to care for her. She suited his purpose when it came to his hunt for a bride, but it was something more than that that made him smile.

They didn't make it as far as their respective staterooms. Something had changed between them. For him, it was unrequited lust and extreme pain in the groin region, while for Samia it was possibly an expression of relief at signing the non-disclosure agreement, which meant they could put their differences behind them and move on, though he liked to think it might be lust on her part too.

They stood side by side but not touching on board the powerboat taking them back. They boarded his yacht without incident, but a tension he knew only too well had started building. It seemed like the most natural thing on earth to link their fingers as they began to walk through the ship. Their steady pace didn't last long, and soon he was pulling her along behind him as if their lives depended on it.

CHAPTER TEN

HER THROAT WAS dry with excitement, her breathing all over the place. This was wrong. *This was right.* She didn't know what the heck it was, but if she waited for the right moment to come along, it might never happen. And if it did, but not with Luca, would she regret missing out for the rest of her life?

Walls, doors, companionways rushed past. Everything became a blur. Then he stopped dead and, whirling her around, he pinned her to the wall with his fists planted either side of her head. She was still in midyelp of surprise when his black eyes asked one question: *Do you want this?*

Having seen all he needed to, Luca continued to lead her on down the corridor. When they reached the companionway leading to the upper deck, he went ahead, and then stopped and turned to face her. Without the slightest hesitation she moved into his arms. Lifting her, he shouldered his way into the first door they came across. Kicking it shut behind them, he secured the lock. Carrying her across a glorious, jewel-coloured Persian rug, in what was a very smart-looking office, he lowered her onto the desk. Nudging his way between her legs, he made her cry out with pleasure at his first touch, and that was just his thigh brushing against her. There was no mistaking

how much he wanted her. Moving deeper, he dipped at
the knees and slowly drew himself up again, so she could
enjoy the full benefit of his erection. Beneath the placket
of his surf shorts, she could feel every inch of his firm
length and incredible breadth. The prospect of knowing
him intimately drew a whimper of excitement from her
throat. The wealth of hard muscle beneath her hands,
together with Luca's knowing attention to that sensitive
place between her legs, gave her an overload of sensation, and before she could stop herself she lost control.

'That's good,' he breathed as she bucked helplessly in
his arms while pleasure rampaged through her body. She
cried out in time to each exquisite spasm, until finally
they subsided and she collapsed, gasping with shocked
delight in Luca's arms.

There was no brushing of lips or tender exploration,
and none needed. Luca drove his mouth down on hers,
and she responded with matching fire. No longer two
people reeling from the unexpected hand of cards that
life had dealt them, a woman fearful of penetrative sex,
and a man mourning the loss of his brother, they were
feral creatures in the prime of life feeding greedily off
each other's hunger.

'I want more,' she gasped, writhing and thrusting to
prove it. Having been denied any semblance of enjoy-
ment in the physical side of marriage, she was desperate to try everything Luca could teach her. The urge to
pleasure him in return was just as strong. Slipping her
hands beneath his top, she pulled up the fabric to kiss
his hot skin. Tanned, salty, and hard with muscle, Luca
was everything she'd expected and more, and the taste of
him pushed her arousal higher. He responded by tugging
down the straps of her sundress to expose her breasts,
but even though she strained towards him, he denied her

his touch where she wanted it, and only teased her with kisses on her neck, and on her shoulders.

'Oh, please, more,' she begged, feeling as if her nipples were screaming for attention.

Luca laughed softly, down deep in his throat, while she urged him on with guttural sounds of need. The way he used his tongue and teeth to tease her mouth, her lips, made heat flash to her core. She was as hungry as if she hadn't experienced the ultimate pleasure only minutes before. It still wasn't enough. She had to feel him skin to skin.

A cry of excitement escaped her throat when Luca ripped off his top and flung it across the room. Holding his fierce stare, she issued a challenge of her own. Pulling her dress over her head, she dared him to mock her as her ex had. *They'll bruise your knees when you're older*, he had used to sneer, referring to her generous breasts, but Luca was openly admiring.

'Magnificent...' he whispered, cupping them and weighing them appreciatively as he chafed her nipples with the lightest of touches.

Throwing her head back, she moaned, 'More...'

'Don't worry, I haven't finished with you yet,' he promised as a sigh of pure pleasure shuddered out of her.

'I need this,' she somehow managed to gasp.

'I know it,' he confirmed huskily.

He understood her need and his voice was pure seduction in itself. When he reached for the catch on her bra, she shifted position to help him. Wriggling out of it, she made his job easy, but if there was one thing she had learned about Luca, it was that he was never predictable. Her knickers were discarded next, and, dropping to his knees in front of her, he parted her legs and brought them to rest on his shoulders. With a groan of anticipation, she relaxed back onto the desk, leaning on her forearms for support. Papers went flying this way and that, and a big red box went crashing to the ground. 'Leave it,' Luca growled as he supported her buttocks to lift her to his mouth.

He was right. Nothing mattered. Nothing could, she reflected dazedly as she drifted into a world where pleasure ruled. Could she survive this? She wondered as Luca explored her with his tongue. The sensation was indescribable. How did he know how to do this, and to do it so well? She ground her body against his mouth, knowing there was no hope of holding on, and no reason to, so she didn't even try. Her world shattered into a rhythmical starburst explosion of sensation, while she cried out as each pulse of pleasure gripped her, with her fingers laced through Luca's hair.

'More?' he suggested wryly when she was finally quiet.

What do you think? banged in her brain, but she couldn't drag in enough air to say the words. The best she could do was to express herself in sensual sounds of need.

'Empty your mind and relax every muscle,' he instructed as he spread her legs wide.

'Yes,' she agreed eagerly. She would agree to anything now.

'Don't hold back,' he advised.

As if she could!

Closing her eyes and thinking of nothing but sensation intensified the experience. Taking his time, Luca teased her back to a state of full arousal where he kept her suspended until she was as hungry for pleasure as if she'd never been fed.

'So, so good,' she gasped as he upped the pace of his

mind-shatteringly skilful lapping. Changing his grip on her buttocks so he could use one hand to pleasure her, he lifted her to a new level with delicate feather-light strokes of his finger pad. That, added to the exquisite pressure of his tongue, tipped her over the edge again, and she fell, shrieking with relief as each powerful pleasure wave gripped her.

She was still hazy minded with the afterglow when he gathered her into his arms. He didn't say anything, he didn't need to, he just held her and stroked her, and kissed her as he soothed her down.

'We will talk later,' he promised in a tone she'd never heard him use before. 'But take your time,' he added gently, 'I won't rush you.'

'Into what?' she asked with a frown.

Pulling back, she stared deep into Luca's eyes. She was calm, and she was drowsy and contented, but when someone went out of his way to be considerate, her past history made her suspicious. Her ex had been a perfect example. When he wanted something, he could be particularly nice. What did Luca want?

'I won't rush you into dinner,' he explained with one of his dangerous smiles.

'Okay.' But something still niggled at the back of her mind.

Scooping up her clothes, Luca held them while she dressed. She couldn't fault him for politeness. Her only concern was that everything seemed to be happening in such a rush. Getting to this stage in a relationship took weeks usually, but with Luca her control was out of the window.

'I'll see you at dinner,' he said as he turned for the door, 'and we'll talk.'

The offer was both a promise and a puzzle. What did

he want to talk about? Her job on board? He seemed in no hurry to assign her any duties.

A leisurely bath and a good think were called for, she decided, to work out where she was going from here. Luca's expression gave her nothing to worry about. It was warm, sexy, brooding…and settled, as if she had inadvertently answered a question. Had he thought she was frigid too? And was that the only thing on his mind? She wasn't frigid, but she was frightened of penetrative sex, and with good reason. Her ex had been a brute and a bully with no thought for anyone but himself.

'Shall I escort you back to your cabin?' Luca suggested, resting his hand lightly on her shoulder.

His comment shook her out of these thoughts and returned a smile to her face. 'I can still walk—just.'

'Don't get lost,' he cautioned, matching the warmth of her smile.

Too late. She was already lost. Now they'd started down this road, she wasn't interested in detours.

Her mood had changed by the time she reached her suite. A feeling of uncertainty was growing. She wanted Luca with a fierce longing, while common sense told her it could never be. His joke about her being a princess was just that—his idea of humour. Why he even wanted to keep her around was a bit of a mystery. It wasn't as if he'd got anything out of their sexual encounter. For her it was an exercise in trust. Giving herself…showing her most vulnerable self to Luca in that moment of release was huge. Trust in another human being didn't come bigger than that. Her ex had planted so many seeds of self-doubt inside her, but if she were that frigid, overweight pain in the ass he'd always called her, why did Luca want to be with her? There could be no faking that run through the ship, when hunger for each other had gripped them equally. And why would he trouble to give her so much pleasure and demand nothing for himself? She'd seen no mockery in his eyes, heard no scathing note in his voice. There hadn't been a single unkind comment. Quite the opposite, in fact.

Throughout everything, she remained a hopeless romantic, she decided, while Luca was a pragmatist with a disciplined, logical mind. Was she just another of the Pirate Prince's casual love affairs, and, if that were the case, was she happy to stick around until he tired of her? That didn't strike her as being captain of her ship and taking her destiny into her own hands.

Maybe she should cut them both some slack, Samia concluded. There was huge change looming in Luca's life. Of course he was living every day to the full. He had advised her to do the same, so why didn't she?

Sex was an exercise at which Luca excelled, and that was all it had ever been to him in the past. Samia had changed that, changed him. He had never been so determined to pleasure a woman, or felt so consumed by desire that common sense had deserted him. The deal between them was supposed to be straightforward, an agreement that brought benefits to both parties. He gained a bride to reassure his people that his days of rampaging were over, while Samia was free to do as she pleased. Free from fear of her ex-husband, who was already being dealt with by Luca's lawyers, and free from money worries for the rest of her life. She would join him in Madlena as a princess of that country for as long as it suited them both.

All well and good so far, but what he hadn't factored into his plan was caring for her to this extent. And now it was too late. Samia in the throes of passion had changed her, but it had also changed him. Her vulnerability in those moments had touched him. After all she'd been through, she had chosen to show her raw self to him. He'd always been able to switch off his feelings before. Why couldn't he do that now? As a child, he had quickly come to understand that he could never be as precious as his brother, the heir. Pietro had helped him to accept this, and when their parents were killed, and first his grandmother, and then Pietro had assumed responsibility for Luca's welfare, Luca's main aim had been not to put any additional burden on his brother. That was why he'd chosen a career in special forces, while Pietro had taken the role that would eventually suck the lifeblood out of him.

He'd been out of the country on yet another covert mission when Pietro took his own life. His brother's note had explained that the pressure of ruling a country was too much for him, and that Luca would make a far better Prince than he had. Luca lived with that guilt, and it made his concern for Samia all the more intense. He'd been on the point of proposing when she broke apart in his arms, but, remembering how impatient he'd often been with his brother when Pietro had doubted himself, he couldn't rush something so important now. Samia was so much more than he'd thought her, but instead of intimacy clearing his head, as it usually did, she had only doubled his distractions. Outwardly vulnerable, even prim, she had a very different side to her character, and he was more determined than ever to set that part of her free.

The discovery of a simple column of ivory silk tucked away between all the glitz and glamour hanging in her dressing room thrilled Samia. Sleeveless and ankle-length, with a boat neck that exposed her shoulders rather than her breasts, it had a split up one side, but only to just above the knee. The fabric felt lovely, and as light as air as she slipped it on over a lacy bra and thong.

She found Luca at the bow rail, dressed in jeans and a top. His hair was still damp from his shower, and the stubble that had abraded her mouth when he'd kissed her was thicker than ever. Swinging around at her approach, he exclaimed, 'Excuse my appearance. I've been up the mast making repairs, and I lost track of time.'

And must have ripped off his clothes and dived under the shower, she mused, picturing the scene as she took in his glorious body.

'You look amazing,' he commented matter-of-factly.

'You like the dress?'

'It's a great improvement on the sparkling cucumber you wore last time.'

She laughed and relaxed. 'That green dress must have cost a fortune.'

'Then someone clearly wasted their money—and I'm sorry to say that was me. While *this* vision of loveliness...' walking up close, he took hold of her hands and held out her arms to admire her chosen outfit '...is worth every penny.'

The touch of his lips on hers, his hands on her body, his clean man scent, and warm minty breath and the fire in his dangerous black eyes were everything she could ever want. When Luca kissed her, she felt complete. He stirred her emotions and filled her with fire.

'I thought we'd eat here on deck,' Luca said, indicating the comfortable casual seating area. 'We can serve ourselves beneath the stars.'

'Perfect.' What could be better, especially when they were both so relaxed?

But he got down to business right away. 'I hope you

haven't had second thoughts about signing that document?' he said as they sat down.

Yes, it niggled. She'd be lying if she denied it. She didn't like being thought of as untrustworthy, but she could see that Luca had to protect himself and his country. 'I can't say I like the necessity of it,' she admitted, 'but if I were you, I'd think it a wise precaution.'

'But you're not me, so how do *you* feel?'

She told him frankly in two caustic words, and he laughed.

'Do you forgive me?' he asked.

'Maybe,' she offered, curving a smile. 'We'll have to see.'

'In the meantime, shall we eat?' he suggested.

As he spoke, Luca teased her lips with a slice of ripe peach, and one thing led to another. Kisses had never been so sweet and delicious as two people shared one slice of peach.

When he sucked peach juice from her mouth she felt a corresponding tug down low in her belly. Then he found the fastening on her gown. Her emotions were all over the place. How could life be so cruel as to allow them to meet, when she was patently unsuited to romancing a prince?

'Hey,' Luca whispered, his lips very close to her mouth, 'anyone would think you were distracted.'

'I am,' she admitted, gasping as he found her nipples through her dress and began to tease them. 'Please stop,' she begged, laughing and moaning with pleasure all at one and the same time.

'You're very sensitive there,' he approved. 'What about here?'

She sucked in a breath as his hand began to work between her legs. Using just his thumb at first, he rubbed gently, but persuasively until his forefinger took over using a more direct approach.

'You know I can't hold on,' she wailed.

'Can't you?'

He sounded so matter-of-fact as he continued to work his magic. 'Relax and open your legs a little more for me,' he instructed.

Obedience was vital and she did so immediately, and was instantly rewarded with the most powerful release yet. It was a long time later when she was finally able to speak, but before she could say anything he began to touch her again. And now it was impossible to concentrate on anything else.

When the waves of her next climax subsided, there was something she had to say.

'I've thought of a way to pay you back.'

'You have? When did I give you the chance to think about that?'

'Earlier,' she chastised softly, 'while I was getting ready for tonight. I thought I could write something for your tourist board to promote Madlena. Advertise the country and its assets.'

She didn't know if she was pleased or not when Luca paused and lifted his head to tell her he thought it a very good idea.

'Well, thank you, kind sir.'

'You're welcome. Now, please allow me to enjoy the rest of my supper...'

CHAPTER ELEVEN

As Samia parted her lips in surprise, he drove his mouth down on hers. She tasted of milk and honey, and it was harder by the minute to remember this was leading to a marriage of convenience. Samia didn't know that yet, although the arrangements were already well under way in Madlena. Meanwhile, her capacity for pleasure seemed endless, which pleased him, and boded well for his scheme.

'Let's go,' he murmured as he soothed her down again and then helped her straighten her dress.

'Yes,' she whispered as he lifted her into his arms.

Her gown was little more than a wisp of material, but even that was a barrier to Samia's lithe and eager body. He wanted nothing more than to rip it off, but was forced to curb the impulse as they crossed the public part of his yacht. Once they were enclosed in opulent silence out of public view, he shifted her position to kiss her, while she clung to him with fingertips made of steel. 'Bed, now,' he growled.

'Or even sooner,' she whispered as he dipped his head to kiss her again. 'Can your crew spare you?'

'I've sorted the problem. They just have to check the sails. This is the real emergency.'

She laughed as he strode on to his stateroom. Shouldering the door, he carried her in. Kicking it closed behind them, he took her zip down and sloughed the dress from her shoulders. 'Step out of it,' he said softly. 'Please,' he added huskily when she gave him a challenging look.

He was beyond impatient to feel her soft warmth yielding beneath him, but willed himself to remain calm. His reward was seeing the need on her face as her shoulders relaxed. She was barefoot and beautiful, and now completely naked; it was Samia's turn to challenge him. 'Undress,' she ordered.

They faced each other. 'You take them off,' he invited. Holding his arms out at his side, he waited. She hesitated a couple of seconds as her desire to strip him warred with a woman who'd been cruelly robbed of enjoying union with a man by her bully of an ex. His will to protect her surged again, even stronger than before.

With no idea of the forces she was unleashing, she began in true Samia style with his belt buckle. 'Stop. This is not the way things should be.'

'How should they be?'

She looked so bewildered, he brought her into his arms. 'Like this,' he said. Kissing her gently, he set her down on the bed. Everything had been racing towards an inevitable conclusion, but suddenly she wrapped her arms around her naked chest and crossed her legs for good measure, hiding her face in her knees. He had never seen a sadder picture. 'If you've changed your mind...' easing his neck, he shrugged '...there's nothing wrong with that. You're frightened. I get it.'

'A little,' she admitted in a small voice.

At that moment, he would have liked to take the individual responsible for doing this to her by the scruff of his neck and bring him to his knees in front of Samia to beg for her forgiveness. 'Did he hurt you very badly?'

'Yes.'

He could barely hear her. 'Every time?'

'Every time,' she confirmed in the faintest of voices.

Gritting his teeth, he lay down beside her and gathered her into his arms. Compared to this, his turmoil was nothing. His emotions had been battered? Not in comparison to Samia's. Any move he made now would feel like a violation. He had to re-evaluate everything.

'Luca?'

'Don't. Don't look at me like that. There's no cause for you to be embarrassed.'

'I've done nothing wrong?' she suggested with a sad little twist of her mouth. 'You must be wondering if you can trust anything I say.'

'No. I believe you.'

'I was running away from his thugs when I blundered into that bar,' she said softly. He stilled, knowing she needed to have someone listen to her. 'He's on his honeymoon with his new young wife, having left instructions to make sure I had a good time too. The only difference is that a good time for me in his eyes is as much pain and suffering as he can inflict. And anyone I turn to will receive the same treatment.' She shook her head in despair and her eyes were stricken as they stared into his. 'I've put you in danger, but I was desperate. I wasn't thinking—'

'You were thinking,' he insisted. 'You needed to get away. And you've put no one in danger, least of all me.'

'He texted me the details of how he'd like to see me beaten up,' she continued, staring blindly into some scene of horror. 'He said I'd never find a hole small enough to hide in.'

Nice, he thought, grinding his jaw. What type of moron did that to a woman, to anyone? Remaining silent, he let

Samia talk. This was therapy for a wounded mind. Her profession was immaterial. All he cared about was the well-being of his bride.

'He could never let go of anything he'd once owned,' she was saying, almost as if speaking to herself. 'Goodness knew, I had enough opportunity to learn that while we were together, but I was blind to it, thinking only that I'd lost my mother and now I had to save my father. I left when my father went to prison where my ex couldn't harm him. I know my father wasn't totally blameless, but he was weak, and that monster took advantage of him. I thought I could protect him, but I was wrong.'

'How were you supposed to stand up to a bully and protect your father, when you could hardly protect yourself?'

'I didn't think. I just knew I had to help him, and I tried.'

'You did your best,' he reassured her, 'and that's all any of us can do.'

'Then, you came along, and yes, while I genuinely didn't know who you were at first, I did see an opportunity to figure out my next move while I was safely away at sea on your yacht.'

He let the silence hang, and then he said, 'Thank you for your honesty. And, for the record? Not all men are the same.'

Relaxing a little, she looked into his eyes. 'I know that now.'

Standing up, he covered her with the sheet and tucked her in, so every inch of her body was covered. He couldn't bear to see her looking so vulnerable. She had nothing to apologise for. It was her ex-husband who should hang his head in shame. Samia was a survivor, and had proved this time and time again. 'I think we both need to take a few deep breaths and step back,' he said.

'What if I don't want to?' she whispered.

When he studied her face, he saw the same appeal that stabbed his heart each time he looked at her. Would this feeling vanish in time, or was it something to build on?

'You're welcome to sleep here,' he told her. 'I'll take a guest suite.'

'Must you?' She held out her hand to him.

'Yes. But first I have a question to ask you.'

'Go on…'

'Marry me.'

'I'm sorry?'

'Marry me. I'll keep you safe, and you'll be doing me a favour.'

Blood drained from her face. 'No,' she told him in a shocked voice.

'No?'

'Do you seriously think I would leave one disaster behind only to walk blindly into another?'

'It would be a sensible arrangement.'

'*Sensible?*' Her expression turned from shock to anger. 'Is that all I am to you? A convenience? I almost believed you.' Her voice broke. Shooting up in bed, she quickly covered herself again, remembering she was naked. 'I think you'd better leave.'

'My room?'

'All right. I'll leave.' Grabbing the sheet, she stumbled out of bed. He reached out to steady her. She knocked his hand away. 'Don't touch me! Don't even look at me! I'll never forgive you for this!'

Throwing his head back, he roared in agony as she left, slamming the door behind her. To say this situation was new to him would be putting it mildly. If he wanted to keep Samia on side, he'd have to act fast, or he might just lose the best thing that had ever happened to him.

She took a shower, which gave her the chance to reflect on Luca's proposal. It was hard to believe he was serious. How could he be? Why choose her? Did he think her so malleable and such a fool that she would marry simply for advantage? Was that what people did in royal circles? Maybe, but it would never be enough for her. But she refused to hide away here. She would confront him. She'd tried and failed to save her father, but she would not fail this test. This was the new Samia. Luca might wield all the power in the world, but she would stand up to him.

She'd calmed down a little by the time she got dressed, and had accepted that family was everything, for her and for Luca, and, as far as he was concerned, Madlena was his family, and he would do anything to safeguard his people, which was where she came in. The Pirate Prince clearly needed a bride to reassure the citizens of Madlena that he was bringing them peace and optimism, not turmoil and uncertainty. But surely he must have a list of princesses waiting with bated breath for his call? Madlena might be small, but it was a fabulously wealthy little island since his parents had arrived at the brilliant solution of turning it into a tax haven. She could only imagine the long line of hopefuls vying for a slice of that.

Perhaps he'd been looking for something more than an avaricious princess?

But I'm no one. Why choose me? What have I got to offer? If I were choosing a bride for Luca...

Yes?

She couldn't even bear to think about it. Which was

ridiculous, remembering their latest encounter. It was
time to find out exactly what was going on—in her head
as well as his.

Still reeling from Samia's refusal, Luca was ready to
concede that he could have put it better, or maybe chosen a better moment, but he was a plain-speaking man.

Leaving the shower with a towel wrapped around his
waist, he used another to towel dry his hair vigorously
before raking it with impatient fingers. He had always
wanted everything yesterday.

She had come back?

He stilled as Samia entered the room wearing a plush
robe she'd thrown on, and had belted carelessly in her
rush to get back.

To him?

Maybe not, he thought dazedly as she launched into
a tirade. *Guilty on all counts*, he mused. She went on to
list all the reasons why she couldn't marry him.

'I'm a divorcee. My father's in prison.'

'He was convicted of fraud. Am I right?'

'You've read his file, I imagine?'

'I have,' he confirmed. 'Further investigation proved
that the mysterious funds in your father's bank account
lead straight back to your ex.'

'Everyone knows that. They were to pay off his gam-
bling debts.'

'No. He had already paid those off.'

'What?'

This new information stripped away her battling front,
replacing it with an expression of hope so intense it was
almost painful to see. 'The funds that put your father in
prison were added to his account at a later date. It's my
belief he was set up, and I intend to prove it.'

'Can you do that?'

'My lawyers can. They seem quite confident.'

'If you could do that, I—'

Never one to miss an opportunity, he suggested, 'You'd marry me?'

'I didn't say that,' she fired back.

'I'm not trying to blackmail you with empty promises. My lawyers are working on your father's case as we speak and whatever answer you give to my proposal, they will continue to work until he's free. That's all I can say at this moment. I can't do anything about your mother's death, and I regret that more than you know. The damage done by your ex-husband was a tsunami that took down everything in its wake. Except you,' he stated levelly.

'Don't do this,' she said, covering her face with her hands. 'I need time to think.'

'You can have all the time in the world—if you make a decision today.'

Choosing to ignore the joke, she raised angry eyes to his. 'You can't heal everything with sheer force of will.'

'But I can try.'

She seemed to accept this, although a lot of seconds ticked by before she started speaking again, and by then she was reflective. 'I don't want to do anything without careful consideration first. My mother always said I rushed into things, but then the real world was a mystery to her, and she couldn't appreciate that sometimes opportunities had to be seized. She was never fitted for enduring reality. Raised in a cocoon of wealth and privilege, she expected that to continue for the rest of her life. I just wish I could have talked to her, to prove how many good things there are away from top show and empty possessions, and all the opportunities she was missing.'

'Some people just don't want to hear the truth. You can't blame yourself for that.'

There was another long silence, and then she admitted, 'I didn't expect you to be so understanding.'

'I'm not. I'm an impatient man with a country to reassure. I'm not proud of my motives, but I ask you to understand them.' Marrying to seal a deal that benefited both parties made perfect sense to him.

'This is marriage we're talking about,' she confirmed.

'Of course.'

'I could give you another list of reasons why I can't marry you.'

'But none of them would make sense.'

'To you, maybe.'

'I don't understand what's stopping you.'

'Your arrogance? Your sense of entitlement? Your assumption that you only have to speak and I will jump?'

'Am I allowed to voice a defence?'

Her jaw worked as she stared at him. 'Here,' she said, tossing him a robe. 'Put this on. You're far too distracting.' No one had ever complained before. 'If this is a serious proposal of marriage, I can only assume you have a touch of sunstroke, and should rest.'

'I can assure you I'm sound in mind as well as body.'

'I can see that,' she agreed, narrowing her eyes.

He'd in no way won her over yet, or made up for his crass proposal, but, catching the robe one-handed, he shrugged it on as they exchanged a searing look.

CHAPTER TWELVE

MUSCLES RIPPLING, his wild hair even wilder than ever following some rough attention with a towel, Luca was nothing short of magnificent. She knew he was mocking her with that smouldering look, but he could afford to take chances. She couldn't, and that was the difference between them. The Pirate Prince was taking one last throw of the dice—and, quite amazingly, it was in her direction—before he settled down to rule Madlena. All this talk of marrying him… What was she to make of it? It wasn't easy to think straight in the face of so much potent male attraction, which he knew. But she would think straight. She was the most unsuitable bride he could have picked. Even forgetting her past, she had no skills in the bedroom, and a rebellious soul, that, now it was free, wouldn't tolerate restrictions made by any man. She couldn't think of a worse choice off the top of her head.

'If you're looking for a bride to inspire confidence in your people, I don't think I'm your gal.'

'I disagree,' he said firmly.

'You would. But there's something else.'

'Go on,' he prompted, angling a chin that needed a good close shave.

'I don't want to be a princess.'

'Because you like your life the way it is? The notion

of jewels and status, and the best seats at every event, travel by private jet wearing fancy clothes, and people bowing and scraping for no better reason than you have a meaningless prefix before your name—none of that appeals to you?'

'No. It doesn't,' she agreed.

'Greeting dignitaries you can't stand?'

'Horrible.'

'What about meeting those who need your support?'

'Well, that's different,' she said as if this were obvious. 'Of course I'd do everything I could to help, if I were in a position to do so.'

'It might surprise you to know I feel exactly the same. I'll do whatever it takes to serve my people and to help build my country into a flag bearer for fairness and equality, but when it comes to endless banquets and court affairs, I'm going to need someone to prod me to make sure I stay awake.'

'And that's my job?' she queried, shooting him a scathing look.

'You can always plead a headache and I'll ask someone else to do it.'

'This isn't a joke, Luca. Seriously. Who wants to be royal? No privacy, no comments you can trust won't be repeated, guarding everything you say while you're surrounded by sycophants pretending to be your friend? I've always pitied those who carry that burden, and have never wished to join them. Don't forget I've had my fifteen minutes of fame—infamy, in my case—and it was a hideous experience.'

'Because you were unhappy, and had no one to support you,' Luca countered firmly.

He was right, but how could she pretend to be something she was not, and could never be? 'I can't just brush my past under the carpet and become a saintly princess.'

'Heaven forbid! Brushing anything under the carpet is the last thing I'd want you to do. You can build on your past experiences, and I'd want you to bring them to bear on everything you do. In that way, you can use them to help others. I've seen you interact with my crew. I've felt your natural warmth and observed how well you relate to everyone. I can't think of a better endorsement for a princess than people taking you to their hearts. I imagine that's the quality that made you such a successful journalist, until your column was corrupted by someone no one, not even you, could control.'

Because my ex owned the newspaper, she reflected ruefully, *as you rule Madlena. Am I heading for Groundhog Day?*

'You're intuitive and empathetic,' Luca continued, 'which draws people to you. I believe that quality would in time make you a much-loved Princess of Madlena.'

'You *are* serious about this marriage proposal,' she said through lips that felt numb and stiff as they formed words she found it impossible to get her head around.

'Of course I am,' Luca insisted. 'I would hardly joke about something like that. All I ask is that you commit to a certain period of time for our marriage—say five years. That should be enough to reassure my people that I can be the Prince they need. You'd have all the freedom you wanted during that time—'

'Let me stop you there,' she rapped out, grim-faced. 'You're putting boundaries on the duration of your marriage?'

'Our marriage,' he emphasised with a look as steely as hers. 'I thought that was what you would want. You don't want to be tied to me for ever.'

Luca was as damaged as she was, Samia reflected as he went on, 'We would need to remain married long enough to reassure my people that I intend to be the stable leader they hope for. Five years should do it.'

'And when those five years are up, I pack my bags and leave to write a book? I'd make millions telling our story, and, of course, I'd live happily ever after.'

'A simple clause in the marriage contract should prevent the writing of a tell-all book,' Luca reflected out loud.

'You expect me to stick around for five years, busying myself by putting my name to worthy causes, and never getting my hands dirty, of course?'

'Now you're being sarcastic,' he observed, 'and I thought better of you. I would never stop you taking a proper role in any cause you felt drawn to.'

'How good of you,' she said sweetly. 'And when I return to the real world—with a pension, presumably, so I never have to work another day in my life—what then? I wear a gag and take up tatting?'

'That won't be necessary,' Luca said stiffly. 'We'll visit the lawyers again and sign the required prenup—'

'Excuse me?' she cut in. '*Who* will sign the prenup?'

'Why, you, of course,' Luca confirmed.

'Of course,' Samia agreed caustically. 'I'd be only too pleased to protect you in every way I can.'

'I knew you'd see sense eventually.'

'*Sense?*' she snarled. 'Have you been indulging yourself sailing around the world for so long you've lost touch completely with reality? In my world, women work and raise families, build homes that are warm and loving sanctuaries, care for others, and improve themselves, all at one and the same time. Not at any point do they sit back and let a man take the helm.'

'I think you misunderstand me.'

'I think I've got a perfect grasp of the situation. You command and I obey.'

'It wouldn't be like that.'

'And my guarantee?'

'Do you need it spelled out?'

'Yes. I think I do. If you have a contract for me to sign, then I'll have one for you as well.'

'So, that's a yes to my proposal, then?'

She had to stop her jaw dropping to the floor at his sheer audacity. This was the Pirate Prince at full throttle, doing what he did best, which was to cut a swathe through all objections. Luca needed her to say yes, and he wasn't too bothered about the form in which her agreement came.

'At no point do you find this preposterous?' she demanded.

'No,' he confirmed, looking genuinely bemused. 'Why would I? Perhaps I could have put it better...'

'Perhaps you could,' she agreed.

'I genuinely think this will benefit both of us,' he insisted. 'I don't consider it outlandish in any way. People enter into arranged marriages all the time. If there are enough common factors and sound foundations to build on, there's no reason why a marriage of convenience can't be a success.'

'For five years?'

'Or for whatever term you state. I'm merely suggesting a minimum of five years.'

She really needed to sit down before her legs gave way. This was so far beyond her ken she didn't have a ready answer, just feelings that threatened to overflow and drown her. 'So here's my take on the situation,' she offered with a deceptively mild expression on her face.

'Please,' Luca invited, opening his arms to encourage her, obviously believing that she was on the point of giving in.

'As my first marriage proved, there are no guarantees in life, and mistakes can always be made, but to walk blindly into something twice would be supremely stupid, and I'm not daft.'

'No. You're a very clever woman,' he agreed, 'or I wouldn't be asking the question.'

'I'm also a dreamer, as you've noted, and my dream is to find the right man to marry so I can build a home and raise children, help others—all those points I mentioned before. At no stage of my dream is there a contract stating when it's time to wake up and find everything I care about has gone. You might find this hard to believe, but I still believe in love, and I still value marriage, and if and when I marry again, it will be with total love and commitment, and with no boundaries or contracts to define the terms.'

'But you accept that a second marriage might not work out for you?'

'Of course I do. I have to. There are two people involved, not just me. There are no certainties in life for any of us.'

'Then, what's the difference between our propositions?' Luca demanded, throwing his arms wide with frustration.

'Mine is made with love, while yours is made with a deal in mind.'

'Maybe you expect too much.'

'Maybe I do,' she agreed.

They were both quiet for quite a while, and then he said the one thing she'd been dreading. 'There's something else behind your reluctance, isn't there, Samia?'

She'd been blunt with him so far. She couldn't back down now. 'I'm no good in bed,' she said, staring him straight in the eyes as if daring him to disagree.

'Surely, that's for me to judge?' Luca said quietly.

'I don't care to be judged.'

'Perhaps judged is the wrong expression,' he conceded. 'What I meant was, this would be a new beginning…for both of us.'

She perched on the edge of the bed to give herself a chance to think. Luca was leaning against the wall with his unbelted robe slipping off one shoulder, which exposed the thick column of his neck, and a wealth of impossibly powerful muscle. That wasn't exactly helpful when it came to clear thinking.

She took her time, and then said, 'It isn't wrong not to like sex.'

'Wrong? No,' Luca agreed. 'I just find it impossible to believe you fall into that category.'

He'd neatly sidestepped the marriage question, she noticed, but his remark was due an answer. 'I don't know why you find it so hard to believe.'

Those shoulders eased in a lazy shrug that made her heart thunder. 'I've seen you come apart in my arms,' he murmured, fixing his gaze on her face. 'I've heard you beg for more. I've felt you respond, and I've tasted your passion. I've seen the tiger inside you unleash its claws, and yet now you're asking me to believe you don't enjoy sex. Forgive me if I don't believe you.'

'But what if I can't…?' A dry throat was bad enough. A strangled throat was worse.

'Can't what?' Luca demanded, refusing to let her off the hook.

'What if I can't go the whole way and give you a proper marriage?' The humiliation of giving voice to her fears was so overwhelming, she wasn't sure she could hold back the tears.

'Like every other couple,' Luca responded in a matter-of-fact tone, 'we'll face that hurdle when we come to it.'

'No,' she said decisively. 'You don't understand. I can't—I really can't.'

'Because...?'

'Because I can't face it—'

'Face what? Go on, say it,' he insisted as she pressed her lips together.

'I can't stand penetrative sex,' she blurted. 'There. You've got what you wanted. I've said it. And why are we even discussing this?' she added before Luca had the chance to say a word. 'Why must you torment me, when it's obvious that marriage between us is a ridiculous idea?'

'I don't agree. We can marry, and we will.' He let that fact settle in, and then he added, 'Are there any other issues you'd like to raise?'

A fist maybe? To plant in his arrogant face. Apart from that...?

Feelings exploded inside her.

'Nothing more to say?' he prompted. 'Then, let me reassure you that you can safely leave those concerns to me.'

'Why bother?' she flared. 'There must be countless women gagging for the job of Princess!'

'But none I want,' Luca said flatly. 'I will marry you. And here's why. I need a bride to reassure my people. You say you're unsuitable. Let's think about that. Who could be more fitting to sit on the throne of Madlena than a woman who's suffered, and experienced life on the outside? You've haven't been hiding away in an ivory tower, you've been working. You've coped with your mother's death, and you did everything you could to help your father, while living through a personal trauma. Who better to mould the Pirate Prince into a decent human being than a tried and tested survivor who has come out on the other side, armed with knowledge and experience? Not only are you ready to help my people, you're eager to do it too.'

'So your argument is, I will influence you in a positive way?'

'My argument is that it will look that way.'

'As I thought. Even you have to admit that's hardly persuasive.'

Luca shrugged. 'If you want to pick holes in my argument, neither of us is a suitable candidate for the throne. We're both tainted, but I believe this can work, if we want it to. With our joint experience of the world, we can make the type of difference Madlena needs. Our people will take you to their hearts and I'll join you on that ride. Who can resist a "bad boy turned good" story?'

'Someone who doesn't see the world from your cynical point of view. You want your people to love you, but you're frightened to give them your heart.'

What chance do I stand? she wondered.

'I'm being realistic,' Luca argued, starting to pace the room. 'Which is what Madlena needs. My brother lived in an ivory tower, where he was aloof and untouchable but adored, because his life was so closely guarded he never appeared to make a mistake. I *want* to get my hands dirty. I want to take risks for the good of my people, and through it all I'm going to be on full view with my bride at my side, taking part in life as a citizen of Madlena. I'll make mistakes. I'm bound to, but I'll do everything I can to put them right, and it's my hope you'll buy into that, because I know you'll be a great asset to the throne.'

'That's a rather cold-blooded assessment.'

'Yes, it is,' Luca admitted frankly. He stopped pacing in front of her. 'I expect the services of a loyal bride with all that that entails, while you get guaranteed safety, along with a life that, I can tell you now, will take all your energy, but that will fully repay you, by fulfilling your every need.'

Every need? She had no expectations of that where the marriage bed was concerned, and even less when it came to some small sign from Luca that one day they might mean more to each other than two parties entering a contract *that made perfect sense*. She was falling for this man, while he'd practically admitted he was incapable of love. This could be her worst dream come true. Perhaps her ex was right. Perhaps she would never be worthy of love. At least, not the type of love she longed for, both to give and receive. She dreamed of a love that had no boundaries, and that spread its light far and wide, and her greatest hope had always been to make that dream a reality.

She had another major niggle too. 'I'm not sure about the *services* of a loyal bride. I would need to know what these services entail.'

Luca's gaze sharpened. 'Before you agree?'

'I haven't decided anything yet.'

'You want me to understand that you bow your head to no man?' Luca suggested.

'Never again,' she confirmed. Her mouth twisted ruefully. 'I tried it once, and look where that got me.'

'Some would say, into a very good place.'

'But not me,' she assured him.

'Let me make this clear. By *services* I mean no scoops in the press, no sudden surprises. I would never stop you writing. I can see the benefits to Madlena. And I would never stop you doing anything you want to do, unless it posed a risk to our country.'

In spite of her doubts, Luca using the phrase '*our country*' gave her pause for thought, and a thrill of anticipation ran through her mind as she considered all the possibilities that weren't connected to wealth or status. If she didn't at least consider his argument, she was being as closed off as her mother. She had to listen and weigh the facts. Only then could she give him her answer.

'Would you want to read everything I wrote and approve it first?' she asked, remembering past shackles. *And then change it?* The words bounced around in her mind. That was her biggest fear. If Luca turned out to be anything like her ex, she really was leaping from the frying pan into the fire.

'If you become Princess of Madlena, I would expect you to have the country's best interests at heart.'

'I would. Don't take that as my answer,' she warned when a flame sparked in Luca's eyes.

'It goes without saying that your ex will never trouble you again,' he added, as set as she was on getting his point across. 'When your father leaves prison—and we have every reason to believe that will be sooner, rather than later—I'll ensure he receives all the help he needs to get back on his feet, as well as a plan going forward. So long as he does nothing to hurt you, he'll always be a welcome guest in our home.'

These offers were wonderful and generous, but Luca had made not one single mention of romance. His suggestion remained a cold-blooded arrangement to benefit both of them. It was hard to argue with a single word he'd said, but that didn't stop her heart aching for something it couldn't have. *Something I obviously don't deserve.* He'd been wholly objective when he laid out the details of their contract, which made his promise to 'sort out her problem' more terrifying than exciting. Could he do that? Could anyone? What if she failed utterly in bed, or recoiled as she had in the past?

Worse. What if she proved to be frigid, as her ex had insisted she was?

And yet... And yet...

Family was everything, and how could she help her father if she didn't have a job, or even a home to go back to? He'd always been weak and easily influenced. Wouldn't it be better for him to be influenced by strong people with good intentions? Could she deny him that chance? She could provide him with all the love in the world when he came out of prison, but nights were cold, and his belly would be empty without the practical support Luca had offered. Wasn't this one thing she could do for her mother, who must have loved her father at some point? Shouldn't she do everything she could to set her father back on his feet?

CHAPTER THIRTEEN

SHE QUICKLY GATHERED her wits. Helping her father was the one unselfish act she could accept as a reason for marrying Luca.

Hadn't she done that once before? What made him different?

She'd learned from past mistakes, and would put safeguards in place. Luca wasn't her ex-husband, but a man of principle. His reputation might be colourful, but she'd seen first-hand his determination to change. Marriage was all part of that long road to redemption, and, though theirs would be a cold-blooded marriage, he was right in saying they both had something to gain from it. But when they went to the lawyers she would not remain silent. There was more than money at stake. There was her father's future, and her dreams at stake.

So I've made my decision?

Her mind was still in turmoil. She might be able to do some good as Princess of Madlena... She'd have a platform, if nothing else... But first, Luca had to hear her conditions. 'I can't take this further until you hear my requests.'

She had thought he might object, but now realised she should have expected the flare of triumph in his eyes. 'I'm keen to hear your views,' he said.

'I'll continue writing, and you can't censor my work in any way.'

'That's easy to agree,' he confirmed.

'I'd be free to travel?'

'It isn't my intention to cage you. You seem distracted?' he observed when she fell silent.

'*If* I agree to your suggestion—and I'm nowhere near close to that yet—I would need to undertake a real, practical role. I could never agree to being a puppet princess, wheeled out now and then for the sake of appearances.'

Luca laughed, and as he threw his head back, making his thick, wavy hair catch on his stubble, she almost weakened.

'I'm sorry,' he said, curbing his laughter with obvious difficulty. 'I realise this isn't the best time for humour, but you in the role of meek, obedient wife? I'm sorry, but that's a stretch too far. And I don't want that,' he insisted. 'I need challenge. I expect you to espouse causes and fight for them tooth and claw. Being "wheeled out," as you put it, on state occasions, is a little harder to imagine. I'll have to rely on your better nature to oblige me when it comes to that. I'd be wasting your talents if all you did was to sit dumbly at my side. I'm hoping you would want to use your royal role for the good of the people.'

'But—'

'There's something else?' he queried when she broke off.

'Yes,' she admitted.

'Go on,' he prompted.

'If I'm hopeless in…'

'In bed?' he supplied.

'If I can't… If I really can't stand it…'

'I assume we're talking about sex?'

Swallowing convulsively, she nodded her head.

'Remember, I do know a little about you.' His lips tugged fractionally, though not in a mocking smile, but with understanding.

They had very few secrets left when it came to her physical responses, she accepted. It was just that life-changing next step she dreaded.

"'You can stop looking so worried. We won't sleep together until our wedding night, by which time you will be—'

'Ready?' she whispered. It was more question than a statement.

Luca shrugged.

Her imagination raced ahead. When it came to wanting him there was no problem. The comfort of his arms around her, and the pleasure of his touch—those were wonderful. But the pain she associated with penetrative sex—

Sucking in a great shuddering breath, she knew for certain that she would never be ready for that.

Crossing the room in a couple of strides, he took Samia in his arms. There could never be sufficient punishment for what that bully had done to this woman. She couldn't accept that a man could be kind? What kind of legacy was that? His negotiations were still under way, but the offer of physical warmth had no conditions. And she was in no hurry to break away, he noticed. 'You'll be fine,' he soothed. 'You'll make the right decision. I won't say anything more, or try to influence you.'

She laughed softly, her voice muffled against his chest. 'You already have influenced me. I tried to fight you, and found I don't want to. Can we just be friends?'

Samia was naked beneath the robe, her arousal plain to see. Her nipples thrust imperatively against the robe, and he guessed the rest of her body would be equally receptive.

'Don't you want me?' she asked. 'Or are you just playing me to get what you want?

Even he wasn't entirely sure about his motives, but he did know he wanted her. 'I want you,' he confirmed as he pulled away. 'But we're going to wait until our wedding night.'

'You're very confident,' she whispered.

'Yes. I am.'

CHAPTER FOURTEEN

HE MET SAMIA again at breakfast the next morning, beneath an awning on deck where an exquisitely dressed dining table with a crisp white damask cloth and napkins, crystal glasses, delicate porcelain plates and silver cutlery was a setting fit for a princess. A role Samia played with consummate ease, and unassuming elegance, he noted as a steward directed her to the chair next to his.

Rising from his place, he rose and stood until she was comfortably seated, then settled himself and eased back in his seat. 'I trust you slept well?'

'I trust you did?' she countered.

He hadn't had a moment's sleep. He'd been too busy making arrangements. The first of these would come to fruition in about half an hour.

'You look refreshed,' he commented. She took his breath away. 'I see you've been raiding the closets again?'

'No point in being coy about it,' she explained with her normal forthrightness, flicking her still-damp hair out of the way. 'I don't have any other clothes with me.'

'I have to say, those simple sundresses look beautiful on you.'

'Someone has very good taste,' she observed dryly. 'And before you ask, I wasn't fishing for information on who that might be.'

'Yes, you were.' It pleased him to think she might be jealous.

'Her loss is my gain.'

Samia's pointed stare reminded him of an opponent in the ring. This tussle wasn't over yet—it was only just beginning. *And it might have a lifetime to run.*

He brushed the thought away as a steward intervened at just the right moment with coffee. Things would never be easy between him and Samia, but that was half the stimulating fun of it. She wasn't exactly immune to him, either, he thought as she moistened her lips and looked away.

'So,' he probed, 'is the Pirate Prince about to become a reformed character?'

'I would have thought that was up to you.'

'My question requires an answer.'

'I haven't decided yet.'

'Then, you should. Time is running out...' As he spoke, they both turned in the direction of an approaching helicopter.

'Visitors?' she said. Shielding her eyes with her hand, she stared up into the harsh early morning light.

'Heralding the start of a day devoted entirely to your pleasure,' he explained.

'I don't understand.' She frowned.

'There's nothing *to* understand. The question is simple. I asked you to be my bride. I'm asking you again—formally asking, this time—and I need your answer now.'

'*Now?* You mean, right now?'

'Right now,' he confirmed.

He was glad he'd chosen an emerald engagement ring to match her eyes. It was the perfect choice. The royal jeweller had excelled herself with a Herculean effort, working through the night to create what Luca considered to be the most beautiful jewel he'd ever seen, and then having it transported by launch at dead of night.

'What's this?' Samia exclaimed as he produced the midnight-blue velvet box from the breast pocket of his shirt.

'A priceless gem, made with consummate skill and the utmost devotion by a world-renowned jeweller in Madlena.'

If he had been the type of man to puff himself up, he would have puffed at that moment, so proud was he of the craftspeople of Madlena. He was confident that Samia would be blown away. He had seen many fabulous pieces of jewellery in his time, but nothing to compare with the clarity, colour and cut of the gemstone currently residing in the palm of his hand. 'Try it on,' he invited.

'Really?' As she pulled her head back it was clear she didn't know whether to laugh or smile. 'May I?'

'Of course,' She should get used to such things.

She took the ring from his hand and stared at it in wonder as a child might on Christmas morning after picking something choice out of a stocking. The priceless stone glowed green like the heart of a rainforest, while the sizeable diamonds surrounding it flashed like Arctic fire. As she held it up to the light, she laughed. 'It looks like green ice.' But then she handed it back to him. 'What a whopper,' she remarked. 'My granny would love it. Oh, I'm sorry,' she blurted, realising she might have caused offence. 'I mean, the ring is absolutely gorgeous, but just not for me.'

The helicopter hovered over them like a noisy black cloud determined to rain on his parade. Denied further conversation, he could only sit and seethe in response to

Samia's unexpected reaction to the ring he had chosen
with such care, as its powerful engines screamed over-
head. His affront would have to wait, he concluded as
the pilot lined up for a pinprick perfect landing on the
Black Diamond's helipad. He had more pressing matters
to attend to now. Prince Luca Fortebracci wasn't noted
for indecision and he saw no reason for their marriage
to be delayed any longer.

'Shall I stay here while you greet your guests?' Samia
enquired as the engines quietened to an agitated purr.
'The ring's beautiful—honestly, it is,' she added, seeing
his closed expression. 'I hope you're not too offended by
what I said? I realise now you probably designed it—and
with me in mind.'

'Who else?' he gritted out.

'If I decide to marry anyone, it won't be the ring that
seals the deal,' she assured him. 'Love and trust would
be enough for me.'

'After everything you've been through?' he queried
sceptically.

'Expensive jewellery wouldn't change any of that, and
it certainly can't be a deciding factor in whether or not I
accept your proposal. I always think a plain gold or platinum band is all that's needed to reflect a circle of love.'

'That's your romantic side speaking for you.'

'Good,' she said. 'It's nice to know I can still rustle up
a few romantic feelings after going ten rounds in the ring,
so to speak.' She chuckled at her own expense. 'Wasn't
it you who said that not all men are the same? Well, not
all women are the same, either, and for me it's what's in
the heart, not on the finger, that counts.'

It was hard to be offended when Samia's smile was
so genuine it lit up her eyes, making them more like precious gems than the ring in the box he was gripping so

tightly it threatened to dent. Putting it back in his pocket, he leaned over to plant his fists on the table. 'Samia,' he said quietly, 'I really do need your answer now. Will you marry me?' As he asked the question the helicopter engines were switched off, and the abrupt silence made him appear to shout.

'I will!' she shouted back, springing to her feet.

He was so shocked by her sudden acquiescence that he barely heard her add, 'I guess I'll get used to the idea eventually—if you give me enough time…'

'There is no time,' he said briskly. 'We'll be docking in Madlena tomorrow morning, and my intention is to arrive with a bride.'

'I'm sorry?' Samia demanded. 'At the risk of sounding like a complete dimwit, who exactly is this bride going to be?'

'The captain of my *floating office block* will marry us tonight. I trust that is acceptable?'

Her mouth worked but she said nothing. Luca took the chance to fill the sudden silence with essential information. 'I will go and greet our guests—hairdresser, make-up artist, fashion designers, and a seamstress to make any necessary alterations to your wedding gown and, of course, my indispensable PA, Domenico, who will direct events. Three of them will act as our witnesses, and then the helicopter will return them to shore, while you and I discuss our future over a candlelit dinner before retiring to our marriage bed.'

Ice gathered in the pit of her stomach. 'I… I thought I would have longer to get used to the idea before we were actually married.'

'Think again.'

It seemed that Luca was done with waiting.

* * *

Numb with shock, Samia was in a state of complete unreality as she allowed herself to be ushered back to her stateroom by an immaculately groomed gentleman who introduced himself as Domenico. Luca's PA wouldn't have looked out of place behind a mahogany and glass counter in Savile Row, but he seemed kind, and funny, and was trying very hard to put her at ease. She'd need something, she reflected as he hustled her away. Everything was happening so quickly she had barely had a chance to breathe.

Left alone to bathe for a scant ten minutes, she exited the bathroom in a robe, ready to be primped and preened by beauticians, who then handed her over to the charge of a hairdresser who, it had to be said, worked wonders with her wilful hair. Though so many pins were required to hold up the heavy mass of gleaming curls, they stuck into her scalp like vindictive darts, reminding her of a lifetime of discomfort ahead. Her thighs tingled as she tensed them. High-heeled shoes and tiaras would be the least of that discomfort. She couldn't deny Luca the physical side of marriage for ever.

'There will be photographers,' Domenico explained as he twitched the yards of filmy fabric that comprised her gown until it obeyed his smallest command. 'I hope you like the dresses I chose for you to try on. Signor Luca insisted they should be understated, or he warned you might consign them to Davy Jones's locker.'

'Toss this in the sea?' Samia queried on a disbelieving breath as she ran her hands down the front of the exquisite gown she and Domenic had finally decided on. 'Never.'

In a flattering shade of ivory, the bridal gown was a dream of a dress, composed of the softest, finest chiffon that moulded her figure like a second skin. It didn't constrict, or stop her leaning over in case she revealed more than she intended.

'I can't believe you've second-guessed my taste like this.'

'That credit goes to Prince Luca,' Domenico informed her as she twizzled around in front of the mirror in an attempt to see the gown from every angle.

'Clothing the body of a beautiful woman requires a very different approach to that of someone who only seeks to impress. Building on Prince Luca's recommendations, I saw instantly that you are a free spirit, but strong, which made my vision for you something that floated as you stamped your mark on the world.'

She laughed. 'You make me sound formidable.'

'Time will tell,' Domenico observed with a sniff. 'The main thing now is that you like it. Prince Luca trusts me, and in this instance with his most important project yet.'

Samia frowned. 'I'm not sure I like being described as a project.'

Taking hold of her shoulders in a light grip, Domenico held her at arm's length. 'Are you sure about this?' he asked with an appraising stare.

'Can anyone be sure about anything?'

'That is not an answer. I can see that Prince Luca has plenty to gain by marrying you, but what do you get out of it? He has no idea when it comes to romance. I imagine he attempted to woo you with some vulgar display of extravagance?'

'Well, I wouldn't call it that, but—'

'It's only because he doesn't know any better. Prince Luca chose to make his home in a barracks, and no doubt imagined that a grand gesture was required when it came to his bride. Don't be too hard on him. He's a good man, and if anyone can soften him, I believe that person is you.'

'A snap judgement?' she suggested.

'That's why he keeps me at his side. I haven't been wrong yet,' Domenico told her.

'I only wish I had your confidence.'

'You should. You're beautiful, and you look stunning in this gown, but, more important than that, you have a good heart and a brave spirit. I've done my investigating too.'

'It seems we're all sleuths around here.'

Domenico smiled warmly. 'Turn around and take another look at yourself in the mirror, and then tell me that you're not a princess.'

She did as Domenico suggested, and found herself looking at a stranger who seemed so poised. The stranger was exquisitely dressed, as if she had stepped out of the pages of one of the fairy tales Samia's mother used to read when Samia was a little girl.

If only her mother had lived to see this day...

Straightening her spine, she lifted her chin. Her beloved mother was gone. She couldn't change that, but she could remember one of the last things her mother had said, which was, the best way to cope with loss was for the survivor to continue playing the role she always had. *Be my daughter. Make me proud. Hold on to that, because then you'll have a purpose that will help you climb out of the dark into the light.* That was what she would do. This was not a time for doubt, but a time to remember she had a father to care for and a life to live. And why not this life? She would embrace the role of Princess wholeheartedly as she did everything else. She'd only ever wanted to help and love and give, and now she had that chance. This new life would be like her column, where her purpose had been to find solutions for other people's problems and make things right, and now she could do that for Luca and his subjects.

'Just your veil now...'

She realised Domenico was still standing there patiently as he waited for her to come out of her temporary trance. He needed to finish helping her dress, and had a band of fresh flowers resting on his perfectly manicured hand, and a foam of twinkling tulle draped across his arm. 'Sorry to keep you waiting,' she apologised with a smile. 'Daydreaming is a terrible habit of mine, and I can't seem to shake it.'

'You should never do so,' Domenico insisted. 'Without dreams, what are we? Without them we'd never strive.'

'Agreed,' she said, 'but must I wear a veil? It hardly seems appropriate under these circumstances, and I'd rather leave my hair free. I'm not even sure I can keep a veil on if we go on deck. Knowing my luck, it will probably blow away.'

'I'd say your luck is about to change for the better.'

'Luca!' At the sound of his voice, she swung around in surprise.

'You don't have to do anything you don't want to do,' he confirmed. 'Thank you, Domenico,' he added pleasantly. 'You can leave us now.'

Breath hitched in Samia's throat as she looked at the man she was about to marry. His hair was still damp from the shower, and his stubble was growing rapidly in spite of a recent shave. Luca Fortebracci was any woman's dream. Tanned, ruggedly good-looking, and built like a gladiator, he was a most imposing sight, a prince amongst men in every sense of the word. In a crisp white shirt and a beautifully tailored pale linen suit, he was impossibly good-looking. So how could she hesitate?

Because she was the girl from nowhere, whose only talent lay with words. And yet, the fact that this man was determined to rush her into this marriage seemed more of a blessing than a curse.

CHAPTER FIFTEEN

'YOU LOOK BEAUTIFUL,' Luca murmured as he held her gaze.

And breathe, she instructed herself firmly as he stopped in front of her—though a disappointingly 'sensible' distance away, as her old headmistress might have said. There were documents in his hand, she registered belatedly. It was time to come out of her dazzled trance and face reality.

'I can't believe this is happening.'

'Rest assured, it is, and to mark the occasion, there are some documents for you to sign.'

To seal our deal, she thought as her happiness dropped away. And why was she surprised, when she had always known what she was getting into? She couldn't think of a single useful thing to say as her heart squeezed tight. If it had been china, it might have shattered into tiny pieces. Luckily for her, she was made of sterner stuff. 'Thank you,' she said, reaching for the papers. 'I'll read them through.'

As she closed her fingers around the stiff vellum, Luca maintained his grip so they were joined by the sheaf of legal papers. Better than nothing, she reflected as they stared into each other's eyes.

'My legal team has already been in discussion with your father, and all things are settled, though he has made one request that, I must admit, I hadn't anticipated.'

'Oh?' She was still shuffling the cards in her brain, only to have this curveball thrown into the mix. 'I'm surprised you didn't tell me sooner.'

'I've only just found out, and time is of the essence.'

'What is the request?' she pressed, fearing the worst, and hoping her father hadn't asked Luca's team for money.

Releasing his end of the legal papers, Luca stepped back to explain. 'He's extremely happy for you, and glad things have worked out. He wants to reassure you that he's keen to leave his old life behind, and his only wish is to live in the Highlands as a crofter where he once owned some land.'

Until her ex stole it from him, Samia remembered unhappily.

'This is a fortunate turn of events,' Luca assured her, 'as I own an estate in Scotland.' Of course he did, she thought incredulously, happily, fondly. 'My gamekeeper and his team are the best of men, and would like to help your father. I hope that's a satisfactory conclusion to your concern?'

It was so much to take in she could only nod her head dumbly. 'How can I ever thank you?' she said hoarsely at last.

A flicker of humour flared in Luca's eyes. 'By marrying me?' he suggested.

The helicopter brought another captain on board. His colleague would marry them, Luca explained when he left Samia reading the documents he'd brought to her stateroom as proof of his intentions. She impressed him by handing over her own document of wishes and reassurances, which she asked him to sign. These were hastily written, not by a legal team, as his were, with endless checks and balances throughout, but emotional, and small. She expected so little. Her bar was set very low, which made him want to give her the world. It was a shame that things had to be so calculated and rushed like this, but he didn't want to risk her backing out once she got to Madlena. After a harsh start in life, stumbling from one crisis to the next as she attempted to shore up her parents' chaotic existence, Samia deserved a proper courtship, and a man who could offer both his undivided attention and unstinting devotion. That man was not Luca. He had a country to put first, a reputation to salvage, and a brother he still mourned. Slim pickings for a bride whose imagination took her on endless flights of fancy, and, in spite of his devotion to duty, he only wished he could offer her more.

Domenico gave her away. They'd formed a bond in the short time they'd known each other, and she'd eagerly accepted his kind offer. Two members of the crew played the wedding march on guitars as she walked across the deck towards her fate, and the rest of the crew had assembled to wish her well. Only Luca's eyes were narrowed as he surveyed her. Was he disappointed in his choice of bride?

Too bad, she thought with what little remained of natural humour on this most daunting of days. *He's got me now. How must Luca be feeling?* she wondered as she closed the distance between them. Was any bride fit for a prince of his standing?

'I do,' she stated firmly when the question was asked. This was her duty. A new life for her father beckoned. If there could be a better outcome, she couldn't imagine what it might be. Luca had been very generous, both with her father's pension, and with his wedding gift to Samia

of a handwritten reassurance from the gamekeeper leading the caring community her father would be joining
on Luca's Scottish estate. She could be confident her father would be given the best possible chance to recover
when he was welcomed into the remote Highland village. She glanced heavenward in what she knew was a
childish gesture, almost as if to reassure her mother that
everything would be okay now.

'I have great pleasure in pronouncing you man and
wife.'

It was done.

'You may kiss your bride...'

Luca had never seemed more imposing or more intimidating as he brushed her lips with his. Sensing the
savage power within his muscular body, as yet supremely
controlled, but due to be unleashed that same evening,
she trembled. So tall he blotted out the sun, and so blis-
teringly masculine she felt swamped in his arms, for a
moment she panicked, wondering how on earth she could
go through with this marriage, and all it entailed.

'Don't be afraid, little one,' Luca whispered in her ear.
'I'll take care of you now...'

Extricating herself from his embrace with as much
dignity as she could muster while they were surrounded
by well-wishers, all of whom—with the possible exception of Domenico—no doubt imagined that they were
witnessing a fairy-tale romance, she smiled up at him
serenely.

'Thank you...' Any further commentary she might
wish to make on Luca's choice of endearment could wait.

'Do you like your wedding band?'

'I love it.' Samia realised she was twirling it round
and round her finger. At least one thing was right about

today. The slim platinum band represented everything she believed about love and commitment. It needed no adornment. It simply was. Or was not, in this case.

'The twist of your mouth suggests otherwise,' Luca observed as they sat at a dining table set for two. He'd dismissed the stewards so they were alone on deck. 'It was better not to have a formal wedding banquet to sit through,' he'd said. He wanted to protect Samia from other people's curiosity. Conversation would be necessarily stilted between the guests, as everyone tried to get up to speed with the bride, and what had happened beneath the radar to result in this hectic wedding. They would wonder where her family was, and if anyone apart from insiders knew this was happening.

'No. Seriously. I love my wedding ring,' she assured him. 'You couldn't have chosen anything better.'

'Then, why are you so quiet?'

She stared at him levelly. 'First, even though I never took the option off the table for myself, I never actually imagined I'd ever get married again. That I did so in such a rush obviously gives me pause for thought. Then, if I'm completely honest, I always imagined that somewhere in my future I might meet someone, and love them as they loved me.'

'That's your romantic side flexing its muscles again.'

'And I'm not ashamed of it.'

'Nor should you be,' Luca said as he topped up their champagne. 'Should I have given you a chance to change your clothes?' he added as they chinked glasses.

'Into something less comfortable?' she teased weakly. 'You look uncomfortable in that formal suit, while this gown is extremely forgiving. Why don't you take your jacket off and relax?'

'Are you ordering me about?'

'Maybe…' Further conversation was halted by the sight of Luca's muscles flexing as he stood to take the jacket off, and the knowledge that, in a very short time, she would be sharing a bed with that big, powerful frame, all of which was built to scale.

'You made an excellent choice of gown.'

Instinctively, she glanced down to where the cut of her bridal gown displayed her breasts. Her ex had always said she should cover them up—

'Forget him,' Luca said, reading her with his usual ease. 'You're married to me now.'

She stared down at Luca's hand covering hers. He was right. 'I'm sorry you read my distraction so accurately.'

'There's no need to be sorry. Just accept you're beautiful and leave it at that. If I tell you often enough, you will eventually believe it.'

'And then my head will be too big to fit through the doors.'

'Don't worry. I can handle you.'

Heat rushed through her as she imagined that promise transferred to the bedroom. She might have her fears and doubts when it came to the marriage bed, but her body was wholly in favour of the idea. As she adjusted the bodice on her dress she caught Luca staring at her. He seemed to understand there was a lot of damage to repair—for both of them, she thought. Remembering how she'd bridled at his throwaway comment, 'little one,' she thought it not worth pursuing. They'd get to know each other and their boundaries gradually as they went along. To challenge him now would be petty. Shouldn't every partner in a healthy relationship want to look out for the other? She had to get used to a new way of thinking to give this unique situation a chance of survival.

* * *

Samia was a beautiful bride. And still a largely unknown quantity. But that would change in time. At this moment, he couldn't believe how lucky he was, or that fickle fate had brought them together. He had needed a bride—almost any bride would do. Then she crossed his path. He considered that to be the most extraordinary piece of good luck.

'You're staring at me,' she remarked with a slow-forming smile.

'Am I?' he queried. 'I wonder why that could be.'

'I have spinach between my teeth?'

He shook his head. 'No. Because that delicate ivory gown is the perfect foil for your hair.' Which, since the brief ceremony, she had unpinned and brushed out so it floated around her shoulders like a fiery cloud.

'I've never worn anything like this before,' she confessed as she smoothed the pale fabric.

Or taken anything like it off before, he guessed as he pictured the moment when he would remove it with the care and deliberation she deserved before he kissed every inch of her naked body. The night-dark sky was like a canopy over a throne crowned with stars, and cloaked in the last rays of the sun. When they returned to Madlena, there would be a blessing of this marriage for his people to witness and then he would be enthroned with Samia at his side.

'Are you listening?' she asked.

'I have to confess, not a word,' he admitted.

She hummed in mock disapproval. 'I was saying that I have to work—a proper job. I need a purpose that goes beyond dressing up.'

Samia seemed oblivious to the fact that she had married into unimaginable wealth. 'Why don't you make a start by redesigning my properties?'

'That's hardly my forte.'

'I have plenty of properties—'

'Let me stop you there,' she said firmly. 'I'm not a practically minded person. If you want me to write a brief, or a wish list, I can do that for you, and willingly, but hands-on renovation will take a team of experts. That's not who I am, and if we're going to go forward successfully and make a positive difference to Madlena, each of us needs to play to our strengths.'

His lips tightened as he considered this, and then he shrugged. 'You're not that person,' he agreed. She was so much more, and only needed the confidence to prove it.

'What's it like to live like this?' she asked as they finished their meal.

'Complicated,' he admitted.

'Nothing's ever as straightforward as it appears, is it?' she observed. 'So, if it's all right with you, after dinner I'd like to discuss some of my ideas going forward.'

After dinner they'd be in bed.

She talked animatedly for a while, until the moment came when neither of them brought up a new topic, and he thought she looked uncomfortable, and guessed she was hunting for a reason to delay their wedding night. Pushing his chair back, he stood. She glanced up, but made no move to join him. 'I'm not tired at all,' she insisted brightly as he eased his neck.

'That's good.'

She froze.

'It's a lot to take in,' he reassured. 'So much has happened in so short a time.'

'Exactly,' she agreed, 'so why the rush?'

'You need to take a rest. It's been a busy day.' She

looked at him with surprise. 'Around midday tomorrow we'll arrive in Madlena, which means we both need our sleep.'

He waited to escort her to their stateroom, but she didn't move. 'You're frightened,' he said. 'I get that.' He should understand, having read the sickening report supplied by his security team. Not only had Samia's ex-husband brutalised her, he had also secretly filmed his depravity.

'Frightened?' she scoffed weakly as she stumbled to her feet.

'Your days of fear are over,' he murmured as he linked her arm through his.

Luca was right, she was terrified of failure, and his kindness almost made it worse. They crossed the grand salon side by side, the handsome prince and his awkward bride, heading for the bridal chamber. By the time they reached the door of Luca's suite, her heart was racing so fast she could hardly breathe. Opening the door, he led the way inside. 'Make yourself at home,' he invited. 'This *is* your home now—or at least one of them.'

'But I don't have anything here,' she said, registering the fact that she sounded utterly panic-stricken for the want of a toothbrush, some nightwear and a change of clothes.

'Domenico will have anticipated your every wish,' Luca assured her with an understanding smile. 'You have your own separate dressing room and bathroom here. Please,' he offered, indicating the doors to these, 'take as long as you want.'

'But I can't…'

'Turn around,' he invited.

His fingers on the back of her neck were like incendiary devices to her senses as he began to undo the tiny buttons that ran the length of her wedding gown to the waist. It was impossible not to react as they brushed her shoulder blades. She quivered involuntarily beneath his touch. When he was finished and the gown slid from her body to pool on the floor, she was naked underneath except for a single wisp of underwear, and shivering.

'Are you cold?'

It was a warm Mediterranean night. She could hardly blame the weather for the white-hot terror surging through her veins. Another man, another wedding night, was playing like a film through her mind. Her ex had never loved her, and she knew that now, though at the time she had still believed in fairy tales. She was nothing more than a means to an end, a link in a chain that led to a weak father and the possibility of a golf course in Scotland. She'd had no idea about pleasing a man in bed, or what was expected of her—she still had no idea.

'Samia…stop it,' Luca said gently as he brought her close. 'I'm not that man.'

No. And for such a big man he could be incredibly gentle. 'I know,' she whispered on a throat so dry her tongue cleaved to the roof of her mouth.

'What do you want? What can I do to reassure you?'

Tenderness, sharing, trusting, all those things, but how to put that into words?

I want you to hold me and lay me down on a newly made bed that smells of sunshine and soap. I want to experience pleasure, but I don't think I can. I want to give you pleasure, but I don't know how. What I dread most is that you will mock me and my body. And I don't want penetration, because I know it hurts.

Sweeping her into his arms, Luca carried her to the bed. Tossing the covers back, he murmured, 'Sleep well,' as he tucked her in.

She glanced up in alarm. 'Where are you going?'

'To the gym.'

As the door closed behind him she knew she'd failed. And before she'd even got to the first hurdle. The weight of that failure pressed down on her like rocks. She lay in bed as stiff as a statue, registering each new sound in the hope that a familiar footstep might return. It didn't, of course. An hour later, there was still no sign of Luca. All she could hear was the slap of the sails and the creak of the ropes, as the wind carried them forward to a destination she could only hope would be better than this lonely place.

Reaching out, she traced the crisp, cool sheets with her fingertips. The ceaseless movement of the waves only acted as a cruel reminder that there was nothing to fear in Luca's bed. Numb and empty inside, she was a bride without a groom, a woman without a purpose. Luca couldn't have made it clearer that their marriage of convenience was just that, a formality that suited him. It would reassure his country, but he felt no obligation to take part, or to carry out his marital duties.

Which should come as a huge relief. But it didn't. Instead, it only underlined the fact that her ex had been right all along. She wasn't desirable. She was incapable of being attractive to a man. She was a failure. When they reached Madlena, how long would Luca put up with that without seeking comfort elsewhere?

What could she do about it? Lie here, feeling sorry for herself, waiting for events to unfold? What about that task she'd set herself to help Luca climb out of his grief? She wasn't going to do that by brooding alone.

Slipping out of bed, she explored the suite of rooms until she found to her pleasure that the dressing room meant for her had been stocked with brand-new clothes, none of which had come from her original dressing room.

She smiled, and knew it was a kindness from Domenico. Now she turned to the sumptuous bathroom, which was fit for a princess, or a woman whose head was whirring with ideas.

Having almost destroyed the punchbag, he lifted weights until he ran out of plates to add, and then set off on the running machine for a straight ten miles uphill. Having exhausted all the possibilities for expending energy in the gym, he took an ice-cold shower that gave him the chance to ponder where he was at, and what he'd done.

Shaking sodden clumps of hair out of his eyes, he planted his fists on the wall and swore viciously. Not only did he have the uncomfortable mix of mourning a much-loved brother, and a personal reputation to salvage, he had a business to run, and a country to reassure, and now a damaged woman, one he cared deeply about, and had married, who had troubles that needing sorting right away. How to best allocate his time to each of these concerns was now his most preoccupying thought.

'Well done, Luca,' he snarled as he switched off the shower and reached for a towel. 'You've excelled yourself this time.'

One step at a time, he concluded as he tugged on his jeans. Which meant, to the great pleasure of the wolf inside him, that Samia and only Samia should be his priority tonight. But by the time he returned to their bedroom, his bride was curled in a ball, breathing at the steady pace of sleep. He stared at her for a moment and then at the couch across the room.

To hell with that!

CHAPTER SIXTEEN

SHE WOKE SLOWLY in absolute blackness, and was uncertain for a moment or two as to where she was. Reaching out her legs and arms to find a cool spot in the bed, she discovered a hot, naked body next to hers, and shot up. Now she was wide awake. Unscrambling her brain, she realised Luca had finally come to bed. Now what?

'It's two o'clock in the morning,' he growled. 'Go back to sleep.'

She couldn't decide if his lack of enthusiasm was her fault, or if he was taking a nap while he could. Angry waves were crashing against the hull, rocking the yacht, so maybe he needed to rest before returning to the business of sailing? He didn't seem unduly disturbed, she reflected as she rested on one elbow to stare down. Sprawled starfish-fashion on the bed, Luca appeared to be sleeping soundly again. How did that make her feel? Surplus to requirements? A necessary evil he'd got himself lumbered with? Maybe he already had a mistress waiting for him in Madlena. The thought pierced her heart and twisted deep like a corkscrew. However dismissive Luca might be, telling her to go to sleep on their wedding night, her feelings for him showed no sign of flagging. Yes, she still dreaded the possibility of him wanting more than she could give in bed, but not having him want anything from her was almost worse.

It was worse, she decided when Luca woke and told her once again to settle down. 'How am I supposed to do that when the boat is rocking like this?'

'I'll anchor you,' he said. 'Now, be quiet and go to sleep.'

'But I—'

'But you nothing,' he said sharply.

Which was how she came to find herself lying next to Luca, as close as it was possible to be, every inch of her naked body touching his spoon-style, her back to his front, and one of Luca's muscular legs anchoring hers, just as he had promised.

His tone should have annoyed her. Pinning her to the bed should have annoyed her more, but against all the odds she found herself gradually relaxing until, with a long sigh, she allowed herself to slip away into the darkness.

He woke to find Samia in his arms with a contented smile on her face. He brushed his lips against her cheek, and then her mouth, where he lingered before pulling back to stare down into her peaceful face. Her eyelids fluttered and then she looked up with surprise. 'Just don't ask me what I'm doing here,' he suggested dryly.

'I wasn't about to.' And then, after a few moments more, she admitted, 'I'm glad you're here. I want us to be together.'

She whispered this, holding his stare steadily. Cupping her face, he kissed her long and slow. When he judged the moment right, he brought her into his arms and drew the covers back. When she attempted to raise them again, he tossed them off the bed. 'You're beautiful. Why would you want to hide yourself?' She made a little sound, al-most like a suppressed sob. He was already kissing her collarbone so she didn't see his expression turn grim. He'd arranged for lawyers to deal with her ex and they were already making great strides to bring him down. It wouldn't be too long before the man faced the justice he so thoroughly deserved. But in the meantime, they could handle it without emotion, which he doubted he could, and anger only provoked a reaction that he wouldn't risk in case it hurt Samia. She'd suffered enough unkindness for one lifetime.

Stroking her to soothe her down, he dropped kisses on her eyelids and her mouth. At first she covered herself with her arms, and crossed her legs for good measure, but gradually, with whispered inducements in his own lan-guage, he encouraged her to loosen up, and, by avoiding any particularly sensitive areas, he finally managed to win her trust. He had no inhibitions, and perhaps it was as well that his brutishly masculine frame was mostly hidden by the darkness of the room. At the same time he wanted her to know every inch of him, as he wanted to know every inch of her. 'Touch me,' he encouraged when she sighed.

She stiffened and whispered, 'I can't.'

His answer was to take her hand and wrap it around him, at least partway around him, as she would need both her hands to encompass him fully, but he judged it too soon for that. Going by the soft sounds she was mak-ing as they kissed, she wasn't frightened now. She tasted so good, so warm and womanly, and her hand on him was starting to move. Running her fingertips lightly up his shaft until she reached the smooth, rounded tip, she brought her hand slowly down again. The sensation was incredible. This was no practised seductress repeating something she'd done countless times, but a woman discovering what she could do. If he thought too much about it, his much-vaunted control would be dust.

'Do you like that?' she murmured with a smile in her voice as he moved her hand away.

'What do you think?' he asked, turning her so now he was on top of her.

'What are you doing?' she asked as he nudged his way between her thighs.

'Appreciating you... Pleasuring you,' he said as he spread her wide. 'Stroking you...'

She cried out when he said this, and thrust her hips towards him in the hunt for more contact. Cupping her buttocks, he lifted her to meet him so he could give her what she needed.

'That feels so good,' she gasped.

'If I were a betting man I'd say this feels even better...'

A cry escaped her throat, and she tensed momentarily as he took her with just the tip of his straining erection. To help her forget her fears, he added a gentle touch of his slightly roughened finger pad until she was exclaiming with pleasure and couldn't help herself.

'Oh,' she cried out with disappointment when he withdrew, so he stroked her again with the tip, without seeking entry.

'Sex doesn't have to be painful or uncomfortable. There's something wrong if it is. It's a natural process where I give you pleasure and you pay me back with more.'

'Sounds good for you.'

'It is...or it will be.'

Taking her search for more contact as his cue, he increased the friction of his finger pad.

'I can't hold on!' she cried out in panic.

'You can and you must,' he insisted calmly.

'Can't I have just a little bit more?' she asked when he pulled back again.

'If that's what you want?'

'I do!'

He gave her the tip and continued to massage her at the same time, and when she arced towards him this time, he entered just by the smallest amount, and sank a little deeper, and moved back and forth before he withdrew.

'Please,' she begged, thrusting her hips up. 'You can't leave me hanging like this.'

He could and he would. 'Not yet. Only when I'm absolutely sure I have your trust.'

'You do—you *do*!' she insisted.

'Once I'm sure, I'll take you every way you want.'

How was she supposed to hold on? 'This is cruel.'

'This is the opposite of cruel,' Luca insisted. 'This has to be right, or it won't happen. Didn't I promise to keep you safe?' he murmured as he kissed her again.

Even his voice was arousing. Everything about him was a seduction. Her senses had never been so keenly tuned. Luca knew how to keep her teetering on the edge, knowing he only had to say the word to send her tumbling over. She lay suspended in his erotic embrace; this was an experience like no other. He tempted her to let go and then withdrew the offer. She wanted to scream and shout with frustration.

'Unless you relax—'

'You'll what?' she demanded, moving restlessly in his arms. She only had to look into Luca's eyes to sense the pleasure in store. He was her ideal, with his thick, inky black hair, and pirate stubble that rasped her skin in such a surprisingly pleasurable way. His body was perfect. Hard, big, powerful, fit, he was ridiculously good-looking with his knowing eyes and his skilful touch. Luca Fortebracci was the most exciting thing that had ever happened to her, and she was aching for him now.

'Soon,' he promised as her hand reached down.

The brush of his warm, hard body against hers, how he tasted—everything about him—made her impatient for him. The clean taste of his mouth, the light salt of his body, mixed with the scent of warm, clean man, was turning this into an experience she would never forget. It was as if he was about to take her for the first time, and with all the care and tenderness she had always dreamed a man would use.

'Do you like that?' he asked as he tested her for readiness.

The slightest bit of friction was all it took to blank her mind. And his hands, long, sweeping strokes to reassure her that she was someone to be valued, rather than a creature to be used.

Having protected them both, he cupped her buttocks in one hand, while using the other to soothe and caress. Samia's thighs parted instinctively, inviting him to take her, a cue he took with the utmost care.

'Ah...yes, *yes!*' she exclaimed when he gave her the tip once more, but this time he didn't stop moving, and thrust gently inside her. Pulling out again, he noted her immediate complaint and took her again, moving a little further in this time. He repeated this as her cries grew more demanding, until finally he was lodged to the hilt. Her eyes widened as he stretched her, and her breathing became ragged, but then he moved his hips in a lazy, massaging motion until she couldn't hold on. She cried out for the longest time yet, rhythmically and fiercely demanding as her inner muscles attempted to milk him dry. The tiger claws he knew she had bit into his shoulders, and even when her release subsided into a series of milder spasms, he could still feel her inner muscles hungrily pumping him. Stroking her hair back from her face, he stared into her eyes as she breathed hectically in the aftermath of pleasure. 'More?' he enquired with amusement.

Her answer was to grip his buttocks with fingers turned to steel, and work her body hungrily against his.

It was a long night, and a surprising one in many ways. As if she'd woken from a long sleep, Samia was clearly intent on making up for lost time. That they wanted each other was never in any doubt. It was the strength of the longing they'd unleashed in one another that shocked him.

'I want you again,' she told him at one point when he was sure she was asleep. 'I want to ride you, and I want you to touch me. I want to feel you deep inside me, and here too,' she said, holding his gaze fiercely as she put her hand over her heart. 'I want to feel you here.'

His heart jerked in response. Had they both forgotten this was a marriage of convenience?

'Don't,' she said when he reached across to the nightstand. 'I don't want anything to come between us.'

He hesitated with his arm outstretched, and then shook his head, and did as he'd intended. 'I will not take advantage of you.' She'd had enough of that, and however cold-bloodedly they had embarked on this arrangement, he would not take more than he needed from Samia, which was to smooth the transition period in Madlena from his brother's rule to his. Then they would decide how to proceed. Until that time came, they could enjoy each other and nothing more.

'Is this just another deal for you—another business contract?' she suggested, pressing her lips down in anticipation of him confirming this in his usual blunt way.

'It's a lot more than that,' he admitted, 'but not enough to risk consequences neither of us are ready for.'

In spite of her turbulent past, Samia had surprised him by being a generous and inventive lover. If he hadn't been such a cynic, he might have said they were made for each other, but these were early days and he knew better than to rush things. Having discovered her fears were unfounded, she had unleashed a passion that was careless of risk. Impatient to try everything, she'd forgotten that for every action there was a consequence, and, though this marriage suited them both for a variety of reasons, there was no guarantee the arrangement would last.

'Luca,' she whispered as she mounted him, 'touch me... Take me deep.'

Now he had protected them both, he was more than happy to do whatever she wished.

CHAPTER SEVENTEEN

As she prepared to disembark the *Black Diamond* the following day, Samia felt as if she were still suspended on a gossamer cloud of amazement. It was hard to believe that, not only was she over all her fears about sex, but that with Luca they had been completely unfounded. She'd had no idea anything could feel so good, or that the giving and receiving of pleasure could bring her so close to someone.

She only wished that Luca felt the same, but he'd given no sign of increased affection, or that particular look one lover gave to another. Did last night mean nothing to him? It meant so much to her. She'd lived with fear for so long. And it was a pledge and a promise on her part that cut deep. She could no more look at another man than she could return to her old life…but did Luca feel anything? She couldn't read his face.

Oh, snap out of it! she told herself impatiently. Whatever happened next, she would throw herself into it with the utmost effort. Her feelings were a gift no one could steal, and not to be taken lightly.

'You're about to set foot in your new country. How do you feel about that?' Luca asked.

She forced something appropriate out of her mouth, and was relieved when someone else distracted him to

brief him about some last-minute changes to their arrival plans. Naturally, the old doubts took the opportunity to resurface. Was she good enough? Could she do
this? Now she was on the threshold of her new life, she
realised that it came with no guarantees. But Luca had
shown her that it was possible to feel safe and wanted,
cared for and cherished by a man, and she could never
thank him enough for that. He'd taken her on a voyage
of discovery proving there were no boundaries where
pleasure was concerned, and no restrictions when it
came to trust.

She was falling in love, Samia realised as she watched
Luca talking to his aide. Her husband was the only man
she could ever want, or admire, or enjoy, and not because he was a prince or a billionaire, but because he'd
made her whole again, and because they had fun together.
She'd learned to laugh and to trust again last night, but
now the business of being a prince and a ruler must take
precedence. As it should, she accepted, but that couldn't
stop her feeling lonely as Luca prepared to walk ahead
of her to greet the crowds come to welcome him home.

The moment Luca appeared the cheers became deafening. Samia hung back, feeling out of her depth and
sinking fast. It was one thing being strong when she
was dealing with the familiar, but everything was new
here—new country, new marriage, and with a man who
might never love her back. Was she strong enough to
deal with that? Only time would tell, but did she want to
spend the foreseeable future aching for something she
could never have?

'Samia?' Luca called, turning back to look at her with
an assessing glance, as if measuring her ability to go
through with it.

'Ready,' she confirmed. People had crowded the quay

to see Prince Luca arrive with his bride, and, however inadequate she might be feeling, she owed it to him and to them to get over her anxiety.

'You look beautiful…and, as always, you've judged your appearance perfectly,' he murmured, clasping her hand.

Was that reassuring squeeze of her hand make-believe? Or the warmth in his eyes all for show? Lifting her chin, she smiled back. She had chosen her outfit with care to show respect for the country's recent grief. The plain grey suit, with its pale blue blouse to soften the tailoring, felt comfortable and relaxed, and she wore her hair tied back loosely—not too severe or, worse, unapproachable. Her only embellishment was her simple wedding ring and the love shining out of her eyes.

'Beautiful,' Luca confirmed with a look that heated her blood. But was there more than hunger in his look?

Don't be so ungrateful! Be satisfied with what you've got.

She could never thank him enough for introducing her to the precious joy of feeling safe, and for however long that lasted, she would cherish every moment. 'Are you sure I look all right?'

'How can you ask a question like that?' he demanded the moment they were enclosed in the royal limousine. 'I thought your days of doubt were behind you. It seems I still have a lot more work to do.'

'We both have a lot more work to do,' she admitted as he embraced her.

Their welcome in Madlena was even warmer than she had expected. The streets were lined with cheering crowds, and the cheers grew even louder when the people caught sight of their new Princess. This was her country now, with the weight of responsibility that entailed, and it made her all the more determined to do everything she could for Luca, who had lost a brother and believed he was to blame. He needed her every bit as much as she needed him.

'They're calling for their Princess,' Luca observed with pleasure.

Samia was thrilled and touched by all the smiling faces, and when she waved back, it was not a regal wave, but an enthusiastic, happy wave. It was still hard to come to terms with the fact that an accident of fate had changed her life to this degree. But it had not changed who she was, and it never would, she vowed silently. She was no better and no worse than she had been before they married.

Luca helped her out of the limousine when they arrived at the palace. Taking her hand, he led her forward to where a podium had been set out beneath a royal canopy. The reception from his people was wild as he turned to face them. It was as if the citizens of Madlena wanted to reassure him that they had grieved with him for the loss of his brother, but now they were ready to move forward, and with a magnificent prince at their head. Dressed in sombre black, as befitted his first day home in the country where his brother had died so tragically, with black diamonds flashing at the cuffs of his crisp white shirt, Luca exuded confidence and reassurance as the crowd chanted his name. And when he opened his arms as if to embrace his people, they cheered him as if they would never stop.

'Allow me to introduce you to my bride,' he said, speaking into the microphone on the podium. Turning to Samia, he brought her to his side. 'Princess Samia will serve our country as I will—'

She hadn't thought it possible for the cheers to grow

even louder, but as Luca's strong, warm hand closed around hers, they did.

'This is a new beginning after the saddest of endings,' Luca promised the crowd. People fell silent at his words, remembering his brother. 'But together,' he added, his glance spanning the crowd before turning to include Samia in its warmth, 'we will take Madlena from strength to strength.'

Samia's ears were ringing with the sound of so many voices raised in support of their new Prince, but her heart ached at the thought that she was only window dressing, and could never be the love of Luca's life. She was the bride brought home to reassure his people, and to warm his bed for as long as it suited them both, but when it came to the sort of lasting love she yearned for, Luca remained unaware, and possibly uncaring, that she longed for more than a convenient deal.

'My people already love you,' Luca enthused as they left the temporary stage.

Yet they were deceiving them with this mock show of a happy marriage, she thought, cringing inside at their dishonesty as she raised a smile in response to Luca's words, but this was his day, not hers, and she had to get over it.

Their first day back in his homeland had been long and tiring for Samia. She would be relieved when he dismissed their attendants. He was looking forward to introducing his bride to their beautiful suite of rooms within the historic palace of Madlena.

He needn't have worried. The moment they walked into their apartment she exclaimed with pleasure. Staring up at the elaborately painted ceiling with its billowing white clouds, clear blue skies and plump pink cherubs circling the heavens on sunlit wings, she turned full circle

with her arms outstretched, fingertips reaching out like a
bird in flight. 'This is absolutely glorious,' she breathed.

'I'm glad you like it,' he said warmly. He'd always
loved the painted ceiling, and believed the artwork in
the palace had inspired his brother's love for design. 'It
has been compared to the work of Michelangelo,' he explained, 'and is praised the world over for its excellence.'

'I'm not surprised,' she mused, but then her face fell
and she looked away.

'Samia?'

'You don't have to keep up the pretence now we're alone.'

'The pretence?' he queried, frowning. 'What do you
mean?'

'Our deal,' she explained. 'I realise you're going to be
busy from now on, and I want to reassure you that you
don't have to worry about me. I'll be fine. I'll have plenty
to occupy my time while I'm here.'

'You certainly will,' he agreed, bringing her into his
arms. She was tired. He must make allowances. But he
couldn't wait another moment to feel her body close to
his. Pressing her back against the heavy mahogany door,
he kissed her hungrily, and after a moment of resistance,
she kissed him back.

'What's wrong?' he queried gently as he brushed her
wild red hair from her face. Her hair could never be contained for long, and however carefully she had arranged
it, the lustrous locks had a will of their own. Just like
Samia, he thought warmly. 'I realise this is all new and
strange to you, but you will get used to it in time.'

'I am not worthy.'

He knew she was trying to make a joke of it, but the
shadows were back in her eyes. 'Don't say that, not even
as a joke.' Kissing her fears away was harder than he'd
expected this time. So strong in so many ways, Samia was

always ready to be hurt. It was as if she expected every rainbow to have a quagmire at the end of it instead of a pot of gold. Anger rose inside him as he thought again about her past, and he silently vowed that, whatever it took, he would make her whole again. 'I can't think of anyone worthier, or more fun and compassionate than you.'

'That's only because you don't know me yet,' she teased with a shrug.

'And who do you think is taking the bigger chance in this relationship?' he asked, dipping his head to stare her in the eyes. 'Me or you?'

Her eyes searched his. 'We both are,' she said softly.

'Then, let me reassure you...'

One kiss to soothe her, and another to arouse, and then he carried her across the room to the bed, by which time her arms were looped around his neck, and her legs had encircled his waist.

He couldn't restrain himself and thrust hungrily against her plumply aroused body. She cried out with pleasure. Rotating his hips, he massaged the place that craved his attention most. That was the starting gun. Reaching for his belt buckle, she made short work of his zipper. Scraps of lace went flying, and moments later he took his beautiful bride thoroughly and completely in one ecstasy-provoking plunge.

Samia had no intention of holding on and came immediately. Shrieking his name, she bucked wildly in the grip of an orgasm so powerful he had to tighten his hold on her buttocks to keep her in place as the pleasure waves rolled on and on.

'*Good!*' she exclaimed, collapsing against him. '*So good!*'

He kissed her to soothe her down, until finally she smiled into his eyes and asked, 'Now, can we go to bed?'

'Whatever my princess desires.'

Having discovered the pleasures of sex, it seemed Samia couldn't get enough, but this was more than sexual attraction for him, he reflected when she finally fell back on the bed groaning with contentment. This was trust and sharing, as he'd never known it before. A good sign for the future, he thought as Samia twined her legs around his and snuggled deep into his arms. 'Can we sleep a little now?' she said groggily.

'Are you finally admitting I've exhausted you?'

Her steady breathing answered the question. Princess Samia was asleep.

Every lifelong relationship had to begin somewhere, he mused as he studied her sleeping face. She looked so innocent. Her moods had run the gamut since they'd met from exuberance to anxiety, on to doubt, and then to this sleeping contentment, which he mightily preferred. It made him feel good to raise her up any way he could. Samia deserved to be happy, and he was fiercely determined to make sure she was.

He had to ask himself, was this love? What was happening to him? He'd never felt such a wealth of feeling before, or such an overwhelming desire to remain close to someone, so he could protect and grow with them for the rest of his life. This so-called marriage of convenience was already so much more, he reflected as he rested back in bed.

It was the best night's sleep she'd had in ages, but her mind remained made up. It was as though sleeping so soundly had finally reconnected the wires in her brain and she knew what she had to do. There was no going back now. Anxious not to wake Luca, who was sleeping soundly with one powerful arm thrown across his face, she crept out of bed and went to the dressing room where she dug out her old backpack and her mother's walking boots, thoughtfully placed there with the rest of her things by Domenico, who had intuited how much they meant to her. She wouldn't take anything she hadn't arrived with, with the exception of her wedding ring, which refused point-blank to budge from her finger.

'What are you doing?'

Shocked to be discovered acting furtively, she swung around to see Luca leaning against the door. 'Leaving you.'

'Leaving?'

'I can't do this. I can't look those people in the eye day after day after day and live a lie. I don't know how I ever thought I could. They deserve more than this empty marriage, and a Princess who isn't fitted for the task.'

'What the hell are you talking about?' Luca's voice was still husky with sleep, and his face was incapable of subtlety while he was only half-awake. He was angry and surprised.

'I'm leaving you,' she said again. 'It's for the best. I can play-act for a while, like anyone else, but I'd mess it up spectacularly in the end. Even you must admit, I'm hardly traditional princess material.'

'Which is exactly the point, and why you're here. I didn't want traditional—I'm not even sure what that is,' Luca growled, knuckling his eyes.

'You should take your time. Choose a bride properly, not just be landed with me because I bumped into you and suited your purpose for a few months.'

Luca's dark eyes narrowed to slits of suspicion. 'You're putting a time limit on our arrangement now?'

'It just ran out,' she fired back. 'This is an *arrangement*, which is *my point*. It's not a love match, and we both deserve more. What happens when you eventually fall in love with someone else and you can't live without them?'

'I'll certainly miss you,' he admitted, scowling deeply. 'Imagine the peaceful lie-in I'd get in the mornings.'

'But we hardly know each other,' she pointed out with exasperation.

'I'd say we know each other pretty well already,' Luca fired back. 'I can't think of any other woman I've been on such a rapid journey with, and I can't say I appreciate hearing that you've taken nothing from it apart from physical gratification.'

'That's not true!' She flared up. 'How dare you turn this around on me?'

'You've just decided our marriage has a sell-by date.'

'You decided that first. It was for five years, you told me. It was never meant to last for ever.'

'Well, maybe I changed my mind,' he growled. 'I hope you're not suggesting I'm as dishonest and manipulative as your ex? I thought we arrived at this agreement together, and that it was for our *mutual* benefit?'

'A straightforward business transaction is what you called it.'

'And now that's not enough. Maybe what has happened since I said that is too much for you? Please,' he said, throwing his arms wide. 'Enlighten me.'

'I don't know what it takes to be a princess, but I'm pretty sure I don't have it,' she insisted stubbornly.

'Just be yourself. That's all anyone would expect from you.'

'I don't know who that is anymore,' she wailed.

'Then, perhaps you should leave,' he said coolly. 'If you can't leave the past with all its doubts and demons behind, then maybe I'd be better off without you.'

'You would be. As I would be better off without you,

because you can't leave the past behind, either, and the sooner you come to terms with that, the happier you'll be. You've said you let your brother down. I believe I let my mother down, when the truth is, we loved them with all our hearts, and would have done anything to make things better for them, but what I've come to realise is, they each left us, not the other way around. I'm right about that, aren't I? About Pietro?'

There was a long silence, and then Luca nodded and said quietly, 'When did you get to be so wise?'

'When I met you and started seeing things as they were, rather than as I dreamed they might be—which was rather terrifying when I discovered you were the infamous Pirate Prince.'

'So why can't you see things as they are now—this minute—right here, right now? You are a princess. Suck it up.'

'Are you kidding? I mean, look at me.'

'You look beautiful to me, though those boots could do with some loving attention from a tin of polish.'

She was still riled up inside, but relieved at the same time that the crisis seemed to be over, and they could part as friends, as she'd hoped. 'This is me,' she said, running a hand down her shabby clothes. This is who I really am. I'll never make a suitable Princess for you. Even you can't fit a round peg into a square hole.'

'No,' Luca admitted thoughtfully, 'but I know someone who can.'

'Who?'

'Not now,' he murmured. 'I've got something else on my mind.'

'What?' Samia shook her head in disbelief. 'Isn't this situation serious enough for you to spare time to discuss it?'

'It certainly is,' he murmured, tapping his stubbled chin with a long finger.

'So, what is this something else?' she asked, weakening with curiosity, even though she knew she should stick to her guns.

'You,' he said wickedly, yanking her close.

CHAPTER EIGHTEEN

AFTER A LONG lie-in and a lazy shower, which involved more activity than the term 'lazy' might suggest, he told Samia to give him the chance to prove she was indeed the perfect Princess for him and for their people.

She insisted on wearing her original travel clothes, while he wore jeans to take her on the back of his Harley to the artists' quarter in town. A tall, undistinguished building occupied most of a cobbled square, and, dismounting from the beast, they jogged up five flights of stairs until they reached the penthouse floor.

'Wow,' she gasped when they walked in.

'I guess the word *penthouse* hardly conjures up the reality of this place,' he admitted. The entire top floor had been knocked into one massive room that could be used for a variety of purposes. 'It's an artists' commune,' he explained. 'Everyone has their own space for however long they need it. They can even sleep here, if they want, and they all have the very best of sponsors in my beloved *nonna*.'

'Your grandmother is a patron of the arts?'

'And an artist in her own right,' he revealed. 'She undertook the restoration of the ceilings in the palace with a team of fellow craftsmen. At almost seventy years old, she lay on her back on top of the scaffold, painting for months.'

'Like Michelangelo! She must be fit—'

'Creaking a little these days, my dear…'

'Nonna!' Swinging around, Luca exchanged the warmest of hugs with a tiny, birdlike woman whose arms barely stretched around his waist. Her abundant grey hair was held up with a couple of paintbrushes, and she was dressed in a shapeless artist's smock, of indeterminate colour beneath a blizzard of paint smears. Her face was old and wise, her smile wide, and her raisin-black eyes full of warmth as they fixed on Samia's with the friendliest of greetings.

'Luca, my naughty boy,' she exclaimed, stepping back from the giant towering over her. 'Why have you stayed away so long?'

'Because, as you told me to, Nonna, I've been searching for a bride.'

'As if you'd do anything I told you to,' his grandmother scoffed. 'But here she is,' she added in a softer tone. Stepping back, she took a shrewd look at Samia. 'Well, Luca, are you going to introduce us?'

'Of course. Princess Aurelia, may I present my wife…?'

'Samia,' Samia broke in, bobbing a curtsey. 'Just plain Samia.'

This comment produced a hearty guffaw from a woman who looked as if a puff of wind would blow her over. 'A kindred spirit! I knew it at once. This isn't one of your painted trollops, Luca, or a namby-pamby milksop, but a down-to-earth woman with sensible boots. How are you, my dear?'

It was Samia's turn for a warm hug. Wrestling with the sharp tang of turpentine overlaid with carbolic soap, she laughed as Luca's grandmother demanded, 'Are you in charge of this man? Keep him on a short leash. I couldn't bear any harm to come to him. He has my heart. Luca *is* my heart.' Returning her attention to her grandson, she adopted a stern face that wasn't quite as successful as maybe she had intended. 'Bad boy. Why did it take so long to come to your senses?'

'Perfect princesses don't grow on trees?' Luca suggested, cocking his head to one side to bathe his grandmother in the warmth of his smile.

'And if they did you'd probably stride past them, silly boy. I imagine Samia bumped into you? Am I right?'

They both stared at her, and then they laughed. 'How did you know?' Samia asked as the princess linked arms to draw her deeper into the busy space where at least half a dozen artists were working, each lost in their work.

'Because Luca feeds off the unexpected, and I can see from the way he looks at you that he's madly in love.'

Samia blinked. 'You can?'

'Of course! How can you doubt it? My grandson never does anything by halves, and the fact that he's brought you to meet me speaks volumes.'

'I'm just not sure that I—'

'Can be a princess?' Princess Aurelia supplied. 'That's what I thought once upon a time. You can see I'm hardly conventional. But if you care for someone—really care—you can expand your heart to encompass everything they care about, even when that means embracing an entire country and its people. The citizens of Madlena need someone like you, as they needed me in my time, to reassure them that their royal family is just as delightfully quirky as theirs. As far as I'm concerned,' she added, smiling into Samia's eyes, 'I'm delighted to welcome you into our family.'

'So what did you think of the last Princess of Madlena?' Luca asked when they arrived back at the palace. Having parked the Harley in the vast courtyard at the back of the building, they strolled through the exquisitely manicured gardens to their apartment.

'I think your grandmother is absolutely amazing,' Samia admitted as they paused in the shade of a rose arbour, where swags of pink roses exuded the most exquisite scent. 'It would be impossible not to love her. You must be very proud.'

'I am,' Luca confessed. 'She helped to bring me up, though she thought I'd be better off with my brother after she was widowed and her life started gravitating towards the artists' community she'd created. Pietro would soften me, she said, while she might lead me astray with her bohemian lifestyle, which in her opinion was the last thing I needed.'

'She's a wonderful woman.'

'And a wonderful princess, adored by the people of Madlena. They see her strength and love her for her eccentricity, and they know her to be deeply caring. She'll do anything in her power to help them, and proves it every year by donating all the proceeds of her work to Madlenan charities. She's a very different type of royal as you and I will be. I'm not going to ask you again if you want to go on this journey with me,' he added as he drew Samia into his arms. 'I'm going to tell you that I'd be nothing without you. I'd be all steel and no heart. You're the love of my life, Princess Samia, and though I'm not too good at expressing things, because I've never felt this way before, I can promise that I'll tell you that I love you again and again.'

'Please do,' she whispered, staring up into Luca's eyes.

'I love you and I want you at my side. You're not just a princess who is more than worthy of the name, you're the woman I adore, and will do for the rest of my life.'

'Love,' she whispered, loving the sound of that word. It made all the difference in the world.

'Adore,' Luca countered. Adopting a thoughtful expression, he added, 'You *love* hamburgers, but I'll give you every reason to adore me.'

'I love *and* adore you.'

'No more than I adore you,' he said.

EPILOGUE

A year later...

THE FORMAL BLESSING of Luca and Samia's marriage was held on Prince Pietro's Day. Starting from this day, Luca's late brother would be honoured every year with an annual public holiday.

The glorious medieval cathedral in Madlena with its soaring vaulted ceiling was bathed in jewelled light streaming through the stained-glass windows. Guests from all walks of life had gathered to celebrate an outstanding first year for Prince Luca and Princess Samia. Not only was the country riding the crest of a wave thanks to the tireless marketing of its many assets by a talented princess who used the home-grown artwork of her grandmother-in-law's artists' collective to enhance her promotion of the country, but Princess Samia was pregnant, which was a cause for general rejoicing.

Domenico insisted on escorting Samia down the length of the aisle to where her handsome prince was waiting, while Princess Aurelia, dressed for the occasion in diamonds and ankle-length shocking pink silk-satin, stood on her other side. Glorious organ music accompanied them, while the scent of white roses filled the air.

'Much as it pains me to hand you back to this brute of

a man,' Domenico murmured as they reached the steps of the altar, 'I have to say, you've improved him a little, but there's still a lot of work to do.'

'A lifetime of work, I hope,' Luca remarked dryly.

Samia's heart swelled with love as she stared up at the handsome prince at her side. In his official regalia of black and gold, with a red silk-satin sash of office pinned with a magnificent jewel running diagonally across his powerful chest, Luca was…quite simply, the man she loved. He had restored her confidence in every way, and set her free to fly. *Which only goes to prove*, she reflected, *that even when a bird flies free, it still returns to those it loves.*

As Domenico and Princess Aurelia melted back into the congregation, Luca stared deep into her eyes. 'You look beautiful…*again*,' he murmured.

The smile they exchanged was both intimate and perfect. Samia's elegant peach-coloured gown was cut cunningly to flatter, rather than to hide her growing bump. They were both so thrilled about the tiny prince or princess that they celebrated constantly—often in the most unlikely places. Who knew a palace had so many nooks and crannies for a love-struck couple to hide away?

'That gown is gorgeous,' Luca said huskily. 'I can't wait to take it off you.'

'Shh!' Samia implored as the thundering organ quietened.

But, with its lace bandeau bodice and filmy long sleeves, it was a fairy-tale dress. It had arrived as a surprise from Paris. 'So you can't refuse to wear it!' Luca had teased his practical bride.

When she'd lifted the filmy creation from its reams of tissue paper, the gown had taken her breath away.

'And I want you to wear this too,' Luca had said as

he'd produced the priceless fringe tiara of sparkling blue-white diamonds that had once belonged to his late mother. 'You'll have to take that off before I make love to you,' he murmured discreetly now. 'Or we'll end the night in the ICU.'

'You're *so* romantic,' Samia remarked with loving irony as the service began.

'Aren't I just?' Luca agreed. 'But I'd do it all *again*,' he insisted.

'And again, I hope,' she murmured back, 'because I love you.'

'As I love you,' Luca responded, smiling into her eyes. 'With all my heart, and my body too…'

'What a coincidence,' she said as Domenico cleared his throat theatrically to draw their attention to the fact that the service had begun, 'because I adore you too, and I always will.'

'Ditto,' Luca mouthed with a wink for Domenico.

* * * * *

COMING SOON!

MILLS & BOON

Coming next month

THE SECRET KEPT FROM THE KING
Clare Connelly

'No.' He held onto her wrist as though he could tell she was about to run from the room. 'Stop.'

Her eyes lifted to his and she jerked on her wrist so she could lift her fingers to her eyes and brush away her tears. Panic was filling her, panic and disbelief at the mess she found herself in.

'How is this upsetting to you?' he asked more gently, pressing his hands to her shoulders, stroking his thumbs over her collarbone. 'We agreed at the hotel that we could only have two nights together, and you were fine with that. I'm offering you three months, on exactly those same terms, and you're acting as though I've asked you to parade naked through the streets of Shajarah.'

'You're ashamed of me,' she said simply. 'In New York we were two people who wanted to be together. What you're proposing turns me into your possession.'

He stared at her, his eyes narrowed. 'The money I will give you is beside the point.'

More tears sparkled on her lashes. 'Not to me it's not.'

'Then don't take the money,' he said, urgently. 'Come to the RKH and be my lover because you want to be with me.'

'I can't.' Tears fell freely down her face now. 'I need that money. I need it.'

A muscle jerked in his jaw. 'So have both.'

'No, you don't understand.'

She was a live wire of panic but she had to tell him, so that he understood why his offer was so revolting to her.

She pulled away from him, pacing towards the windows, looking out on this city she loved. The trees at Bryant Park whistled in the fall breeze and she watched them for a moment, remembering the first time she'd seen them. She'd been a little girl, five, maybe six, and her dad had been performing at the restaurant on the fringes of the park. She'd worn her Very Best dress, and, despite the heat, she'd worn tights that were so uncomfortable she could vividly remember that feeling now. But the park had been beautiful and her dad's music had, as always, filled her heart with pleasure and joy.

Sariq was behind her now, she felt him, but didn't turn to look at him.

'I'm glad you were so honest with me today.' Her voice was hollow. 'It makes it easier for me, in a way, because I know exactly how you feel, how you see me, and what you want from me.' Her voice was hollow, completely devoid of emotion when she had a thousand throbbing inside her.

He said nothing. He didn't try to deny it. Good. Just as she'd said, it was easier when things were black and white.

'I don't want money so I can attend the Juilliard, Your Highness.' It pleased her to use his title, to use that as a point of difference, to put a line between them that neither of them could cross.

Silence. Heavy, loaded with questions. And finally, 'Then what do you need such a sum for?'

She bit down on her lip, her tummy squeezing tight. 'I'm pregnant. And you're the father.'

Continue reading
THE SECRET KEPT FROM THE KING
Clare Connelly

Available next month
www.millsandboon.co.uk

LET'S TALK
Romance

For exclusive extracts, competitions
and special offers, find us online:

MILLS & BOON

THE HEART OF ROMANCE

A ROMANCE FOR EVERY KIND OF READER

MODERN

Prepare to be swept off your feet by sophisticated, sexy and seductive heroes, in some of the world's most glamourous and romantic locations, where power and passion collide.
8 stories per month.

HISTORICAL

Escape with historical heroes from time gone by. Whether your passion is for wicked Regency Rakes, muscled Vikings or rugged Highlanders, awaken the romance of the past.
6 stories per month.

MEDICAL

Set your pulse racing with dedicated, delectable doctors in the high-pressure world of medicine, where emotions run high and passion, comfort and love are the best medicine.
6 stories per month.

True Love

Celebrate true love with tender stories of heartfelt romance, from the rush of falling in love to the joy a new baby can bring, and a focus on the emotional heart of a relationship.
8 stories per month.

Desire

Indulge in secrets and scandal, intense drama and plenty of sizzling hot action with powerful and passionate heroes who have it all: wealth, status, good looks…everything but the right woman.
6 stories per month.

HEROES

Experience all the excitement of a gripping thriller, with an intense romance at its heart. Resourceful, true-to-life women and strong, fearless men face danger and desire - a killer combination!
8 stories per month.

DARE

Sensual love stories featuring smart, sassy heroines you'd want as a best friend, and compelling intense heroes who are worthy of them.
4 stories per month.

To see which titles are coming soon, please visit

millsandboon.co.uk/nextmonth

JOIN US ON SOCIAL MEDIA!

Stay up to date with our latest releases, author news and gossip, special offers and discounts, and all the behind-the-scenes action from Mills & Boon...

 millsandboon

 millsandboonuk

 millsandboon

It might just be true love...